INCREDIBLE ACCLAIM FOR

WATCH THE GIRLS

"Fast-paced and involving." —*People*

"One can't help but become ensnared...With dark woods, missing women, eccentric locals, unsettling wolf masks, secret messages and nighttime stalkers, WATCH THE GIRLS has all the nightmare fuel of great horror movie camp mixed with an absorbing mystery...There is no denying WATCH THE GIRLS is 'nervously-eat-an-entire-box-of-cookies-without-realizing-it' good."
—*Shelf Awareness* (**Starred Review**)

"A devastating novel that evokes Ingmar Bergman and David Lynch....This disturbing, surrealistic thriller will keep readers spellbound."
—*Publishers Weekly* (**Starred Review**)

"Sibling rivalry and Hollywood obsessions collide...Fast-paced and fraught with suspense, WATCH THE GIRLS unravels like a perfect summer-night movie." —*BookPage*

"It's a fascinating setup, and while it seems like it may be nothing more than a fun romp, don't let looks deceive you. This takes dark and unexpected turns, culminating in an ending fit for its own horror movie. Liv is a compelling protagonist with a distinct voice—snarky and vulnerable, tough and persevering—and the book as a whole takes clever swipes at the Hollywood culture that has pervaded our lives. I'm anxious to see where Wolfe takes us next—either with this character or the next. Frankly, I'm willing to follow her anywhere." —*Crimespree* Magazine

"WATCH THE GIRLS is one of those books—it gets under your skin and stays with you long after you've devoured the last page. It's the perfect dark, chilling thriller for the age of social media and ubiquitous reality TV that's anything but real. Jennifer Wolfe's damaged heroine toes the thin and ever-blurry line between truth and fake Hollywood glitz, right up until the devastating conclusion."

—Nina Laurin, author of *Girl Last Seen*

"Make no mistake: Wolfe's got the goods. Timely, harrowing, and vividly imagined, WATCH THE GIRLS is a wild ride with style to burn."

—Chris Holm, Anthony Award winning author of *The Killing Kind*

"Twisty, tense, and addictive, WATCH THE GIRLS is like a great horror flick, a classic mystery, and an edgy piece of social commentary—all wrapped up into one dark, delicious package. Jennifer Wolfe is a huge new talent. Welcome to the book everyone will be reading this summer."

—Brad Parks, author of *Closer Than You Know*

"[A] campy debut thriller...with [a] twisty and twisted ending." —*Kirkus Reviews*

WATCH

THE

GIRLS

WATCH

THE

GIRLS

JENNIFER
WOLFE

GRAND CENTRAL
PUBLISHING
New York Boston

Copyright © 2018 by Jennifer Wolfe
Jacket design by Elizabeth Connor
Jacket photo © Severin Matusek / EyeEm / Getty Images
Cover copyright © 2018 by Hachette Book Group, Inc.

Hachette Book Group supports the right to free expression and the value of copyright. The purpose of copyright is to encourage writers and artists to produce the creative works that enrich our culture.

The scanning, uploading, and distribution of this book without permission is a theft of the author's intellectual property. If you would like permission to use material from the book (other than for review purposes), please contact permissions@hbgusa.com. Thank you for your support of the author's rights.

Grand Central Publishing
Hachette Book Group
1290 Avenue of the Americas, New York, NY 10104
grandcentralpublishing.com
twitter.com/grandcentralpub

Originally published in hardcover and ebook by Grand Central Publishing in July 2018
First Mass Market Edition: June 2019

Grand Central Publishing is a division of Hachette Book Group, Inc. The Grand Central Publishing name and logo is a trademark of Hachette Book Group, Inc.

The publisher is not responsible for websites (or their content) that are not owned by the publisher.

The Hachette Speakers Bureau provides a wide range of authors for speaking events. To find out more, go to www.hachettespeakersbureau.com or call (866) 376-6591.

Library of Congress Cataloging-in-Publication Data

Names: Wolfe, Jennifer, 1978- author.
Title: Watch the girls / Jennifer Wolfe.
Description: First edition. | New York : Grand Central Publishing, 2018.
Identifiers: LCCN 2017041740| ISBN 9781538760840 (hardcover) | ISBN
9781549169199 (audio download) | ISBN 9781478974246 (ebook)
Subjects: LCSH: Women private investigators--Fiction. | Missing
persons--Investigation--Fiction. | Psychological fiction. | BISAC: FICTION
/ Suspense. | FICTION / Contemporary Women. | FICTION / Psychological. |
FICTION / Romance / Gothic. | GSAFD: Suspense fiction.
Classification: LCC PS3623.O5528 W38 2018 | DDC 813/.6--dc23
LC record available at https://lccn.loc.gov/2017041740

ISBNs: 978-1-4789-7423-9 (mass market), 978-1-4789-7424-6 (ebook)

Printed in the United States of America

OPM

10 9 8 7 6 5 4 3 2 1

ATTENTION CORPORATIONS AND ORGANIZATIONS:
Most Hachette Book Group books are available at quantity discounts with bulk purchase for educational, business, or sales promotional use. For information, please call or write:

Special Markets Department, Hachette Book Group
1290 Avenue of the Americas, New York, NY 10104
Telephone: 1-800-222-6747 Fax: 1-800-477-5925

To my agent, Doug Stewart,
for liking it weird.

Celebrity is a mask that eats into the face.
                              —John Updike

OLIVIA HILL

2003

17 YEARS OLD; 109 LBS.

1.

I've been watched nearly as long as I've been alive. I was used to being stared at. Observed. Followed. Probably why I didn't notice we had a shadow until Miranda, the younger of my two little sisters, twisted around in the passenger seat and said, "That car's been on us since we left the house."

A glance in the rearview mirror told me she was right. A black SUV hung back a hundred yards. I would have tried to lose him, but Mulholland Drive—a snaky, two-lane strip of road balanced on the ridgeline of the Santa Monica Mountains—was no place for evasive maneuvers, especially at night. Below us, Los Angeles was a blanket of rusty stars, but Mulholland was lit only by the occasional lights of foliage-cloistered, multimillion-dollar homes.

"One of the usuals?" I asked, referring to the gaggle of photographers who stalked my other sister, Gemma, and me so regularly we had their license plates memorized. We knew their nicknames. Their *girlfriends' and wives' names. Even a few of their birthdays.*

"He's too far away. I can't tell." Miranda faced forward again. "We should go back."

"Gemma needs us."

Miranda snorted. It was an ugly sound. Too bitter for her age. Fourteen and already jaded, but justifiably so.

"Neither of us can give Gemma what she needs." She dug absently at the dime-size hole she'd gouged in her arm that morning. There were others hidden from view on her legs and back. A few years ago, Desiree (I stopped calling her Mom after she appointed herself my manager) took Miranda to a Beverly Hills psychiatrist to find out what was wrong with her. What she really wanted was to know why Miranda wasn't like Gemma and me. Why didn't she want to act or sing or dance or model? Why didn't she cooperate and justify her existence in Desiree's life? Why didn't she earn?

Anxiety, depression, perhaps a dash of ADD and a sprinkle of OCD. That's what the shrink proclaimed, and wrote several prescriptions. But no combination of pills would change Miranda's circumstances. With a different mother, a different set of sisters, growing up in a different city, she might have been a different girl. One who didn't pick at an unblemished canvas of skin until it was spattered in sores. Who didn't wake up every morning knowing the woman who gave birth to her would have traded her in for another model if she could have, preferably a model who wanted to model.

Behind us, the road went dark. I checked the rearview again and sighed in relief. The headlights were gone.

"She wouldn't lift a finger for you unless it was scripted," Miranda said, continuing to scrape at her wound. There was no love lost between my sisters. Gemma followed Desiree's lead and treated Miranda with the same cold dismissal as our mother did. So I wasn't sure why I'd dragged Miranda with me to retrieve Gemma, except there had been something in Gemma's voice when she called, a note of terrorized, alcohol-slurred desperation, and I didn't want to go alone.

Olivia, can you come get me? I'm at a party. I don't know whose. I just need to get out of here. Don't tell Desiree. Please hurry. I want to come home. I can't live like this anymore. I can't be this person anymore.

She had said it in an urgent whisper, like she was afraid someone might overhear. What was I supposed to do, tell her no? I'd never heard her sound like that. Weakened. Vulnerable. If Miranda had heard her, even she might have softened toward Gemma.

I can't be this person anymore...

I'd waited a long time for Gemma to say those words. I hoped she still meant them when she was safe and sober.

So here we were, after midnight, racing toward some sleazy Hollywood party in the red BMW Desiree had bought me for my seventeenth birthday. A car I hadn't asked for, purchased with money from my trust fund that I was not allowed to access until I was eighteen, just a few months away, thank God. At the rate Desiree was spending the money Gemma and I earned on our show, there would be nothing left by the time we were able to touch it. Desiree claimed there was plenty to go around, and it wasn't like Gemma and I *were going to stop working, so we ought to enjoy our success. Gemma didn't argue with Desiree. She already had a taste for Dom Pérignon and four-hundred-dollar shoes. She owned handbags that cost as much as a semester at UCLA.*

Maybe it was because Gemma didn't get her first job until she was nine years old, and all of this—the attention, the money—still seemed new and shiny to her, whereas I'd been working nonstop since before I could eat solid food. I'd heard Drew Barrymore got her first job when she was eleven months old because a dog bit her during an audition, presumably because the producers were afraid her mom would sue if they didn't cast Baby Drew. I got my first job in a national diaper spot because the casting director said my tiny baby nipples were the perfect color. Pink, but not too pink. Desiree reminded me of this every time I stipulated I would never do a topless scene.

Miranda picked up the Post-it note on which I'd scrawled the address Gemma had given me. "Why didn't she call Desiree? She always calls her when she needs to be evacuated."

This was not the first time Gemma had gotten hammered at a party and needed an exit strategy. But Miranda was right. Gemma always called Desiree, and tonight she had specifically asked me not to tell our mom, which was easy since I didn't even know where our "momager" was. Probably schmoozing it up at some studio exec's mansion, working an angle to get Gemma or me or both of us cast in a teen rom-com or a slasher movie. I'd play the final girl, Gemma the one who has sex first and is promptly slain, if anyone would cast her these days with all the

rumors circulating that she was a drunk and a lia-
bility. Yet another teen star destined for rehab. There
was talk that Gemma might be written off the show
we'd starred in for two seasons, and Desiree was
frantic to segue her little moneymakers into film.

A flash of light in the rearview. The SUV was back,
following more closely now. I jammed my foot down
on the gas pedal, accelerating past the speed limit as I
envisioned a telephoto lens snapping rapid-fire pictures
of me crutching my wasted sister to the car. If a single
one of those photos ended up in People or In Touch or
US Weekly, it would be the end for Gemma. I didn't
want that for her, even though I had a strong suspicion
that she wouldn't mind if I derailed my career and disappeared from the spotlight.

The road curved suddenly. I made the turn too fast,
and Miranda sucked in a sharp breath. I spotted a line
of cars parked along the road and pulled over abruptly,
killed the engine, cut the lights. The SUV rounded a
curve behind us and sped past without slowing. I exhaled a breath and reached for the door handle.

"I'm staying here," Miranda said, crossing her arms
and glaring out the windshield.

I left the keys in the ignition, too tired to argue. Too
proud to tell her I didn't want to go in there alone.

"Keep the doors locked. And if you spot that SUV
again, duck."

Halfway to the house, I felt a crawling sensation between my shoulder blades. I paused, looked around,
expecting to spot the manic, lidless eye of a telephoto
lens clicking at me from the bushes. I saw nothing.
Heard nothing.

But the feeling remained.

LIV HENDRICKS

2018

32 YEARS OLD; 139 LBS.

Facebook Fans: 6,019

Twitter Followers: 17,156

Instagram Followers: 4,590

2.

If I feel like I'm being watched, it's usually because I am. Someone has recognized my face, but they can't quite place me. They glance my way when they think I'm not looking. They don't realize I'm watching them back, waiting for the moment when they'll either lose interest or muster the courage to approach and say—

"Hey...I'm sorry, but are you Olivia Hill?"

It was that desperate time of night when everyone was trying to get a drink at the same time. If only it was the bartender who couldn't keep his eyes off me instead of this woman. Barely a woman, really. Her pixie cut framed a cherubic face and fleshy, flushed cheeks. Her slender stem of a neck didn't look strong enough to support her globe of a head. Aspiring actress, I guessed. In this town, weren't they all?

"Nope," I told the girl.

"Oh. My mistake." She started to withdraw into the crowd, and then halted, stepped forward again, determined. "You're Liv Hendricks, from *Bullshit Hunters*!"

My eyes shifted to the comforting rows of bottles shelved above the bar's backsplash, the amber liquid in them that would grant my only wish: an end to the day's sobriety.

The baby-faced girl kept standing there, waiting for me to confirm what she already knew. I felt sorry for her because there were so many of her in Los Angeles. Girls who all wanted the same thing, who *almost* had what it took to get it. These girls would have killed for the opportunities I'd cast off like an itchy sweater, the kind that made you miserable every second you wore it.

What I had learned about girls like this one was that most of them didn't want to act, or sing, or model, or whatever it was they'd ostensibly come to LA to do. They wanted to be seen. They didn't exist until observed, the pretty-girl equivalents of Schrödinger's cat. Living online wasn't enough for them. Twitter and Facebook and Tumblr and Instagram, Periscope and YouTube and Snapchat and blogging and all the rest were not enough. Would never be enough to make them feel like they were real, like they mattered on a planet of six billion people and counting.

"Yeah," I admitted. "I'm Liv Hendricks."

"Oh my God, I'm such a huge fan! I watched your show every day in junior high. I mean, they were reruns, but I was *addicted*. I'm serious. It was my crack."

I hailed the nearest bartender, a twenty-something hipster with a high and tight haircut, wearing a vest and an antiquey, collarless shirt with the sleeves rolled up. He looked like he'd come to work straight from the set of *Boardwalk Empire*. "Old-fashioned," I called to him. I could have been describing him.

The girl's mouth kept moving. I could barely hear her,

but I knew what she was saying. The same things these girls always say.

I didn't trust her motivations, but then I didn't trust most women. As a teenager, I'd never had girlfriends who didn't treat me like a prize, someone who could get them into places they wanted to go, introduce them to the celebrities they wanted to meet, buy them clothes they couldn't afford. But once the money and the celebrity were gone, so was my entourage.

Women had an agenda too often for my comfort. So did men, but theirs was predictable. If a man asked to buy me a drink, I knew he wanted to fuck me, or at least talk me into giving him a blowjob. If a woman did the same thing, I couldn't be sure what she wanted from me, only that it was probably something I'd rather not give.

By the time the aspiring actress took a break from gushing, I had my cocktail. The whiskey heat settled into my hollow stomach. I counted what I had eaten that day. Coffee for breakfast. A cup of yogurt with blueberries for lunch (150 calories). Three slices of deli turkey before I came to the bar (60 calories). Two hundred and ten calories for the entire day. *It's all about the calories.* The words were branded on my brain. That's what happened when your mom put you on your first diet when you were seven.

I finished my drink, completed my buzz. Started feeling good. Chatty, even.

"Hey," the girl said. "Can I buy you a drink? It would be such an honor for me, and there are so many things I want to ask you. Please say yes!"

"Sure," I said. "Why not?"

3.

LA FEMME ONLINE
A Star Burns Out:
Whatever Happened to
Olivia Hill?

Freya McBride
4 hours ago—Filed to CELEBRITY
378 Likes—78 Comments

Last night I learned a valuable lesson. If you ever spot your teen idol in a bar in Silverlake, think twice before asking her if you can buy her a drink unless you want your image of her to be shattered. #LAproblems #amiright

As a teen, I developed a cultish obsession with reruns of a TV show called *The Hills Have Pls*, a faux-reality mystery about two teenage sisters/teen stars (played by real-life sisters/teen stars Olivia and Gemma Hill) attending high school in Hollywood and investigating a series of suspicious events surrounding the disappearances of several classmates. It's sort of like *Twin Peaks* meets *Veronica Mars* set in LA, but filmed like it's a documentary à la *The Office*. The show first aired in 2001, and ran for two seasons, but was canceled before the overarching mystery was resolved. Gemma Hill signed on for another season, but Olivia Hill refused due to her distress over the disappearance of the youngest Hill sister, Miranda (not on the show). Among fans, it's been speculated that Miranda's disappearance was a publicity stunt staged to increase *The Hills Have PIs'* ratings, but it's been fifteen years and Miranda Hill remains a gone girl.

Which brings me to Liv Hendricks, aka Olivia Hill. While Gemma went on to climb her way up the alphabet toward A-list status (she hovers around a B+), Olivia dropped out of the spotlight for so long that most people forgot about her.

But not me.

When I saw her last night, I couldn't resist the opportunity to tell her how much I'd loved *THHPI*. And, yes, I will admit that as a contributing blogger for *LA Femme*, I thought I might squeeze an interview out of her. Let me assure you, it was not my intention to get her wasted and then film our conversation. Maybe a part of her wanted this to happen. She clearly had some things to get off her chest.

Watch Video ▶

Comments

1NeverApologize And the Crazy Bitch Award goes to...*3 minutes ago*

MCrush OMG! I forgot about this show! I used to watch all the time. RIP Olivia Hill's career *5 minutes ago*

Megasm Could she just make a sex video already? All I wanna see is dem tittays!;) *9 minutes ago*

> **CryFace20** Not funny, asshole *7 minutes ago*

WolfKing18 Liv Hendricks is the best thing about *Bullshit Hunters*. She deserves her own show. I'd watch that. *18 minutes ago*

> **1NeverApologize** Like anyone would give this train wreck her own show—*15 minutes ago*

> **WolfKing18** She doesn't need anyone to give it to her. All she needs is a camera. She should pitch something on Kickstarter or Shot in the Dark. I'd back her. *13 minutes ago*

CryFace20 I feel sorry for her. Her life was a nightmare. *24 minutes ago*

1NeverApologize Wah wah wah poor me! Suck it up bitch. We all got problems. You used to be rich and famous, and you threw it away. Get over yourself. *26 minutes ago*

> **1NeverApologize** Sucks about her missing sister, though. That'll fuck you up good. *25 minutes ago*

4.

I woke to a shrill ringtone next to my head and fumbled weakly for my phone, needing to stop the sound before my skull shattered. When I peeled my eyes open, I found Gemma's name floating on the screen, and thought I must still be drunk. Gemma and I didn't talk on the phone. We didn't talk in person. We didn't talk period.

"Hello?" I mumbled into the receiver, sounding every bit as disoriented as I was. Why was she calling me? How had I gotten home?

"What were you thinking?" Gemma demanded in greeting.

"Can you be more specific?" I pulled the sheet up over my head. The sunlight felt like lemon juice in my eyes, stinging and acidic.

An extended silence, and then, "You don't know?"

Her ominous tone would have made me sit up if I were capable of such a feat. I tried and failed and curled into the fetal position instead. "Just tell me."

"It's better if you see for yourself. I'll text you the link."

"Is that all?" I didn't ask what the link was to. I wasn't ready to know.

"Jesus, Liv, you sound wrecked. Are you shooting today?"

"It's not *Bullshit Hunters* without Liv Hendricks."

Another long silence, and then, more gently, "You can't keep on like this." I would have been touched by her concern if she hadn't followed with, "It's not just affecting you anymore. What you did last night is bad for me, too. My publicist is doing her best to contain the situation, but she's not a miracle worker. You need to fix this. Make a statement. Apologize and promise you're getting help. Say you lied. Just do *something*. I'm sure Desiree would be happy to—"

I ended the call, and then lay there for a few minutes, waiting for the throbbing in my skull to die down. If a bottle of Advil had appeared in my hand, I would have chewed the pills like Pez.

What had I done?

I was used to waking up to this question—both existential and literal—but whatever I had gotten up to last night must have been particularly scandalous.

My phone dinged with a text from Gemma, a link to something on *LA Femme Online*, LA's premier feminist lifestyle and entertainment blog. I didn't click the link, nor did I look at any of the other texts waiting for me. I was already running late.

When I finally managed to sit up I discovered that I was naked beneath the blankets. Which was shocking because I never slept naked, certain that one of these days an earthquake would drive me from my apartment in the middle of the night. The last thing I needed was for someone to snap a nude photo of me and post it to one of the Tumblr boards devoted to *Bullsh?t Hunters,* the title spelled with a question mark so we could get away with cursing on cable.

I attempted to revive myself with a cold shower, trying not to read into the tenderized ache between my legs. I shut off the faucet and reached for my only clean towel. I needed to buy new linens one of these days, sheets and a duvet that weren't as rough as diner napkins. Towels that weren't permanently stained with self-tanner and mascara.

I'd moved into my studio loft just after I was cast on *Bullsh?t Hunters*, and had always intended to do an apartment overhaul but never quite got around to it. Most of the downtown loft-dwellers were creatives—artists and designers, filmmakers and screenwriters—people who transformed the interiors of their homes into shrines to edgy art and hipster culture. They made passionate, personal, pretentious statements with their walls, their carefully chosen vintage furniture, their choice of CB2 shower curtains. I didn't even *have* a shower curtain, just the clear plastic sheet that kept the spray contained, and my loft was bare but for a few pieces of Ikea furniture I'd bought on Craigslist to avoid having to put anything together. I had yet to hang a single picture. My exposed-brick walls and stainless-steel appliances deserved better than what I had to offer.

I started a pot of drip coffee brewing and got to work on my hair and makeup while I waited. The *Bullsh?t Hunters* production team used to include a hair and makeup department, but after a recent bout of budget cuts our producer, Danny, started asking the cast to arrive camera-ready.

The hardest part about being my own hair and makeup department was covering the three-inch scar slashing my forehead, a memento from the night Miranda had gone missing. A branch of the tree that had caught my BMW thrust through the windshield and carved a trench from my right eyebrow into my hairline, so deep the white of my skull had been exposed. I got a reminder of the worst night of my life every time I looked in the mirror. A night I barely remembered.

I dressed in one of my "investigating" outfits, a short pleated skirt, lacy camisole, tight cardigan, and argyle knee socks. The wardrobe was my least favorite part of the job. The only time a woman in her thirties should wear a costume like this is if her lover has a schoolgirl fetish. But *Bullsh?t Hunters* had been pitched to the network as reality Scooby-Doo for adults. As the "Daphne" of our merry band of paranormal investigators, my look represented femininity and girl-next-door sex appeal. In other words, I was something for the predominantly straight, male viewership to masturbate to.

By the time I was ready I had only twenty minutes to get to set. I requested an Uber so I could read the day's pages on the way. Balancing a travel mug of coffee, my bag, and the pages, I opened my front door to find my down-the-hall neighbor, Elliot, standing on the other side, his hand raised to knock. When he saw me he grinned and shoved his hands into the pockets of pants so tight they would have fit me better than they did him. Elliot was cute in a deliberately slovenly way, but he was almost ten years younger than me, and I had a strict anti–*Melrose Place* policy not to get involved with anyone who lived in my building.

"Elliot, I'm running *really* late. Can we talk later?" I skirted around him without waiting for an answer, striding fast toward the elevator and stabbing the button repeatedly.

A hand came to rest on my hip. I twisted away, my heart crashing against my chest and an irrational scream trapped behind my lungs.

"Whoa! What's wrong?" Elliot held his hands up in surrender.

"I just...you surprised me." And I didn't like being touched in intimate places without giving permission, which should have been a given.

"I'm sorry. After last night, you know, I thought—"

Fuck. Literally.

Elliot scratched the beard he was growing to make him look older than his twenty-three years. He claimed youth was getting in the way of his directing career. He didn't understand Los Angeles yet. Any second grader in this town could direct a film if he was a big enough asshole. Elliot was too nice.

"I-I just thought we were...something," Elliot tried again, his eyes full of puzzled hurt.

"Right..." Somewhere in the blackout-edited filmstrip of my memories was probably a scene that depicted me running into Elliot in the hall, inviting him in, offering a drink. The rest was easy enough to figure out.

The elevator dinged. I jumped inside. "I'll see you later. Gotta be on set in thirty."

The doors closed in his face.

Alone in the elevator, I leaned against the back wall and closed my eyes, willing the balloon of guilt in my chest to deflate, telling myself it was just sex. A random hookup. It didn't mean anything. Elliot was old enough to know that, if nothing else.

Besides, according to Gemma, I had more important things to feel guilty about.

5.

The Uber driver, Jake, picked me up in a Scion the size of a shoe box. We drove north on the Hollywood Freeway toward the Valley, where the temperature would instantly increase by at least ten degrees. It was October, but LA was in the grip of a heat wave. It hadn't rained in months, and the sky was brown with brushfire smoke and exhaust.

"Could you turn up the air-conditioning?" I asked Jake. His car smelled faintly of cigarettes overlaid with vanilla air freshener, and that, coupled with the heat and the cramped interior and the way Jake was weaving through traffic, had me one lurch away from vomiting in the car and losing another star on my passenger rating.

"Of course!" Jake said with unbridled enthusiasm, and cranked the AC. "Is that better?"

I met his eyes in the rearview mirror. He was smiling, eager to please. He'd been trying to start a conversation ever since he picked me up.

"It's great. Thanks."

I gave up on memorizing my pages and shoved them

into my bag. I said basically the same thing in every episode anyway. I could wing it. I took out my phone to check the link Gemma had sent.

"Do you want to listen to your music?" Jake asked. "I could plug in your phone."

"Yours is fine."

Jake signaled and wove into another lane to bypass a slow driver in a beat-up Buick. I could see the driver's silhouette, a helmet of tight curls and a hunched back. An old woman. The weather aside, this was not a city for the elderly. LA was for the young and poor, the young and rich, or the middle-aged and *really* rich. I wondered if I still counted as young and poor. Maybe I didn't belong here any more than the woman in the Buick.

Another wave of nausea rolled over me. I held my breath, waiting for it to pass.

Jake cleared his throat. "Um. I'm probably not supposed to do this, but I wanted to let you know I think what you said was really brave."

"Thanks?" I had no idea what he was talking about.

"It's crazy," he went on. "There's no privacy anymore. I mean, you never know when someone's got a camera pointed at you. The whole world is a fucking reality TV show now. Sorry. *Effing* reality TV show. And you're *on* a reality TV show, so now it's like you're on a show within a show. I actually wrote a screenplay about this. I've had a lot of meetings, but I think I want to try to get funding myself. I'm doing a Shot in the Dark campaign. I've almost reached my goal."

My cell vibrated, and I thanked all the gods when I saw Chris Wheeler's name on the screen. "Sorry, I have to take this," I said, relieved to put an end to the one-sided conversation. "Hey," I said into the receiver.

"Tell me you're on your way," Wheeler said.

"I'm on my way. It's been a rough morning."

"I'll bet." My friendship with Wheeler had blossomed out of a shared loathing of the versions of ourselves we played on *Bullsh?t Hunters*. I, the perky hot girl. He, the cowardly burnout. He'd never taken so much as a single hit of marijuana, but even he had to admit he was a bit spineless. At his request, I'd had to call his last girlfriend to break up with her for him; otherwise he would have ended up married to her. She was a manipulative tyrant who reminded me of Desiree, so I considered it role-play therapy.

"I guess you saw the post on *LA Femme*," Wheeler said.

"Not yet," I admitted.

"How do you even know this Freya McBride person?"

"I don't. Who the hell is Freya McBride?"

"Some blogger," he said. "But apparently you thought she was an aspiring actress, and you took it upon yourself to warn her about the perils young women face in Hollywood."

A milky, impressionistic memory began to take shape in my mind, a fangirl who approached me while I was trying to get a drink, gushing about how much she'd loved *The Hills Have PIs*.

Wheeler covered the phone, but I heard a muffled, irate voice in the background. "Danny wants to know where the fuck you are," Wheeler said.

"Does Danny know about the post?"

"Everyone knows about it."

"Did he say anything?"

"He didn't have to."

* * *

Almost an hour late, my Uber pulled to the curb across from the day's location: a run-down house with its windows boarded up and its exterior tagged with decades' worth of spray paint. Production vehicles congregated along the street, the cast and crew milling around the canopied craft service table.

I reached for the door handle, but Jake craned around. "Hey, can I ask you a favor? Any chance you'd tweet about my Shot in the Dark campaign?"

I stared at him blankly.

"You know, the crowdfunding site?"

He told me the title of his project. I'd forgotten it by the time I closed the door. If I were a slightly bigger asshole I'd deduct a star from his rating.

I stood there on the sidewalk, the sun baking my shoulders. I clicked on the link Gemma had texted me, but my cell signal was weak, and the *LA Femme* post refused to load. It would have to wait.

Danny spotted me walking toward him as he was jamming a lid onto a paper cup of coffee. He pushed too hard and crushed the lid, sloshing coffee onto his sleeve. "Where the fuck have you been?" he snarled, shaking brown liquid from his fingers. There were streaks of white on his ruddy skin from hastily applied sunblock. He was one of those unfortunate people with skin so pale he could get a melanoma from the moonlight.

"There was construction on the 101."

"I took the same freeway to get here, and I managed to arrive on time."

"It won't happen again," I promised.

"Liv," Danny said, taking a breath, growing eerily calm, "after we wrap tonight, you and I need to have a talk."

*   *   *

"Get your shit together, Liv. We're losing our light, and we need these shots or the narrative won't make any sense."

I would have laughed if I had the energy. The narratives never made sense, but now was not the time to point that out to Danny. Whatever patience he had reserved for me had been used up. I'd flubbed my lines only twice before he took me aside for some light verbal abuse and shaming, his directing method of choice.

"And keep your hands off Blitz," Danny added when he was finished giving me my talking-to. "He's supposed to be Wheeler's dog, not yours."

Blitz, the seventy-five-pound Doberman pinscher who accompanied us on our investigations, chuffed at his name. I removed my hand from where it rested on his back. It had become habitual to touch the dog if he was within reach. There were few things more comforting than being adored by an animal who could rip your throat out if it wanted to.

Danny stormed off to powwow with the director of photography, the back of his shirt Rorschached in sweat, and I returned to my mark. The crew glared at me as I passed by, muttering to each other. I'd spent most of my life on set, but I had never learned to ignore the grumbling disapproval of a cranky, impatient crew.

I took my place with my co-hosts at the bottom of the porch. Before we entered the dilapidated house, we had to deliver exposition and backstory about the "disturbances" experienced there, and try to make the scripted lines sound natural. *Bullsh?t Hunters* was considered reality TV, but it was no more real than the campy cartoon that had inspired it. Our viewers weren't stupid. They believed because they wanted to believe, just like people who watched *The Bach-*

elor chose to buy into the idea that people could find true love during a competitive bitchfest, or that the biggest losers on *The Biggest Loser* actually kept the weight off and lived skinnily ever after. If reality TV viewers didn't willfully deceive themselves, how could they accept a woman in her thirties going mystery debunking in a schoolgirl uniform?

The current age of television was considered a renaissance, but from where I stood it looked more like everyone was scrambling to keep an increasingly jaded public entertained. People had seen it all. The biggest explosions! The fastest cars! The landmarks destroyed! The goriest carnage! The most elaborate fight scenes! The most gruesome deaths! All the twists you never saw coming! Split personalities! Imaginary friends! Faked deaths! Evil twins! Evil twins having sex!

Every genre had been milked dry, and now the only thing left to do was recycle the same spectacles.

But reality TV, no matter how scripted, still managed to reel in viewers so long as they deluded themselves that people like me and the other Bullshit Hunters were real, and that they were flies on the wall, watching an unlikely group of friends banter and bond as we explored our strange hobby.

"Back to one, everybody!" Danny called.

"How are you holding up?" Wheeler asked when I was beside him again. We hadn't had a chance to talk much since I arrived. His mournful eyes were red and glassy, the lids more swollen than usual, like he'd recently sobbed. But that was how his eyes always looked, because he refused to take his allergy medication. His puffy, watery eyes were the main reason he'd been cast to play our "Shaggy." Without antihistamines, he looked perpetually stoned.

"I'm fine," I lied. I was exhausted and nauseated, and

a headache thundered behind my eyes. The relentless heat wasn't helping. If anything, the temperature seemed to be rising as the day waned.

"Have you eaten anything?" he asked.

"Uh-huh." Another lie. Wheeler knew it but chose not to argue.

Sasha—our "Velma"—made a face at me that would have seemed sympathetic if I didn't know her. "When I'm hung over I eat bacon sandwiches with butter. It's a miracle cure, swear to God."

"I'll try that." I had no intention of trying it. Sasha would love for me to stuff myself with fat and carbs in the hope that I would show up to the next shoot a couple of pounds heavier. In my wardrobe, every ounce I gained was apparent, and the Twitterverse was not afraid to call it out with cruel hashtags. Ever since a photo of the backs of my thighs made the rounds on #celebulite (a photo I was certain had been taken and leaked by Sasha), I had resumed my old habit of counting every calorie.

The fourth member of our gang was Tate, our "Fred" on steroids. His biggest claim to fame before being cast on *Bullsh?t Hunters* was coming in fourth place on *American Ninja Warrior*. He rarely spoke other than to ask craft service if they had Muscle Milk, or to recite his lines on camera, and that was probably for the best. No one who exercised that much had anything to say that the rest of us wanted to hear.

"All right, everybody," Danny called, clapping his hands in a halfhearted attempt to energize the crew. "We need these exteriors before sunset, so we have just under an hour."

My right eyelid began to twitch rhythmically. I took a deep breath and let it out, trying to ignore the pain.

"Sound speeds," the sound recordist called.

"Action!" Danny barked. On our limited budget, he was both producer and director.

"Wow" I said, in manufactured wonder. "Looks like something straight out of a horror movie!"

"Guys, I don't know about this one." Wheeler followed, dopey and tremulous. "Maybe we should hit the road. The sun is going down, and I don't want to be in there after dark."

Tate punched Wheeler on the shoulder. "You can't wuss out now, bruh. We've been to scarier places than this." Every show was the same formula. First I stated the obvious: that the place we were about to enter looked creepy. Then Wheeler tried to back out of the investigation. Tate followed with a show of machismo toward Wheeler, which he segued into an opportunity for logical Sasha to deliver the exposition. At the end of the investigation, if we found the circumstances to be fraudulent, we would declare, "This one's bullshit!"

Sasha launched into her educated-skeptic monologue. "Well, this house does have quite a dark history..."

When she was finished, Tate led the way up the porch steps and opened the door, a Steadicam operator on our heels.

I made it about three steps into the house before the smell hit me: wood rot, decay, rodent shit in the walls. My stomach heaved. Then I was on my hands and knees, emptying what was left in my stomach onto the dusty floor.

"Cut!" I heard Danny shout over the sound of my miserable retching. "Fucking cut!"

6.

I guess it's time for us to have that talk," I said.

Danny leaned against the production van next to me, arms folded, staring down the quiet street. The sky was dark now, and the temperature had finally cooled to a tolerable eighty degrees. After I had finished being sick, we'd continued with the shoot, and had made our day by a hair.

"Why did you do it?" Danny asked after a long, tense silence. "Why did you give that interview? Why can't you just show up and do your job and be a professional?"

There were many answers I could give to this question, but all of them felt like none of his goddamn business.

"You know, I never wanted to hire you in the first place," Danny continued when I didn't speak. "I'd heard the rumors about you and your family. I knew you'd be trouble, but the network thought casting a washed-up child star from a cult hit would increase our ratings. But no one cares about you anymore, *Olivia*. You had your moment, and this attention you're getting online . . . it'll be over by tomorrow, but you'll go on being a fucking pain in my ass. My job is hard enough without having to babysit you." He looked at me, and although we'd worked together for five years I felt no warmth from him, no familiarity. It was like he'd already forgotten me.

I should have begged for my job, told him I could change. But hearing him give voice to my worst fears ignited my last spark of dignity. "Go to hell, Danny," I said instead. This man thought he knew me, but he had no idea what I'd been through. No idea how much worse I could have ended up.

Danny laughed tiredly and rubbed his eyes. I noticed an abnormally shaped mole on the back of his hand that he ought to get checked out, but I wasn't about to point it out to him.

"Your contract expired last week. It's over, Liv. I'm cutting you from the show."

It took a few seconds to find my voice. "You can't replace me. My character's name is Liv Hendricks. She's *me*."

"I have no intention of replacing you. We can't afford four leads anymore. And to be honest, you're too old to be wearing these outfits."

He put his hand on my shoulder, trying for a comforting gesture, but it felt more like a shove out the door.

"I'm sure you'll land on your feet."

*   *   *

Wheeler called three times as I rode home from my last shoot as a member of *Bullsh?t Hunters*. Thankfully my Uber driver didn't speak much English and made no effort to engage me in conversation. I didn't want to talk, not to a stranger and not to Wheeler. I let his calls go to voicemail.

At home, I filled my favorite chipped coffee mug with bourbon, downed it in three swallows, hardly felt the burn. My hangover began to dissolve. I poured another drink and collapsed on the couch, feeling numb. I sipped the bourbon as I scrolled through my text messages and Twitter notifications, which had multiplied over the course of the day. Most of the text messages were from Wheeler, but there were a few from Gemma, amounting to: *What are you going to do about the video?*

The video.

I couldn't hide from it forever.

I clicked on the link Gemma had texted that morning, and Freya McBride's blog post loaded. I skipped the text and scrolled to the video, clicked PLAY. My face filled the screen, my eyes glazed and my cheeks flushed. But my speech was barely slurred. I became strangely articulate when I was blackout drunk. Articulate and angry.

The video was eight minutes and twenty-three seconds long.

By the time I finished watching it, I was quite certain that no one in this town would ever hire me again.

◆　◆　◆

I quit acting after Miranda went missing. Cold turkey. Done. I turned my back on it forever. Or until I ran out of money, which took about ten years. My retirement would have lasted longer if I had left Los Angeles, bought a little house in Arkansas or North Dakota, somewhere no one wanted to live.

In truth, the money wouldn't have lasted that long even if I had moved to a cheaper city. The network sued me for breach of contract after I quit, so by the time I turned eighteen and could access my trust fund there was only $332,000 left. I invested half of it, and lost most of that when the market crashed.

By twenty-seven I was broke. I hadn't worked in a decade, hadn't gone to college. I refused to ask Gemma or Desiree for money, so I did what any out-of-work actress would do: I waitressed.

That was when Mac Patrick "discovered" me, working at an Italian restaurant in Mar Vista, where every sauce tasted the same and the pasta was always overcooked. The restaurant was empty when the fat man with the cell phone glued to his ear walked in, seated himself, and waved wildly for a menu. He commenced to bark into his cell for the next thirty minutes. By the time he hung up, he'd gone through two baskets of bread and four Diet Cokes.

"Bowl of linguini Bolognese and a Caesar salad, extra dressing, extra Parm. More bread." He hadn't even bothered to look at the menu. He was looking at me, instead. He glanced at my body, appraising, but not in a lascivious way. His eyes settled on my face.

"You've got a look," the fat man said. "Who reps you? Whoever it is, they're worthless if you have to work in this dump. The food is barely edible, the bread is stale, and I've seen better atmosphere in an Olive Garden."

"Then why did you come here?" I asked.

"Because I knew it would be empty, and there's nothing a fat man hates more than having a room full of people stare at him while he eats. You didn't answer my question. Who reps you?"

"I'm not an actress."

The fat man reached into his suit pocket to pull out a card. "Doesn't matter. I know the look when I see it. When you decide to do something with your life, give me a call. I don't know if you can act, but you're interesting to watch, and that's enough to get started."

He inhaled his food and left without saying goodbye. I tossed his card in the trash and didn't think about it until a month later, when Mac Patrick returned to the restaurant. By then the constant smell of garlic and stewed tomatoes was getting to me. I couldn't sleep unless I got drunk first, and even then nightmares left me more tired than when I'd gone to bed. I needed to do something more stimulating in my waking life to distract me from what was in my head. It was time to come out of retirement.

I sat down at Mac's table and told him my name— my real name—with the caveat that he not use my former celebrity to shoehorn me back into the industry. I was Liv Hendricks now.

Mac signed me right then and there while he ate spaghetti and splattered sauce on the paperwork. A month later, after a steady stream of auditions, during which no one recognized me (the thirty pounds I'd gained since I was seventeen helped), I began landing jobs, mostly little things at first, regional commercials and featured extra work. The more I worked, the fewer nightmares I had, and the fewer nightmares I had, the less I drank. By the time I was cast on *Bullsh?t Hunters*, I was almost not miserable.

Then, a year ago, Mac Patrick was found dead in his Woodland Hills home. Heart attack. Big surprise to no one.

I hadn't signed with another talent agent. I told myself it would be a betrayal to Mac's memory. If Mac's ghost manifested in front of me now, he would have covered his eyes and shaken his head, muttering, "Liv, Liv, Liv . . . what am I going to do with you?"

* * *

I emptied my second mug of bourbon and poured another, spilling a little on the kitchen counter, and a little more on the floor.

I didn't have a savings account. I had four thousand dollars in checking, but that wouldn't last a month in LA. I needed to get a new manager, start auditioning again. But I was thirty-two now, geriatric in Hollywood years. The best roles would go to actors ten years younger than me, and they would play women my age.

Plus, there was the *LA Femme* video. The nail in my career's coffin. I would be deemed an insurance risk and a publicist's worst nightmare.

My phone vibrated. I checked the screen. A text from my neighbor Elliot.

Can we talk?

I didn't even remember giving him my number. I responded:

Come over.

In less than sixty seconds, there was a tentative knock on the door. I let him in. He looked me up and down. I was still wearing my schoolgirl costume.

"About last night..." Elliot said, hanging his head and hiding his hands in the pockets of a slouchy maroon hoodie. "I guess we were both pretty drunk, so I don't know if it meant anything, but...we should at least talk. Right?"

"Have you seen it?" I asked, and Elliot's brow furrowed in confusion.

"Seen what?"

I sighed, removed my cardigan, let it fall. There was only one thing this costume was good for anymore.

I took Elliot's hand and led him to my bed. I still had a strict policy about not sleeping with anyone in the building, but I wouldn't be able to afford my loft much longer anyway.

7.

It wasn't the best sex of my life, but it gave me something else to think about for ten minutes. I wasn't sure I'd ever gotten the hang of sex. Or maybe the problem was that I had never dated anyone long enough to get comfortable asking for the things I wanted. The things I didn't want to want.

Tie me up and hurt me. Make me beg for it to stop. Make me suffer.

Afterward, Elliot rolled onto his back and sighed in that contented way men do after sex, like all of their problems have been solved. He walked naked to the bathroom. I listened to him pee, hoping he would make some excuse to leave.

The toilet flushed and the sink ran. Elliot walked back into the room. His penis was still semi-hard. He got back into bed and pulled me down to snuggle on his chest. His breathing deepened as he prepared to fall asleep. I wriggled out of his hold and into a T-shirt.

"Where are you going?" he asked.

"I need a drink. You want something?"

"I'll take a beer."

"I don't want to open a beer if you're going to fall asleep." Alcohol was a precious commodity now. It must be conserved.

"I'll stay awake, then," he said, eager to please. I knew I should be flattered that a good-looking guy with a decade less cell degeneration than I had wanted to get something started with me. But his sycophantic sucking up left me wondering if his attraction had more to do with my celebrity status, minor as it was these days.

In the kitchen, I poured myself another bourbon and grabbed a bottle of hefeweizen from the fridge. I walked back to the bed and handed it to him, but I stayed standing. I was restless again, crawling out of my skin with anxiety. Maybe it was time to give up drinking and become a pot-head.

Elliot twisted the cap off the bottle. "Can I ask you a favor?"

"Depends on the favor."

"I need to shoot something next week. I was hoping you'd be in it."

"Are we making a sex video already?" Maybe that would help jump-start my career.

He laughed and shook his head, but I noticed the definition of his penis straighten beneath the sheet. "Just a scene to help get funding for my feature. You know that crowd-sourcing site Shot in the Dark? I'm going to post a video about my project and see if I can get enough backers to start shooting. With you in my video, I'll get way more views."

So there it was, the real reason he was interested in me. Sure, he probably thought I was pretty. Sure, he probably enjoyed having sex with me. But my face and body could be put to far more advantageous uses. I should have pegged him as a star-fucker the second I found out I'd slept with him.

"Is there anyone in this city who *isn't* doing a Shot in the Dark campaign?" I asked.

Elliot shrugged, but he looked hurt.

"I'll do it," I muttered. It wasn't like I had anything else going on.

His smile told me I'd just made his night. At least I'd made one person happy today.

"Come back to bed." He held out one arm and offered that part of his chest so many women loved to use as a pillow, the fleshy hammock between pectoral and shoulder. I set my bourbon aside and slipped into bed next to him. Elliot began stroking my back. He rolled toward me, cradling my head, and kissed me. His warm, beery tongue filled my mouth, and his hands drew my hips closer to his. My mind wandered to one of the comment threads under the *LA Femme* video that had gotten me fired, someone saying I deserved my own show. That all I needed was a camera, and I could crowdfund the whole thing.

I sat up. "How does it work? Shot in the Dark, I mean."

"You want to talk about this now?"

"Yes."

Elliot propped himself on an elbow. "You have to propose a project on the site. Most people shoot a scene or a short film as proof of concept, or make a video where they talk about the idea, kind of do a sales pitch and outline their reason for choosing this project and why it inspires them. Then you post your video and state how much funding you're looking for. Once it's all set up, you blast it out to social media and spread the word. If backers meet your goal, then you get to keep the money. If not, your project doesn't get funded."

I nodded, thinking this over. Crowdsourcing sites like Kickstarter and Indiegogo and Shot in the Dark were a last resort in the entertainment industry for those seeking funding, but tended to be effective if some kind of recognizable celebrity was attached to the project.

Now that I'd outed myself as Olivia Hill, I might as well benefit from all the negative attention I was receiving. Danny had said that by tomorrow everyone would have forgotten about me already. If that was true, I didn't have time to waste.

"Go get your camera and tripod," I told Elliot.

"What are we doing?" He sounded hopeful, probably thought I was serious about the sex video. But I wasn't that desperate. *Not yet.* I was, however, desperate enough to try something I'd never considered before. All I needed was a project. I didn't have one, but maybe it didn't matter. I'd leave that up to the Internet to figure out.

8.

I woke to a ringing phone, a thunderous headache, and the regret that I hadn't stopped on my way home from getting fired to buy a new bottle of Advil. I went through one of the big ones every month, the kind they sold at office supply stores that were supposed to treat the migraines and menstrual cramps of an entire company.

I retreated beneath my blankets, waiting for my cell to stop ringing. I intended stay in bed until it was time to sleep again. It wasn't like I had a job to go to.

This thought made me sit up abruptly. My recollection of what happened after I got home last night was foggy, but not missing entirely. A brownout, not a blackout. It would come back to me if I didn't think too hard about it. I had a strobing, fragmented memory of inviting Elliot over and having mediocre sex with him to distract myself. But I must have sent him home afterward, because I was alone.

My cell started to ring again. This time I reached for it, saw Wheeler's name. I answered.

"So..." he said. "You seem to have landed on your feet. How long have you been planning this coup?"

"I don't—" I stopped talking as the jumble of memories I'd been missing began to come back to me. "Wheeler, I'm going to call you back."

I hung up and got out of bed, scrambled around my loft until I found my laptop on the coffee table. I picked it up and opened it. The last webpage I had visited was the first thing I saw, a project listing on shotinthedark.com. *My* project page, which included the video I had made last night with Elliot's help, and the amount of funding I was seeking for my project ($10k). Beneath my estimated backing number was the amount that had been pledged thus far and the word: BACKED!

$27,000.

I blinked and read it again, but the number didn't change.

I barely breathed as I watched the video I had posted on Shot in the Dark. It was short and to the point, unlike the video of me Freya McBride had posted on *LA Femme*. And although I had definitely been drunk when it was recorded, I doubted anyone could tell. I was *on*.

"My name is Liv Hendricks, and as many of you now know I used to go by the name Olivia Hill. Up until a few hours ago I was one of the hosts of a reality TV show on which my friends and I investigated unexplained mysteries, urban legends, ghost stories, and weird tales. But I'm on my own now, and I want to offer my services to you—to all of you—as an investigator of unsolved mysteries, specifically those that involve missing persons. If you choose to back my project, you can suggest a mystery, but the backer who contributes the most will have the right to assign my investigation. I will document each investigation on camera and post video updates, so you'll be a part of the experience from start to finish."

In the video, I paused, and my hand strayed momentarily to the puckered line of scar tissue that cut across the right side of my brow, no longer concealed. I must have removed my makeup so it would show. I wanted to think the choice wasn't deliberate, that I hadn't consciously decided to milk my sister's disappearance for sympathy backers, but I knew myself better than that.

"When I was seventeen, my younger sister Miranda disappeared," I said to the camera. "I may never find out what happened to her, but if there are questions out there that I can answer for someone else, I want to try. Thank you for your support."

After the video ended, I sat there thinking about what I had said. What I was offering, and the genuine earnestness with which I had offered it. So unlike me, this kind of public sincerity. But apparently it had worked.

I clicked on BACKERS and perused the list. Several hundred people had offered pledges of between ten and a hundred dollars, along with their suggestion for the mystery I should investigate. There were a few facetious suggestions—Stonehenge, the Bermuda Triangle, my balls, my ass, my taint—but most were serious cases involving missing people. One woman pledged five hundred dollars for me to track down her teenage daughter, who'd gone to a party with her friends and never come home.

If I'd had the choice, I would have taken her case, but the backer whose pledge I had to honor was the one who had donated the most. This particular backer had identified himself as Red_Stranger. He wanted me to investigate a series of disappearances on a place called the Dark Road, and he was willing to pay me twenty thousand dollars to do it.

Twenty. Thousand. Dollars.

It had to be a joke.

I clicked on the button to privately message Red_Stranger and typed:

Is this a serious offer? If so, I'll need some kind of verification.

I went to the bathroom and brushed my teeth. By the time I returned to my laptop, Red_Stranger had responded.

Ms. Hendricks,

Allow me to introduce myself. My name is Jonas Kron. I don't know if you remember, but we almost worked together many years ago. You were my first choice for the lead in one of my films. You passed on the project, but I assure you there are no hard feelings, and I think you'll find that I am a reputable backer for your project. No doubt you are wondering why I'm making such an extravagant offer. Let me explain.

I have, just this year, revived the Stone's Throw Pie and Film Festival in Stone's Throw, California, where I reside part-time. Unfortunately, this town's reputation has suffered due to a series of disappearances that took place on what people call the Dark Road. Here is a link to a recent article about the Dark Road published on a popular blog.

http://www.2scared2sleep.com/darkroad

As to your question, your backers' funds are verified before the totals contribute to your goal. The source of my funds is legitimate. If I am your highest backer—and I do believe I will be—I require only two things: that you start your investigation immediately, and that you keep my identity private.

Yours,

Jonas Kron

By the time I finished reading Jonas Kron's message, I was biting the inside of my cheek hard enough to leave tooth marks. I had to force my jaw to relax. I knew exactly who Jonas Kron was. His bizarre, experimental horror films were an acquired taste, but he had a rabid cult following that worshipped his work. The cult of Kron went by a variety of names. Kronites. Kronophiles. Kronopheliacs. There was even a form of cosplay called Kronsplay, in which people dressed up as characters from Kron films. Kron was the darling of prestigious international film festivals like Cannes and Toronto, but his work regularly drove audience members from theaters. His first film, *Anathema*, about a twisted, incestuous family who had the heads of wolves, inspired a murder that had made headlines twenty years ago. A man stabbed his wife and dog to death, sawed off both of their heads, and switched them. When they were all arranged on the sofa with *Anathema* playing on TV, he put a gun in his mouth and blew out the back of his skull.

Another of Kron's films, *The Reddest Red*, which involved a series of ritual murders of small-town, menstruating, redhead virgins, had inspired a copycat killer to go on a murder spree through the Bible Belt. The copycat had never admitted that he was inspired by Kron's films, but he had a quote from the film tattooed on his back: *Good girls don't bleed*.

And then there was *The Girl and the Wolf*, the film Kron's casting director had approached me to star in. I hadn't actually turned him down. Desiree had done that, worried playing a part in one of Kron's films would damage my wholesome-teen brand. I remembered fighting with her about turning down the role without asking me, which was not to say I would have accepted the offer. Kron was notorious for his improvisational directing style. He wrote the story and the script as he filmed, so his actors never knew ahead of time what they were agreeing to do on screen. Still, a part of me had always regretted not accepting the lead in *The Girl and the Wolf*, which had become renowned in the horror canon. After that film, his career began to decline. He still made movies, about one every three years, but the problem with his shocking art house films was that he had raised the bar too high. He couldn't out-shock himself. His later films began to seem like cheap imitations of his own work.

Regardless, the man was a legend. And this director, whose work had inspired more than one mimic to translate fictional murder to real-life murder, would be choosing my first crowdfunded investigation.

9.

THE DARK ROAD

Chuck Jones
7/10/18—Filed to MYSTERY
17 Comments

There is a road in central California on which few people drive, especially if they know its history. Dag Road leads to an out-of-the-way tourist town named Stone's Throw (pop. 1,507), although what the town is a stone's throw away from no one seems certain. This secluded mountain village is known for several attractions—its apple orchards, its wolf sanctuary, its annual pie and film festival, and, most notably, its Jonas Kron film locations. The Norwegian film director, who built his career on elevated shock value, shot two of his most celebrated movies in Stone's Throw, *A Stranger Comes to Town* in 1994 and *The Girl and the Wolf* in 2003.

But after disappearances began on the road in 2006, Stone's Throw's reputation as a popular getaway destination (especially for Kronophiles) suffered and tourism declined. Now, instead of being famous for the best apple pie in the state and a wolf sanctuary boasting over twenty wolves, Stone's Throw is known for its Dark Road.

That's what people call it now. The Dark Road. It literally is a dark road, boxed in by the remains of a once thriving forest that was ravaged by fire in 2003, the trunks of the trees blackened by flames. Still, the forest is so dense that if you drive the Dark Road at night, it will appear as if you're traveling through an organic tunnel that stretches for miles. In the early 20th century, the Norwegian immigrants who settled Stone's Throw restricted the road's access after dark, which is how the road got its name. *Dag* means "day" in Norwegian. No one is entirely sure why nighttime travel was prohibited on the road. Probably it was because of the risk for accidents due to the way the bowing trees block moonlight (remember, this was before automobiles, so most travelers rode on horseback or in wagons and carriages). But it could also have been due to a series of animal attacks that took place on the road, most likely involving wolves or mountain lions.

It's hard to imagine a more appropriate place for several women to mysteriously vanish, leaving behind their vehicles and belongings but little evidence of what befell them. The most recent disappearance occurred only a few days ago, on July 5, 2018, when thirty-three-year-old Ana Newman's vehicle was found abandoned on the shoulder of the Dark Road, near a popular hiking trailhead, frequented by backpackers and Kronophiles alike. Local law enforcement launched an investigation that quickly hit a dead end, as have the previous investigations into the cases of three other missing women. But Ms. Newman's disappearance has been the highest profile. She was formerly known as Annika Kron, niece of Jonas Kron and star of *The Girl and the Wolf*. After filming for *TGATW* wrapped, she remained in Stone's Throw for several months, living with her uncle, but she left the town abruptly and it is rumored that she never spoke to her uncle and his family again. Over the years, she has been sighted by the occasional Kronophile, but not often. She changed both her name and her appearance, dyeing her long blond hair black and cutting it short. No one, including Jonas and his son, Soren, knows why Annika returned to Stone's Throw after more than ten years of living in anonymity.

"Residents of Stone's Throw are shocked to learn that another woman has vanished on the road," says the new sheriff, Brian Lot, less than a year into his first term, "but we want to assure prospective visitors our town is a safe and happy place."

That someone kidnapped these girls from the Dark Road seems to be the most likely theory, but there are others in circulation, including alien abduction, cults, witches, human trafficking, human sacrifice, and doorways to alternate dimensions. Some even think the girls were taken by the *Ulv Konge*, a hulking, nightmarish creature with the head of a wolf featured in *A Stranger Comes to Town*.

Some think the missing girls merely stopped to hike and got lost, a likely enough theory, as their cars were found parked at a hiking trailhead. As to what really happened to the girls on the Dark Road, all we can do is speculate, because none of the women who disappeared were ever seen again.

But one man is determined to save Stone's Throw from being blacklisted, despite this most recent tragedy involving one of his own family members. That man is Jonas Kron, whose first film premiered at the Stone's Throw Pie and Film

Festival in 1970. Kron resides in Stone's Throw part-time. He has chosen to organize the festival this year (co-organized by his son, Soren Kron) in an effort to draw a larger crowd.

Who knows if anyone will dare to show up?

Comments

WonderLust9000 The Ulv Konge is going to get you!!!! PS this article didn't mention that one of Kron's locations for "A Stranger Comes to Town" is in the woods where the girls disappeared. *32 days ago*

> **BurntToast63** "A Stranger Comes to Town" fucked me up for life *32 days ago*

Smokethisplease Human trafficking. That's what's happening here. Those girls are probably on a ship to Iran or something by now, all addicted to heroin. Too bad none of them had Liam Neeson for a dad. *37 days ago*

> **TeamEnigma** This is central CA, not Mexico *37 days ago*

> **Smokethisplease** Is it? IS IT? *37 days ago*

NotReal89 I've been on that road. There's something wrong there. You can feel it. The whole area creeps me out. *38 days ago*

> **NiceGuyXOXO** That's bullshit. The town is adorable, way less touristy than Solvang. The pie is amazing. Everyone should visit at least once. Stay at the Eden Tree Inn. *38 days ago*

> **NotReal89** I think it's YOU *38 days ago*

MistressPayne Know what I'm never going to do...go to Stone's Throw. Not worth it for all the pie in the world. And I fucking love pie! *43 days ago*

GrrowlBop Okay, I'm obsessed with this. It's gotta be Jonas Kron, or another of his copycats. It can't be a coincidence, right? This director who makes the MOST fucked up movies just happens to live in a town where a bunch of women go missing? Come on. He's involved. RIGHT? *44 days ago*

> **NiceGuyXOXO** Way too obvious. *44 days ago*

10.

When I finished reading everything relevant I could find about the Dark Road, I texted Wheeler to ask if he could meet me for breakfast at our regular downtown café, Ledlow Swan. The only available table was on the patio, where we could enjoy the view of a homeless woman across the street pulling her hair out in handfuls and throwing it in the trash.

"I'm having second thoughts," I said, setting my menu aside.

Wheeler eyed the homeless woman. "Yeah. I'm losing my appetite, too."

"Second thoughts about Shot in the Dark. I might call it off."

Wheeler twitched the hair out of his eyes and blinked hard at me, mole-like. He needed glasses or contacts, but he refused to go to the optometrist and get a prescription, claiming he didn't have enough time or insurance to bother, but I knew it was because his worsening eyesight made him feel his age. There was nothing like being in entertainment to convince a person that the thirties were the new eighties. Ironic since LA was a city of immature adults who made a living (or attempted to) playing pretend. But it wasn't the same for male actors as it was for females. Male actors in their thirties were still cast in adaptations of young adult novels to play the actual *young adults*, while female actors were left with mommy, politician, or dystopian despot roles.

"Talk to me," Wheeler said, so I told him about the Dark Road disappearances, leaving out nothing except that Jonas Kron was my backer.

"I'm not a real detective," I finished. "I can't do this."

Our waitress—a translucent-skinned girl with blue-gray hair and a neck tattoo of a koi fish—appeared to take our drink order. She had toothpick-shaped slashes of scar tissue up her forearms. A former cutter. If Miranda was still alive out there somewhere, I imagined this is what she would look like.

"Everything okay?" the waitress asked, and I realized I was staring. We ordered and handed over our menus.

"So what are you going to do?" Wheeler asked when the waitress had sauntered away, clearly in no hurry to put in our order.

I held up my hands. "I don't know. I made almost thirty thousand dollars in my sleep last night. If I don't follow through with the project, I don't get to keep it. And if I don't keep the money..." My gaze wandered to the homeless woman across the street, who had finished pulling her hair out, and now had both hands down the front of her pants and a beatific grin on her face. She looked familiar. I was nearly certain she'd starred on a sitcom in the 1990s.

"What would Big Mac tell you to do?" Mac Patrick had been Wheeler's talent agent as well as mine. He'd discovered Wheeler under similar circumstances: while getting a beer at a dive bar in Culver City at two in the afternoon.

I fidgeted with the napkin on my appetizer plate. "I don't know."

"He would tell you to take risks," Wheeler said.

"I'm not sure this was the kind of risk he meant. Police have been investigating this road for years. If professionals couldn't figure it out, how can I?"

"Maybe you're exactly what it needs. Fresh eyes. An outsider perspective. And this is what you do, investigate weird shit."

"Pretend to investigate weird shit."

"Whatever. You know the routine. Is there really that much difference between being a detective and playing one on TV?"

"Probably, yeah."

"Our country elected a reality TV star president. If that can happen, you can make the jump to private detective."

I sipped my coffee in thought. The constant rattle and roar of traffic on 4th Street felt like shrapnel tumbling around in my brain. I wished we'd gotten a table inside. It was impossible to think clearly with so much noise in my head. I bet it was quiet in a little tourist town like Stone's Throw. It would be nice to get away, go somewhere peaceful for a while. Peaceful except for the Dark Road.

"It's not like you're helpless," Wheeler continued. "I've seen you on the gun range. You're a better shot than I am."

That was an understatement. Back when Wheeler and I were still auditioning, Big Mac had suggested that we learn how to handle guns so he could add that to our "special skills." I was a natural.

If it came down to it, I knew how to protect myself.

* * *

After breakfast, I headed back to my loft, weaving around slumbering homeless people and dodging piles of dog crap. It seemed everyone who lived downtown had a dog, despite the scarcity of grass. Every time I stepped over an exceptionally large mound of shit, I thought of Blitz and wondered if I'd ever see the big dog again in real life, or if I would have to tune in to *Bullsh?t Hunters* to spend time with him.

When I was back in my loft, I closed the door and leaned against it, surveying the few hundred square feet that I called home. If I didn't accept the Dark Road challenge, I would be broke in a month, and I would lose the walls I had never gotten around to decorating. I'd rather go back to waitressing than ask Gemma or Desiree for money. I promised myself a long time ago I'd never resort to that, no matter how bad things got.

I brought my laptop to my threadbare Craigslist sofa and opened my Shot in the Dark profile. At the top of the page, near my name, was a tiny envelope symbol, my inbox for private messages. I clicked on it and scrolled through the messages, but didn't read any until I came to a new one from Red_Stranger, aka Jonas Kron.

Ms. Hendricks,

Are you waiting for another backer to beat my offer? Or perhaps you've educated yourself about the Dark Road, and you are getting cold feet. If so, let me tempt you further. The $20k I pledged is still on the table, but if you succeed in discovering who is behind the disappearances I will add another $20k to the sum with one proviso: You must conclude your investigation before the commencement of the Pie and Film Festival. That gives you three days starting now.

In addition, I will book your accommodations and cover the bill for your entire stay. I expect to hear from you soon.

Yours,

Jonas Kron

I sat back, bewildered. Forty thousand was a lot of money for me these days. And even for someone like Jonas Kron, who was clearly loaded, it was a lot of money to pay an out-of-work actor to do a job she was unqualified to do. Why was he so eager to throw this sum at me when he could hire an experienced private investigator to do a much better job? Maybe because he knew I couldn't succeed, and he'd never have to pay me the second half.

I responded:

Mr. Kron,

Before I accept your offer I have to ask, why are you willing to pay me so much to investigate the Dark Road? It's unlikely I'll solve this when the police couldn't.

Liv

I hit SEND and waited. It occurred to me that Kron might be the one who'd been abducting women (including his niece), as had been suggested by a commenter on the 2scared2sleep thread. This scenario seemed far-fetched, but I filed Kron away under possible suspects, and realized as I did so that I was already getting started. I was actually eager to set my mind onto a task more challenging than reciting hackneyed dialogue and pretending to be scared. My alcohol-soaked brain had lain dormant long enough.

I didn't have to wait long for Kron's response.

Ms. Hendricks,

There are three reasons I have chosen to put my faith (and my funds) in you. The first is simple and should be evident to anyone who watches my films: I have a taste for the sinister and the bizarre, and I think a web series investigation of the Dark Road will be to my taste.

The second and most important reason is my niece, Annika, who was the most recent victim of the Dark Road. In case you are wondering if I am actually the person responsible for the disappearances of these women, you needn't bark up that tree. As a particular kind of auteur, I am a likely suspect. However, my alibis are ironclad. I was on location during three of the disappearances, including Annika's. This has all been well documented. Still, people wonder, and my reputation has been damaged. I would prefer to be remembered for my films, not unfounded suspicion. If you were to uncover the truth about the Dark Road, my name would finally be clear. The police tried and failed to provide answers. The private detectives I hired to find Annika failed, as well. At this point, I'm willing to put my faith in a different kind of investigator, an outsider if you will. Perhaps you will see what they could not.

The third and final reason is your sister, whom you mentioned in your pitch video. You understand the torment of living with the unknown. Perhaps if you were able to solve this case you would have some measure of peace in regard to her disappearance. Your tragic story intrigues me, and I believe it is deserving of a satisfying conclusion.

Yours,

Jonas Kron

When I finished reading Kron's message, I hit REPLY immediately and typed back before I could change my mind:

I'll do it.

His reply was just as rapid.

The first $20k will be deposited into your account immediately. The future of the second installment depends entirely on you. Remember our agreement. Keep my identity as your backer between us, and get started immediately.

11.

"Are you sure you don't want me to come with you?" Elliot asked, heaving a suitcase into the trunk of my car. "I could be your all-purpose camera, grip, sound, lighting guy. Whatever you need."

I shoved the suitcase to the side to make room for my newly acquired camera bag, the least costly of my recent purchases. When Jonas Kron's twenty thousand dollars—now *my* twenty thousand dollars—appeared in my bank account, I'd gone straight to Samy's Camera and dedicated a couple of thousand dollars to necessities: a digital SLR camera, extra batteries and cards, a tiny GoPro that would be good for on-the-move footage, a tripod, and a body camera the size of a button, the kind used on hidden camera shows and reality TV. We'd occasionally used them on *Bullsh?t Hunters* when we'd needed to steal shots. Now I wished I'd stolen one of the body cameras before I was fired.

"If I can't hack it, I'll call you," I told Elliot, and slammed the trunk closed. I *had* considered asking him to come with me to Stone's Throw, where Jonas Kron had booked a room for me at an inn called the Eden Tree. According to the inn's website, it was situated at the edge of a vast apple orchard, where guests were free to pick and eat as many apples as they could stomach.

But Elliot would not be joining me unless I got desperate for help. His neediness had already begun to suffocate me.

Elliot frowned and kicked one of my tires with the toe of his shoe. "You were supposed to help me with that scene, remember?"

I slapped my forehead. "Shit. I completely forgot. I'm sorry." I fished my keys out of my purse. "When I get back we can do the scene. I promise." It was a promise I meant. Despite his ulterior motives for attaching himself to me, I did appreciate his help shooting my Shot in the Dark video last night, and I wanted to pay him back.

He followed me to my car door and opened it for me, stood in my way so I couldn't get in. He licked his lips to moisten them. I turned my head away, feeling a surge of revulsion. I'd enjoyed kissing him last night, but that was when I was drunk and needed a distraction. A lot of things seemed like a good idea after half a bottle of bourbon.

But I didn't want to get into this with him right now. When I got back, I would do his scene, and then I'd let him down easy if he actually had feelings for me. I would tell him I did not do relationships, which was true. Relationships required emotional intimacy, and I didn't want to inflict mine on anyone worth dating. It wasn't them, it was me. It was most definitely me.

I allowed Elliot a dry, sisterly kiss, but he turned the kiss into a hug and nuzzled his nose into my hair.

"I'm worried about you," he said. "You'll be all alone up there."

I could have told him about the Glock 19 semi-automatic pistol stowed beneath my front seat, which I'd bought for the practice range. I'd never had call to use the Glock in real life, but Wheeler was right. I could handle myself if it came down to it. I wondered if Elliot, whose parents paid his rent, could say the same.

"I like being alone," I said. "Don't worry about me."

•   •   •

It was hard to believe that only a few hours had passed since I'd accepted Jonas Kron's deal, but there had been no time to waste. I had three days to wrap up this investigation if I wanted to double my money. I didn't have time to second-guess my decision, agonize over the pros and cons. And when it came right down to it, what the hell else did I have to do?

During the drive to Stone's Throw, I downed two ventis of strong, black coffee and thought through what I had learned about Stone's Throw and the Dark Road, formulating a plan for where to begin my investigation.

Stone's Throw, founded in 1881, was first settled by three wealthy Norwegian families—one of them the Krons, ancestors of Jonas—who pooled their money to purchase a large plot of land, sight unseen. They were told that the land was a mere "stone's throw" from San Francisco, when in fact it lay more than two hundred miles to the southeast.

It was a town founded on a lie, but it thrived nevertheless, thanks first to the apple orchards and later to the film industry.

Because the town was only a four-hour drive from Los Angeles, it became a getaway destination for Golden Age film stars, writers, directors, and executives, which necessitated a magnificent movie theater. The stars needed some-where to watch themselves on screen when they were staying in Stone's Throw. The movie theater was christened the October Palace, because in Stone's Throw the high season was October, when the townspeople threw their annual Pie and Cider Festival, which later became the Pie and Film Festival. Jonas Kron debuted the films he shot on location in Stone's Throw at the festival, which increased its notoriety significantly, although the extreme nature of his films changed the overall ambience of the town.

In 2003, a wildfire razed an expanse of the dense woods that fronted Dag Road, leaving behind miles of charred forest, and Dag Road became the Dark Road. The woods, I learned online, were called the Wolf Woods. Apparently, before they were hunted down and killed, the mountains and forest around Stone's Throw were teeming with wolves.

The disappearances began in 2006.

The first girl to go missing was Allison Sargent, age eighteen, a freshman at UCLA who, according to her friends, had intended to major in film studies, and had been an avid fan of Jonas Kron's films and also of mushrooms and LSD. Her car was found parked at the hiking trailhead, where it sat for several days before anyone called to report it. If there had been any trail, it had gone cold by the time local law enforcement got around to investigating.

No sign of Ms. Sargent ever surfaced. No new evidence emerged. The people of Stone's Throw were shocked that something like this could happen near their town, but it was an isolated incident. There was no body. People assumed she had made a pilgrimage to Stone's Throw to worship Kron at some of his locations, and had gotten lost in the woods and died of exposure. Animals would have taken care of her remains. Everyone moved on.

Four years later, Camille Banks, also eighteen, vanished under similar circumstances. The only real difference between the two cases was that Camille had been on her way to Stone's Throw for the Pie and Film Festival. She was an actress who lived in Los Angeles, and was making her debut in one of the films being screened, although she was little more than a featured extra.

The next victim, in 2012, was Mary Elizabeth Woodson, nineteen years old, an art school dropout who worked at a tattoo parlor and was living out of her car in San Francisco at the time of her disappearance. She had no close friends, and her co-workers had no idea why she went to Stone's Throw. The owner of the tattoo parlor claimed he had given Mary Elizabeth his old laptop, but the laptop was not in her car when it was found.

Jonas Kron's niece, Ana Newman née Annika Kron, was the fourth girl to go missing in the summer. Annika had been living in a suburb of Salt Lake City, Utah, working from home as a freelance translator for the publishing industry. People online speculated that she had chosen to live in Salt Lake City because it was less likely she would be recognized there. Mormons eschewed the extreme sex and violence in Kron's mostly NC-17 and unrated films.

The one person who had regular contact with Ana Newman/Annika Kron was a psychiatrist who prescribed her mood stabilizers and antipsychotics for bipolar disorder.

Annika's car was found in the same place all the others were: parked at the hiking trailhead. Annika was thirty-three, by far the oldest of all the women who'd gone missing.

Jonas was filming on location in Eastern Europe when Annika's car was found.

It wasn't much to go on, but I was just getting started.

My investigation would begin at a gas station called Fill 'r Up, located half a mile from the turnoff to Stone's Throw. It was the last place the Dark Road victims had been seen alive.

12.

There was nothing sinister about the Fill 'r Up, a vintage gas station that belonged on a retro cover of the *Saturday Evening Post*. I pulled up to the antique pump station and killed the engine, then got out and set up my camera on a tripod facing the gas station. It was a disappointingly pretty picture, nothing like the abandoned carcasses of buildings I'd explored on *Bullsh?t Hunters*. But cute could turn menacing with the right sound design. A few ominous tones would make the Fill 'r Up seem like a backwoods rape shack.

When the camera was ready, I positioned myself in the picture, standing to the right of the frame. One of the gadgets I'd bought was a wireless remote for the camera, so when I was ready to record I hit the button.

"Hi everybody. I'm Liv Hendricks, and this is the first stop on my investigation of the Dark Road. Since 2006, four women have gone missing on this road. The most recent disappearance occurred three months ago. As far as anyone knows, Raymond Talbot, who owns this gas station, was the last person to have contact with the missing women. Mr. Talbot has agreed to talk to me about those encounters."

This last part wasn't exactly true. I'd called Mr. Talbot's store several times during my drive to ask if he would be willing to let me interview him, but he never answered the phone.

I ended the recording and packed up my gear. When I turned toward the gas station, I saw Mr. Talbot standing in the doorway.

He wasn't smiling.

＊　　＊　　＊

"You don't have a permit to film my station. I'm going to have to ask you to delete that footage."

These words might as well have been the kiss of death. I'd hoped Stone's Throw was far enough from Los Angeles that the locals would be ignorant of the rules. Anything filmed for commercial purposes required a permit. Many a rogue production had been shut down for the lack thereof.

"Are you Raymond Talbot?" I asked, and he nodded reluctantly, dark, button eyes squinting above his ruddy round cheeks. Talbot looked to be in his early sixties. He was at least a hundred pounds overweight, with a blizzard of white hair and skin the color of something that's been left in the oven too long, Santa Claus just back from vacation along the Mexican Riviera.

"I'm Liv Hendricks." I held out my hand and Talbot squashed it in a swollen fist.

"Liv Hendricks?" His head cocked, and he leaned uncomfortably close to examine my face. His breath was piney with gin. It was three in the afternoon. I wasn't judging, only filing this information away. Day drinkers were generally alcoholics unless they reserved their habit for Sunday brunch, and alcoholics liked to run their mouths. I should know.

Talbot's eyes widened with recognition. "I know you! I've seen you on TV!" He glanced past me. "Where's the rest of the gang?"

"They'll be along later," I lied, not wanting to burden him with the complicated truth. "In the meantime, can I ask you some questions about the girls who went missing on the Dark Road? On camera," I added, and produced a talent release, hoping he wouldn't read it and realize I wasn't actually interviewing him for *Bullsh?t Hunters*.

I released my breath silently when he glanced at it for less than a second and waved me inside.

"Is there anything in particular you remember about your encounters with the missing women?" I asked Talbot, who opted to stand behind the counter with his palms planted on the Formica countertop, the sleeves of his flannel shirt rolled up to show meaty forearms like holiday hams.

"Well, the thing is, I didn't know any of them were going to go missing, so I didn't pay much attention," he said. "They were all pretty, though, I can tell you that. All of 'em blond and pretty and young. But I only remember that because their pictures were in the paper."

I smiled at him and nodded encouragement to let him know he was doing great.

"Do you live in Stone's Throw?" I asked. I was starting with the easy questions, the ones that would put Talbot at ease. It was a tactic I had learned on *The Hills Have PIs*. The frog-in-a-pot-of-boiling-water technique. By the time the suspect realized he was being interrogated, he was already cooked.

"Oh yes," Talbot said with a big smile that showed a row of small teeth as yellow and crowded as ripe corn. "Lived there all my life, and I never plan on leaving. Great little town. It's a shame what these disappearances have done to our economy, though."

"You must drive on the Dark Road often to get to your gas station here. Does that ever make you nervous?"

"Absolutely not," he said, puffing out his chest.

"Because you're not a woman, and only women vanish?"

"Well...yes. But my wife drives on Dag Road, and I don't worry about her, either. Remember, there's no proof those women were abducted. For all we know, they went hiking and got lost. It's easy to do if you leave the trail, and there's not much cell phone reception in this area."

"Has anyone who isn't young, blond, and pretty ever wandered off in the woods and gotten lost?"

He scratched his head. "Well, there was Jonas's niece. She was in her thirties, I think, and her hair was dark. I didn't recognize her when she came in. She must have dyed it. I'd seen her around town a few times when she was shooting that wolf movie with her uncle, and her hair was so blond back then it was almost the same color as mine."

He smiled and patted his snowy hair. I tried not to take offense at his implication that a woman in her thirties was no longer young, and focus on the fact that Annika still fit the profile, at least partially. She was a natural blonde, and regardless of her *decrepit* age she was still attractive. The picture that had accompanied news of her disappearance showed a woman with flawless bone structure framed by a severe, blunt-cut bob. She didn't celebrate her beauty, but she maintained it. Still, I understood why Talbot didn't relate her to the other victims. The rest were young enough that they could still be labeled as girls.

In my research, I'd found a promotional photo of Annika and an actual, live wolf that had been taken by a now dead and famous photographer (a friend of Kron's, I assumed) and was featured in a coffee table book of the man's work. In the picture, Annika had been a glowing nymph of a teenage girl. She wore her wardrobe from *The Girl and the Wolf*, a white, lacy baby-doll dress with a Peter Pan collar and red knee socks. Her pale hair framed a round, open face and ran the length of her spine. Her coltish legs went on for miles. She had looked, to me, almost identical to Gemma when she was that age, although if this same picture had been taken of teenage Gemma she would have posed, pushed out her lips and her chest, sexualized the photo in some way. It would have gone from art to something closer to child pornography.

"Annika is the only victim who ever lived in Stone's Throw, is that correct?" I asked.

"Yes," Talbot said, a hint of hesitation in his voice.

"And you knew her?"

"I don't think I ever spoke to her," he said. "I just... noticed her. Not...I mean, I didn't..." His skin flushed a deep, high-blood-pressure red. "Everyone knew who the Krons were, that's all."

"What do you think of the Kron family?"

"Oh..." Talbot's gaze shifted to the ceiling. "Jonas is always polite. He stops here to gas up that vintage car of his. Looks like what Alfred drives in the old *Batman* show. I don't think it gets more than a few miles to the gallon, and it doesn't have any of the new features like cars have now, not even a tape cassette. But Jonas, well, he's an eccentric. Wait till you see his house. The Red House, he calls it."

"Are you a fan of his films?" I asked.

Talbot's mouth tugged down at the corners, but he forced a laugh. "Me? Oh no. I saw one of them and didn't sleep for a week."

"Does it bother you that someone who makes those kinds of films lives in your town?"

His smile was rigid. "Stone's Throw probably would have dried up a long time ago if it weren't for Jonas."

He'd skirted around the question, but that told me enough.

There was a crunch of tires on gravel outside. I glanced out the window to see a black convertible speed up to the pump.

Talbot stared out at the convertible, his expression almost pained. "Well, much as I'd like to gab all day..." He trailed off, and I got the hint.

It was a good beat on which to end the interview. I cut, thanked Talbot, gathered up my equipment, and departed with my signed release before he could start asking questions.

As I was leaving the store, the driver of the convertible held the door open for me, and I was forced to acknowledge him with a smile. The social contract between men and women demanded it. But when I met his eyes, I stopped abruptly, stared at his face, which was startlingly familiar. Where had I seen him before? He looked about my age and was over six feet tall, with slicked-back blond hair and eyes the color of a glacier. He was good-looking enough to be an actor. Maybe I'd met him on set.

I was about to ask his name when his eyes lowered to my chest, and then returned to my face, smiling approval of what he found there. While I wasn't offended by the idea that men couldn't help their compulsory tit-checks, this felt different, like he did it to make me uncomfortable. To remind me what I was to him, a body that existed for his visual enjoyment.

I ignored him and went on my way, but he called from behind me, "Hey." I turned back around. He held out Talbot's talent release. "You dropped this."

I tried to take it from him, but he withdrew the paper, grinning at me. "What do you say?"

For the briefest of moments, his gall left me speechless. Sometimes I forgot that men like this still existed in the world. Men who took pleasure in extorting power away from women in the most trivial ways.

I snatched the release out of his hand and stuffed it into my camera bag, turning to walk away without saying thank you. Fuck the social contract.

"It's nice to see you again, Olivia," he said from behind me, and I froze, turned back around, squinting at him.

"Do I know you?"

"We've met."

I smiled thinly at him. "I don't remember you. That's probably for the best."

I kept walking, and behind me I heard him laugh.

It wasn't until I was in my car, heading away from the gas station, that I remembered where I had seen the man: in a photograph with Jonas Kron, accompanying an online article I'd read that morning about the Stone's Throw Pie and Film Festival. The man I'd just encountered and insulted was Soren Kron, Jonas's son, whom I most definitely needed to speak to in regard to the Dark Road disappearances.

I was about to flip a U-turn and head back to the Fill 'r

Up to see if Soren was still there. I could, I supposed, un-clench my jaw long enough to give a convincing apology to the arrogant bastard. But before I had a chance his convert-ible blew past me on the highway, driving at least fifteen miles an hour over the speed limit.

So I kept going. I'd see him in Stone's Throw.

13.

When I reached the turnoff to Stone's Throw, I pulled to the shoulder of the road and attached my GoPro to the driver's-side window. I started recording. The sun was about to set, and the light would only be good for another fifteen minutes.

And then I was on the Dark Road. I drove five miles under the speed limit so I could take it in. I could have slowed to a crawl and no one would have been bothered. Mine was the only car on the winding road that slithered through ubiquitous forest, the trees packed in tight on either side.

After ten minutes, the wall of trees thinned, shifting from brown and green to charred black, branches grasping and interlocking overhead, creating a tunnel of scorched fingers.

The Wolf Woods.

I had been here before, I realized. I'd visited this place through Kron's film *A Stranger Comes to Town*, lauded as one of his most arcane and troubling. In it, a mysterious woman with amnesia wanders into a bucolic town. She doesn't know who she is or where she came from. A family welcomes her into their home. They feed her, house her, make her a part of their insulated, picturesque world. But the woman begins to suspect that the town isn't as charming and virtuous as it seems. The townspeople smile constantly, and eat pie for every meal, and they talk about little other than the weather. The woman wakes one morning to discover that a section of her long blond hair has been snipped off in the night. She catches the family she's staying with spying on her through holes in the walls, then discovers a group of people holding a masked vigil in the woods at night. She decides to try to escape the town, but her plan is discovered. She is captured, bound hand and foot, and taken to a clearing in the woods, in the middle of which stands a fairy-tale cottage. The woman is deposited outside the cottage door, the townsfolk offering her as a human sacrifice to the monstrous god that lives inside—the *Ulv Konge*, a towering chimera with the head of a wolf. With the smiling townsfolk picnicking in the clearing on red-and-white-checkered blankets, eating dripping cherry pie, the creature eats the nameless woman alive. When it's finished, the townspeople pack up their picnics and disperse, like they've done this a thousand times.

A film studies teacher might say Kron's film was a feminist (or possibly anti-feminist) allegory, or a commentary on the microcosm that was small-town USA, on the distillation of secrets and myths within insular communities. Fancy ways of saying the film was about a group of people willing to feed an innocent girl to a monster, as long as it was *their* monster. As long as they got to go home and sleep in their own beds at the end of it all, and it wasn't their own daughter being swallowed, they could justify their complicity.

Or something like that.

I pulled over on a section of the road where a long swath of the shoulder had been widened to allow for a parking lot. I didn't realize why until I saw the wooden signpost at the edge of the trees, indicating a trailhead.

I picked up my camera and got out. The sun had set, casting grim blankets of shadow over the road, the charred matchsticks of the trees. I filmed for a few minutes, but the wind was sharp and biting, and I was shivering too hard to keep the camera steady. I took a few photos and short video clips with my iPhone to use on Instagram and Snapchat, noticing that I had no cell reception on the Dark Road. Not a single dot.

I opened the trunk to retrieve my tripod so I could keep my camera steady and record some decent footage. The wind picked up then in a gale so forceful it made me lose my balance, and I had to brace myself against the bumper. A doleful, low-pitched moan of wind wove through the trees, shuddering in currents of air. The forest alive and twitching. I knew I should start filming, capture this classically eerie footage, but I felt frozen where I stood. I kept thinking of the first scene from *A Stranger Comes to Town*, in which the main character, the amnesiac ingénue, walks right up the center of this road. She's only wearing one shoe. In the film, she can't remember what happened to the other one. She has scrapes on her arms and face, and her little toe has been severed, or possibly bitten off. It drools blood as she walks. In the film, no attempt is made to call the police or find out what happened to the woman, and she never speaks, not one line of dialogue. Perhaps she traded her voice for a set of legs, minus one toe, Little Mermaid–style.

I whirled at a scraping sound behind me, a cry clawing

up my throat, only to find a stray, blackened branch being dragged across the road by an invisible force. The wind. Only the wind. But then came the howl. At first there was only the sound of one mournful, lupine wail, but it was quickly joined by others until the howling seemed to surround me. Logic told me that the wolves were caged at the sanctuary and couldn't hurt me, but they sounded so close, their howls echoing off the sides of the mountains and settling in the valley. My brain was not capable of believing logic at that moment. My fight-or-flight responses were kicking in, and they were leaning heavily toward flight.

I slammed the trunk, climbed back into my car, hit the locks, and stomped on the gas pedal. I was still shivering, chilled to the bone, so I cranked the heat up as high as it would go.

I'd come back later, I told myself. I would check into my hotel, and then I would return to the Dark Road. Not tonight. Tomorrow morning, when darkness was as far away as it could be, and the wolves were quiet.

14.

The Dark Road spit me out into Stone's Throw, and instantly the irrational terror that had gripped me evaporated. It could not survive in the face of such charming surroundings. Queen Anne houses with gables and turrets and front porches with rocking chairs. Fairy-tale cottages tucked into hillsides, guarded by frilly trees. Traditional Nordic houses painted primary colors, their lines so simple they were like a child's drawing of a house made literal. By now, most of the stores and cafés had locked up and turned their signs to CLOSED. Still, the old-fashioned, wrought-iron lampposts were lit, and twinkle lights hung from the trees. The place was like a holiday greeting card come to life. No wonder Kron had chosen to film his most famous movies in Stone's Throw. The production value was through the roof. It was impossible to frame a bad shot.

I drove around the village, getting the lay of the land, experiencing that same urgent sense of déjà vu I'd had on the Dark Road, like I'd dreamed this place before ever setting foot here. That wasn't the case, of course; it was familiar to me because I'd seen *The Girl and the Wolf* and *A Stranger Comes to Town*.

It had been over ten years since I'd watched *The Girl and the Wolf*. It had been released shortly after Miranda went missing, and at that time I couldn't stand to watch anything. No movies. No TV. All of it reminded me of the life I'd left behind, and I wanted to separate myself completely from my former existence. But after finally seeing *The Girl and the Wolf*, I had to admit I was relieved I hadn't been involved in the project. The film featured two seemingly perfect teenagers—Jack and Joelle (played by Annika Kron in her first and only role)—who form a destructive friendship when they discover a mutual fondness for anonymously tormenting their friends and enemies in a variety of sick and twisted ways.

The idea that Jonas Kron had not only cast his niece as the lead, but also improvised the story—which required a great deal of nudity and, it was rumored, actual sex—was appalling. It was no wonder he'd never been able to top *The Girl and the Wolf*'s shock value. I had always wondered how the story might have been different if I'd starred in it instead of Annika. Would I have inspired Kron to go in an entirely different direction? I supposed I would never know.

The main thoroughfare in the village was not a straight line but a vast circle, a sort of expanded roundabout with buildings in the center. The trees that lined the sidewalks held colorful bouquets of gold and red and orange fall leaves, still clinging to the branches for dear life. There was not a single chain store, no Starbucks or Coffee Bean, no Subway or Pinkberry or Urban Outfitters. The shops and cafés had cutesy, clever names like Humble Pie and To Pie For and Tarts and Tins.

But no matter how quaint the town appeared to me in real life, I could not shake the sense of malicious familiarity from Kron's films. I wondered if the decline in tourism had as much to do with how Kron depicted Stone's Throw as it did with the Dark Road.

I pulled to a stop in front of the October Palace, right at the center of the circle. The theater was magnificent, baroque, the marquee reading:

> STONE'S THROW PIE AND FILM FESTIVAL
> IT'S BACK!

I parked and got out to film B-roll footage of the village, though it would most likely be underexposed, too dark and grainy to use. The wind had died down, and the evening was bracingly crisp, smelling of fall, a kind of musty smokiness glazed with butter and sugar from the pie shops.

I cut and let my camera hang on its strap around my neck as I wandered around the deserted village. I walked to the October Palace's entrance and tried the doors. Locked. I cupped my hands to the glass and peered in. There was flickering light coming from behind the theater doors, just visible from the entrance. This was the kind of theater with only one screen. I'd always preferred this type of theater to the megaplexes that overwhelmed people with choices, mostly movies no one wanted to see. Theaters like the October Palace had no choice but to be picky, as they could only show one film at a time.

And there was definitely a film playing at that moment, though the theater was closed. Probably someone preparing for the festival. I knocked lightly, but no one appeared, so I gave up and returned to my car. Only then did I glance up at the hillside overlooking the town and notice a large, dark shape huddled in the trees, a congealed blood clot of a house. This had to be Kron's part-time residence, the Red House. I'd seen a picture of the Red House that morning while I was researching the Dark Road, a sprawling monstrosity in the style of the Queen Anne houses that were so popular in Stone's Throw, only Kron's was entirely red. The roof was red. The trim was red. The turrets and gables were red. The whole thing appeared to have been dipped in blood.

The Red House clashed unapologetically with the town's sickly sweet aesthetic, and I guessed Kron himself did, too. Did the people of Stone's Throw welcome him, or merely tolerate the eccentric director because he kept the town alive? Small towns in America were supposed to be havens of safe normality, and Kron lived on the other end of the spectrum.

I checked the time on my phone. It was almost seven p.m. I was starving, but food could wait. I had one more stop to make before I checked in to the Eden Tree.

Stone's Throw was too small to justify its own police department; it had only a sheriff's department and a few deputies. The sheriff who'd presided over the first three disappearances had to step down after he succumbed to Alzheimer's. Sheriff Brian Lot was currently serving his first term, which meant he'd been acting sheriff during only the most recent disappearance. That would have to be enough.

*　　*　　*

"Is Sheriff Lot available?" I asked the gray-haired woman working the front desk at the sheriff's station.

"We're about to lock up for the night," the woman said, smiling curiously at me. "Do you have an appointment?"

"I left messages on his voicemail, but didn't hear back."

Her smile remained fixed in place, but her eyes cooled as she asked, "Are you a reporter?"

"No." She waited for me to offer more information, which I did not.

Finally she picked up the phone. "Sheriff? A woman here to see you. A blonde," she added, eyeing me with unfathomable suspicion. She listened a moment before hanging up and opening the divider that separated me from her side of the desk. "This way."

Sheriff Lot's door swung open before I had a chance to knock. I had expected someone older, maybe with a flabby paunch and a non-ironic mustache. But the sheriff was in his mid- to late thirties, with no signature facial hair, though he could have used some to cover the acne scars on his cheeks and neck. Somehow they didn't detract from his attractiveness. Coarse hair the color of shoe polish. Intense black eyes. Broad shoulders and arms thick with muscle. He was the kind of man who could have sex standing and not make his woman feel like she was going to make him throw his back out.

He held out his hand. "You must be Liv Hendricks. I got your messages. Sorry I didn't have a chance to get back to you."

"It's no problem," I said, shaking his offered hand. He squeezed hard enough to make me wince.

"Come in," he said. "We have a lot to talk about. Something to drink? It's after seven, so technically I'm off duty."

"I'm sorry to keep you," I said, taking a seat.

He rummaged in a mini fridge under his desk and came up with a beer bottle that had no label. He cracked it open and set it in front of me. "Brewed it myself," he said.

My hand moved involuntarily toward the bottle. I

wanted to keep my mind clear, but I didn't want to offend him by refusing his beer right before I asked him if I could take a look at his case files. One drink wouldn't do me in, I told myself. But I couldn't remember the last time I'd had just one drink of anything that had an alcohol percentage, even kombucha.

I took a delicate sip, and the sheriff's upper lip curled.

"Why can't women appreciate beer? It's all white wine and Skinnygirl cosmos."

"I'm not here to do a tasting," I said, setting the bottle aside.

"I'm well aware of that. I know exactly who you are and what you're up to."

He took a long swallow of beer, then set the bottle aside and linked his hands behind his head, pulling his uniform taut against his chest. I found him annoyingly sexy. He had a sort of raw, unadorned masculinity that I didn't encounter much in LA. Guys in Los Angeles tended to be more like Elliot and Wheeler, neurotic and creative and soft around the edges. Sheriff Lot was a man's man, the sort who'd roll his eyes and leave the room if a woman mentioned her period.

"What is it I'm up to?" I asked, raising an eyebrow.

"You're here to do my job for me. Or to try."

"That's not exactly—"

"Do you know how much I make per year?" he cut in. "Thirty-two thousand. How much are you making off this little charade of yours?"

"That's not really your business," I said.

"No," he said. "But the Dark Road is, and you want a piece of my business. Did you think you could waltz into my office and I'd tell you everything I know about the disappearances? That I'd hand over my files to you and invite you into the investigation?"

I decided to take one more drink of beer, a bigger sip this time (20 calories). This was not going well. "Are you saying you want money for information?"

"I don't want your money."

"Then what do you want?"

"For you to go home. Just walk out the door, get in your car, and drive away."

"That's not happening."

"You're wasting your time."

"I just got fired. I have nothing but time." I leaned toward him, summoning my acting skills to cover the fact that this guy intimidated me. I needed him to think my balls were as big as his. "What bothers you more, the fact that I'm here to do your job for you, or the fact that I'm a woman here to do your job for you?"

He smirked, took another swig of beer. "Get the hell out of my office," he said nicely.

"Fine," I said. "But I'm not leaving town. There's no law against me asking questions about the Dark Road."

"That's true," he admitted. "But it *is* against the law for you to film for commercial purposes without a permit. So if I catch you, I'm going to seize your equipment and hit you with a fine." He smiled. "Just doing my job."

15.

The Eden Tree Inn stood at the edge of a seventy-acre apple orchard, a couple of miles east of Stone's Throw Village. It was the inverse of Kron's Red House, the same Queen Anne architectural style, a whimsical, wooden castle, but painted white with green trim instead of gore red. It was almost identical to a dollhouse Desiree had given me when I was six, my prize for landing my first big film role as the president's daughter in an action movie. I remembered peering in through the windows at the pretty, perfect world inside the dollhouse walls and understanding for the first time that I was not the girl who played with the dollhouse. I was the girl who lived inside one, being observed by everyone else. I existed for the amusement of other people. My life was theirs to watch.

I had told Desiree I didn't want the dollhouse, that she should take it back. The dollhouse was wasted on me. I was never going to play with it. I barely had time to play with any of the toys I already had. I was always working.

Desiree had gone cold when I rejected her gift. She

never yelled, rarely even raised her voice. She turned to ice, and that was worse. Any love she had for me didn't prevent her from the little cruelties she saw as necessary for molding me into the perfect package. Part of her job. My punishment for declining the dollhouse didn't come for three days. She waited long enough that I thought maybe she would let me off the hook this time. Sometimes she did that...tormented me with waiting for the ax to fall. And sometimes it never did. But not this time.

I didn't realize what she was doing until it was too late. I had an audition for a TV musical, and the morning of the audition Desiree insisted that my voice sounded raspy. She gave me glass after glass of apple juice to drink, first at home, and then in the car. By the time we reached the casting office, I had to pee so badly I was squirming, but Desiree insisted we were late, there was no time for me to use the bathroom. She rushed me into the casting office, my bladder screaming by that point. I stood in front of a row of mildly interested adults in a small room, a camera pointed at me. I told the camera my name, my age, my weight. They asked me to sing the song I had memorized and practiced for over a week. I had just reached the first chorus when it happened. My bladder simply let go, not in a trickle, but a rush. I was wearing tights, but they didn't hold in the deluge of urine. I'd probably drunk a gallon of apple juice. Piss splashed onto the floor at my feet, drenching my shoes, spreading in a wide puddle. The sharp scent of it filled the room, and I just stood there, stunned by what had happened, humiliated by the gasps from the casting director and her assistant, the disgust on their faces.

But I was relieved, too. Relieved because I saw the

smirk on Desiree's face, and I understood that my wait was over. This humiliation was my punishment.

I didn't get the part, and Desiree didn't take the doll-house back to the store. She gave it to Gemma, who tried to eat one of the dollhouse's dining room chairs and nearly choked to death. After that, Desiree finally got rid of the thing.

There were only two other vehicles in the lot, and both bore the Eden Tree's name and logo. It appeared I was the sole guest.

I had barely pulled to a stop when a tap on my window made my heart rocket into my throat. A man's face peered in at me. He had a disarming smile and a brown mop of wavy hair that dangled vine-like over the rims of his oval, wire-frame glasses, the kind that had never been in style, even when they were. I guessed his age to be anywhere between thirty and forty, but he had one of those vaguely forgettable faces that was hard to focus on. He resembled a hundred other people I'd known. He wasn't bad looking, just...plain.

He pointed at the name tag pinned to his dark-blue blazer: PORTER MORRISON, MANAGER.

My heart rate stuttered back toward normal, and I released my breath in a rush, my face hot with embarrassment. On *Bullsh?t Hunters* I'd played a version of myself that jumped at the word *boo*, but letting a person see me in a state of real alarm felt like being caught masturbating.

"Sorry I startled you," the man said when I rolled down the window. "I saw your headlights on the road. Thought I'd come out and help with your luggage."

I opened the door and climbed out. The manager adjusted his tie, though it was perfectly straight already, pinned to his shirt by a silver tiepin with a black circle in the center, very James Bond, but it wasn't the most appropriate accessory to pair with a hotel blazer, khaki pants, and brown loafers.

Grinning, he thrust his hand at me. "You must be Liv Hendricks. I'm a big fan."

"Really?"

"*Really* really. Pretty sure I've seen everything you've ever done. I'm kind of an entertainment fanatic, and I was obsessed with *The Hills Have PIs* when I was in high school. I even ordered one of those signed headshots of you from the network."

I laughed, warming to him. "Do you still have it?"

He grinned, showing teeth that were perfect on the top, slightly crooked on the bottom, as though his parents hadn't been able to afford a full set of braces. "Will you think I'm weird if I say yes?"

"I already think you're weird."

"Then yes."

Normally this kind of devotion would have creeped me out, but I couldn't help feeling flattered. This was just the kind of ego boost I needed after being fired.

Walking to the front doors of the Eden Tree, I caught the distant sound of wolf howls again, and chills raced up my back. "Do they do that every night?" I asked Porter. "The wolves, I mean?"

"No, no. Not every night. Just most nights." He winked at me, and I forced a weak smile.

Inside, Porter parked the silver dolly carrying my suitcase and camera gear next to the registration desk and went around behind the sternum-high counter. He'd left a plate of apple pie steaming in a bath of vanilla ice cream beside his computer. The smell of it made my stomach gurgle with hunger. I hadn't eaten since breakfast with Wheeler, and I was running on coffee fumes.

"I have you down for an open reservation," Porter said. "Is that correct?"

"I'm not sure how long I'll be here, so yes."

He raised his eyes. "I guess that means you're not in town for the festival." His tone was still friendly, but I detected an edge to it. All the bad press about the Dark Road must have been hard on the people who lived here.

"Not exactly," I admitted. "I'm investigating the disappearances on the Dark Road."

"Just you? Not the rest of the Bullshit Hunters?"

"I'm kind of... doing my own thing at the moment."

He nodded, returning his eyes to the computer screen. "I'm sorry, it's none of my business. I don't mean to pry."

"Don't worry about it," I said, and changed the subject. I wasn't here to talk about me. "Have you always lived in Stone's Throw?"

Porter nodded, and when he spoke the tension had lifted from his voice. "Born and raised. The Eden Tree has been in my family since it first opened. I inherited it after my mom died." He cleared his throat and turned away to grab a key from a shelf of numbered cubbies on the wall. From what I could see, there was not a single key missing. I was, indeed, the only guest.

"Are you expecting a full house during the festival?" I asked.

"Oh yeah," Porter said, turning around, an old-fashioned key dangling from his finger by its ring. "We're completely booked for the duration of the festival. Enjoy the solitude while you can. Tonight it's just you and one other guest." He checked his watch and frowned, mumbling, "She should have arrived by now."

Our eyes met, and I read the worry in his gaze before he shook his head and brought back his pleasant smile. "I'm sure she'll be along any minute," he said. Translation: I'm pretty sure she didn't disappear on the Dark Road. "Let me show you to your room."

Porter led me past an ornate tearoom to a long hallway, the walls papered in an intricate, somewhat dated design. I stopped abruptly.

"Kron filmed a scene from *A Stranger Comes to Town* here, didn't he?"

Porter raised an eyebrow at me, surprised or impressed or both. "You must have watched the deleted scenes. Most of what he filmed here didn't make it into the theatrical release version. That's why the Eden Tree isn't on the map for the Kronophile tour. Even in the deleted scenes, you only see this hallway for a few seconds." He smiled over at me, looking delighted in the way a geek does when he's encountered one of his own.

"So you're a fan?"

He laughed. "A fan, but not a Kronophile. I don't *worship* him, but I admire his process. Did you know he writes the script as he goes? That's why sometimes it takes him years to finish a film. The production for *A Stranger Comes to Town* went on in Stone's Throw for two years. A lot of the cast and crew stayed in the Eden Tree. It was great for business." His smile faltered. "We could use another Jonas Kron production to stimulate the economy."

"Have you ever considered moving somewhere else? Starting over?"

He shrugged. "I used to dream of moving to Los Angeles to become a screenwriter, but that business is too cutthroat for me. I don't think I'd last long."

"Do you write?" I asked, and then regretted it. I didn't

want to encourage this nice man to write. What he did here seemed far safer and less soul sucking. Most of the writers I'd known were narcissistic hacks or self-loathing geniuses.

"Let's just say I've never finished anything." He stopped in front of room nine. "This is you."

He unlocked the door and opened it for me. I stepped inside the room and did a slow turn, taking it in. The space was larger than my entire loft, with a settee, an antique roll-top desk, and a king-size sleigh bed. The mismatched furniture looked to be a hundred years old. There were shuttered double doors leading out onto a private porch, and beyond that into the orchard. On the desk sat a wooden pie box and two tall bottles of hard cider.

"Apple?" I guessed, lifting the lid of the pie box.

"Baked fresh this morning. And the cider is from a local distillery." He lifted my luggage off the dolly and set it upright near a mahogany wardrobe, which looked like something I could use to transport myself to a fantasy world filled with talking animals. "Is there anything else I can do for you tonight?"

I shook my head and reached for my wallet, but Porter held up his hands, backing toward the door.

"No, no, no. No tips. It's bad enough that my mom named me Porter, you know what I mean?"

"Fair enough." I walked Porter to the door, a wave of impending loneliness cresting over me. Once he was gone I'd be alone. No Bullshit Hunters. No Wheeler or Blitz or Danny. No clingy Elliot. Just me, and this insane task I'd undertaken, one I was almost guaranteed to fail.

"Is there a Wi-Fi password?" I asked, stalling.

"Yes! Glad you reminded me. You're going to need it. It would be generous to say the cell service in the area is unreliable." He took out a card and a pen, wrote the password on the back. "If you need anything, don't hesitate to call the front desk," he said. "And if you want someone to show you around, or get coffee with you, or dinner..." He trailed off, smiling shyly, and handed me the card. "Just ask. I know everything there is to know about Stone's Throw."

When I took the card, our fingers brushed, and my stomach did a giddy, urgent leap. It had been a long time since my body reacted to someone with such intensity. I had to remind myself why I was here. Not to make dates with innkeepers, no matter how nice and normal they seemed, but to find out what had happened to four missing women who were most likely dead.

Porter withdrew his hand, his eyes still on my face, more specifically on my forehead. His brows drew together. I knew he was looking at my scar.

"I was in an accident," I told him. "A long time ago."

"I know," he said. "I'm sorry. I didn't mean to—I'd just never noticed it before."

"The magic of makeup."

Porter cleared his throat and stepped through the door. "Well...good night, Ms. Hendricks."

"Call me Liv."

"Good night, Liv."

As soon as he was gone, I got to work.

*　　*　　*

I finished editing my first webisode just after midnight. It was only four minutes long, but brevity was what worked for web content. The Internet had a short attention span.

I uploaded the webisode to my Shot in the Dark profile,

which connected to all the major social media sites. I tweeted:

> Ride with me on the Dark Road as I search for the truth.
> #DarkRoad #ShotintheDark #LivHendricks #STFilmFest
> #creepy #unsolvedmysteries #horror #missingperson

Then I got a slice of apple pie and ate it while I watched Twitter light up in response to the video. I didn't even count the calories.

Even though I was exhausted, I didn't think sleep would come easy that night. I hadn't fallen asleep without the aid of at least a glass of wine in months, perhaps as long as a year. And my brain was *alive*. I was doing something. I had started something. For the first time in a long time, I didn't crave the numbness that set in after a few drinks. I was *occupied*.

There was no TV in the room, so I downloaded *The Girl and the Wolf* and *A Stranger Comes to Town* onto my laptop. I started playing *Stranger*, feeling the need to brush up on my Kron films, although I had no idea whether they'd come into play.

The film opened on the Dark Road, a static shot of the nameless girl in the distance, walking slowly toward the camera. She wore a retro 1950s swing dress, narrow at the waist with a skirt made for twirling. The fabric was white, covered in abstract red splotches. Only when she drew closer to the camera did the audience see that the red pattern on the dress was blood. This was one of the most popular Kronsplay outfits fans donned for Halloween and various cons.

I watched for an hour before fatigue dragged my eyes

closed. I didn't open them again until the movie was over and my room was as silent as a deprivation chamber. So silent that the creak of a floorboard was like an alarm that yanked me out of sleep.

I was sure before I even opened my eyes that the sound came from inside my room.

16.

I snapped awake and sat up, eyes scouring the room as I waited for them to adjust. I heard a wheezing, sucking sound, an asthmatic inhalation. My mind went blank with terror until I realized the sound was coming from the doors that led out onto my private patio.

One of the doors was open, just a crack, allowing the wind to hiss through.

My heart still thudding, I switched on the bedside lamp, flooding the room in yellow light. As far as I could see, I was alone. But the sound that had woken me wasn't the wind wheezing through the crack in the door. It was the groan of a cranky floorboard. I heard the sound again as I padded across the room to peer outside, and startled when I saw an ember of light glowing in the darkness fifty feet away.

Someone was out there smoking in a garden gazebo. All I could see of her was her blond hair. She was dressed in dark clothing that blended with the night, so her hair seemed to levitate like a wig hanging from fishing line, once the gold standard in special effects.

I glanced back at the clock on the nightstand. It was two thirty in the morning, and the temperature outside had to be forty degrees, plus windchill factor. Was she that desperate to smoke, or had she been the one to open my door?

After turning on all the lights in my room and checking every conceivable hiding place, I glanced outside one more time to see if the smoker was still there. If she was, I intended to confront her. But the woman had vanished.

I rubbed my eyes. Had I imagined her? Perhaps the creak I'd heard had merely been the sound of the building settling. Perhaps the door hadn't been closed properly, and the wind had blown it open.

To satisfy my paranoia, I picked up the room phone and called the front desk, disappointed when a woman answered instead of Porter. He must have gone home for the night.

"Hi, I'm in room nine. I was just wondering..." I trailed off, unsure what to ask. "I was wondering if my friend checked in yet. The other guest staying at the inn tonight? I tried to wait up for her, but I fell asleep."

"Oh yes," the woman said brightly. "Ms. Stone Maretto arrived safe and sound."

Everything in me went still. "Ms. Stone Maretto, you said?"

"Yes. Suzanne Stone Maretto. She's the only other guest we have on the books."

"Could I get her room number?"

"Room ten, right next to yours. She requested it."

"Thanks." I slammed the phone down and covered my face with my hands.

Suzanne Stone Maretto was the character Nicole Kidman played in the 1995 film *To Die For*, about a fame-obsessed sociopath who enlists three teenagers to kill her husband. She was one of Gemma's favorite characters when we were teenagers, and I guessed she still was.

Suzanne Stone Maretto was the name Gemma assumed when she checked into hotels and wanted to remain anonymous.

17.

"When did you start smoking again?" I asked when Gemma opened the door, the scent of Pall Malls wafting from her clothes. There was no question in my mind as to the identity of the smoker in the gazebo.

"I indulge in the occasional cigarette," Gemma said, and stepped back to allow me in. "I don't make a habit of it."

Gemma had started smoking when she was thirteen. Desiree didn't try to stop her. It helped her keep her weight down. As far as I knew, she'd quit smoking (along with everything else) after Miranda disappeared. After she became me and I became her. If I was honest with myself, the main reason I avoided Gemma was because I felt like she had stolen my life, my identity, and I couldn't stand the juxtaposition of being in her presence.

Gemma closed the door behind me and sat on her bed. I stayed standing, my arms folded.

"Nice room," I said. "Mine is bigger, but I guess you know that."

She blinked at me and cocked her head. "Why would I know that?"

"Because you were in it about ten minutes ago."

She shook her head, and I couldn't tell if her baffled expression was genuine or feigned. That was the problem with a good actor, and Gemma *was* good. Always had been. A good actor and an even better liar. But they amounted to the same thing.

"I was not in your room," Gemma said slowly and carefully, as though she thought I might not understand her language.

"Then it must have been a coincidence," I said. "I wake up because I hear someone in my room, find my patio door open, then see *you* outside smoking. Yes. All of that sounds like pure coincidence."

Her eyes stayed on mine, her gaze steady as she repeated, "I was not in your room."

"Did you open my door?"

"Of course not. Why would I?"

"Why would you follow me to Stone's Throw?"

She didn't have a ready answer for that. She pressed her lips together, stood again, and turned slightly away from me, toward her own patio doors. "I was worried about you," she said, and looked offended when I barked a laugh.

"Come on, Gemma. You can do better than that."

She faced me, folded her arms. "After I heard what you were doing, I read about the Dark Road. I think I have a right to be worried. But I also have a few friends whose films are debuting at the festival, so I already planned on attending. I rearranged my schedule so I could head up a couple of days early and keep an eye on you. Besides... I'm considering doing a Kron film, and I've never met him.

This seemed like a good opportunity to kill all the birds with one stone."

"I'm not interested in being one of your birds," I said. "I'm doing just fine on my own."

"I'm sure you are. But maybe we could spend some time together anyway."

Again, I had to laugh. "Are you dying or something? Why the sudden interest in spending quality time with me? And why did you sneak up here in the night instead of telling me you were coming?"

"Because I knew you'd tell me not to come." She sighed and ran a hand over her face. She looked more exhausted than I'd ever seen her, and she was too thin. Her head looked like a lollipop on her twig of a body. Desiree was probably delighted.

Thinking of our mother, I narrowed my eyes at Gemma. Where Gemma went, Desiree followed like a malevolent shadow. "You didn't bring Desiree, did you?"

"No," Gemma said firmly. "I told her not to come."

"Since when does anyone tell her what she can or can't do?" I shook my head at Gemma, disgusted. "If you ruin this for me—"

"I won't," Gemma insisted. "I swear, Liv, that *LA Femme* interview you did...at first I was angry with you, but then it made me realize how bad things have been for you, how much you've suffered, and I'm so sorry for that. I just want to have a relationship with you again. You're the only sister I have."

"Whose fault is that?" I asked, and walked out, slamming the door behind me, not caring that the sound reverberated through the halls of the Eden Tree. We were the only guests, after all.

* * ◆

Back in my room, I did one final check to make sure no one was hiding in the wardrobe or behind the shower curtain. Then I climbed into bed with my phone and laptop, too angry with Gemma to attempt sleep right away, lest she follow me into my dreams.

It was just like her—the old her—to show up and try to be best sisters right when I was having a moment. Back when we were costars, she took any opportunity she could to hog the limelight, which was fine with me. It was never what I wanted. It was never why I worked. But the attention was like sunlight to Gemma, activating her, bringing her to life, making her stretch and grow. I used to wonder if part of the reason she began to party destructively was in the hope of getting caught. For a little while, she would be the center of attention. But she must have known that kind of public fascination was fickle. That after it faded she would be left unemployable and unwatched.

I piled a slope of pillows behind me and leaned into them while I skimmed through texts I hadn't bothered to check that day. Most were from Elliot.

Miss you

Did you make it OK?

Starting to worry

Why are you ignoring me?

Are we OK?

I sighed and texted him a cursory message:

All is well. Not ignoring you, just busy.

I silenced my phone and put it on the nightstand. I decided to check my email one last time for the night so I could put it off again until tomorrow afternoon.

The most recent email was from Danny, a quick message that left me smiling smugly.

Liv, can we talk tomorrow? The network is starting to wonder if letting you go was a mistake.

Letting me go. Like I'd been the one struggling to extricate myself of them, and they had reluctantly set me free. Danny and the network would have heard about my Shot in the Dark project by now, and realized the exposure I was getting was exactly what *Bullsh?t Hunters* needed to keep it relevant. If they wanted me back, would I go? My Shot in the Dark project might keep me afloat for the moment, but what if that moment passed and I found myself in the same position I'd been in after I was fired?

I typed a quick response to Danny.

We can talk.

There. Nice and noncommittal. Talking didn't mean I was coming back to the show. I needed time to think about it.

I clicked on the next message. It had come from an email address I didn't recognize. The subject line read: FOLLOW THE WHITE WOLF. But there was no message, only a link to a YouTube video.

I hesitated a moment, thinking it might be spam, but curiosity got the better of me. I clicked on the link and a YouTube page loaded. The video began to play.

The footage was infrared and shook with each step the cameraman took toward a sleeping figure. She lay with her back to the camera, but I didn't need to see her face to recognize her. I knew the messy blond hair, the jeans and gray sweater she wore.

They were the ones I'd dressed in that morning. The ones I was still wearing.

The girl in the video was me.

The cameraman reached out a black-gloved hand and gave my hair one quick stroke. In the video, I stirred and muttered something unintelligible.

The video abruptly ended.

For a moment, all I could do was stare in shock at the black screen. My hand shaking, I moved the curser to click PLAY again.

But the video wouldn't play.

It had already been deleted.

OLIVIA HILL

2003
17 YEARS OLD; 109 LBS.

18.

I was underdressed and underage for this party, but I moved through the room like I belonged among this cattle call of hungry women. Hungry in every sense of the word. Their little black dresses hung on brittle clavicles and crucifix shoulders, surgically altered tits hard and hoisted. They outnumbered the middle-aged males five to one. The men—producers, I guessed— were soft-bellied, balding, bespectacled. But they had penises and power, and could take their pick of these ambitious wannabe starlets lining up to audition with an enthusiastic blowjob.

It was the kind of party I went to great lengths to avoid, and that even Gemma tended to steer clear of. We were not like these girls, the ones who would do anything for their big break. We didn't need this scene. So what was Gemma doing here?

I would be sure to ask her while she was still drunk. Alcohol made people honest, and Gemma lied as easily as she told the truth. I hadn't trusted her since she learned how to form simple sentences.

Curious glances shifted my way, but I didn't think anyone recognized me. I looked like a different person before the hair and makeup department prepared me for camera, teasing out my best features, my absent father's high, round cheekbones, my mother's cornflower-blue eyes, the pouty mouths Gemma and I shared. I'd heard us referred to as the BJL—blowjob lip—sisters. Such lips were a hallmark of any child star worth his or her salt, whether we used them or not. I did not. I wasn't so sure about Gemma.

A quick tour of the first floor turned up no sign of Gemma, so I moved to the lower floor. The tiered house was built into the hillside, with a living room on the second level, as well. When "The Big One" hit, this house would most likely topple like it was slapped together with Elmer's Glue. The lights were dim downstairs, the music louder, the crowd younger, hotter. A dozen people were dancing, making out, groping whatever was within reach. A blonde slumped on the couch, passed out with her legs slightly parted, giving anyone who looked at her from a certain vantage point a view up her dress. For a moment I took her for Gemma, but on closer inspection I realized she was a cheap imitation of my sister. I tried to wake her up anyway, ask her if she wanted me to call her a cab. She was in bad shape. Her breath, when she muttered a request that I gofuckaway, was vodka and vomit.

The lower-level party guests were more Gemma's crowd, but I didn't see her anywhere. I had explored all of the common areas in the house, which left only the bedrooms. I'd saved those for last, hoping I wouldn't have to play "what's behind door number 1, 2, 3, 4, etc...."

The repetitive thump of house music switched abruptly to dreamy Portishead. "Sour Times" plunged the mood of the party into something darker, more surreal. I caught two guys staring at me from across the room. They were around my age, one tall with a striking, angular face ruined by terrible, home-dyed maroon hair chopped at his chin, a Kurt Cobain clone; the other unremarkable in every way except his eyes, which were a radioactive shade of green. I felt a magnetic pull to the one with the eyes. Growing up surrounded by professionally good-looking people, average looks had always struck me as exotic. I craved a nice, normal boy, a beta male who went to public school and maintained a B average, someone who didn't know what he wanted to do with his life, had no big dreams, no great expectations. This guy would have seemed my type, but this was not a party for ordinary guys.

"Hey," Maroon Hair said, approaching me with more swagger than most guys his age could muster. A momentary swoon of heat passed through me at the smell of his cologne, the kind designed to make girls' stomachs flip. It was probably full of pig pheromones, something that would disgust me if I knew what I was inhaling.

"Are you looking for Gemma?" he asked.

I blinked in surprise. They recognized me. Did they know Gemma? Had she asked them to keep an eye out for me?

"Where is she?" I asked.

"She left with a couple of older dudes. She was

pretty out of it, though. She could barely walk. We tried to get her to stay, but she wouldn't listen."

"Shit," I muttered. Had Gemma blacked out and forgotten I was on my way? "How long ago did they leave?" I asked.

"Fifteen minutes, probably," Green Eyes answered. "They went to another party. Something exclusive." He glanced at his friend as though for permission before saying, "We know where it is. We can take you there if you want."

"Thank you," I said, overcome with relief. "I need to find her."

Maroon Hair shrugged, starting toward the stairs. "We were about to leave anyway. This party sucks."

I hesitated, turning to Green Eyes. I had already decided he was the one I could trust. His friend had a smarmy vibe that put me off, reminding me of studio executives and agents, the kind who didn't see a person when they looked at me, only a value. What value did I have to Maroon Hair? Bragging rights for screwing a famous chick? Perhaps he thought that's how I would repay him if he helped me find my sister. He would be disappointed. In some ways, I'd lived more in seventeen years than most people did in eighty, but one thing I had not done was have sex. I wasn't giving my first time away to some random guy I barely knew. Call me old-fashioned or uptight or even a prude—and Gemma had—but I was holding out for something more meaningful than a hookup.

"How do you know Gemma?" I asked Green Eyes.

He looked momentarily confused, and then seemed to deflate a little, his shoulders sagging. "You don't remember us."

I squinted at him, as though trying to bring his face into focus, and then smiled. "Oh my God, I'm so sorry! Yes, of course I remember you. We met at that thing. When was that?" I had no idea where we'd met, but I didn't want to offend him.

Luckily, he seemed to buy my act. "Last month," he said. "It's okay if you don't remember. We only talked for a few minutes. I'm Jimmy, by the way. And that's Russel."

Russel stood at the foot of the stairs, waiting with an expression of vapid impatience.

"Jimmy and Russel. Yeah, I definitely remember you guys." And I actually thought I did. Sort of. The names sounded familiar. "It's just—" I gestured around at the darkened lower level of the house. "Different context."

"Sure, don't worry about it," Jimmy said. "It's weird we ran into you here. This doesn't seem like your kind of party."

"I'll take that as a compliment," I told him, though I thought it strange that he presumed to know what my kind of party was. "I could say the same about you," I said, moving through the crowd toward the foot of the staircase.

"Gemma invited us," Jimmy said, and then in a smaller voice, "Not us, really. She invited Russel, and I tagged along."

"So they're…friends?" As far as I knew, Gemma didn't have friends. She had a stable of beauty foils, wing girls half as attractive as her that she clubbed with, and a few preening teen heartthrobs she occasionally pretended to date for celebrity gossip's sake. But she did not associate with the likes of Russel and Jimmy, nobodies who couldn't advance her career.

Jimmy didn't get a chance to answer my question. We reached Russel, and he slung his arm around me. "You get to ride shotgun. Sorry, Jimmy."

He said it as though I ought to feel privileged at such an opportunity. I noticed his eyes were red and watery, too wide open. He was on something. Maybe Russel was Gemma's drug dealer.

I slid out from under Russel's arm. "I'll follow you in my car. It's easier that way." And I wasn't about to get into a vehicle with two strange guys, whether they were Gemma's friends or not.

I was leaning toward not.

LIV HENDRICKS

2018

32 YEARS OLD; 142 LBS.

Facebook Fans: 9,002

Twitter Followers: 37,443

Instagram Followers: 7,413

19.

I emerged from my room at sunrise the next morning. I hadn't slept since watching the video that had been emailed to me. I didn't know if I'd sleep again for the remainder of my stay in Stone's Throw.

Porter was stationed at the front desk, his laptop open in front of him. He drank coffee from a delicate teacup with a filigreed design around the rim, and seemed completely comfortable doing so, though I could imagine someone like Sheriff Lot ridiculing him for it. When he saw me, he stood, smiling.

"Good morning. How did you—" His question cut off. Anyone could tell just by looking at me how I'd slept. My eyes were nests of red veins. "Was the room all right?" he asked, concerned.

I hitched my camera bag up onto my shoulder, hesitating. I'd had a lot of sleepless hours to consider whether or not to tell anyone about the YouTube link. Since the video had been taken down, I had no proof there'd been anyone in my room. I'd tried responding to the email, demanding to know who had sent the link, but the message immediately bounced back to me, undelivered. If I went to Sheriff Lot, he would probably tell me it served me right. I had even considered that he might be behind it, that this was an attempt to scare me away.

Then there was Porter. It was my responsibility to keep him informed about potentially criminal activities taking place in his hotel. But without proof he might think I was lying to sensationalize my project. Besides, an investigation into the safety of his hotel right before his busiest time of year would be bad for business, and I liked him too much to do that to him.

I wrenched my lips into a smile. "The room was fantastic. Five stars. If I look tired, it's because I worked late."

"Ah. I'm a night owl, too. Or maybe insomniac is a more appropriate description. But who needs sleep when we can binge-watch *Black Mirror* all night, which is what I did. I've already had a couple of these." He nodded and lifted his teacup. "Speaking of which, there's coffee, tea, and pastries in the tearoom. And apples from our orchard, picked fresh this morning."

All I'd eaten since arriving in Stone's Throw was apple pie, so a breakfast of apples and pastries didn't sound appealing. But I needed something in my stomach, and I could definitely use the caffeine.

The Eden Tree tearoom was every little girl's fantasy location for a date with her dollies. There was a fireplace at one end, flames flickering inside the hearth, and a huge mirror above a mantel, crowded with old clocks and figurines. A crystal chandelier overhead reflected fragments of morning light around the room like an ethereal disco ball. A banquet table offered baskets of croissants and Danishes, bowls of apples, coffee carafes, and stacks of elegant china.

Feeling guilty that all of this had been laid out for just Gemma and me, I changed my mind about the pastry and grabbed a golden croissant. I stuffed it into my mouth (450 calories), catching my crumbs with a napkin. I put two apples into my camera bag and filled a teacup with coffee. I drank the whole thing in one searing gulp, then filled the cup again and returned to the front desk.

"So, I was thinking...I'd like to take you up on your offer." Porter's gaze remained blank. Had I misread his signals? "You said if I needed someone to show me around town—"

"Oh!" he broke in. "Of course!" He knuckled his forehead, a gesture that made him look like a ten-year-old who'd forgotten to do his homework. "Sorry. I'm a little distracted at the moment. I seem to have over-booked for this weekend. I'll have to cancel a few of the last-minute reservations. Hopefully they can find accommodations elsewhere in town, but there aren't a lot of options."

"At least you'll have a full house. That's a good thing, right?"

"Absolutely. I had to hire extra staff, just for the duration of the festival."

"I guess that means you'll be pretty busy over the next few days."

He smiled. "I'm on the desk until four, and then I'm all yours."

"Fantastic," I said as brightly as I could manage through the haze of my exhaustion. "Oh, one more thing. You wouldn't happen to have a map for local hiking trails, would you?"

Porter disappeared behind the desk for a moment, and reappeared with a single page covered in a network of squiggly lines. Bold letters declared at the top: THE WOLF WOODS. He laid the map down on the counter and grabbed a pen. "There's some great hiking in the mountains, but I assume this is what you're interested in." He circled a trailhead off the Dark Road, and made another circle in the woods. "This is the trailhead where the missing women's cars were found. It connects to a lot of other trails, so keep this map with you. It's easy to get lost. Oh, and keep an eye on the weather. It's supposed to rain today, and when it rains here it *really* rains."

"Thank you," I said, giving him a look. "I didn't think you'd be so forthcoming about all this."

He tapped his pen nervously against the map. "Last night, after I checked you in, I googled you and found out about your project. I'm sorry to hear you won't be on *Bullshit Hunters* anymore. You were the best part of the show."

I smiled, thinking of Danny's email last night. "You never know. They might miss me too much and bring me back."

He cleared his throat and set the pen aside. "I'll be honest, I think what you're doing could bring more negative attention to the town…unless you actually figure this whole thing out. And that's what I'm hoping for. An ending. A happy one, if possible."

"Then we want the same thing." I exhaled some of my tension, relieved to have him on my side. He'd lived his entire life here. If anyone could help me get started, it was him. It didn't hurt that I already liked the guy more than I liked most of the people in my life. His sweet, enthusiastic nerdiness toward entertainment reminded me that a lot of people out there lived for what I took for granted. And his protective instincts toward the town, although potentially inconvenient for me, were chivalrous and strangely honorable.

I pointed to the second circle he'd drawn on the map. "What's this?"

"That's a landmark, in case you do get lost. It's the Wolf King's cottage."

"The Wolf King?" I raised an eyebrow at him, and his pale skin flushed.

"You know, from *A Stranger Comes to Town*. The *Ulv Konge*. That's Norwegian for 'Wolf King.' I know, I sound like a Kronophile. Anyway..." He tapped the circle he'd drawn. "This is the actual location where Kron filmed the final scene. It was also in *The Girl and the Wolf*, if you remember."

I nodded. The cottage was where the malevolent teenage tricksters lured two of their unsuspecting classmates in order to trap and torment them.

"It's in the burnt woods, and it's a bit scorched but otherwise still standing. Kronophiles used to go out there at night and hold ceremonies to summon the *Ulv Konge*, but I don't know if that happens much anymore. Not since the disappearances started."

"But it's just for fun, right?" I asked. "No one actually believes the Wolf King is real, do they?"

He smiled, but there was something forlorn in his expression, like I'd brought up a painful memory. "Most people don't know this, but Kron's Wolf King is inspired by a local legend about a creature that lived in the woods and had the head of a wolf. Supposedly this creature attacked travelers on the road, but if the travelers made some sort of offering it would let them pass. When I misbehaved as a kid my mom used to threaten to drag me into the woods and offer me to the *Ulv Konge*. Needless to say, I was a very well-behaved little boy." He forced a laugh. "It was harmless for the most part. I'm sure your mother had her own terror tactics to keep you in line."

He had no idea.

The phone rang loudly then, making us both jump.

"Sorry. I have to—" Porter put his hand on the phone.

I stuck the map in my jacket pocket. "Thank you for this. I'll see you later."

My cell buzzed with an incoming call as I was walking out into crisp fall air. I paused on the wraparound porch and checked the screen. It was Danny. I let the phone ring until the last possible second before answering.

"Liv," he said stiffly. "How are you?"

"Fantastic, actually."

"Let's not belabor this," he said. He sounded like he was speaking through clenched teeth. "You know why I'm calling. The network wants you back. This buzz you're getting…it would be good for the show. People are responding to the new you. So how about we join forces on your Dark Road investigation?"

My smug smile flickered out. Danny didn't just want me. He wanted the Dark Road.

When I didn't respond, he continued. "What you're doing is not sustainable in the long run. You need to be realistic, Liv. You know that. You can't do this on your own."

"You've had your budget cut three seasons in a row," I said. "Maybe it's what *you're* doing that's not sustainable."

"Are you seriously going to throw this opportunity away?"

I thought of how spooked I'd been on the Dark Road, and about the person who'd trespassed in my room last night and filmed me sleeping. I couldn't even feel safe in my own hotel room, but if Wheeler and the others were with me...

I opened my mouth, about to tell him yes. I wanted to come back. I wanted to be part of the team again. Then Danny added, "Do you know how many out-of-work actresses would kill to take your place?"

"I'm not an out-of-work actress," I said instead, and hung up before I could change my mind.

In the parking lot, Gemma's silver Mercedes was parked just a few spaces away from my Fiat. Gemma sat in the driver's seat, looking down at something in her lap. I walked toward my car, then realized Gemma's car wasn't running and she still hadn't looked up. Was she asleep in her car? I knocked on the passenger-side window, and Gemma's head jerked up. For a moment she stared at me as though I were a stranger. Then she hit the UNLOCK button and I opened the passenger door.

"Are you okay?" I asked, not really caring about the answer until I saw the object on her lap.

It was a mask. Not the cheap, plastic variety sold in drugstores for Halloween. This was the work of an artisan, a handmade wolf mask, rendered in such careful, precise detail it looked like it had been peeled from the face of a once living animal, an incomplete taxidermy.

Looking at the mask, my arms began to tremble. Saliva filled my mouth, and my stomach lurched. I felt the sudden, violent urge to empty my stomach onto the ground. I swallowed back the bile stinging my throat, and my mind reeled backward into a black space, a missing reel, clawing at a memory I couldn't summon. A memory of a mask like this one. Where had I seen it before? In Kron's first film, *Anathema*, in which the main characters had the heads of wolves? No. That wasn't it. I hadn't seen that film since I was a teenager, and while I remembered it being disturbing, I hadn't felt anything in this ballpark of visceral abhorrence. This was something different. Something buried so long ago I couldn't reach it.

"Why do you have that?" I asked, my voice thin, choked.

"It was in my car," Gemma said. "I found it on the seat."

"It's not yours?" I asked, confused, though I should have grasped right away what she was saying.

"No," she said, and I saw her hands were trembling. "Someone put it here last night."

20.

Gemma waited in her car while I did a quick survey of the parking lot to check for security cameras, but as far as I could see the inn was free of surveillance. I was not surprised. Whoever put the mask in Gemma's car was too careful to allow himself (or herself) to be recorded in the act, because that person was probably the same person who'd been in my room filming me in the middle of the night.

When I was hidden from Gemma's view around the corner of the building, I couldn't hold it in any longer. I evacuated the contents of my stomach—pie and pastry and acid—behind a bush. Afterward, I felt blessedly empty, both emotionally and physically. Washing my mouth out with water from a half-empty bottle I had in my purse, I told myself all that pie last night hadn't agreed with me. On my way back to Gemma's car, I glanced through the windows of my Fiat to see if a mask had been deposited on my seat, too.

There was no sign of a mask in my car, but I thought

of the subject line of the email I'd received: FOLLOW THE
WHITE WOLF.

I opened the passenger door and climbed back into
Gemma's car. Gemma had set the mask on the dashboard
and was now watching it warily, like it might make a move
on her if she took her eyes off it.

"Are you sure your car was locked?" I asked.

She nodded. "They must have jimmied it."

"What about your car alarm? Why didn't it go off?"

She shrugged, holding up her hands in helpless dismay.
"I have no idea." She looked at me. "Why would someone
do this?"

I picked up the mask. It was lighter than I'd expected,
probably made from papier-mâché. I barely felt the weight
of it. "Maybe just to mess with you," I said.

"No one knows I'm here. I checked in under a false
name."

"I know you did, Ms. Stone Maretto. But you have a
pretty recognizable face. Maybe someone saw you in town
and decided to leave you a gift."

"I didn't stop anywhere in town. I came straight here.
Besides, this doesn't feel like a gift. This feels like a threat,
or... I don't know. A bread crumb."

"A bread crumb?"

"Yes, Liv, a bread crumb. A clue. Whatever you want to
call it. Isn't that what you're here to find?"

Her sudden hostility took me aback. I stared at her, not
speaking, until she took a breath and sighed.

"I'm sorry," she said. "I didn't sleep much last night, and
I'm feeling a bit frayed. I came out here this morning thinking maybe I would just go home, and then I found that on
my seat, and I just... I don't know what I'm doing here. I
shouldn't have come."

As usual, I was having a hard time figuring out whether or not Gemma was full of shit. For as long as I'd known her, she'd been trying on different versions of herself. Obedient daughter. Party slut. Dedicated actress. Polite talk-show guest. Who was this new version? Sister filled with regret, hoping to mend our relationship after years of dysfunction? I'd never met this Gemma, but I decided to give her the benefit of the doubt that she wasn't trying to manipulate me in some way, just to see what would happen.

"Last night, after we talked, someone sent me this." I showed her the email and the link, and explained about the video, and how it had disappeared after I'd watched it.

"So there really was someone in your room." She was quiet a moment, and then looked at me, her blue eyes round and serious. "We should go to the police."

"No."

"But, Liv—"

"I've met the sheriff. Trust me, he's not going to do anything about this."

"Why not?"

"Because he hates me and wants me to leave town. For all I know, he's the one who sent the video *and* left the mask. Think about it. He's a cop. I'm sure he knows how to get through locked doors without being detected."

She raised a professionally plucked, disbelieving eyebrow. "He must really want you gone to go to that much trouble. You do have a way with people."

"My way with people is just fine."

She laughed. "As long as they aren't female, family, your producer, or, apparently, members of law enforcement. But I guess that's always been your thing, butting heads with authority figures. My therapist says it's because you lacked a strong male role model, so you need to test people's boundaries."

"That actually has nothing to do with it. Also, stop talking to your therapist about me."

Gemma cocked her head. "You don't talk to yours about me?"

"I don't talk to anyone about you, Gemma."

My sister's face fell, and she sat back heavily in her seat. She was quiet a moment, and I thought she must be mulling over hurt feelings until she spoke. "What if the person who was in your room and who put this thing in my car is the same person who abducted those women on the road? Then aren't you obligated to tell the police?"

It was an angle I'd already considered, and rejected. "It doesn't fit the pattern."

"Neither do you," she pointed out. "So maybe it's not the actual perpetrator of the abductions, but someone who knows something and is trying to point you in the right direction. Remember the pilot episode of *The Hills Have PIs*?"

In the pilot, I learn that my best friend, Angel, has disappeared in the middle of the night from the bedroom of her Hollywood Hills home. A few days later, someone leaves a mysterious item in my locker at school, a clue to Angel's whereabouts. I enlist my younger sister Gemma to help me find her.

Gemma gazed at me with a hopeful look in her eyes. "I could help you," she said. "It'll be like the good old days."

"I don't need help. And the good old days weren't all that good."

"Fine, then I'll take this back." Gemma attempted to grab the mask, but I wouldn't let go. "You can have it if you let me help you. Just for today, and then I won't bother you anymore. Please?"

There were tears in her eyes. As she waited for my answer, one slipped free and she wiped it away hurriedly. I wondered if she was having a midlife crisis. She was nearly thirty-one. That was forty in actor years.

"Fine," I said, and she released the mask. "If you're coming with me, you need to change clothes. Did you bring hiking boots?"

She nodded and began to open the door, then turned back. "Can I ask where we're going?"

"Do you need to?"

She shook her head, her expression darkening. "I'll be quick."

"I'll drive," I said, and got out, too.

Gemma glanced back at me as she was walking toward the Eden Tree. "You better not leave without me."

"I won't," I promised, feeling guilty because I had considered it.

As I sat in my car waiting for Gemma, I set the mask aside and pulled out Porter's map, scanning the network of trails. When I saw the name of the first trailhead that he'd circled, the skin on my back began to prickle.

White Wolf Trailhead
15.5 mi

Follow the White Wolf.

21.

There it is." I swerved onto the gravel parking area next to the White Wolf Trailhead. It was the same place where I had stopped the previous evening on my way into town. Now, with honeyed morning light spearing through knots of cloud, it was hard to remember why I'd been spooked. Still, I reached into my jacket pocket, reassured by the hard, angular shape of my Glock. I didn't have a concealed carry license—wasn't sure they were even legal in California—but there was no way I was going into those woods without my gun.

"Don't freak out," I said, and pulled the gun out to check again that the safety was on.

"Liv! What the fuck!" Gemma planted her back against the passenger-side door like I'd pointed the gun at her. "Why do you have that?"

"The Second Amendment."

"Do you even know how to use it?"

I slid the Glock back into my pocket. "Better than most."

"Did you bring one for me?"

I laughed and opened the door. Gemma followed me to the trunk, where I retrieved my digital camera and hung it around my neck on its strap. Then I got out my GoPro and the accessory kit I'd bought to go with it. I attached the GoPro to the head strap and handed it to Gemma.

"Put this on," I told her. She stared at the head strap like I'd given her a pair of my dirty panties to wear. "You wanted to help. You get to be B camera."

"Oh." She didn't complain, but I saw a flicker of haughty displeasure in her eyes, a look that said very clearly, *I'm Gemma Hill, and I am no one's camera B.*

I hid a smile as she pulled the strap over her head. Then I stood back to examine her and nodded, trying not to laugh. She looked ridiculous.

"What am I supposed to do?" she asked.

"Nothing," I said. "Just walk. The camera will do all the work for you."

Gemma's frown deepened, and I knew what she was thinking, that she was wasted behind a camera. She belonged in front of it.

Not today, sister dear.

By the time I locked up the car, a layer of ink-dark clouds had become visible along the western horizon, on a collision course with the sun. Rain was an hour away, maybe two, but I couldn't wait around for good weather. A twenty-thousand-dollar clock was ticking.

I turned to Gemma. "If I'm filming, try to stay out of the shot, okay?"

"Why?"

"Because you haven't signed a talent release, and even if you did I'm sure Desiree would lose her mind if you ended up on something as low-profile as my web series. I don't want to deal with her or your lawyers, so just do what I'm telling you to do, okay?"

She held up her hands. "You're the boss." A shiver shook Gemma. In the shade of the black trees that arced above us, the temperature seemed near to freezing. It was barely nine o'clock, but suddenly it looked like night was about to fall.

I pressed a button on the GoPro to start it recording, then turned to the faded wooden sign that marked the trailhead.

"White Wolf Trail," Gemma read softly behind me.

"You may have been right about those bread crumbs," I admitted.

* * *

Wind whistled around the stark, burnt trees. Everything around us was shifting. Rattling. Shivering. I kept my eyes moving, scanning the looming trees, the tangled ground cover, but as far as I could tell there was nothing to see. Each acre of the woods looked the same as the next. Mile upon mile of brittle, baked stalks. The forest floor had begun to come back to life in a green tangle, but the blackened trunks served as a constant reminder of the fire that had blazed through the area.

"Do you know what started the fire?" Gemma asked from a few feet behind me.

I answered without looking back. The trail was overgrown, roots and branches waiting to trip me every time I took my eyes off the ground. "The articles online don't mention the origin," I called back. "But the disappearances didn't start until after the fire. Maybe there's a connection."

"How long after the fire?" she asked.

"Three years. The first was in 2006."

"I don't know, Olivia. That sounds like a stretch."

I stopped abruptly and turned to her. "Why did you call me that?"

She blinked at me, head cocked. "What?"

"Olivia."

She shrugged. "It's your name."

"It's not my name," I said, my chest tight. "Don't call me that. *Ever.*"

"Sorry," she said faintly as I revolved and marched forward.

Gemma and I didn't talk for a while after that. We trudged ahead through the shuddering gauntlet of branches and leaves, the lower halves of our faces tucked into our scarves for warmth. Abruptly, after we'd walked for close to an hour, the trail curved, revealing a clearing and the Wolf King's cottage Porter had told me about, nestled among the trees. For once, a Kron location did not immediately strike me as familiar, but only because the cottage had been transformed by the fire, given a scorched makeover. No walls had toppled, but an oak tree as tall as a three-story building had collapsed onto the roof, caving in a large hole. The tree remained propped against the cottage, its trunk the color of a cold campfire. At some point the structure would likely buckle beneath the weight of the oak.

I filmed as I moved toward the devastated structure, but stopped when I remembered Gemma. This footage would be more compelling with me in it. It needed a focal point, a narrator. I turned to ask Gemma if she would take over camera A and film me giving exposition and exploring the cottage, but she wasn't on the trail.

"Gemma?" I called, turning in a circle. I scanned the forest in all directions, searching for a flash of the bright-red anorak she'd been wearing. It should have been easy to spot. "Gemma!" I listened for her voice, realizing that the wind had died down as abruptly as my sister had vanished.

Now there was only silence and the watchful remains of the trees.

22.

Gemma!" I called again, but she still didn't answer. Could she have fallen so far behind, she was unable to hear me? She was in far better shape than I was. She would have been able to match my pace hopping on one leg. Maybe she'd seen something and stopped to check it out, and I'd gotten ahead of her. Or, more likely, this was a trick to get back at me for making her wear a GoPro strapped to her head. It was the kind of thing Gemma was known for when we were teenagers, petty pranks to show her displeasure. Stealing my bras and throwing them into the pool in the backyard. Calling a guy I liked and pretending to be me, telling him I wanted my first time to be with him, but only if we did anal. Tearing out the last chapter from a book I was reading, so I'd never know how it ended unless I went out and bought the book again.

Then there was option number three, the one I didn't want to think about...that something had actually happened to Gemma.

I told myself to stay calm, not to let my imagination run

away with me. I touched my gun for reassurance, my eyes scanning the woods, searching for movement, for a glimpse of blond hair and red jacket. They stopped abruptly on the Wolf King's cottage.

On the door easing open.

On the man stepping out into the gray light.

He was dressed plainly, in a chambray shirt, jeans, and boots. As to what his face looked like, I couldn't say, because he wore a mask identical to the one Gemma had found in her car.

A white wolf.

My breath quickened. My heartbeat boomed in my ears, a rhythmic thunder. I wanted to draw my gun, but I couldn't move. I felt numb and on fire at the same time. I could not take my eyes off the wolf's face. For the second time that day, bile burned in my throat. My stomach cramped, and I nearly doubled over. My mind ran in circles of blind panic, but this fear felt old somehow, dated. Like I'd carried it with me for years, waiting for its conclusion.

But this time my fear of the wolf mask was not entirely irrational, because there was someone behind the mask, and I was alone in the woods with him, and Gemma was missing, and none of this was good.

The man in the mask took a step toward me. At the same moment, a scream shredded the air, a sound so high and shrill and piercing it ripped me from my paralysis and set everything moving at once. My muscles unclenched and instead of pulling my Glock I found myself sprinting through the woods, away from the man in the wolf mask, hurtling through trees and undergrowth. Then the scream came again, and I realized I was running toward it, not away from it.

I slowed when I crossed from blackened forest to living

again, fumbled for my gun, was about to yank it free when the man stepped into my path. I barreled into his chest. He grabbed me by the shoulders. I tried to wrench free, but he held me tight.

"Whoa, whoa, whoa," the man said. "Calm down. I'm not going to hurt you." His voice was kind, with a musical Scandinavian accent.

I swallowed a cry for help and focused on his face, no longer concealed by the wolf mask. He was grandfatherly, yellow-white hair thinning, skin as leathery as a cowboy's, and electric blue eyes filled with genuine concern. He wore safari colors, a beige shirt with a logo stitched on the breast pocket and army-green cargo pants, not jeans.

I realized he was not the man from the cabin. Not unless that man had found time to change clothes before teleporting ahead of me. I'd run so far I'd left behind the burnt section of forest.

"I...heard screaming," I panted. My heart felt like it might explode. "My sister...she was right behind me, and then she...was gone. And there was a wolf...at the cottage."

"A wolf?" the man repeated.

"Not a wolf. A man in a wolf mask."

The blue-eyed man released his grip on my arms, his brow furrowed with concern. "I don't know about the man you saw, but the scream was Tocsin."

"Toxin?"

"Tocsin," he repeated, pronouncing it *tuk-seen*. "It means 'alarm' in Norwegian." He smiled gently. "Tocsin is a mountain lion. She's our only big cat at the sanctuary. They make the most awful noises sometimes. Don't worry," he added, seeing me tense. "She's in her habitat, not roaming the woods." He pointed into the distance, and I made out the diamond pattern of a high chain-link fence.

The wolf sanctuary. One more of Stone's Throw's charming little attractions.

"I'm Anders, by the way," the man said. "Anders Larsen."

"Liv," I said distractedly. "My sister. She's still out there in the woods with that man."

"You saw him at the cottage, you said?"

I nodded.

"Probably just a hiker."

"No. I told you, he wore a mask." Even saying the words, I felt my stomach clench. The image was burned on my brain, but the source of the aversion remained entombed, somewhere deep in my subconscious.

Anders nodded as though encountering a masked man in the woods was nothing special. "A fan of Jonas Kron, then."

I blinked, remembering what Porter had told me about the cottage: that Kronophiles sometimes visited and held ceremonies in masks to call on the *Ulv Konge*. It hadn't occurred to me that I might stumble upon one such pilgrimage to worship at Kron's altar.

I looked down at the camera hanging around my neck on its strap. It was still recording. I must have caught the man in the wolf mask on camera, as well as the extreme shaky-cam footage of me bolting through the woods like a maniac. Whether the man in the wolf mask had anything to do with the Dark Road or not, the footage would play well in my next episode.

Anders's eyes moved past me. "Is that your sister?"

I turned to see Gemma scrambling up the trail with the GoPro still strapped to her head.

"Liv! There you are. Jesus, I've been looking all over for you!"

I grabbed Gemma by the arms, held her back to look at her. The knees of her jeans were dirty, a tear in the left one showing a swipe of red.

"Are you hurt?" I demanded. "What the hell happened? Where were you?"

"Where were *you*? I tripped and scraped my knee. I called for you to stop, but when I looked up you were gone."

"Didn't you hear me shouting your name?"

She shook her head, glancing toward Anders. "I didn't hear a thing until that screaming."

Anders explained again about the mountain lion. "I own the wolf sanctuary," he continued. "My wife, Helene, and I." He glanced from the camera around my neck to the GoPro on its head strap. "What is it you two were doing in the woods?"

"We're in town for the film festival," I said, not ready to explain the real reason I was here and risk an adverse reaction. "We just got some new camera gear and wanted to test it out."

"I see." Anders rubbed his hands together and shivered, raising his eyes to the sky, where the clouds were now the color of lead. "It's going to rain soon, and I imagine you two are a few miles from your vehicle. Come back to the sanctuary and warm up, then I'll drive you to your car."

Gemma smiled tightly. "Oh, thank you. But we don't want to trouble—"

"We'd really appreciate that," I cut in, and silenced Gemma with a look. Anders and his wife practically lived on the Dark Road. If anyone had seen something suspicious happening on the road, it was them.

23.

"Kron shot a scene for *The Girl and the Wolf* right here, didn't he?" I stopped in front of a habitat the size of a banquet hall that appeared to contain nothing but boulders and dirt, though a sign on the fence claimed this was the home of a pack of arctic wolves.

Anders paused to look back at me, frowning. "It's what we're famous for." His tone implied a sigh.

"You get a lot of Kronophiles coming through, then?"

Anders smiled stiffly, nodding. "I suppose I should be grateful we get as many visitors as we do. I only wish they were as interested in the animals as they are in re-creating the scenes that were shot here and posting their pictures and videos on social media. I don't like when visitors in their 'Kronsplay' do that in front of children. Most of our guests are bused in from local schools. These reenactments are highly inappropriate for young eyes."

I nodded agreement. The wolf sanctuary scenes were of great significance in the canon of horror films, right up there with the shower scene from *Psycho* and the Satansex dream sequence from *Rosemary's Baby*. The sanctuary scene featured the two lead characters, Jack and Joelle, at the beginning of their transformation. The setup: Jack, a rule-following good boy, is on a first date with the prim, chaste Joelle. They stroll through the sanctuary, chatting benignly about homework and prom decorations and favorite ice cream flavors. Then they stop in front of a habitat housing two enormous wolves, a male and a female, both of them white as new snow. That is where things take a turn. It's feeding time for the two wolves. They huddle around a bloody slab of meat, ripping and tearing at it, their muzzles stained red. The point of view shifts: Seen through Jack's eyes, the slab of meat is no longer a slab of meat. It's Joelle, alive and writhing in pleasure as the wolves tear her entrails from her stomach. Jack blinks and Joelle is no longer in the pen, but right in front of him. He presses his body against her back, forcing her up against the fence, and begins whispering in her ear while he works on the button of his pants. He gets them down, lifts Joelle's skirt, pulls down her modest white panties, and begins fucking her right there, while they watch the wolves feed.

We never see Joelle's face, but once Jack begins thrusting into her, there is another POV shift. Through Joelle's eyes, we see an alternative fantasy of what's happening in the wolf's pen. She sees herself naked, crouched over the body of a dying wolf, its throat and belly torn open. Joelle lowers her mouth to the wolf's stomach and begins to feed voraciously. The camera zooms in on Joelle's eyes, hungry and feral. Something has woken her.

A film studies professor would most likely interpret this as the "Adam and Eve eat from the Tree of Life" scene.

I appreciated why Anders tensed at my mention of the scene. I'd heard that Kron's films had inspired an entire genre of Kron porn, bestial homages to his stories in which the stars all wore animal masks. Curiosity had gotten the better of me, and during one drunk, lonely evening I did an Internet search for this horror porn. I watched less than a minute of a re-created scene from *The Reddest Red* in which the would-be murderer has rough, bloody sex with a barely legal redhead on her period before I had to shut it off. There was, supposedly, far more disturbing and illegal Kron porn floating around the Dark Net, involving minors and actual animals. It was rumored that Kron snuff films existed out there in the world. I had never been moved to seek out any of these things.

Anders kept walking. I picked up my pace to walk beside him.

"Are you expecting a lot of visitors during the film festival?" I asked, and Anders instantly brightened.

"Oh yes. Things always pick up during the festival. I already have a number of tours scheduled."

"How many wolves do you keep here?"

"Twenty-two. Plus Tocsin, the mountain lion. Her stay is temporary. She's recovering from a gunshot wound. Once she's fully back on her feet she'll be moved to a big-cat sanctuary in Washington."

"That's a lot of animals to take care of. Do you have many employees?" What I really wanted to know was how many people worked this close to the Dark Road.

But Anders shook his head. "My son, Niklas, and I manage the day-to-day chores and take care of the animals. A local veterinarian donates her time pro bono to see to their health, and my wife handles the business side of things. We operate on charitable contributions and government grants, for the most part. Speaking of which, it's feeding time for the animals and I know my son could use a hand. Do you mind if we make a stop? Then you can get a look behind the scenes, so to speak."

"Not a bit," I said. "Do you mind if we film?"

Anders hesitated. "Most people don't ask first, but since you did I have to decline. We have rules about professional photography. You'd need to fill out forms and pay a fee. If it were up to me I'd say go right ahead, but my wife is very strict about the rules."

"No problem," I said, and when Anders's back was turned I pushed the RECORD button on my digital camera and positioned my scarf so it hid the red light but left the lens unobscured. Gemma noticed and frowned in disapproval of my rule breaking. This from a girl who'd had a dealer on speed dial when she was fifteen.

The fenced animal enclosures were built in a side-by-side row against a hillside, their covered dens at the back of each enclosure. We followed Anders to a door that opened into the hill itself, and entered a humid tunnel that smelled very monkey house—a pungent combination of urine, straw, feces, and musty animal funk. I resisted the urge to cover my nose and mouth. For some reason that seemed rude, but Gemma had no such qualms. She pulled her scarf up over the lower half of her face, so she looked as if she were about to rob a stagecoach.

Each enclosure had its own "care station"—as Anders called them—a sectioned-off room at the back of its den where the animals were fed and received medical check-ups. I had thought Gemma and I would wait in the tunnel, but Anders invited us into the care stations to observe.

And there, on the other side of the metal bars, less than ten feet away from us, stood a shaggy gray wolf, her eyes somewhere between blue and silver. She gazed at us calmly, assessing. There was something so human in her eyes, I could almost believe she might open her mouth and start speaking English.

"This is Frost," Anders said. "She's new to the sanctuary."

"You keep her alone?" Gemma asked. It was the first time she'd spoken since we entered the sanctuary.

"Yes, for now," Anders said. "We tried introducing her to a pack, but they rejected her."

Gemma frowned. "Why would they do that?"

"A variety of reasons," Anders said. "She's lame. One of her legs was broken when she came to us. Wolves do not appreciate weakness."

Anders donned rubber gloves and opened the lid of a small cooler in the corner. He picked out a piece of slippery purple meat, opened a slot, placed it inside, and then pushed it through. Frost didn't move, didn't even glance at the food. She kept her eyes on mine, her gaze mesmerizing.

Anders marked a clipboard hanging on the wall that the wolf had been fed, and then gestured toward the door. "She will not eat if she's watched. She's private, this one."

I followed Anders through the door, feeling a great deal of empathy for Frost, rejected by her peers, judged weak and fragile, didn't like anyone watching her eat. She was my kind of wolf.

We moved on to Tocsin's care station next. I hesitated at the door, unsure whether I wanted to be trapped in a small space with the animal that had emitted those banshee screams I'd heard in the forest. But the inside of Tocsin's care station was twice as large as some of the others, giving those of us on the freedom side of the bars room enough to keep our distance.

There was a man in Tocsin's care station already, bent over her feeding tray, whispering to her and filling her tray with raw meat while the big cat paced restlessly on the other side of the bars. Tocsin's wheat-colored coat was sleek, her movements lithe and graceful. Her watchful, pale-gray eyes appeared lined in black pencil, and her paws, which had to be as wide as my own hands, made no sound padding across the straw, though the animal had to weigh close to two hundred pounds. As I watched the big cat move, I realized she limped ever so slightly, and I noticed a large patch of missing fur on her left flank, and a round, ugly scar, where I assumed she'd been shot at one point.

There was a tranquilizer gun in a rack on the wall in the care station, but I didn't think a tranquilizer dart would have left a scar like that.

"We don't know who shot her," Anders said. "She almost died in the wild because she couldn't hunt. When she came to us, you could see her ribs through her fur, but we nursed her back to health."

The man who had been feeding Tocsin had his back to us. After pushing her tray through the slot, he turned around, and I had to choke back a gasp at the sight of his face.

The man kept his eyes and head lowered, so mostly what I saw of him was his unkempt blond hair, which hung to his shoulders. But it was impossible to hide the pink mass of scar tissue that marred his forehead and cheek. The man didn't say a word, just stood there for an awkward moment looking trapped before he headed for the door and slipped out into the hallway.

"Please excuse Nik," Anders said in a quiet voice. "It's difficult for him to meet new people."

"Of course," I murmured, the next obvious question burning on my tongue. *What happened to his face?* But I already knew at least part of the answer. I'd seen enough prosthetic burn scars in movies to recognize the real thing. And living this close to the burnt woods, it was a logical assumption that Anders's son had been caught in the fire.

We moved on to the next care station, for a pair of timberwolves, one black and one white. Inside their care station, I could see them peering out at us from their den, eyes the sickly yellow of dehydrated urine. The sight made my mouth go dry and paralysis seize my limbs again, even though I knew I was safe on my side of the bars. I wanted to run. To just get the hell out. I would have thought my reaction was instinctual, simple lizard-brain predation fear taking over, but I'd had the same flood of adrenaline telling me "flight" was the best option when I saw the wolf mask in Gemma's car, and the man in the woods wearing his mask. Did I have an irrational fear of wolves I'd never realized? But why? What was the origin? Maybe it was time for me to start therapy again. I'd seen a pill-happy shrink after Miranda's disappearance, but quit when he implied that I was lying about the events I *did* remember from the night of the accident. I'd been self-medicating ever since.

Anders removed a large bag of something bloody from a blue cooler and dumped the contents into the wolves' feeding bin. Moments later, the two wolves crept forward into the light. They stalked toward the feeding bin as though there were a chance their prey still had the capacity to elude them. When they reached the bin, they dove at the meat and wet, ripping sounds ensued.

"The black one we named Brutus," Anders told us, stuffing the bloody bag back into the cooler. "He's the male. The white one, Tispe, is female."

"Tispe," I repeated, mimicking Anders's pronunciation. *Tiss-pay.* "Is that Norwegian?"

"Yes," Anders said, glancing away, his cheeks reddening. "It means 'bitch.' Helene named her. I told her it was crude, but she insisted the name was fitting."

"How?" Gemma asked. She looked pale, and I wondered if it was the smell bothering her, or something else.

"We had two female wolves come to us at the same time from rescue organizations," Anders explained. "We put them in a pen together, separate from Brutus, but that was a mistake. Tispe...well, she must have smelled a male nearby. She wounded the other female so badly the first night that we had to put her down. But Tispe gets along quite well with Brutus," he added with forced cheerfulness.

I glanced furtively at Gemma, thinking that maybe Brutus had nothing to do with Tispe tearing the other female apart. That was simply what happened when certain females were locked in a cage together.

We watched the wolves devour their meat a moment longer, soaking their muzzles with blood, until Gemma couldn't take it anymore.

"I need some air," she said, and bolted from the room.

"She doesn't have a very strong stomach, does she?" Anders said, mildly amused.

I gazed after her. "It used to be a lot stronger."

24.

It was a relief to breathe fresh air again. Leaving the cavern that housed the care stations, Anders and I found Gemma standing in the rain, her face still pale beneath the hood of her red raincoat. I ceased recording and zipped my jacket over my camera to protect it.

"My truck is parked at the office," Anders said, beckoning us to follow him up a dirt path away from the wolf enclosures. His body was proportioned like a pair of scissors, his legs the blades, long and straight. They seemed barely to bend at the knees as they carried him up the road. Gemma and I had to jog to keep up. I wanted to question Anders about the Dark Road, but I wasn't sure how to open that conversation. I'd have to shout the questions at his back.

We crested a rise, at the top of which stood a minuscule cabin—practically a "tiny house"—with a sign posted out front that read:

Stone's Throw Wolf Sanctuary
Office Hours: Mon–Sat, 10–5
Call for private tours

"I need to get my keys and check in with Helene," Anders said. "Do you mind waiting a few more minutes? I can offer you coffee."

"Sure," I said. "No rush." Beside me, Gemma sighed. I wondered what her hurry was. For all her ardent words about wanting to heal our relationship, she seemed impatient to be anywhere but at my side.

As we neared the cabin, a modest, two-story house came into view about a hundred yards behind it. It was the least fanciful home I'd seen since arriving in Stone's Throw.

"Is that where you live?" I asked Anders, nodding at the house.

"Yes," he said. "When we first moved here from Norway, we lived here, in the cabin, but that was a very tight fit." He opened the door wide for Gemma and me, and we stepped inside.

The cottage smelled like coffee and burning wood. A fire crackled in an old-fashioned stove, and the air inside was so warm it made me realize just how chilled my hands were. My numb fingers tingled to life.

"This is my wife, Helene," Anders said, gesturing to a statuesque blond woman sitting behind a desk covered in neat stacks of papers and file folders.

But what I noticed first was not the woman. It was the series of handcrafted wolf masks that hung on the wall behind her, a sign above them stating: WOLF MASKS $75. There were four colors: black, gray, brown, and white. The white mask was identical to the one that had been left in

Gemma's car, and that the man in the woods had worn. Looking at them, my stomach began to turn again.

The woman glanced up from her work, smiling warmly. She saw where both Gemma and I were looking and said, "We also offer T-shirts and mugs."

She was not what I anticipated for a woman who owned an animal sanctuary. She had the same azure eyes and yellow-white hair as her husband, but where Anders's skin was sun-browned and weathered, hers was mannequin-smooth, and her thick hair was wound into a bun on the back of her head. She wore a crisp white button-down shirt, gray cardigan, and fashionable, plastic-frame glasses, and looked more like an executive assistant in a corporate office than someone who ran a small-town animal preserve.

She stood, revealing her height, which had to be six feet, maybe taller. In the tiny cottage with its low ceiling, she reminded me of Gandalf stooping to fit inside Bilbo's hobbit hole. She loomed over us as she offered her hand, first to Gemma and then to me. But even when she shook my hand her eyes remained fixed on my sister. "Are you...oh my, are you Gemma Hill?"

"I am..." Gemma smiled politely.

Helene's hand flew to her heart, like she was about to salute Gemma. "I wasn't going to say anything, but I had to know. I loved you in, well, in *everything!*"

Gemma lowered her eyes as though humbled by this praise, even though I knew she was used to far more effusive ass kissing. "Thank you. That's always nice to hear."

Anders blinked at Gemma in confusion. It was clear he had no idea who she was. Who *either* of us were. Helene still hadn't spared a glance for me, probably assuming I was Gemma's assistant. My ego bristled.

"Do you want to arrange a tour?" Helene asked, eyes

bright, looking like she wanted to jump up and down and clap.

"They're not here to see the animals," Anders cut in. "I ran into them in the Wolf Woods. They were hiking and got lost. I'm giving them a ride back to their car."

"Oh, I see," Helene said, sounding disappointed. "Well, it's easy to get lost in those woods if you leave the trail."

That was my cue to bring up the Dark Road. I opened my mouth, but Anders interrupted.

"I'll get coffee," he said, and disappeared into a tiny kitchen off the main room.

"Make a fresh pot!" Helene called to his retreating back. Then her eyes fell on Gemma's bloodied knee. "You're hurt!"

"It's nothing," Gemma said. "Just a little scrape."

"Nonsense. Let me clean it for you."

Gemma tried to protest, but Helene wouldn't take no for an answer. She hefted a first-aid kit the size of a professional tackle box out of the cupboard behind her desk and told Gemma to take a seat.

"We're always patching up little scrapes and bites around here," she chattered as she swabbed the scrape on Gemma's knee with antiseptic. Gemma winced but didn't complain.

While the Norwegian woman worked on my sister, I moved closer to the display of masks. On closer inspection, I was assured that whoever made these had also made the mask Gemma found in her car. They didn't look manufactured. The detail was too precise. These were made by an artisan.

"Beautiful craftsmanship," I said. "Is it all right if I touch them?"

"Of course," Helene said. "And thank you. I'll pass the

compliment along to my son. He makes them. It started out as a hobby, but they've become a very popular souvenir."

"I'll bet," I muttered, and picked the white wolf mask off the wall to study it, feeling that same swell of revulsion and dread in my guts that had driven me to empty my stomach back at the Eden Tree. I carefully replaced the mask on the wall and turned away from them, taking deep breaths to still the anxiety shaking me like a snow globe, sending my insides into a chaotic flurry.

This time Gemma sensed my distress. She caught my eye and mouthed over the top of Helene's head, *Are you okay?*

I nodded, though I didn't feel the least bit okay.

"What brings you to Stone's Throw?" Helene asked Gemma, clearly assuming she was the reason we were here. "Are you in town for the festival?"

"Gemma's here for the festival," I said. "I'm here for the Dark Road."

Helene glanced back at me, blinked once, slowly, and then, to my frustration, turned to Gemma again. "Are you two sisters? I just realized how much you resemble each other."

Gemma smiled. "Yes, Liv is my older sister."

"By eighteen months," I said, feeling the neurotic need to clarify that I wasn't *that* much older.

Anders chose that moment to return with two paper cups of coffee. He went out of his way to hand Gemma hers first, and once I had mine in hand I considered throwing the steaming-hot coffee in all of their faces.

"Did I hear you say something about the Dark Road?" Anders asked warily.

"Yes," I said, sipping the coffee and scalding my tongue. "I'm doing a digital series about the disappearances."

"A web series," Anders repeated, nodding in thought. "That explains the cameras."

"Actually, it would be great if I could film an interview with you two," I said. "Since you live so close to the road, I figure you have a unique perspective."

"We can't help you," Helene said flatly. "All of that business with the road has been very bad for us. I'm sure you understand why we're reluctant to draw more negative attention to it."

Gemma cleared her throat, and I thought she was about to suggest that we drop the subject before I made the situation more awkward. But she surprised me by saying, "One thing we were wondering about is what started the fire that burned those woods. It must have been terrifying, a forest fire so close to the sanctuary."

I cast a quick, grateful smile in Gemma's direction, suddenly glad that she was with me. Instead of worrying about her getting in my way, I should be making use of her. To Helene, I might as well not exist, but she'd probably do an interview naked if Gemma asked her to.

That was what I thought until I saw the way Helene's expression had pinched in fury, and I remembered her son…the old burn scars on his face.

Helene thrust her finger at the door. "Get out," she ordered. "Both of you. *Now.*"

25.

Helene slammed the door behind us, hard enough to make us both jump.

"So much for *that* interview," I said, glancing up at the sky. The rain had ceased for the moment, but the clouds looked heavier than ever. I started walking down the path toward the main road.

"Liv, I'm sorry," Gemma said, following after me, looking dazed. I wondered how long it had been since someone besides me had dared to be that rude to Gemma Hill. "I shouldn't have asked about the fire. I wasn't thinking. Their poor son…"

"It's fine," I told her. "I don't think either of them would have talked to me about the Dark Road anyway."

"You're not mad at me?" Gemma asked, disbelieving.

"I know you were trying to help."

Gemma smiled over at me. "This is good for us."

I rolled my eyes but allowed her a small smile in return. "Whatever you say."

"So what did you think of—" she began, but cut off at the sound of crunching footsteps. We turned to find Anders jogging toward us, looking harried. I guessed he'd just gotten an earful from his wife.

"I'm sorry if I said something to offend you both," Gemma offered when Anders reached us. "That was not my intention *at all*."

Anders waved both of his hands in front of him. "Helene thought you knew, but I told her it's a misunderstanding."

"What's a misunderstanding?" I asked.

Anders hesitated. "About Nik. That he started the fire. It wasn't in any of the papers, but people in town know. No one wanted to press charges. His injuries were punishment enough."

At that moment, the clouds let go and the rain came pelting down in a fury.

"Let me give you a ride to your car," Anders said. "It's the least I can do."

By the time we backtracked to Anders's truck, rain was shooting down in sharp, cold bullets, and we were soaked. We climbed into the cab, which just had one bench, so I ended up sitting in the middle with my knees in the way of the gearshift. Anders tried to reverse, but the truck tires spun out in the mud of the unpaved drive, and then caught so suddenly that the truck whipped backward.

Driving past the cabin, I saw Helene glaring out the window, watching us depart.

Anders drove in silent concentration, but I didn't want to waste my last minutes with him. I had to keep him talking.

"Why did you leave Norway?" I asked.

Anders slowed to steer around a deep pothole. "We love our country," he said. "But winter was intolerable. No sun for sixty days. It can feel like sixty years. It takes a toll on the mind, and it is especially difficult for children like our son." Anders glanced over at me, hesitating, but after a pause he continued. "Nik had . . . developmental problems. So when we had an opportunity to leave Norway, we decided that would be for the best. And it was good here for a while . . . until the fire. And the disappearances."

The windshield wipers could barely keep up with the rain, it was pouring down so fast now. Ahead, I spotted my car, a smudge of black through the downpour. And there was another vehicle parked next to it near the trailhead. A sheriff's sedan. A man in a tan uniform and a black anorak bent to peer through the windows.

Shit.

Anders pulled up behind the sedan. The uniformed man peering in through the windows straightened and turned in our direction. Sheriff Lot smiled grimly and gave me a cheerful, mocking wave.

"Thank you again for the coffee and the ride," I said to Anders, and Gemma echoed my gratitude. We hopped out and hurried toward my car.

The sheriff grinned at me from the cave of his hood. "Nice to see you again, Ms. Hendricks. How about you two follow me back to the station, where we can dry off and have a conversation?"

"About what? We haven't done anything wrong." Our cameras were hidden inside our jackets. He couldn't know we'd been filming.

Lot made as if to tap the glass of the driver's-side door of my car, but there was no sound. I stepped closer to the car and realized why. There *was* no glass. Someone had broken the window. Glass shards littered the ground and the driver's seat.

"Figured you'd want to file a report," Lot said.

I pushed past him and threw open the door, but a cursory search only confirmed what I already knew.

The wolf mask was gone.

26.

On the way to the sheriff's station, I had to shout over the wind blowing in my face to tell Gemma about the man in the wolf mask at the cottage. When I was finished, Gemma cranked up the heater a few more notches, but the warm air went straight out my broken window.

"Do you think it was the mask from your car?" Gemma asked, her teeth chattering.

"I don't know. It looked like the exact same one. But was there time for the man to break into my car, steal the mask back, and then get ahead of us on the trail? It seems unlikely. And it's not like that mask was unique. At least now we know where it came from." I used my sleeve to mop raindrops from my face. Pointless, as rain just kept spraying through the window. "I feel like I'm following a trail of bread crumbs someone purposely left for me."

"A lot of people know you're in town, and they know why you're here. Maybe someone is trying to tell you something."

"Or maybe they're just fucking with me."

"The mask was in my car. If they're fucking with you, they're fucking with me, too."

I glanced over at her. "Who knows you're in Stone's Throw besides Desiree?"

She paused to think. "Not many people. My agent. My personal assistant. A few producers and directors I made plans to meet during the festival."

"Jonas Kron?" I asked. Gemma didn't know about my connection to Kron, and I didn't intend to disclose it. I trusted Gemma more today than I had yesterday, but that wasn't saying much, considering that yesterday I hadn't trusted her at all.

She nodded. "He's the main reason I'm here. I mean...you, too."

"But mostly him."

"Liv...don't be like that."

"It's fine, Gemma. I know where your priorities lie."

She reached over and put a hand on my arm. "You're my top priority right now," she said so earnestly that it was hard not to believe her. The backs of my eyes stung with a hot flood of emotion. Was I this starved for sisterly affection?

I cleared my swelling throat, and Gemma removed her hand.

"Anyway," I said, "it sounds like plenty of people know you're in Stone's Throw, and who knows how many people those people have told?"

"Do you think whoever broke into your car wanted the mask?" Gemma asked.

"I think whoever broke into my car wanted it *back*."

"You should tell the sheriff. About all of it, I mean. The mask. The email. The man in the woods. Even if it is just to mess with you—with *us*—whoever's behind it might be dangerous."

"I'll think about," I said, but I knew Gemma was right. That bothered me almost as much as the idea of waking up tomorrow morning to another emailed video of me sleeping. I didn't want her to be right. I didn't want her to be helpful. I didn't want to want her back in my life.

"You really didn't hear me shouting for you when we got separated?" I asked, watching Gemma from the corner of my eye.

She sighed. "Liv, I know we have our issues, but come on. Why would I pretend not to hear you?"

I shrugged, but I was thinking about a common tell I'd learned back when I was playing a teen detective on *The Hills Have PIs*, how responding to a question with a question was a good indication that someone was lying.

27.

Entering the building that housed the sheriff's office, my cell service kicked in and my phone buzzed repeatedly with arriving texts. I started to check them but was distracted by Lot, sauntering by with his cell phone pressed to his ear.

"Coming?" he said, and vanished into his office, leaving the door open.

I started after him, but Gemma stayed where she was, looking at her phone. "Mind if I sit this one out? I need to return some messages while I have a signal."

"Sure. Whatever," I said, but I felt a twinge of disappointment. I hated to admit it, but it had been kind of nice to have Gemma around. I reminded myself not to get used to it. My sister had a history of pulling the rug out from under me.

I closed Lot's office door behind me. He was already seated, still on the phone, but his smug arrogance had been replaced by an expression that read to me as exasperated. A moment later he hung up with a cursory,

"Fine," and turned his attention to me, grinning as he regarded my sodden hair and damp clothing. "You look like you had a fun morning. I hope your camera didn't get wet while you were filming without a permit."

I tensed, but Lot waved his hand. "Relax. I'm not going to take your camera away. I just got off the phone with Soren Kron, calling on behalf of his father. As of five minutes ago, a film permit for all public property in Stone's Throw has been secured in your name. Apparently you have friends in high places. Or one friend. The only one who matters around here."

I nodded and exhaled in relief. I should have thought to ask Kron for help with a film permit immediately. Lucky for me the director seemed to think of everything.

Lot leaned back in his chair and linked his fingers behind his head, revealing Pac-Man–shaped sweat stains tucked into the armpits of his shirt. It wasn't hot in there. Maybe I made him more nervous than he let on. Or something else was making him nervous.

"I want to make a mutually advantageous deal with you," Lot said. "If you learn anything significant about the Dark Road, let me know, and in return I'll let you in on a bit of what I know."

It took a moment for his offer to sink in. "Why the sudden change of heart?"

He lowered his arms and leaned forward on his elbows, looking me in the eye. "After watching your first *episode*, or whatever you want to call it, I decided you might be more effective than I gave you credit for. You got Ray Talbot to talk to you in a way he's never talked to me or the previous sheriff. You've got a knack for subtle manipulation that I, sadly, do not have."

"Don't sell yourself short," I said. "I think you're plenty

manipulative." He laughed, and on that note, I asked, "Can I look at your case files?"

His laughter ceased immediately. "So much for subtlety," he said. "You first. Did you learn anything this morning?"

I pretended to mull over the question. "Does 'white wolf' mean anything to you?"

"The White Wolf Trailhead is where the missing girls' cars were found. This is not news. Try again."

"Does a white wolf *mask* mean anything, then? Because someone broke into my sister's car last night and left one on her seat. It was the only thing taken from my car by whoever broke the window, which seems significant since I left my purse in the car." I almost told him about the email and the video, but Lot cut me off.

"You could have mentioned that at the scene," he snapped.

"True," I said. "But I wasn't going to tell you because you're such an asshole, and now you're being semi-decent. So what's the significance?"

Lot shrugged. "The sanctuary sells wolf masks as souvenirs."

"I know. I saw them. What I want to know is why someone would go out of their way to put one in my sister's car and then break my window to steal it back."

"Maybe it wasn't the same person. People's cars get broken into at that trailhead all the time. There's a sign warning about it."

I stared at him, waiting for more, but he pressed his lips together and smiled.

"Fine," I said. "Your turn, Clarice. Quid pro quo."

"Shouldn't I be Lecter?" he asked.

"Nope. You're the cop, so you get to be Clarice. Don't be sexist. Can I have a look at your case files?"

"There's not a lot in the files that'll help you," he said, but he opened a drawer and took out a slim stack of folders. "The previous sheriff wasn't much of an investigator. I would go so far as to say he couldn't find his own dick if it was in his mouth. Great guy to have a beer with, though. Or he was before his brain turned to mush."

I reached greedily for the folders.

Lot withdrew them. "Pick one," he said.

"That's a cheap trick," I said, scowling.

"I shouldn't be letting you look at any of them. This stays between you and me, by the way. Now pick one before I change my mind."

"Annika Kron," I said without hesitation, hoping Lot was a better investigator than his predecessor. She was the only missing girl whose investigation he'd overseen.

"Of course," he said, but made no move to hand it over. "I'll have one of my deputies make a copy of the file. You didn't think I'd let you run off with my original, did you?"

"Thank you," I said. "Really. I owe you."

"Yes, you do. Got anything else useful to tell me?"

I chewed my bottom lip in thought. "Did I forget to mention the man I ran into in the woods today?"

Lot leaned forward. "What man?"

"He was at the Wolf King's cottage."

The sheriff shrugged. "It's a popular trail. Lots of people visit that cottage."

"He was wearing a wolf mask exactly like the one that was stolen from my car."

Lot's eyebrow went up. "Another detail you conveniently forgot to mention. Did you talk to him?"

"No."

"Why not?"

I found a fascinating spot on the wall behind Lot to focus on. I didn't want to admit that I'd bolted. "He scared me. I was alone and—"

"I thought you were with your sister."

"I was. We got separated. That's part of why I was freaking out. I thought something might have happened to her."

"Did it?"

I shook my head, and Lot smiled that infuriating smile of his, the one that was always laughing at me, even when no sound came out of his mouth. "I wouldn't worry too much about the man you saw. People running around in those woods wearing masks doesn't register as unusual here. You know about the fanatics who perv around Jonas Kron's film locations?"

"I'm aware of them," I said. "Are there any regulars? Have you ever investigated any of them?"

"There's no one in town I would call a true Kronophile, and the visitors aren't breaking any laws. Usually." Lot glanced at his watch and stood. "I hate to cut our session short, but I have to run. This is a busy week for me with the festival starting."

"But I just gave you something. Where's my something in return?"

"Did I forget to specify? It needs to be something I can actually use." He reached across the desk and plucked Annika's file from my hand. "Come back in an hour and I'll have a copy of the file ready for you."

"Nice doing business with you," I said, standing and moving toward the door. I stopped with my hand on the knob and turned back to him. "Do you watch Kron's movies?" I asked.

"I can't say I enjoy them, but yeah. I've seen them."

"What do you think about the idea of a copycat? It

wouldn't be the first time someone tried to make life imitate Kron's art."

"I think it's one possibility," the sheriff allowed.

"You know that in *A Stranger Comes to Town* the townspeople feed an innocent blonde to a wolf creature that lives in the forest."

"Who said the blonde was innocent? We don't know her name or where she came from or how she lost that toe. Even she doesn't know those things. We shouldn't assume she's innocent."

"Riiggghhht. Blame the victim."

He shrugged. "If she's to blame, then sure. We simply don't know. So is that your top theory?" he asked. "That we're all in on the disappearances? Everyone in Stone's Throw is culpable?"

"I'm just saying there are similarities. And maybe you're so used to this town you don't realize how strange it is here."

"This coming from a woman who's lived her entire life in LA. You probably experience more weirdness in an afternoon than I do in a year. Believe me, the weirdest thing in Stone's Throw right now is you."

28.

Back in the sheriff's office lobby, Gemma was nowhere to be found. I'd just begun to mentally berate her for abandoning me—and myself for starting to believe she might do otherwise—when the office assistant asked, her eyes filled with envy, "Are you looking for Gemma Hill? She said to tell you she went to one of the cafés to get lunch. I recommended the Upper Crust, just down the street. How do you *know* her?"

"I don't," I told the office assistant, and took a small amount of pleasure in watching her face fall before walking away.

I found Gemma in the Upper Crust, the only café on Main Street that wasn't eerily deserted. It was noon, but the sidewalks were vacant, and most of the restaurants and cafés I passed were empty or close to it. Half the shops hadn't bothered to turn their CLOSED signs to OPEN. The town reminded me of a standing TV set on a studio lot between seasons, which, in a sense, it was.

The décor of the Upper Crust was as adorably twee as

the rest of the town, with a creaky, hardwood floor, lacy curtains, and mason jars with daisies on vintage wooden tables painted robin's-egg blue. Gemma sat at a table near the window, a half-eaten salad and a cup of black coffee in front of her. She barely managed to tear her eyes from her phone to acknowledge me when I entered.

I was ravenous and wanted a feast, but I didn't want to see the look on Gemma's face as she mentally calculated the calories in a sandwich, fries, and a slice of pie. So I ordered a cup of tomato soup, which I figured would help to warm me up. I was still damp from the rain, and couldn't wait to get back to the inn to take a hot shower and change into dry clothes.

I sat down at the table across from Gemma and slumped against the chair back, my lack of sleep from the last two nights gaining on me.

"How did things go with the sheriff?" Gemma asked, returning her phone to her jacket pocket. I wondered if she'd been texting with Desiree. As far as I knew, Gemma was Desiree's only client, and she kept said client on a short leash.

"Slightly better than yesterday," I said. "Which isn't saying much, because yesterday was a disaster."

She took a delicate sip of her coffee. "He's kind of sexy," she said. "The sheriff."

"Not my type. Maybe yours, though," I said, thinking of the bad boys Gemma used to gravitate toward, usually men a decade older than she was, putting them firmly in statutory territory.

Gemma ignored my comment. "Did you tell him about the mask and the email?"

"The mask, yes. The email, no."

She pursed her lips. "Liv, there was someone in your

room last night *filming you while you slept*. You need to do something about that."

"I will." Tonight I'd make sure all the doors were locked, and my gun was within easy reach.

My cup of soup (200 calories) and mug of coffee were delivered to the table by a teenage girl wearing weather-inappropriate booty shorts that showed off eternally long, grasshopper legs. She barely seemed to have a torso. Just legs and breasts. I watched her walk away, feeling envious of those smooth, dimple-free thighs.

"I remember when I had legs like that," Gemma said, pushing the remainder of her salad aside. Her tone was wistful, but something about it rang false, like she was only saying it to bond with me.

"You still have legs like that," I said, and forced a spoonful of soup past my lips. I hated this. Hated eating in front of most people, but Gemma more than anyone. Hated that being around her made me feel inadequate. The soup was sweet and salty, crusted with a layer of Parmesan. I could recognize that it was delicious and not enjoy a single bite of it at the same time.

"It's a lot harder to keep the weight off now," Gemma said softly, staring into her coffee. "Ever since I turned thirty, I've had to be a lot more careful."

"You've been on a twelve-hundred-calorie-a-day diet since you were nine," I reminded her. "How much more careful can you be?"

She shook her head. "Desiree wasn't like that with me."

"Yes, she was." I choked down another spoonful of delicious soup.

"No, Liv," Gemma said, eyes serious. "She really wasn't. You were the one she was always pushing. You were her golden child. I was your understudy. She didn't care what I did as long as you performed. Don't you remember?"

Don't you remember?

My least favorite words. They'd been posed to me over and over again by police and journalists in a thousand different variations after Miranda disappeared. Don't you remember where you went after the party? Don't you remember the make of the SUV that was following you that night? Don't you remember anything about anyone you spoke to? Don't you remember a single thing that could be the least bit helpful in finding your sister?

No, and no, and no. Massive head trauma and brain swelling took care of that. The only thing I remembered clearly from that night was getting the call from Gemma. I had a fuzzier recollection of driving on Mulholland with Miranda, of suspecting that we were being followed. And after that…nothing until I woke up in the hospital days later with my head carved open and Miranda long gone.

But Gemma claimed she had never called. She was adamant on that point. Yes, she had been at a party, but she said she got home shortly after the time Miranda and I would have left. The police checked call records to our house and found that a call *had* been made at the time I remembered Gemma calling, but it was from a burner phone. No way to track it.

I had no proof that Gemma was lying, no idea what motivation she would have to do so. But my memory of her phone call was the only anchor I had, so I couldn't let it go. Maybe she simply didn't want to be involved or blamed. Maybe she was afraid that her party reputation would be connected to Miranda's disappearance and the press would condemn her. But Gemma hadn't changed her story in the fifteen years that had passed, and I doubted she ever would.

"Can we not talk about this?" I said, retreating from a conversation that should not be had in public.

"Why not?" Gemma asked. "We never talk about what it was really like back then. Desiree made a lot of mistakes with you. She was too hard on you, I completely admit that. She was too young when she had you, and she didn't know what she was doing. She was just trying to survive. To provide for you. For all of us."

"I don't want to talk about this," I said through my teeth. "There's no point."

"I think there is."

"I don't care what you think!"

Heads turned in our direction. Gemma was probably wishing she had a floppy hat and a pair of large sunglasses to hide behind.

"Don't yell at me," Gemma said, her tone low and warning.

"Or what? You'll tell Desiree on me? You'll finally leave me the fuck alone? What will you do, Gemma?"

She stood and stared down at me, saying nothing, though it seemed there was something she wanted to say. But then she shook her head and walked out of the café. I resisted the urge to go after her, apologize, tell her I hadn't meant what I said.

But I meant every word.

29.

I had a little time to kill until I could swing by the sheriff's office and pick up the copied file on Annika Kron/Ana Newman's disappearance. I decided to stay put at the Upper Crust in case Gemma came back. I figured she would fume for ten minutes and then return and apologize. That was what the new Gemma would do, anyway, because the new Gemma wanted us to be a family again, as though that were even possible when we'd never really been one in the first place. We'd been colleagues. Costars. At home, we avoided each other like strangers. We had never been sisters. We'd only played them on TV.

But Gemma didn't come back to the café, and I couldn't make up my mind how to feel about that. Either relieved or disappointed, or maybe a little of both. I would have preferred to feel nothing at all when it came to Gemma.

The woman who'd taken my order stopped by my table to refill my coffee. "How was everything, sweet pea?" she asked. "You need anything else? Slice of pie maybe?" She was middle-aged, round and ruddy-cheeked, reminding me of a cheerful Irish maid from a PBS historical series, the kind who was always ready with an anecdote.

"Nope, I'm good," I told her, but she didn't leave. She put her hand on her hip and stared down at me, scrutinizing my face.

"You look *very* familiar. Are you an actress?"

I don't know what I am anymore, I thought, but nodded. Her question did not necessitate a nuanced answer.

"Is this your first time at the festival?"

"Yep."

"That's exciting! I hope you remembered your mask."

"What?" I said, giving her my full attention for the first time.

"Your mask," she said brightly. "For Mr. Kron's opening-night gala. It's a masquerade party. But don't worry," she said, stacking empty plates on her forearm. "There are a few shops around town selling them, and I hear he'll have masks available at the door for anyone who didn't bring one."

"Thank you for the heads-up," I said, and smiled. I would message Kron when I got back to the Eden Tree and request an invitation to his gala. I wasn't sure how it would help my investigation, but it seemed like the perfect opportunity to scope out the people with whom Kron associated. There had to be a lot of weirdos in his circle, and one of them might be the weirdo I was looking for.

I finished my coffee and got up to leave, waving goodbye to the friendly waitress on my way out the door. A man tried to enter the café at the same moment. I looked at him through the glass and stopped dead, struck by yet another wave of déjà vu. Only this time the moment felt familiar because I had already experienced it the previous day at Raymond Talbot's gas station.

"We have to stop running into each other this way," the man said, smiling with large, square Chiclet teeth that had to be veneers. He wore stylish gray jeans, a black V-neck sweater, and a black motorcycle jacket. He looked like what a good-looking man was supposed to look like, but somehow he avoided actually being attractive. His face was too symmetrical to be interesting, his hair too artfully molded, like a living Ken doll. His perfection made him bland. A slightly crooked nose or a few forehead creases would have made him irresistible.

"Soren Kron, right?" I said, thinking of what he'd claimed at the gas station, that we'd already met, though I still couldn't remember where or when.

His smile dimmed a few watts. "I knew it would come back to you." He didn't sound pleased by the idea.

"It didn't. I saw your picture in an article online."

"Ah," he said. "Of course."

I decided to play nice now that I knew who Soren was. He was at the top of my list of people I wanted to interview. He'd grown up in Stone's Throw, his cousin was the most recent victim, and he'd lived his entire life in Jonas Kron's shadow, peering into the sinister worlds his father created. That had to have a strange effect on a person, and yet Soren appeared to be nothing more than an arrogant playboy who'd grown up with a rich daddy. There had to be more to him than that, and if there was, it meant he was hiding it, and if he was hiding it, there had to be a reason why.

"Maybe you can remind me over coffee how we know each other. Are you busy now?"

He checked his watch and made an exaggeratedly disappointed face. "I have a meeting in a few minutes. I'm organizing the festival this year. Not sure if you're aware."

He said it like his volunteer position at a small, local film festival was akin to being appointed vice president of Sundance.

"Sounds like a lot of work. But maybe you could find time later this afternoon? Or tonight?"

"Don't you have plans with Porter?" Soren asked.

Ghostly pinpricks raced up my spine, and my eyes narrowed automatically. "How do you know that?"

It didn't seem possible for Soren's smile to get any wider, but he managed it. "Word travels fast in a town this small. I ran into Porter about ten minutes ago. I asked if he wanted to get a drink with me tonight, but he said he had a date...with you."

A date? Was that what he thought it was? And what did it mean that Soren and Porter were on casual drinking terms? How did they know each other?

"Did Porter tell you why I'm here?" I asked, wondering if Soren might already know, if Jonas had told him about backing my investigation, or if the director was keeping our arrangement a secret even from his son.

"Oh yes. You're here to crack the case on the Dark Road."

"Maybe you can help me out," I said. "I'd love to arrange an interview. It won't take long. I'll work around your schedule."

He reached into his jacket pocket and withdrew a silver card case, handed me one. "Give me a call." As they had yesterday, his eyes did a quick, obligatory appreciation of my body before returning to my face with a smile. "We'll work something out."

I suppressed a chill of revulsion, though I got the feeling that was exactly what Soren Kron wanted me to feel.

* * *

I stopped by the sheriff's station to retrieve Annika Kron's file, hoping for another chance to talk to Lot, but his office manager said he was on an errand. She would not tell me where.

My car with its broken window was parked on the street. I headed for it, giving up on the idea that Gemma was still skulking around Stone's Throw Village, waiting for me to find her. How would she get back to the inn? Stone's Throw was too small to offer a cab service, much less Uber. But when I spotted a white Suburban cruising past with the Eden Tree logo on the side, I waved until the vehicle pulled up to the curb next to me, pleased to find Porter behind the wheel. Gemma wasn't with him.

Porter rolled the window down. "Hi there," he said, adjusting his tie. He really was paranoid about that thing remaining straight. Or maybe it was just his nervous habit. We all had one. In my early teens, mine had been excessive smiling. I walked into every casting session looking like the Joker. Now it had shifted to excessive consumption of alcohol.

I went to the window, feeling self-conscious about my stringy hair and the mascara grime beneath my eyes.

"I got rained on," I said before he could comment.

He nodded sympathetically. "I figured you might."

"Have you seen my sister Gemma? She's staying at the inn, too. She might have called to request a ride."

"You mean Ms. Suzanne Stone Maretto from *To Die For*?"

I was impressed. "Most people don't catch that reference."

He shrugged, nonchalant. "I'm a database of useless

film knowledge. But, no, I haven't seen your sister. I did notice her car was gone from the parking lot when I left."

I leaned against the side of the Suburban. "Didn't you say you were working the desk until four?"

"I arranged for someone to take my shift so I could pick up pie for the new guests. Hey, you didn't tell me the rest of the Bullshit Hunters were going to be part of your Dark Road investigation. I thought you were on your own now."

I felt the blood drain from my face, leaving my cheeks cold and numb.

"I am," I said. "And they aren't."

30.

I drove back to the Eden Tree, ignoring the speed limit, wind blasting my face through the empty space where my driver's-side window used to be. The first thing I saw when I careened into the parking lot was the Bullshit Hunters' van, a slightly more tasteful variation on the psychedelic Scooby-Doo Mystery Machine.

Porter pulled into the parking space beside mine. He got out and watched in helpless dismay as I pounded my fist on the side panel of the van. "Open up, Danny!" I shouted.

"I think they're in their rooms," Porter said softly, coming up beside me, holding a stack of wooden pie boxes in his arms. "They had just checked in before I left."

Wheeler's room was a few doors down from mine. I convinced Porter to let me deliver his pie. It took Wheeler less than two seconds to open his door after I knocked. He must have been expecting me.

It seemed like weeks had passed since I'd seen Wheeler. I wanted to throw my arms around him, but I had a pie box in my hands, so instead I shoved it into his and stormed inside.

"I tried to warn you," Wheeler said, setting the pie box on his desk. "Didn't you get my texts?"

"There's no fucking service in this town," I snapped, misplacing my anger directly onto him. "Not that it would have done me any good. But whatever. I'll have a dozen episodes online before you guys can air a single one."

Wheeler cleared his throat and lowered his eyes. "Actually, um...Danny decided to try something new for this investigation."

"Let me guess. He's going to post mini episodes online instead of waiting for them to air on TV. Brilliant. I wonder where he got that idea. You know he's only doing this to get back at me, right? This morning he tried to rehire me. I turned him down."

Wheeler's eyebrows climbed his forehead. "He didn't tell us that, but I'm not surprised. You're getting a lot of attention. Not all of it good, but there are always haters."

"What haters?"

"It's nothing," he said. "Ignore them."

"Ignore *who*?"

He took a deep breath and sighed. "Some people on social media feel like you're taking advantage of the crowdsourcing system. That you're making money off them, not just funding your series." Wheeler took me by the shoulders, forcing me to look at him. "Don't listen to the trolls. You're doing great! Just keep filming. Pretend we're not even here."

There was a knock on the door then, and a voice that made every muscle in my body clench called, "Wheeler, let's go. Daylight's burning."

I pulled away from Wheeler and headed for the door, grabbing the pie out of the pie box on my way.

"Liv, don't—" Wheeler said, but there was no stopping me now.

I opened the door with my free hand. Danny stood on the other side, eyes affixed to his phone. He didn't notice me until I spoke.

"Welcome to Stone's Throw," I said, and when he looked up I smashed the pie in his face.

I walked past him and disappeared into my room, leaving him sputtering in the hallway, bits of crust and sticky apple chunks plopping from his shoulders to land on the carpet at his feet. I'd feel bad about the mess later. For the moment, all I wanted to do was get my next webisode online before Danny and the Bullshit Hunters shot a single thing.

*   *   *

I went straight to work on my next webisode, cutting together footage from my DSLR and the GoPro. After viewing Gemma's footage, I decided I believed her story about how we'd come to be separated. She did trip (or she appeared to). The camera angle jolted when she fell. I heard her curse, and then call out to me to wait. She began following the trail, her pace increasing as she continued to call my name with no response. Then the camera picked up the distant sound of Tocsin the mountain lion shrieking. Gemma ran toward the sound, the footage so shaky it was almost unusable.

Once I finished the rough cut of my episode. I did a quick polish to tighten it up, and used my laptop mike to record some explanatory voiceover, which I laid in, accompanied by eerie stock music I'd downloaded for free.

All in all, the edit took me close to two hours. The final product probably needed another polish or three, but I didn't have time for that anymore, not with Danny in town trying to scoop me and almost a full day gone from the three I had to solve this thing and double my money. I posted the episode with all the relevant hashtags and blasted it out on social media.

Then I took a deep breath to steady myself and looked at my Twitter feed, scrolling through all the tweets I had missed since that morning.

A minute later, I opened the well-stocked mini bar under my desk, chose a bottle of Maker's Mark bourbon, and drank it like it was Gatorade and I was a dehydrated marathon runner.

The Internet had turned on me. Last night, enthusiasm for my project had been through the roof, but around noon today people had begun to question whether what I was doing was ethical or just a self-serving grasp for attention and quick cash, and their questioning came in the form of an angry Twitter mob wielding hashtags like pitchforks and torches: #LivGreedy #entitled #getarealjob #BullshitBitch.

The hashtags were one thing. The tweets themselves were the truly malicious part.

@LivHendricks Someone should make YOU disappear.

@LivHendricks I would love to knock you the fuck out. Shatter your teeth and hope you choke on them.

@LivHendricks You think you can get away with this? Buckle up. The rape-mobile is heading straight for you.

@LivHendricks I know where you are. Watch your back.

@LivHendricks Greedy bitches need to be tied up and fucked in their fat bitch asses until they bleed. Blood makes the best lube.

Who wants to see a video of @LivHendricks choking on my dick until she agrees to give our money back?

On and on and on. Dozens of them. Threats against my life. Threats to "tear up every hole in my body." Accusations that I was an entitled, greedy, attention-seeking, substance-abusing, not-skinny whore and I deserved every violent act committed against me.

I responded to none of them, but I read all of them. Once I started, I couldn't stop. Was it a coincidence that the Internet hadn't turned on me until today, after I declined Danny's job offer? Maybe Danny had started an anti-Liv hate campaign in retaliation.

It took ten minutes of scrolling, but I found ground zero. The author of all my social media contempt. @Director_ ElliotHoyt

Elliot Hoyt, my neighbor, had tweeted in the early afternoon:

Listen up @LivHendricks is using you to pay her rent after getting fired. Don't fall for her bullshit like I did. #darkroad #entitled

I leaned back in my desk chair, the emotional numbness finally setting in. I should have been furious, but I only felt dazed and ashamed.

I picked up my phone and texted Elliot with clumsy fingers:

Why?

I didn't really need an answer. I already knew. I'd ignored his texts, flaked on acting in his scene, rejected his needy advances. Apparently I'd been wrong about Elliot being too nice to make it in Hollywood. He had a long and illustrious career ahead of him.

I waited, watching my cell screen. The word READ appeared, followed by an iPhone ellipsis telling me Elliot had received my message and was texting me back. Then, just as quickly, the ellipsis vanished and did not reappear. I didn't think I'd be hearing from him again.

I set my phone aside and returned my attention to my Twitter feed. I scrolled back through, rereading tweets, tallying up those still in support of me, and there were some. A few followers had even gone to bat for me, countering the violent tweets with rational, reasoned responses. But those replies were met with escalating scorn and vitriol, threats of rape and violence against my defenders, who could only take so much before they gave up and left me to fend for myself.

They're just trolls, I told myself. Just a bunch of lonely, bitter men who live in their mothers' basements and can't get laid, so they take their anger out on me. I wasn't the first prominent female who'd been vilified on social media, and I wouldn't be the last.

As I reached the top of my feed, a new tweet arrived from someone with an anonymous human head avatar, but a twitter handle that gave me chills when I read it. @AnnikaKron tweeted:

@LivHendricks Follow the white wolf

I slammed my laptop shut and shot to my feet, turning in a circle, my eyes darting to every hidden nook and corner. I searched my room, checking behind the furniture, under the bed, in the wardrobe, in the bathroom. I even looked in my suitcase, like I might find someone folded inside, waiting to crawl out and pounce when my back was turned. That had happened in a Kron film. I couldn't remember which one.

The room was empty. I was alone. I sat back down.

Follow the white wolf.

Whoever had tweeted this must be the same person who was in my room last night. The same person who broke into my sister's car and left the wolf mask, then broke into my car and took it back. I had serious doubts it was the real Annika Kron, but I didn't rule out the possibility entirely.

I fished a mini bottle of Jack Daniel's out of the fridge and drank it in a single, continuous gulp. The warmth shushed my nerves, and I opened my laptop, checked @AnnikaKron's Twitter profile. There was only the one tweet. No bio.

I clicked on the arrow to respond.

@AnnikaKron Who are you?

I waited five minutes. There was no response.

I removed the rest of the mini bottles from the fridge and lined them up next to my laptop. I drank the vodka and then hit FOLLOW on @AnnikaKron's profile so we could take our conversation offline.

LH: You were in my room last night. You emailed that video.

AK: Yes.

LH: Are you really Annika Kron?

No response.

LH: Are you the white wolf?

No response.

LH: What do you want?

AK: I already told you. Follow the white wolf.

LH: I did that already.

AK: You didn't go far enough.

LH: If you really are Annika Kron, tell me what happened to you.

No response.

LH: What will I find if I follow the wolf?

AK: Answers.

LH: Will I find out what happened to you and the other women who disappeared?

No response.

LH: What the fuck do you want me to do?

A long pause, and then her response came in the form of an attached image, a photograph of the white wolf mask that had been taken from my car. At least I thought it was the same one. Even looking at the picture of the mask made my stomach acids churn and my mouth fill with saliva. I swallowed repeatedly, willing myself to remember whatever it was my subconscious wanted to tell me about these masks, but nothing came to me. Not a single shred of memory.

Jennifer Wolfe

LH: You want me to follow the mask, not the trail?

AK: It starts with the mask. Byeeee! Signing off now.

I tried several more questions, but @AnnikaKron did not respond, and I finally gave up. I studied her answers to my questions, homing in on the last thing she'd written.

It starts with the mask.

So where did the mask start?

Helene, at the wolf sanctuary, said her son, Niklas, made the wolf masks they sold as souvenirs. Her son, who worked in close proximity to the Dark Road, whose face had been disfigured by the fire he had started in the woods as a teenager. And who, according to Anders, had some kind of mental health issues as a child. As far as suspects went, he was as good as it got. Had he ever been investigated in regard to the disappearances? I'd have to have another chat with Lot about that.

I felt galvanized by this new direction. I needed to find out more about Niklas, and then I needed to talk to him away from the protection of his parents. I'd never get him to open up with his mother and father present, but I was also not keen on the idea of being alone with the guy. Maybe I could convince Gemma to accompany me as I tracked him down. But first I'd have to apologize to her.

I picked up my room phone and asked the woman at the front desk to connect me to Gemma's room. The phone rang and rang without answer. I tried her cell phone, but it went straight to voicemail. I started to leave a message telling her to call me, but a knock on my door interrupted me. "Never mind. That's probably you," I said, and hung up.

But when I opened the door, it was not Gemma I found on the other side. It was Porter. Instead of his Eden Tree polo, he wore a dark-gray blazer over a checkered shirt with a plain black tie, complete with the silver tiepin that was still too fancy for the rest of his ensemble. He reminded me of a kid who'd dressed up for picture day at school.

"Hi," he said, brow furrowing as he noticed I was clearly not ready for whatever he had in store for me, which, judging by his attire and the hearsay from Soren, was an actual date.

"Hi. Come in," I said, waving him inside, hoping he didn't notice my slurred speech. "I'm running late."

His eyebrows rose slightly at the empty array of mini bottles on my desk, and his nostrils flared the tiniest bit, detecting the alcohol fumes on my breath.

"There's something I need to talk to you about before we go," he said, standing awkwardly in front of my desk, glancing at my laptop screen. I snaked around him and closed it, then swept the mini bottles into the trash.

"Happy hour," I explained. "It's been a long day."

"I, uh..." He laughed, just one short *huh*, and scratched the back of his head, stalling. "I've had a complaint about you from one of the other guests."

"Danny?" I guessed. Of course Danny would tell on me.

"He said you smashed a pie in his face," Porter pointed out.

"I'm really sorry about that," I said, lowering my eyes in a display of shame. "I lost my temper. I'm completely to blame."

"I understand you being upset with him," Porter said, taking a step toward me, close enough that my body lit up like a Christmas tree in proximity to his. I got that giddy, rolling, weightless sensation in my stomach that accompanies effortless chemistry. I didn't remember ever experiencing such attraction to another person who wasn't doing anything to elicit it. This was pure magnetism.

Porter touched my arm to comfort me, and I had to restrain myself from grabbing him by the back of the neck and pulling his mouth onto mine. My sudden desire for him seemed almost pathological. I sat down on the bed to put some distance between the two of us, but Porter sat down beside me, his thigh grazing mine. I crossed my arms and trapped my hands in my armpits.

"I hope you don't think this makes me sound like a stalker, but...I was looking at your Twitter feed and I read some of the things people are saying. Are you okay?"

"I'm f-fine," I choked out, my throat suddenly choked with emotion.

Porter turned so he was facing me, one knee up on the bed. "Tell me how I can help."

"Don't kick me out of the inn for the pie thing with Danny?"

Porter shrugged and smiled a shy, boyish smile. "Believe it or not, you're not the first guest of the Eden Tree to behave badly." His smile dimmed and he glanced away. "Actually, I feel like I'm the one behaving badly right now. I must be violating some innkeeper code of conduct, sitting on your bed with you."

"Is there such a thing as an innkeeper code of conduct?"

"Not that I know of."

"Good," I said. And I kissed him. I didn't know I was going to do it. Maybe it was the mini bottles I'd drunk, or the stress of reading all those hate tweets, or maybe I just wanted him, and I was tired of not getting what I wanted. I didn't know, and at that moment I didn't care.

Porter froze for a moment, unsure, and I pulled back. We looked at each other, heat building between us. Finally, Porter leaned in again, and his soft lips found mine in a gentlemanly kiss. A lingering, patient, Jane Austen kiss. But I wasn't a Jane Austen sort of girl.

I used my lips to open his, not caring anymore that my breath was flammable. I teased Porter's tongue out of his mouth and was gratified when he finally moaned in submission and let me have him. Keeping my mouth on his, I climbed onto his lap, straddled him with my knees on the bed, and felt the hard length of his cock fighting against his slacks.

The rest of it happened as it happens. Shirts peeled off and pants were hastily yanked down. Breasts were cupped, fondled. Nipples licked, sucked. We took turns between each other's legs. I tried not to feel self-conscious about the fact that I hadn't showered since that morning, while Porter's very fine, perfectly sized penis still smelled faintly of soap from his last shower.

And then, the main event.

I'd already cum with assistance from Porter's capable tongue, so I didn't expect to again, but I was pleasantly surprised by the innkeeper's skills as a lover. He thrust into me at just the right angle. He'd clearly had practice. He wasn't as innocent and straitlaced as he seemed.

When it was over, I flopped back on the bed, sweaty and sated and fighting regret, the kind that always hit me after I fulfilled a craving and rational thinking became possible again. But Porter rolled toward me and smiled, making the skin around his eyes crinkle. His glasses had been tossed aside at some point, and he looked even younger without them. He reminded me of someone, and no one.

Porter laid a hand on my bare hip and kissed my shoulder.

"If there really is an innkeepers' union, I think you're going to be in trouble," I said, my eyes drifting closed against my will.

"You're exhausted," Porter said, moving his hand to my hair and brushing a sticky lock of it back from my face. "Take a nap. I'll come back to pick you up for dinner at seven thirty, okay?"

I knew I should rouse myself, get back to work. There was plenty I needed to do, including read Annika Kron's file. But I was already sliding toward sleep, and I needed to shut off my mind, just for a little while. I wouldn't be able to see straight unless I did.

I nodded at Porter and closed my eyes, felt him rise from the bed. He pulled the comforter around me, wrapping me tight like a burrito.

"You're so nice," I murmured, barely conscious. "Will you make sure the doors are locked?"

"Of course." He laid a kiss on my brow. On my scar, I thought.

And then I was out.

OLIVIA HILL

2003

17 YEARS OLD; 109 LBS.

31.

*I*s she coming?" Miranda asked when I was back behind the wheel.

"She's not here anymore." I started the engine, watching the two boys from the party—Jimmy and Russel—walk to their car. Jimmy glanced toward my car and waved, but it was so dark I doubted he could see me or Miranda. I waved back anyway, and kept my eyes on the two guys as they climbed into a gray Toyota.

They pulled onto the road and I followed.

Miranda turned to me. "We're not going home?"

I shook my head. "Gemma went to some other party. Those guys know where."

Miranda heaved out an angry breath and sat back heavily in her seat. "This is stupid."

"Gemma was in bad shape, and the man she left with is way older than she is. She's in over her head."

Miranda snorted a laugh so bitter it made her sound like she'd already lived an entire lifetime of disappointment. "Do you know what I caught her doing a few days ago?"

"What?" I wasn't sure I even wanted to know. I kept my eyes fixed on the treacherous, twisting road, the taillights of the Toyota as it braked at a stop sign before turning right, descending into a hillside neighborhood. The sloping road plummeted at what seemed like a ninety-degree angle.

"I was up late reading, and I heard noises coming from the kitchen. I thought maybe you were awake, watching TV. I got up to check, and I found Gemma with some guy. He had her bent over the dining room table. He was screwing her right there. Right where we eat. The guy...he saw me and smiled like it was the funniest thing, me seeing them. He grabbed Gemma's hair and yanked her head back so she had to look at me. And she was just...empty. Like she wasn't even in there. She was just a body. I ran back to my room and locked the door. I didn't sleep all night. I could still hear them out there."

The story left me feeling sad and sick. I never asked for details about the things Gemma did when she was out. Listening to Miranda's story, I realized how much effort I put into trying not to think about it. I had compartmentalized imagining Gemma's private life into a back room in my mind, figuring that as long as she didn't get caught, as long as she didn't bring any scandal home with her, it was none of my business.

But apparently she had brought it home with her in the most literal sense.

Up ahead, the Toyota pulled over to park on the side of the road. I did the same. At least it was easy to find *parking. There was only one house at the end of this street. The rest of the land around the house looked too treacherous to build on.*

I unfastened my seat belt and reached for the door, but Miranda grabbed my arm, held on so tight her fingernails dug in painfully, even through my jacket. "You don't know those guys. You don't know what kind of people will be in there. Let's just go home. Gemma can take care of herself. This is where she wants to be."

I wasn't so sure about that. Gemma was out of control, and I was partially to blame. I had always resented the way Gemma cooperated with Desiree, playing any part our mother asked her to play. I resented her for choosing Desiree over me. So I had washed my hands of her, maybe out of spite. If I had tried harder to help her swim through the shark-infested waters we'd been submerged in our entire lives, maybe she wouldn't be feeding herself willingly to these hungry animals. It wasn't easy, the life we lived in public, constantly scrutinized, our weight and fitness routines and beauty regimens discussed in magazines. Our relationships speculated upon. Our outfits critiqued, labeled successes or fails. We couldn't leave the house without wondering if there was a photographer following close behind, or hiding behind the bushes at a restaurant, waiting to snap a picture of Gemma or me eating something that would make us fat. Gemma acted as though she enjoyed every second of it, but she was an actress, and she was good at what she did. She had convinced me she loved what she was. Maybe she'd even convinced herself.

"I'll be fine," I told Miranda. "I'll grab her and we'll

be on our way. If she's as drunk as I think she is, she won't be able to put up much of a fight."

"What about the guy who brought her here?" Miranda asked. "He might be the one putting up a fight."

"I won't be alone," I reminded her, gesturing to Russel and Jimmy. I was suddenly very glad they'd be with me, even though they were hardly more than kids themselves.

"You don't even know them," Miranda said again.

"No, I do. I've met them." I decided not to tell her they were friends of Gemma's, or that I didn't actually remember meeting either of them.

Miranda sighed. "Please hurry," she said. "I just...I have a bad feeling about this."

"You have a bad feeling about everything. Don't worry so much."

The words left my mouth easily enough, but meaning them was a different story, especially when I followed Russel and Jimmy to the house and saw the black SUV parked out front. I was certain it was the same make and model as the SUV that had followed Miranda and me to the first party, but that didn't mean it was the same vehicle.

"Hold on a sec," I said to the guys, and peered in through the SUV's tinted windows. I rapped sharply on the driver's-side window, but there was no response. There was no one inside.

I returned to the guys. "What was that about?" Jimmy asked, and I shook my head.

"Doesn't matter," I said. "Let's find my sister and get the hell out of here."

LIV HENDRICKS

2018

32 YEARS OLD; 141 LBS.

Facebook Fans: 11,002

Twitter Followers: 46,712

Instagram Followers: 7,677

32.

I woke with my head pounding, the room pitch-black. I lunged for the lamp switch, winced against the sudden brightness. I made a bulky toga from the comforter and then crept through the room, checking every conceivable hiding place before I could breathe easy. I shouldn't have dared to fall asleep before making sure the doors were locked, but I'd been too deliriously exhausted to keep my eyes open.

When I was assured no one had trespassed in my room while I slept, I turned my attention to the headache making my brain pulse like something about to hatch. I swallowed four Advil with a glass of water and jumped into the shower. It was already seven. I'd slept for two hours, longer than I'd intended, but at least I felt revived and wide-awake.

After showering, I wrapped myself in the complimentary white spa robe I'd found in the wardrobe, and toweled my hair dry while I tried calling Gemma again. She didn't answer her room phone or her cell. At this point, it was obviously that she was avoiding me. Our brief experiment in sister bonding had concluded, and the results were in. It wasn't going to work out.

I didn't have time to crack Annika's file, but I promised myself I would do so as soon as I got back from dinner.

I wasn't sure how to dress for my unanticipated date with Porter. It hadn't occurred to me to bring anything to Stone's Throw other than casual basics, jeans and T-shirts and sweaters. I dressed in black jeans, Frye boots I'd bought when I was financially stable, and a black top and hoped Porter wasn't taking me anywhere too fancy. In lieu of carrying my digital camera around all night, I decided to wear my body camera. I attached it inside my jacket pocket but didn't have time to test it was working before someone knocked on the door. I assumed it would be Porter, but I cracked the door and peered outside to make sure before removing the chain.

"You look beautiful," Porter said, smiling at me in that slightly gleeful way men do when they're fairly certain they'll be getting laid at the end of the evening. I wished I could find that kind of contentment from the thought of guaranteed sex, but I was a woman. I could have sex pretty much whenever I chose to. There was no "if," only "when." But the idea of another go with Porter made me feel something I wasn't used to: a sense of feverish elation, like all my cells were vibrating in tune with his. That was new. Normally the only thing I felt after sex with a near-stranger was regret and a vague sense of violation, like something had been stolen from me. Like I'd lost another vital piece of the puzzle that was Liv Hendricks/Olivia Hill.

"Thank you," I said demurely to Porter's compliment, and I closed and locked the door behind me before my will weakened and I pulled Porter inside for round two.

In the parking lot, Porter clicked the keyless entry button

to unlock his car, a nondescript sedan that said absolutely nothing about his personality, unless it was that he simply didn't care about cars.

"So where are we going?" He opened the door for me, and I folded myself into the passenger seat.

"To the best restaurant in town. Come tomorrow, it'll be impossible to get a table there until the festival is over. Since I have no idea how long you'll be in Stone's Throw, I figured I'd better not wait."

Driving through the lot, I noted that the Bullshit Hunters' van was absent, which probably meant they were shooting somewhere. I wondered whether Danny intended to "produce" a few scares to keep his endeavor interesting, or if he was going to infuse his bullshit reality show with some actual reality.

"How did things go today?" Porter asked. "I saw you uploaded a new episode, but I didn't get a chance to watch yet."

"Good," I said. "I have a few leads."

He arched an eyebrow, impressed. "That was fast. Anything you want to talk about?"

"Actually, yes," I said. "I visited the wolf sanctuary today and talked with the people who run it, Anders and Helene and their son."

"You talked to Nik?" Porter gave me a skeptical look. "Nik doesn't really talk."

"Right," I said. "I talked to his parents. I only saw him in passing. Poor guy."

Porter gave a derisive little snort. "Yeah, poor Nik," he muttered. The reaction seemed uncharacteristically callous. From the moment I met him, Porter struck me as one of those absurdly laid-back people who didn't have a spiteful bone in his body, but apparently he had one for Nik.

"You don't like him?" I asked.

"I have nothing against him," Porter said, but his flat tone implied otherwise. "I just don't feel sorry for him."

"Because it was his fault? The fire, I mean?"

"How do you know that?" Porter glanced at me, clearly surprised.

"Anders told me. He said people in town know, but the cause of the fire wasn't in any of the papers. Do you know why he did it?"

"Not really. But there was always something off about Nik. I didn't know him that well. He was a couple of grades behind me in school, so I never had classes with him. All I know is that he almost never spoke or made eye contact with anyone, and he had a few...I guess you would call them fits at school."

"What kind of fits?"

"Tantrums. Emotional outbursts if people got too close to him or messed with him. That sort of thing. If you want my opinion, he's definitely on the autism spectrum, but back then people didn't really understand much about that, including his parents. Maybe if they'd gotten him appropriate treatment things would have been different." Porter frowned over at me. "In case you're wondering, the previous sheriff already investigated Nik and his family."

"Why did he investigate them?"

Porter shrugged. "I guess because they live closer to the trailhead than anyone else in town. And because of Nik's history."

"Did the sheriff bring in cadaver dogs?"

Porter nodded. "They didn't find anything. Not anything human, anyway."

"What about regular search and rescue dogs?"

"Are those different from cadaver dogs?"

"Cadaver dogs find dead humans. Other types find a living trail. The girls may have been abducted here, but if they weren't killed here, then a cadaver dog might not find them."

Porter raised an eyebrow at me. "You seem to know a lot about this stuff."

I shrugged. "Blitz's handler told me a few things. And I've been on a lot of police procedural shows. Plus, I was a teen detective, remember?"

"How could I ever forget?" He smiled, but the smile faded fast. "Just be careful with the Larsens. Nik isn't my favorite person, but I know he's been through hell. The whole family has. You've seen the burn scars on his face, but not on the rest of his body. He's had at least half a dozen skin graft surgeries since it happened, and a few times his body rejected them. He's spent years of his life in a hospital bed."

"The Larsens must have good medical insurance. That sounds expensive."

"I'm sure it is. So, you know, go easy on them."

"I'm just asking questions," I said. "If I ask enough, eventually they'll be the right ones at the right time." I cringed, realizing I had just quoted an exact line of dialogue from *The Hills Have PIs*.

"Just be careful you don't drag innocent people's names through the mud," Porter warned.

I smiled sweetly and quoted another line from *THHPI*. "That would be easier if I knew who was innocent."

33.

A hanging wooden sign out in front of the restaurant announced the name CORE in engraved tavern scrawl. The interior was as warm and cozy as a cabin at Christmas, with knotty-wood floors and tables arranged around a cobblestone fireplace, where flames crackled behind the iron grate. The dining room was half filled with patrons. It was the busiest Stone's Throw establishment I'd encountered thus far.

The hostess led us to a table near the fireplace and divided the dinner, drink, and specials menus between us. When our server arrived, Porter ordered a bottle of wine. "I hope that's okay," he said when the server had gone. "I should have asked if you prefer red or white. Or if you even like wine. I'm a bit nervous. I don't know if you can tell. I don't do this often. Dating, I mean. Not dating celebrities."

I reached across the table and put my hand over his. "You don't need to be nervous. And I'm really not much of a celebrity."

He ran a thumb lightly over the back of my hand, and I shivered with involuntary pleasure. "Did I take advantage of you?" he asked softly.

I had to laugh at that. "Did I take advantage of *you*?"

"Of course not."

"Just because you're a man doesn't mean I can't take advantage of you."

He glanced left and right to make sure no one at the nearby tables was listening. "I feel like what I did was...disrespectful."

What he'd done was get me off in the most satisfying way I could remember. He hadn't been rough with me, but he'd taken control. At one point he'd held my wrists above my head and wouldn't let go when I tried to move them. He'd kept them trapped there as he moved on top of me, only releasing me once he came.

And then...he'd gone back to being the man sitting across from me. Sweet. Considerate. Just the right amount of nerdy.

I smiled, but felt something grow heavy in my chest. "Sometimes women like to be disrespected." Sometimes we needed it. Or *I* needed it. I wasn't sure what other women wanted. I didn't have female friends to talk to about this sort of thing to find out if I was normal.

Our server appeared and listed the specials. We ordered, and then fell into an easy, conversational rhythm, which consisted of me gently probing him with benign questions while avoiding talking about myself. As far as first dates went, it was nice, especially considering that we'd rutted like animals a few hours earlier. What I realized by the time we'd finished our appetizers was that Porter hadn't done much actual living. Most of his experience of the world had been through a screen.

"Do you think you'll ever move away from Stone's Throw?" I asked as I ate the last of our fried calamari (800 calories).

Porter picked up a piece of bread and tore it in half, but didn't take a bite. "Do I need to?"

The question confused me. "Need to?"

"Am I missing something? I've lived thousands of lives, all over the world, in every period of history. Why should I leave my comfortable existence?"

"Ohhh. I see. You think watching life on TV and in movies is the same as experiencing it."

He smiled. "Not at all. I just prefer it that way." He set his bread aside and leaned toward me. "I went on this amazing vacation once, traveled all over Europe for a month. I saw all the things people said I should see. Ate all the local foods. Bought a bunch of souvenirs..."

"And?"

"And I was bored out of my mind. There was no story to follow. No narrative. I'm addicted to plot. I kept waiting for something exciting to happen, and it never did. That being said, if something exciting *had* happened I probably would have run the other way."

I laughed, but Porter's attitude made me sad, because millions of people shared it. Real life rarely measured up to a great story, and a great story could never hurt you the way real life did. I had no room to judge Porter, though. I'd lived most of my life as other people, taking their stories on and off from one job to the next. And the truth was that I had, for the most part, stopped living after Miranda disappeared. I couldn't deal with real life, and I couldn't hide in characters anymore. I was stuck in limbo.

"Let's talk about you," Porter said after our dinner plates

had been cleared away, probably realizing that I'd told him next to nothing about myself.

"Maybe you could just read my Wikipedia page," I said, polishing off my third glass of wine. Porter wasn't even finished with his first. I'd better slow down.

"I don't believe half of what I read online."

"Which half do you believe?"

"The good half."

"That is either sweet or very naive. Oh, I forgot to mention, I ran into a friend of yours today," I said, deflecting the topic away from me. "Soren Kron? You didn't tell me you were in with the Stone's Throw elite."

Porter took a sip of wine, pausing before answering. "I guess I don't think of him that way. We've been friends since we were kids."

I raised an eyebrow. "That explains a lot."

"What do you mean?" His easy tone had gone stiff.

"I don't know. You two just seem like very different types of people."

Porter's eyes shifted past my shoulder and he smiled. "Speak of the devil."

I twisted around, already knowing who I would see. But I wasn't nearly as interested in Soren Kron at that moment as I was in the man who accompanied him. Soren's companion was in his late sixties, with thinning, white-blond hair and marionette grooves around his mouth. He was so tall I had to tip my head back to look at his face. He wore a dapper herringbone suit and had the look of a mad concert pianist, his hair combed back from his high forehead, while Soren reminded me of the alpha-male villains in John Hughes's movies, all blond arrogance and icy eyes and smirking mouth.

Porter stood and hugged the two men warmly, then stepped back. "Liv, I'd like to introduce you to—"

"Jonas Kron," I finished for him, rising from my chair. "It's so nice to meet you."

"The pleasure is mine." Jonas clasped my hand in both of his, held it rather than actually shaking it.

The hostess hovered behind the Krons, cradling their menus.

"Can we switch to a table for four?" Soren asked her.

"Porter is on a date," Jonas reminded his son. His voice was musical and clipped at the same time, with only a hint of an accent.

"Come on," Soren said, slapping Porter on the back. "I never get to see you anymore. Spend some quality time with me. Besides, I want to tell Liv embarrassing stories about what you were like as a kid."

Porter started to shake his head, but I cut in. "I'm game. Bring on the stories."

"Excellent," Soren crowed, clapping his hands fast and silent. There was something slightly manic, even flamboyant about Soren. He oozed charm and vitality, but seemed like the kind of person who could drain the energy of those around him if they spent too many consecutive hours in his company. And at the same time there was an emptiness about him. I'd worked with hundreds of actors of all different calibers over the course of my career, and I'd learned to recognize the ones I privately thought of as "gloves" within seconds of meeting them. They were the vacant ones who almost seemed like inanimate objects when they were at rest. They had little personality of their own. They required a writer and a script and a director to bring them to life.

Soren wasn't an actor as far as I knew, but he had a quality about him that made me think his personality was more constructed than innate.

The hostess moved us to a larger table, and Jonas ordered a bottle of French wine. I could tell by the way the server's eyes widened that it was likely the most expensive they offered.

"And four shots of aquavit," Soren added, then rubbed his hands together. "Now for those stories."

"He's got nothing," Porter said, smiling across the table at his friend. "He just said that to lure you in."

"That's true," Soren said. "Porter was and still is a perfectly boring human being. It's maddening, really. I spent years trying to get the stick out of his ass, but it remains there to this day. Do you know I took him to Europe once for an entire month, and he couldn't wait to get home to Stone's Throw?"

I smiled at Porter. "You don't say."

"I do say!" Soren almost shouted. It was possible he'd arrived at the restaurant drunk.

Jonas was silent throughout this conversation, busy perusing the menu. I wasn't sure he was even listening.

Soren turned to me. "Porter could be my wingman, traveling the world with me, meeting exotic women, getting kicked out of the best bars and hotels. Instead he stays here in Stone's Throw acting like the mayor of Whoville." Soren shook his head in good-humored disgust. "Boring."

"There's nothing wrong with Stone's Throw," Jonas said, setting his menu down as our server arrived with the wine and aquavit shots.

"You and my father always see eye-to-eye," Soren said to Porter. "That's why he prefers you to me. Then again, he prefers most people to me."

"Soren..." Jonas said in warning.

"What? It's true. Just the other day I overheard you telling someone on the festival committee that I have no work ethic."

"That is not what I said," Jonas replied in an even tone, staring with those cool blue eyes at his son. "I said I blame myself for your lack of work ethic."

"Same thing," he said, and winked at me. He was acting like the subject didn't bother him, but I detected a raw edge to his jaunty attitude. "It isn't easy living in the shadow of a great man like my daddy. I'm sure you understand." He raised his shot glass. "Skoal."

I was the last to drink, too busy mulling over the implications of what he'd said. Was he referring to Gemma and me, and if so, who was casting the shadow—her or me?

I knocked back the aquavit, which tasted like licorice-flavored paint thinner. I chased it with the wine Jonas ordered and almost fell over backward in my chair. It was that good.

"So what brings you to town?" Jonas asked me. His facade was perfect. I could almost believe he didn't know why I was there.

"The Dark Road," I said. "I'm investigating the disappearances."

Jonas feigned confusion. "But aren't you an actor like your sister?"

"I'm trying something new," I said, playing along with the ruse that he knew nothing about me. "Speaking of my sister, she mentioned you might work together on your next film."

He shook his head. "We had a meeting set for tomorrow, but she canceled it, said she had to return to Los Angeles. The next time you do see her, tell her I don't have time to waste on unreliable actors. If she can't keep her appointments, I have no interest in working with her. This is the second time she's canceled on me, and she is hardly the commodity she used to be."

"What are you talking about?" I asked, feeling a twinge of defensiveness on Gemma's behalf.

"She's overpaid and uninspiring," Jonas said with cruel bluntness. "The last three movies she starred in lost money. There is nothing particularly interesting about her look, nor does she bring any true sense of gravitas or nuance to her performances. The only reason I considered working with her is because your mother called and begged me to give her a chance. Apparently I am not the only director who holds this view of your sister."

I blinked at this revelation. Desiree had *begged* Jonas to cast Gemma in a Kron film? Desiree didn't beg anyone for anything. She demanded. At least she used to. I didn't realize Gemma had fallen so far out of favor in the studio system. Desiree must be desperate, which did not bode well for Gemma's career. A desperate actor was an out-of-work actor.

Jonas leveled his rain-colored gaze on me. "I'm sorry if my honesty offends you. At my age, you realize you have no time left to waste mincing words."

"It's fine," I said smoothly, though his tirade rankled. "Gemma and I aren't close."

"We had a ticket reserved in her name for a private screening," Soren said. "You'll have to take her place. And you must come to the opening gala tomorrow. You could be Porter's plus one. Or mine if Porter already has a date." Soren winked, and Porter rolled his eyes before turning to me.

"Would you like to be my date for the gala?" he asked, touching my leg under the table, sending a little jolt of electricity up my thigh.

I opened my mouth to answer yes, but was distracted by the sound of wailing sirens as two sheriff's cruisers with flashing red and blue lights sped past the restaurant.

I stood abruptly, slinging my bag over my shoulder. "I'm so sorry, but I need to go."

Porter didn't argue, just nodded and stood, opening his wallet, but Jonas waved for him to put his money away. "I will take care of it."

The director met my eyes and flashed a brief, grim smile. "I'll see you both at the gala. Don't forget your mask."

34.

The second I spotted the strobe of blue and red lights ahead on the Dark Road, I commanded Porter to pull over. He reacted slowly, seeming dazed as he veered gently onto the shoulder.

"This can't be happening again," he said for possibly the sixth time since we'd left the restaurant. This was clearly too much "plot" for him to handle in his own life. He put the car in park but didn't turn off the ignition. I reached for the door handle, and Porter put a hand on my arm. "If they found another abandoned car, it'll be a crime scene. They won't let you walk into the middle of it."

"I need to find out what's happening," I insisted. And capture it on video if I could. My body camera's resolution wouldn't be great in low light, but it was better than nothing. "You don't have to come with me. Turn off your headlights and wait for me here."

I threw open the door and climbed out, not waiting for his decision. A second later, Porter's headlights turned off, and I heard his car door open and close softly. He didn't say anything, just shoved his hands in his pockets and started walking toward the blue and red lights.

A soundtrack of howling wolves accompanied our progress. I tried to shut out their doleful cries, but the sounds seemed to come from everywhere. Strangely, their howls did not make me feel as though I were falling into myself the way the sight of the masks did, but this was not the moment to ponder why.

As we drew closer to the sheriff's station cruisers, I hit RECORD on my body camera, which was supposed to automatically switch to night-vision mode when it detected that the light levels were low enough. I motioned for Porter to get behind a tree. He sighed but followed my lead as I partially concealed myself behind another tree, leaning out to keep filming. From where we stood, I was able to make out the hood of a silver car. I crept closer, trying to see more detail. And once I did, my breath stopped.

I heard Porter's near-silent footsteps behind me, and I turned to him, the blood gone from my face.

"It's Gemma's car," I said.

And then, from somewhere in the darkness, a shadow rumbled and moved toward us in great, loping strides. There was no time to run, or do anything except brace for impact. The running shadow leapt, sailed past me. Porter let out a grunt as his body slammed the earth. Raised voices and rapid footfalls headed in our direction.

Only then did I recognize the shadow.

"Blitz!" The Doberman stayed standing over Porter, a growl vibrating in his throat, but when he saw me his mouth opened and his tongue lolled out in a happy pant. He stepped off Porter and trotted to me. I knelt down in front of him and let him lick my face.

"It's Liv," Danny said disgustedly when he reached us.

"Anytime the fucking dog misbehaves, Liv Hendricks must be nearby."

I straightened, keeping my hand on Blitz's neck.

Sheriff Lot, Wheeler, Sasha, Tate, and a couple of deputies I didn't recognize surrounded us.

Wheeler wore a slouchy hipster beanie cap—the kind that looked like a deflated soufflé—a flannel shirt, and sloppy, barely laced sneakers. He was in costume as Bull-shit Hunter Wheeler. Real-life Wheeler was a meticulous dresser who ironed his jeans.

"Morrison?" Sheriff Lot said, peering into the darkness. "Is that you?"

"Yeah." Porter climbed to his feet, brushing dry leaves and pine needles from his clothing. I should have helped him, but I felt powerless to do anything besides hold on to Blitz. That car...that silver car.

"What are you doing out here?" Lot asked Porter, but I answered for him.

"He's with me. We saw cruisers, and followed." I swallowed hard. "Is there any sign of her?"

Lot shook his head.

My heart began to pound in heavy thumps. It was happening again. Another sister, gone. Another sister vanished on another dark road. Blitz whined and pressed against my leg, seeming to sense my distress.

"We've got officers searching the woods," Lot said. "And we'll get a search party out here at first light. In the meantime, I need all of you to stick around to answer questions." He looked at me, eyes narrowed. "Especially you, Ms. Hendricks."

*   *   *

Porter tried to lure me back to his car to wait while Lot and his deputies did their thing, but I was determined to keep an eye on the local law enforcement, make sure they did a proper crime scene analysis. I'd played a teen detective and myriad cop roles. I knew enough to be critical, if not expert. But as far as I could tell, the locals did a thorough, professional job, which was not to say they got results.

After nearly an hour of barking orders at deputies and grilling the Bullshit Hunters, who'd been first on the scene, Lot turned his attention to me.

"How're you holding up?" he asked, his voice low and gruff, as though he was chagrinned by having to check on my feelings.

"I'm worried. Obviously."

"You don't seem that worried. Were you and Gemma close?"

I hesitated. "Not really."

"Then why was she here?"

"She came for the festival, and to meet Jonas Kron. But she canceled their meeting. She had to go back to LA for some reason."

"Hm." Lot scribbled something in a tiny notebook and then turned to Porter. "Mind if I have a word with Ms. Hendricks alone?"

"Sure. I'll wait in the car." Porter squeezed my hand and smiled reassuringly, but I got the impression he couldn't wait to be away from the scene.

When Porter was out of earshot, Lot raised an eyebrow. "You and Morrison, huh?"

"Can we focus on my missing sister, please?"

"Right. Sorry. So, that guy, Danny…he had some interesting things to say about you." I opened my mouth to protest, but Lot held up a finger. "Let me finish. There is obviously bad blood between the two of you, and that makes anything he says unreliable. But here's the thing, Liv…I know about your younger sister, what's her name—"

"Miranda."

"Right. I read about her disappearance the day you got to town. The circumstances here aren't exactly the same, but…it's a big coincidence, don't you think? Two sisters vanishing the way they did?" He took a step closer and lowered his voice. "All I'm saying is if this is some publicity stunt or a hoax or part of your web series, I need you to end it now, before this goes any further."

35.

Porter and I didn't speak much during the drive back to the Eden Tree. He seemed to sense I wasn't in the mood. I hadn't told him Sheriff Lot basically accused me of orchestrating my sister's disappearance as a publicity stunt. It sounded too plausible, even to me, and I didn't want to put that idea into more heads than necessary.

It was after midnight by the time Porter walked me to my room. When we arrived at my door, he kissed me chastely on the cheek.

"You're not coming in?" I asked, not even sure I wanted him to.

"It's going to be a madhouse here tomorrow. I have to be up in five hours."

"So do I. For the search party."

"Right." He took my hand. "Listen, I really want to help you find your sister, but I don't know if I'll be able to make it out for the search party."

"That's fine," I said. It didn't feel fine, but Porter didn't owe me anything. He was just a guy I'd had sex with, and dinner—in that order. A guy I would never see again once I left Stone's Throw, because he had no interest in real life. I'd sensed a palpable change in him since discovering Gemma's car on the Dark Road. He was distant, behaving as if he was more in shock than I was. The safe, protected bubble he lived in was being threatened again. If he were watching all of this on a screen, he would have been just fine. But the bubble had burst all over both of us.

"Is there anything else I can do?" he asked.

I decided to take a page from Jonas Kron's book and stop wasting time mincing words. "Gun to your head, you have to name a suspect. Who is it?"

He shook his head. "I don't—"

"Just say a name. One person you think could be behind all of this."

He opened his mouth and closed it again, shoving his hands in his pockets. "If I had any idea, don't you think I would have told someone?"

"My sister is missing. You've lived here your entire life. You were here when the disappearances started. You said it yourself, you know everyone in town. You have to have some idea. A guess. Anything."

"Liv, please…"

I shook my head. "Let's call it a night."

I opened my door and shut it without a real goodbye.

Then I took out my cell phone and called my mother.

*　　*　　*

"Olivia? Why are you calling me? It's after midnight. Is something wrong?"

I hadn't spoken to my mother in years. Hearing her voice now made every muscle in my body clench. My mother's voice was her *thing*. It was how she commanded a room, controlled people who didn't want to be controlled. Even when she asked a question, she did so in a way that said she already knew the answer. Her voice never rose slightly before the end of a sentence, that upward lilt men found so reassuring because it meant the speaker was uncertain of herself. If there was one thing I admired about Desiree Hill, it was her ability to make every sentence a statement, even the ones she'd just barked at me.

I opened my mouth to respond, but the words lodged in my throat.

"Did something happen to Gemma?" she said when I failed to find my voice. "Olivia, tell me. I know she was with you."

Funny how it didn't occur to her to ask whether *I* was all right, whether *I* might be the one who was in trouble. The only daughter she cared about was the one who did as she was told. Who performed on a caliber that kept Desiree in hundred-thousand-dollar cars and two-million-dollar homes. Because Desiree herself had no actual talent beyond making other people do what she wanted. She had tried, when she was younger, to act, and had been told by every director, producer, and costar she worked with that she needed to find another line of work. Lucky for her, she had been beautiful enough to convince her costars to sleep with her, even if they didn't want to act beside her. My father had been one such costar. Desiree had convinced him to plant his talented seed in her womb. After that, she had no use for him.

Which was not to say Desiree hadn't passed any genetic assets down to her daughters. Bitch was in our blood.

"She was here," I said after a lengthy pause. "But she left to go home and... they found her car on the side of the road."

"I don't understand," Desiree said, and although I knew better than anyone that Gemma was the most important person in the world to Desiree, I didn't detect the level of panic in her voice that I'd expected.

I did my best to explain about the Dark Road, not sure if Desiree understood the gravity of the situation.

"So this road," Desiree said when I was finished. "This road you've been *investigating*...you got Gemma—*my Gemma*—involved, and now she's missing. My *daughter* is missing."

Another of your daughters is missing, I mentally corrected, but didn't have the nerve to say it out loud.

Maybe I wasn't the only common denominator here.

"This is your fault," Desiree said, and then hung up on me.

I slumped into the desk chair and let my head fall into my hands. I was bone-tired and had to be up before first light to meet the search party, but sleep was out of the question. If Gemma was out there somewhere, then I needed to find her. And if there was one thing she had going for her that the rest of the missing women didn't, it was that the world knew who she was, and actually cared.

I set up my camera on its tripod, facing the sofa. Then I turned on all the lights in the room, hit RECORD, sat down facing the lens, and started to speak.

"Another woman went missing on the Dark Road tonight, and this time you know her. I know her. Everyone knows her. Her name is Gemma Hill. She's my sister."

I recapped what had happened that night, giving all the information I had about Gemma's disappearance, which wasn't much. "They found her car and nothing else. No sign of a struggle. No blood. No evidence. But Gemma's disappearance doesn't fit the pattern. The last woman went missing only a few months ago, where in the past there has always been a gap of several years between disappearances. It doesn't make sense. Something must have changed—"

Me. I'm the change.

"—which is why I think there's still a chance to find my sister, and I need your help to do it. If you know anything— *anything at all*—use the hashtag #FindGemmaHill to contact me. This is not a hoax. This is not a publicity stunt. This is real, and my sister is in danger."

I paused before segueing into the other topic I needed to address. If Internet trolls had one kryptonite—and that was debatable—it was sincerity. So that was what I would give them.

"A lot of you out there have taken issue with the ethics of what I'm doing, and you've expressed your feelings in no uncertain terms. I'm not going to pretend it doesn't hurt to be the target of so much vitriol or to have my personal safety threatened, but I'm also not going to let it stop me from doing what I came here to do. Maybe I'm not the most qualified person to find these missing women, but the qualified people haven't been effective, either. Now the Bullshit Hunters are in town investigating the Dark Road, too. They think we're in competition, but we have two very different goals. Theirs is to entertain you. Mine is to make sure no women vanish on the Dark Road ever again."

I uploaded the video without a single cut and let it loose on social media. At this time of night, I didn't expect a big response, but apparently people didn't sleep anymore.

The tweeted responses to my newest episode started pouring in a few minutes after I posted it. Mostly the tweets were exclamations of concern or outrage or consolation, though a number of trolls made sure to let me know I was still number one on their rape list.

After about thirty minutes of watching my #Find GemmaHill feed, my eyes starting to glaze and weariness taking hold of my body, I received a tweet that roused me.

@VincentMaguireWrites tweeted:

@LivHendricks DM me. #FindGemmaHill

I followed @VincentMaguireWrites so we could message privately.

> **LH:** Do you know something?

> **VMW:** I don't know. Maybe. It may have nothing to do with your sister.

> **LH:** I need all the help I can get.

> **VMW:** I'm not supposed to say anything. I could get in trouble.

> **LH:** Please . . . my sister's life is at stake.

VMW: OK. Again, I have no idea if this is relevant, but you're in Stone's Throw, and the Krons are in Stone's Throw, so . . .

VMW: I should mention I'm not actually Vincent Maguire. I'm his wife. I use his account. But this is about Vincent.

LH: OK. Go on.

VMW: A couple years ago, Vincent self-published a book of short stories. Hardly anyone read them. He just put them up so they . . .

VMW: . . . didn't end up in a drawer. But Soren Kron plagiarized one of the stories. He adapted it into a short film without buying the rights.

VMW: Vincent decided to take legal action. He sued Soren Kron, and it got ugly. Soren made threats. He played weird tricks on us. It scared our kids.

VMW: I guess I should say, I don't know for sure it was him. Maybe it wasn't.

LH: What sort of tricks?

VMW: It's really messed up...we have a cat. We let her out at night sometimes. One morning she came back...

VMW: Someone cut off her ears and tail. The next day, they were in our mailbox.

VMW: After that, Vincent decided to settle out of court. Soren paid him and made him sign an NDA so he couldn't tell anyone.

LH: But you didn't sign it?

VMW: No, I did. Please don't use this on your series.

LH: I won't. I promise.

VMW: It's just that... I keep tabs on Soren. I know

he's in Stone's Throw for the festival. You need to watch out for him.

LH: Would Vincent be comfortable talking to me on the phone?

VMW: No. Please don't tell anyone what I told you.

LH: I won't. I promise. Thank you.

*   *   *

With nothing left to distract me, I finally opened Annika Kron's copied file. There wasn't much to it, because not much was known about her. She was born in Norway, but Jonas brought her to Stone's Throw when she was seventeen, after her mom was hospitalized following a suicide attempt. Annika's mother, Sara Kron, had been belatedly diagnosed with bipolar disorder, which she'd been living with for much of Annika's youth. That couldn't have been easy on her daughter. Several years ago, I'd borne witness to the kind of havoc bipolar disorder could wreak on a person's life. I was cast for a small part on a made-for-TV movie that had been canceled mid-production when the lead—who had gone off her meds—experienced a manic episode. She'd come to set one day in a frenzy, talking a mile a minute, laughing hysterically, then sobbing, and finally declaring she had decided to quit acting because God spoke to her and told her he had great plans for her. I had stood helplessly with the rest of the cast and crew watching the actress be escorted from set by her manager. She never returned to the screen. I heard she went off her meds every time she started to feel better, and the cycle would begin again.

With no father in the picture and a mother who couldn't be trusted to take care of herself or her daughter, it was decided that the best option was for Annika to move to America and live with Jonas and Soren, where she could pursue her dream of acting. Jonas hadn't intended to cast her as the lead in *The Girl and the Wolf*, but after seeing what she could do (and what she *would* do) he handed her the opportunity of a lifetime. An opportunity that must have come at a cost, because shortly after a grueling year of shooting wrapped and Annika turned eighteen she left Stone's Throw without so much as a goodbye.

Her family never heard from her again. They speculated that she, too, suffered from bipolar disorder. That she was living on the streets somewhere, in need of proper treatment. After her car was found this past summer, it took a week for the police to connect Annika and Ana Newman. Annika had changed her name. Changed her look. Somehow she acquired documentation to prove she was who she pretended to be. She never married. Never went to college. She didn't have friends. She was a ghost.

Annika's car—a 2014 Toyota Camry—was parked at the White Wolf Trailhead for at least twenty-four hours be-

fore anyone called to report it. No sign of a struggle. No
evidence. Lot brought in a search and rescue dog to help
find her, but there was no scent trail leading from her car.

It was when the police searched her apartment in Salt
Lake City that they discovered Ana Newman was Annika
Kron. They found a number of journals handwritten in
Norwegian, but mostly the journals documented how Ana
was feeling from one day to the next. On occasion, probably when her medications needed adjusting, her writing
became more manic. She began to chronicle dreams of
being stalked or raped or eaten by the *Ulv Konge*. The
journal entries around the time of her disappearance were
barely legible scribbles, rants about seeing the *Ulv Konge*
peering in her window at night, watching her sleep. Of
receiving phone calls from it, telling her she owed it
a sacrifice. Police checked phone company records and
found no calls to her cell phone (her only phone) that
matched with the dates when she wrote about receiving
calls from the *Ulv Konge*.

At the family's request, this information had not been
released to journalists covering Annika's disappearance.
Lot made a note that Jonas—who'd been made her legal
guardian after her mother's attempted suicide—felt that
Annika's legacy would be tarnished by revealing her mental illness. Though to me, it seemed more likely that her
legacy would be tarnished by her actual legacy, *The Girl
and the Wolf*.

The final page in the file was a medical report from
when Annika was a teenager. The report came from a
hospital in San Francisco. She'd been treated for second-
degree burns on both of her hands that she claimed were
caused by a cooking accident. It was the date of her treatment that struck me.

March 5, 2003.
Three days after the fire in the Wolf Woods.

* * *

After reading Annika's file, I tried to sleep, but the second I closed my eyes they jumped right back open again, my ears straining for noise, transforming every minute creak into a footstep. I turned the lights on and checked the locks, even though I'd already checked them multiple times, and they couldn't have come unlocked by themselves. Finally, I positioned a chair under the knob of the door that led to the hallway, and pushed the heavy coffee table with its wrought-iron frame in front of the patio doors, just to be safe. Then I placed my gun on the nightstand, within easy reach.

I climbed back into bed fully dressed and stared at the ceiling until an hour before I was set to meet the search party at the White Wolf Trailhead.

Using the complimentary coffee machine, I brewed a pot of coffee and drank the entire thing as I scrolled through my #FindGemmaHill feed, searching for anything that might be helpful. I was about to give up and leave when my laptop dinged.

I had a message from @AnnikaKron.

AK: Gemma found the White Wolf.

LH: Is she alive?

AK: For now.

LH: Why did you take her?

AK: I didn't take her. But she is with me.

LH: Please don't hurt her.

AK: I'm not the one you have to worry about. But you better hurry. If you don't find her soon...

LH: How do I find her?

No response.

LH: Please help me!

No response.

LH: Maybe I should show these DMs to the sheriff. Find out who you really are.

AK: Don't waste your time with the search party. They won't find anything. They never do.

LH: Is Niklas Larsen the White Wolf?

A long pause and then:

AK: If you tell anyone about me, I'll disappear for good, and so will your sister.

36.

It was still dark outside when I left my room at the Eden Tree. The foyer was empty. It was too early for the festival guests to start arriving, so the inn remained as quiet as an after-hours library. Porter was nowhere to be seen, which was a relief after our awkward parting last night.

I should have expected what would await me outside the Eden Tree. After all, I had announced on the most public forum in existence that Gemma Hill was missing.

Cameras flashed bright as bomb blasts in my face the second I stepped out the doors. I put up a hand to shield my eyes, blinking my whitened vision back to color. A group of disheveled men ringed the porch, all of them similarly dressed in baseball caps and jackets with excessive pockets in which to store their camera gear. All of them with cameras held up in front of their faces.

Paparazzi. I scanned the parking lot, but didn't see any real reporters, only these vultures.

"Hey Liv, look over here," one of them said, and snapped his fingers at me like I was a toddler getting my portrait taken at Walmart. The cameras began flashing again.

Instead of pushing past them and making a run for my car, I wordlessly raised my own camera and hit RECORD, panning across the lot of them. I hid my face behind my camera as I filmed them right back. I kept filming as I walked to my car, and only cut when I was behind the wheel.

As I drove away, I wondered if I had made a huge mistake, enlisting the Internet to assist in finding Gemma. I reasoned that the paparazzi would have found out anyway, but perhaps they wouldn't have gotten here quite so soon. They must have hit the road as soon as they watched my video.

But who knew? Maybe the paparazzi would prove useful for once. The more people in town looking for Gemma, the better.

* * *

Despite @AnnikaKron's insistence that I shouldn't bother, I had no intention of skipping my sister's search party. Not only would that look bad, but I didn't trust @AnnikaKron. Whoever she really was, it was clear she was playing some kind of game with me, and until I knew the rules I didn't intend to play by them.

When I arrived at the White Wolf Trailhead, there were already a dozen vehicles parked along the road, including the Bullshit Hunters' van. I spotted Helene and Anders Larsen among those milling about, waiting for Sheriff Lot to call everyone to attention. I waved to them, and Anders nodded hello, but Helene turned her face away. Clearly, I was not forgiven, but Gemma must be since Helene had come out at the crack of dawn to look for her.

Niklas was not with his parents, nor had I expected him to be, which meant he was probably at the sanctuary. Alone. This might be my only chance to talk to him on his own without anyone intervening.

I parked and slung my camera over my neck before getting out. The sun had risen, but its light was blocked behind a bulky sweater of clouds. Another storm was coming.

Danny appeared to be milking my sister's disappearance for all it was worth. He had the Bullshit Hunters interviewing search party members on camera. I made my way toward my former co-hosts. Their backs were to me, so I stood a few feet behind them, listening as they interviewed a woman with hair the color of tomato soup, the one I'd spoken to at the café where Gemma and I had lunch the day before.

"Brenda, you were one of the last people to see Gemma Hill alive," Sasha stated. "What can you tell us about that final encounter?" She made it sound as though Gemma going missing was instant confirmation of her death.

"She came into the shop with another woman, a blonde," Brenda said. "They looked like sisters, but things were tense between them. They got into a fight and Gemma— Ms. Hill—left abruptly without finishing her lunch."

"Do you know what they were fighting about?" Sasha asked.

"I think—oh." Brenda's eyes had found me, and her cheeks reddened to match her hair. "That's her right there."

Danny and the rest of them revolved toward me, still recording. Danny whispered something to Sasha. She nodded.

"Liv," Sasha said. "What were you and Gemma fighting about yesterday before she disappeared?" She had adopted some kind of perky "interviewer" voice a couple of octaves higher than her natural voice, trying to merge my character from *Bullsh?t Hunters* into hers. She'd added blond highlights to her brown hair, and had traded her usual dowdy ensemble for a curve-hugging bodycon dress and lace-up boots.

I looked Sasha up and down. "Nice dress. Good choice for a day of serious searching in the woods."

I kept walking past them, catching Wheeler's eye briefly and nodding when he gave me a covert thumbs-up.

Sheriff Lot stood next to his cruiser, talking to two deputies. I approached them, and they fell silent. Lot gestured for the deputies to give us some space, and they drifted away toward a pickup truck with its tailgate down. The owner had been kind enough to bring a catering-size thermos of coffee and an array of pastries.

"What's the plan?" I asked the sheriff.

"We'll wait a few more minutes for stragglers to arrive, and then we'll get started," Lot said.

"How many more people do you expect?"

"This might be it. The call went out late last night. More searchers will join us throughout the day."

"I hope so." For someone like Gemma, I would have thought the entire town would show up. But maybe after four previous victims vanished without a trace, they felt there was no point in looking. I did notice that several of the paparazzi had followed me, but had yet to emerge from their vehicles. They stayed put in the driver's seats, telephoto lenses at the ready. I had a bad feeling there would be nothing for them to capture and sell to TMZ.

"If there's nothing else—" Lot turned away to consult the map laid out on the hood of his cruiser, but I stepped in front of him.

"I need to ask you something."

"I'm busy. Make it quick." He'd been more impatient with me since Danny suggested to him that I'd set this whole thing up for the benefit of my series. I'd done my best to convince Lot otherwise, but he didn't fully believe me. Maybe if I spilled my guts, told him everything I'd been holding back, I could get him on my side again. But @AnnikaKron's last message stopped me.

If you tell anyone about me, I'll disappear for good, and so will your sister.

I couldn't risk what might happen if I defied her, or whoever was pretending to be her.

"I read Annika Kron's file," I said.

"You got it all figured out, then?" Lot asked.

I brushed off his sarcasm. "Was she in the Wolf Woods during the fire? Is that how she burned her hands?"

The mockery in his eyes shifted to uncertainty. "What does that have to do with anything?"

"I don't know, Sheriff. That's what I'm trying to figure out."

He lifted his shoulders in a shrug, but shook his head. "As far as I know, there's no connection between her burns and the wildfire."

"But she went in for treatment three days after the fire. Doesn't that strike you as a notable coincidence?"

He narrowed his eyes at me. "Of course," he said tersely. "That's why I contacted the doctor who treated her to ask if he remembered anything about her visit. It was over fifteen years ago, so he didn't have much to say. The only thing he could tell me was that she seemed numb to the pain, and didn't make a single sound as he cleaned and dressed the wounds. He said it was like she didn't even feel it." The sheriff paused a moment, chewing the inside of his cheek, and then added, "I asked him if he thought the burns were fresh, or if Annika had waited to get treatment. He admitted it was possible, but it was a long time ago. He couldn't say for sure."

I nodded. "What's the closest medical center to Stone's Throw?"

His answer was reluctant. "There's a general practitioner in Stone's Throw who could have treated the burns."

"Then why do you think she felt the need to drive over two hours to a hospital in San Francisco?"

"Maybe she didn't trust small-town doctors."

"Or maybe she wanted to go somewhere no one knew her. Somewhere she could be anonymous."

"Fine. But I still don't see what any of this has to do with the Dark Road."

"What was Annika's relationship to Niklas Larsen?"

"They knew each other. She spent a lot of time at the wolf sanctuary, filming for that movie, and Niklas was there."

"Were they friends? They were around the same age."

"Nik didn't really have *friends*. His parents didn't know it at the time, but he's severely autistic. Not quite Rain Man, but definitely not high functioning. But he and Annika talked, mostly in Norwegian. As far as I know, their shared first language was the only reason they spoke."

"Can you think of any reason why Annika and Niklas would have been in the woods together the night of the fire?"

"I cannot." He rubbed his eyes with his thumb and forefingers. "Look, you clearly have some kind of theory you're running down. Do you have any evidence to support it, whatever it is, or is all of this just speculation?"

"I don't have any *yet*, but—"

"See, that's the pesky thing about real police work in comparison with reality TV. You need more than guess-work. Let me know when you have something solid. In the meantime, I need to get back to doing my job. Or don't you want me to find your sister until you're good and ready for her to be found?"

"I have nothing to do with Gemma's disappearance," I hissed at him.

He leveled his black eyes on me. "I can't ignore coincidence," he said.

"Neither can I."

"Fair enough."

"Sheriff," one of the deputies called. "We're ready over here."

Lot snatched the map off his hood and started toward the deputy, but I grabbed his arm. The muscle felt hard as glass under my hand. Lot looked at me, eyes simmering. "Something else?"

"What's your opinion on Soren Kron?" I asked.

"My honest opinion? You should stay away from him. Morrison, too."

"Porter? Why?"

"Because you don't get one without the other, and Soren Kron makes Donald Trump seem virtuous."

My cheeks heated, thinking of Soren's unabashed leer-ing. "Why are he and Porter still friends?" I asked.

"That's a question you'll have to ask Morrison," Lot said. "Best guess, it's because Morrison has a hard-on for Soren's daddy."

I let my hand drop, and Lot walked away. I watched him until the crowd of searchers closed around him. When he was out of sight I reached into my coat's breast pocket to adjust my body camera. I had been recording since the moment I arrived. I couldn't use the footage for my series without getting everyone to sign a release, but I didn't care about that anymore. It was for me, so I would have a record of what was said. So I could review the footage later to see if I'd missed anything.

By the time Lot gathered the searchers, there were about twenty-five people present. The deputies handed out walkie-talkies while Lot explained the system, how we were to fan out in teams of two to cover as much ground as possible. When he said this, my eyes flew desperately to Wheeler's, but he gave me a helpless look and gestured to Danny, mouthing, *I can't.*

I watched the remainder of the searchers pair off with people they knew. There was an odd number. I had no one with whom to partner. I glanced at Lot to see if he noticed, but he was addressing the group again, paying no attention to me.

"One last thing," Lot said. "Unfortunately, many of you have done this before, and you know the drill. If you see anything—a strand of hair, a scrap of clothing, a footprint, a drop of blood—I need you to use the walkie to radio me directly, but do not touch anything. I repeat, do not touch *anything*. I have to stay behind to wait for the canine unit. It looks like there's weather coming our way, so we don't have any time to waste. Let's get moving."

The searchers headed into the woods on either side of the road. I started walking, avoiding Lot's eyes, hoping he wouldn't notice that I didn't have a partner. When I heard my name, I froze, caught, but the voice didn't belong to Lot.

I turned to find Porter jogging after me, in a heavy anorak and hiking boots.

"I thought you had to work," I said when he reached me.

"I do, but this is more important. I can only stay for a couple of hours, but I want to help." He reached out as though to pull me in for a kiss hello, but my expression stopped him. "You don't look happy to see me," he said.

I wasn't sure how I felt about his sudden arrival. I kept thinking about Lot's caution to stay away from Soren, and Porter, too, by association. But I needed to know more about Soren, especially after learning he had plagiarized and possibly terrorized a writer and his family. Maybe Porter was too goodhearted to realize that his best friend was a bad guy. And maybe that could work to my advantage. If Porter didn't think Soren was guilty of anything, it might be easier to coax potentially damning information out of him.

"I am," I told Porter. "I'm happy to see you. I'm just worried about Gemma."

"I can't imagine what you're going through right now," he said, brows drawn together in sympathy. "Did you get any sleep?"

I shook my head, willing my eyes to fill with tears. I rarely cried genuine tears, but I could summon the fake ones when I needed them, something Gemma and I had in common.

"I have to find her," I told him, and he put his arms around me, pulled me in for a hug, which felt strangely inappropriate considering Porter's dick had already spent time inside of my vagina. But somehow this hug felt more intimate than sex, and the intimacy felt too sudden, like we'd skipped a few essential steps. Sex without intimacy I could do, but sex without intimacy that then led to an actual emotional attachment...I wasn't sure what to do with that.

Porter's hand moved to the back of my neck, massaging

lightly. His touch felt good, but I had to resist the urge to recoil from him.

"We should get moving." I pulled away and started into the blackened trees in a different direction from the rest of the search party.

"Aren't we supposed to be going the other way?" Porter asked, hurrying to catch up with me. He pointed toward the few searchers we could still see through the trees. "They're all headed south and east."

"I know," I said. "That's why we're going west. To cover more ground."

"Is that what Lot said we should do?"

"Trust me." I gave him a reassuring smile. "This is the way we need to go."

37.

Are you sure you're okay?" Porter asked as we walked side by side through trees the color of burnt toast.

It was the second time he'd asked this question since we started walking. I knew I seemed too calm, and that was part of the reason Lot and Danny suspected I had something to do with Gemma's disappearance. I'd never been one to externalize my emotions. I could play an emotional character because I saved my own, bottled them up and let them age like wine. Even after Miranda went missing, I had not freaked out. I hadn't raged and cried and beaten my fists against the walls. I had shut down instead. I drank instead. I went home with men I barely knew instead.

"I'll think about me once I know Gemma is safe," I told Porter.

"It's not your fault, you know," he said in a gentle, probing voice that made me feel like I was being handled with kid gloves. Like he thought that any moment now I was going to break down and collapse into tears.

"Gemma wouldn't have been here if it weren't for me,"

I said. "She wouldn't have been a target. She wouldn't have been on that road. Yesterday I said some things to her that maybe I shouldn't have said, and so she left. If I'd controlled my temper, everything would have been different."

"You can't think that way," Porter said, cutting off my self-recrimination. "Sisters fight. It doesn't mean you're to blame."

Yes. Normal sisters fought. They fought about sweaters borrowed without permission, and secret diaries violated. But Gemma and I weren't your average sisters, and what was happening to us was a thousand miles from normal.

We walked in silence for a moment, keeping our eyes on our surroundings, though as far as I could tell there was nothing helpful to see. In the distance we could hear the rest of the search party members calling out, "Gemma! Gemma! Gemma!" on repeat. Porter kept trying to delve deeper into the woods, toward the voices, but I subtly steered us back in the direction I wanted to go.

"So," I said, breaking the silence, "how did you come to be close with the Krons?"

Porter glanced at me, but I didn't detect any caginess in his demeanor. "Soren was on set when Kron filmed that scene from *A Stranger Comes to Town* at the inn. We were the same age—nine or ten, I guess—and since we were the only kids on set, we started hanging out. Movie sets can be pretty boring if you don't have a job to do."

"Believe me, they can be boring even if you do. So you didn't know Soren before that? You didn't go to school together?"

"Jonas doesn't believe in conventional education, and even if he did I doubt he would have found our local public schools up to his standards. Soren had a private tutor who lived with them, so technically I guess he was homeschooled. I think it was lonely for him, though, living in this mysterious red mansion on the hill. Most kids in town didn't know what to make of him. He seemed like a different breed of human, so they avoided him, but not on purpose. Not maliciously."

I nodded. "I can relate to that." Like Soren, I hadn't attended traditional school. I'd had on-set tutors. And I hadn't had friends growing up. I'd had sisters, and I'd had costars, and every once in a while I made the mistake of thinking I'd made a real friend, only to discover I was being used for my money or my closet full of designer labels on loan, or so my faux BFF could meet the swoony boys who ran in my circle, most of them egomaniacal, floppy-haired monsters.

"So Soren didn't have a lot of friends before you?" I asked.

"I don't think he had *any* friends before me. Lucky for him, I wasn't the most popular kid, either. You may find this hard to believe, but I was kind of a geek." He flashed a smile at me.

"I have no idea how anyone could get that impression," I said, smiling back, feeling the urge to lean over and kiss him. Not a fuck-me kiss, but a kiss for the hell of it. A kiss to say, *I like you, that's all.* I resisted the impulse. The distraction. The feelings.

"And we had a lot in common," Porter went on. "I was into movies, and Soren practically grew up on set."

It was the segue I'd been waiting for. "Did Soren ever consider going into film, following in his father's footsteps?"

"He made a few halfhearted attempts, but I don't think Soren's got the attention span for making movies. It's a point of contention between him and Jonas, as you might have detected last night. Jonas wanted him to carry on the family legacy. Soren wrote and directed a few short films, but they've never seen the light of day, which is probably for the best."

"Why is that?"

"Let's just say Soren did not inherit Jonas's gift for narrative. He's not a storyteller. He can imitate someone else's style, but he's got none of his own."

I studied Porter's expression, his body language. Was he holding back? He didn't seem to be. Maybe he didn't know what happened between Soren and Maguire, the writer he'd supposedly plagiarized.

"So what *does* Soren do?" I asked.

Porter shrugged, burrowing his face down deeper in his scarf. "He's helping organize the film festival this year. And he's executive produced some projects that are in the works. Other than that, let's see...he travels. He spends money. He has sex with exotic women on yachts. The usual wealthy-playboy stuff. It's funny, the Krons have always been rich. Jonas grew up just as wealthy and privileged as Soren, but he became this brilliant auteur. He was always driven. It seems like some people are just born with the spark. Soren wishes he had it, but that's not who he is."

I sighed inwardly. If Soren didn't have the attention span to make a decent short film, could he be ambitious enough to abduct a series of women over the course of fifteen years and get away with it?

Porter ducked under a branch, and then paused to look at me. "Is there a reason you're asking so many questions about Soren?"

"I've always been curious about the Krons," I said, shrugging like it didn't matter to me either way if we changed the subject. "They're Hollywood royalty, but no one actually knows that much about them. Except you," I said, and kept walking in the direction I wanted to go. "What about Annika? Was Soren happy when she came to live with them?"

Porter hesitated a moment before responding. "He was thrilled to have her there at first. So was I."

I looked at him. "At first?"

He nodded, frowning a little. "Annika was kind of a train wreck. Her life before she moved here had been unstable, but it didn't necessarily get less erratic once she started working with Jonas. Debuting as the lead in one of Jonas's films was a lot of pressure for someone that young. For anyone, actually. He's hard on his actors. It was out of the frying pan and into the fire for her."

Into the fire, indeed, I thought.

"I'm sure she was working through what happened with her mother, too," I pointed out. "The suicide attempt, her mental illness..."

Porter's eyes cut to me again, and this time lingered a little longer. "Not many people know about that," he said after a pause. I ignored the subtle question in his tone. *How do* you *know about that?* "This is hearsay, but supposedly Annika had several breakdowns while shooting *The Girl and the Wolf.* She wanted to see a doctor, but Jonas was afraid they'd prescribe her medication that would flatten her and affect her performance. So instead of going on happy pills, she drank and did drugs to get through it. She kept her self-medicating secret, but Soren knew because... well, I shouldn't say."

"Because he was the one getting it for her," I guessed, and Porter nodded, looking at the ground. I had played a bipolar character on a three-episode arc of medical drama, and had done some research about it to prepare. Drinking and hard drugs exacerbated bipolar disorder, as they did with most budding mental illnesses. Her use may have tipped her over the edge she was already teetering on.

"It wasn't Soren's finest moment," Porter continued. "I would have tried to stop him, but he didn't admit it to me until after Annika was already gone." Porter reached into the pocket of his anorak and withdrew a balled-up pair of black gloves. He inserted his hands into them, squinting up at the sky, the denim-colored clouds looking heavier by the minute. "I wished I could have gotten to know her better, maybe at a different time in her life. She was a mess, but she had real talent. I'll admit I had a little bit of a crush on her, along with every other guy in town. You've seen her picture, I'm sure."

"She was stunning," I said.

"She was," he agreed, and smiled ruefully. "But she didn't give me the time of day. Not surprising. Even the other actors she worked with couldn't get close to her. As soon as a take was finished, Annika ignored them, went completely cold."

My cheeks heated as I remembered doing this same thing, not because I was a snob or a bitch or any of the things I seemed to be, but because sometimes, after finishing a scene, all I felt was emptiness. I had nothing left to give to the people around me. I gave it all to the camera. Hearing about Annika, I felt a growing connection to her, even down to the fact that she hadn't been allowed to take any medication to help mentally stabilize her. Desiree had done the same thing to me, while simultaneously loading Miranda up on prescription meds.

"So Annika didn't have any close relationships with people on set? No friends or boyfriends?"

"The only guy I ever saw her pay any attention to besides Jonas was Niklas Larsen. Nik spoke Norwegian, but I think there was more to it than that. Something about him fascinated her. Maybe it was his lack of fascination *with* her. Unlike every other guy I saw, he didn't try to get close to her. He didn't want anything from her. He was too wrapped up in his own isolation. Keep in mind, I'm just speculating here. Oh—" he said, and stopped walking. "I guess we should head in another direction."

"Why?"

He pointed into the distance. "There's the fence for the sanctuary." He checked his watch, his brow scrunched in worry. "I need to head back soon. The festival guests have probably started to arrive, and my staff is going to be overwhelmed."

"You should go back," I urged him. "Take care of things at the inn. I'll be fine out here."

"Absolutely not," he said, shaking his head adamantly. "I'm not leaving you alone out here."

"Do you really think whoever took Gemma is prowling the woods right now?"

"Doesn't matter," he said. "You could get lost."

"Fine, but I'm not going back yet, and if you're going to stay with me, then you need to do what I say and not try to stop me."

"What are you planning on doing?" he asked, his eyes wary.

In answer, I started walking again, straight toward the sanctuary.

38.

We entered the sanctuary through the same gate Anders had taken Gemma and me through the previous day. This morning, Tocsin either was in a better mood or hadn't detected our presence yet, because she didn't emit her ear-piercing shriek.

"Liv," Porter said, trailing reluctantly after me, "what are we doing here?"

"We're looking for Niklas."

"Why?"

"Because I need to ask him some questions."

Porter caught up to me and grabbed my arm, probably harder than he meant to. It hurt just a little. "This is a bad idea," he said. "If you want to talk to him, wait until Helene and Anders are back."

"No," I said, pulling away. "That's exactly what I don't want to do."

Porter let his arms fall to his sides. He looked like he wanted to argue, but I held up my hand to stop further protests. "I told you, you don't have to come with me. You can go back and join the rest of the search party. But if you're staying, then help me instead of getting in my way."

"All right," he said, sighing. "What do you need me to do?"

"Help me find Niklas, and then tell him he can trust me. He knows you, right? He might listen to you."

"I don't know about that," Porter said, sounding miserable. "But I'll do my best."

"Thank you." I took hold of his coat and pulled him close so I could kiss him. I owed him a show of affection. Our lips were cold, our breath steam. The kiss went on a second too long, and intensified. Porter's arms slid around me, his tongue finding its way into my mouth, one gloved hand snaking under my shirt. I shivered at the rush of chill air on my back and pulled away, but Porter's grip was firm. He drew me back against him, kissing me in that desperate, impatient way people do when they go mindless with lust. I could feel him wanting me, not just his cock hard against my leg, but his whole being. It was like a force field emanating from his body, a crackling energy that matched my own. Porter removed his glove. His bare hand moved to the front of my jeans, neatly popping the button and dragging down the zipper just enough so he could get his hand into my underwear. I gasped as his fingers found their target. If the circumstances had been different, I would have let him finish me right there, but I opened my eyes and saw the wolves, Tispe and Brutus, standing at the fence of their enclosure, watching us intently. My mind flashed to that scene from *The Girl and the Wolf* in which Annika, playing Joelle, lets her boyfriend fuck her from behind while they watch the wolves eat. My stomach rolled with a mixture of nausea and heat, disgust and pleasure.

I turned my head away sharply, breaking the kiss. "We

can't do this now." My body disagreed. I was so horny I could barely stand. My knees were water as I zipped and buttoned my jeans.

Porter blinked at me, dazed. He shook his head. "God. Sorry. I'm not usually like this." He let me go and stepped away from me, like he couldn't trust himself to be within touching distance. I certainly didn't trust myself. He added in a soft voice, "It's been a long time since I was...with anyone. And even longer since I felt an actual connection."

I smiled at him, feeling dizzy and discontented, the crotch of my underwear soaked and sticky. "Me too," I said, referring to the connection, not how long it had been since I'd had sex. But it had been a long time since I'd had the kind of sex I'd had with Porter. Maybe I'd never had that kind of sex with anyone *but* Porter, and the missing ingredient had been that connection, the spark that had seemed to exist between us from the moment we met.

Porter cleared his throat, scarlet to his hairline. "It's early," he said. "Nik may not have started work yet, but he lives with Helene and Anders. We should try the house first to see if he's there."

I nodded, and we started walking up the gravel road toward the house, passing the wolf enclosures on our way. Brutus and Tispe watched us with keen interest as we passed by. Tispe stared at me with intense yellow eyes and licked her chops, like the sight of me made her hungry.

"Has anyone ever seen a wild wolf in this area?" I asked Porter, not taking my eyes from Tispe, who had begun to follow our progress along the fence line.

"There are occasional sightings, but they're probably coyotes, not wolves. I'm pretty sure all the wolves in this area were hunted out of existence decades ago."

"What about other predators? Mountain lions? Bears?"

He shrugged. "There's a lot of wilderness out there. If only one or two people had gone missing, I would guess it's possible they were attacked and dragged away. But all of them women... all of them blondes. It doesn't add up."

"You haven't told me what you think happened to them," I said.

"Because I have no idea."

"But you have to have a theory."

He thought a moment before speaking, and when he did he kept his eyes on the Larsens' house, a hundred yards ahead of us. "If I say it out loud, you'll think I'm crazy."

"I won't," I said. "I promise."

"Okay," he said, taking a deep breath and exhaling out a cloud of frosty air. "It has something to do with the *Ulv Konge*. You know, from *A Stranger Comes to Town*."

"You think a fictional creature is abducting women on the Dark Road?"

"The *Ulv Konge* doesn't abduct women. The *Ulv Konge* accepts sacrifices."

"So you think someone is abducting women and sacrificing them to a fictional creature?"

"I told you you'd think I'm crazy," he said.

But I didn't. It was the best theory I'd heard thus far.

*   *   *

I rang the doorbell of the Larsens' house repeatedly and waited, but there was no answer.

"Guess he's not home," Porter said, sounding relieved. He turned to go, but I wasn't ready to give up so easily. I knocked until my knuckles stung.

"Maybe he's back in the care station feeding the

wolves," Porter said from the bottom of the porch steps, inching backward down the path. "We should check there."

If Niklas was inside and saw a stranger at the door, he probably wouldn't answer, but I had a feeling Porter was right and he wasn't home. I decided to test that theory. I tried the knob, and it turned in my hand. I opened the door a crack and peered inside.

"Liv, what are you doing?" Porter hissed behind me.

"Hello?" I called. "Anyone home? Anders? Helene? Niklas?"

No one responded, so I swung the door open and stepped inside. Porter grabbed my jacket.

"You can't go in there," he said, eyes dark and stern behind the lenses of his glasses.

"I just want to take a quick look around," I told him. "Wait here and ring the doorbell if you see anyone coming."

I didn't wait for his permission or listen to his continued protests. I stepped inside and closed the door behind me. Out of Porter's sight, I checked my hidden body camera to make sure it was still recording. It was.

I turned in a circle, taking in the modest living room, the simple Scandinavian furnishings. The paint colors on the walls were soothing tones of eggshell and moss and haze, the décor a mixture of antique and modern. Framed photographs graced the walls and surfaces of sideboards and accent tables, most of them of the family and of Niklas when he was a child, before the burn that ruined his face. I picked up one framed photograph of Niklas, which appeared to have been taken when he was about ten years old, his neatly combed hair a shade darker than platinum, his eyes serious and distant. He would have grown into an attractive man if he'd had the chance.

I moved farther inside, unsure what I was looking for, but certain that I would know it when I saw it. The construction of the house was more modern and cookie-cutter than most of what I'd seen in Stone's Throw. It was roomy for three people, with a home office and what appeared to be a guest bedroom on the first floor. There was nothing of note in the guest bedroom other than a bed and a dresser, its drawers empty. The home office was OCD-tidy, and looked like it was hardly ever used. I didn't see a computer or a file cabinet, which led me to the assumption that most of the office-style work done in the family happened at the cabin where the wolf sanctuary office was housed.

I moved to the small white desk pushed up against one wall. The surface was entirely bare, but the desk had one slender drawer, which I opened, finding neatly arranged pens and pencils, a calculator, and a stack of printer paper. I was about to close the drawer when I caught a glimpse of something else pinned beneath the printer paper. I opened the drawer all the way so I could remove it, and discovered a slim ledger, the kind I thought no one used anymore in favor of digitized versions. But apparently Helene was old-school in her bookkeeping style. I pulled out the ledger and flipped to the last page. Helene hadn't actually used the ledger in a number of years. The last entry was in 2010. A quick scan of the entries showed that this ledger was for home expenses. Once a month, almost every month, Helene had entered a deposit in the amount of three thousand dollars into their personal account, the money coming from the Stone's Throw Wolf Sanctuary. Three thousand seemed like an incredibly modest amount of money for a family of three to exist on, but I supposed living in a town like Stone's Throw was a lot cheaper than living in LA. Three thousand dollars was rent for a one-bedroom apartment in Santa Monica. But I noticed occasional larger influxes of money on the ledger. Every few years the sanctuary paid the Larsens sums of anywhere between twenty and fifty thousand dollars. But that money was quickly paid out to a plastic surgery center in San Francisco, most likely for reconstructive surgery to Niklas's face. Had the Larsens saved up for the occasional surgery, or were these times when they'd received a larger-than-usual donation in order to afford it? I wondered if there was something questionable about these payouts. The wolf sanctuary was a privately owned business, but it operated on government grants and donations, according to Anders. They wouldn't be able to rake up enough money for this kind of cash flow by putting a couple dozen wolves on display.

Unless the sanctuary had a very wealthy patron. A very wealthy patron who had shot one of his most famous scenes here at the sanctuary. A very wealthy patron who had a strange obsession with wolves.

With my cell phone, I took pictures of a few of the pages in the ledger showing the irregular payouts, and then put the ledger away. I needed to move faster. Porter was probably losing his mind out on the porch.

Moving quickly, I headed back down the hallway toward the staircase leading up to the second floor, where I assumed the master bedroom and Niklas's room were located. But I stopped when I saw a closed door next to the staircase. I opened it and found a wooden staircase leading down into an unfinished basement. I was running out of time. Niklas, or Helene and Anders, could return any minute. I had to make a decision. Upstairs or downstairs. I couldn't do both.

When I thought secrets, I thought basement.

I stepped into the darkened stairwell leading down, feel-

ing for a light switch on the bare boards. I found the
switch and flipped it on. Dusty yellow light flickered from
a naked bulb, illuminating the stairs and the cement basement floor below. I tried creeping down the steps, but each
one creaked the second I put weight on it.

"Anyone home?" I called, and when there was no answer I descended quickly.

When I reached the bottom, I felt for another light
switch, but when I flipped it on nothing happened. The
basement remained dark but for the glow of a strand of
twinkle lights hanging from the ceiling on the other side of
the space, their illumination diffused by a white sheet, also
suspended from the ceiling like a makeshift wall. It was the
only wall in the unfinished basement.

I took out my cell phone and turned it on flashlight
mode. When I shone the light around I saw, in another corner, a long table covered in an assortment of bottles and
cans, some sort of workshop.

I crossed to the table and shone my light over the items
crowding its surface: stacks of newspaper, tubes of paint,
an array of brushes, bottles of glue and a jar of turpentine,
hobby knives. In the center of the table was a half-finished
wolf mask. The basic shape was there, but it had yet to
be painted. I picked up the mask, feeling that familiar rip-
pling lurch in my stomach, and put it down again quickly.
I turned away from the table, my breath coming faster, my
pulse pounding in my neck. This physical, visceral reaction
would have made more sense if I'd found a pile of arts and
crafts materials consisting of human hair and skin and fingernails, but that was not the case.

So why do you feel like you want to scream?

I closed my eyes tight, trying to calm down, but that
only made things worse because I felt the knowledge, the

memory, rearing up behind me, and it was something terrible. Something that would ruin me if I turned to face it.

I wasn't ready to know. I wasn't ready to be destroyed all over again.

I opened my eyes again and moved away from the table, toward the area set apart by the hanging sheet, where I found a bedroom. There wasn't much to it. A bed covered with a rustic patchwork quilt, a standing dresser, a bedside table. But what sat on top of the table intrigued me: a projector hooked up to an old DVD player that looked like a relic from the early days of the transition from VHS to discs. I didn't see a remote, so I pushed POWER on both and hit PLAY on the front of the DVD player. For a moment, nothing happened. Then light beamed across the room, revealing thousands of dust flecks in the air, and a blurry, moving image appeared on the sheet.

I recognized the scene immediately. It was the first turning point in *The Girl and the Wolf*, when Annika and her teenage lover have sex in front of the wolf enclosure. The perspective was through Annika's character's eyes as she watches herself devour a white wolf inside its cage, tearing open its stomach and yanking out loops of intestines, then lowering her face to the wolf's bloodied fur, this imagined self keeping her gaze locked to the true self's eyes as she bites into raw muscle. I remembered hearing that Kron had insisted on using real blood and entrails for the scene, although they'd come from a pig, not a wolf. It was no wonder Annika had had a breakdown.

Annika's face comes up dripping red, and she licks at the blood on her lips and smiles into her own eyes, but she appears to be looking right at the viewer.

Right at me.

That was when the doorbell rang.

39.

The sound was so faint that for a moment I thought it had come from the film. But then the doorbell rang again, and my heart flung itself against the wall of my chest.

Someone was coming.

In a panic, I bolted for the stairs, then realized I had left the movie playing, and dashed back to the projector to hit the POWER button.

I was three steps from the top of the stairs when I heard the front door open. I crept the rest of the way, flinching at every creak, and peeked through the doorway to see if the coast was clear. There was no one in sight, but I could hear a low voice from the front entryway. I couldn't tell who was speaking, or what was being said, but I assumed Porter was attempting to stall while I found my way out. I edged out of the basement and into the hallway, praying the house's floorboards wouldn't make a sound as I stole toward the kitchen at the back of the house, where I'd seen a back door. I held my breath as I eased the door open and slipped through into the biting October air.

Throbbing with adrenaline, I shot for the tree cover behind the house and disappeared into its safety. When I was sure I was hidden from sight, I stopped and bent over to catch my breath, slow my racing heart. I looked back toward the house and saw Porter on the front porch, talking to someone in the doorway, but I couldn't see who. The other person was already in the house. Then Porter stepped inside. I took out my phone to text him, tell him I had made it out, and then remembered that I had no cell service out here. So I stayed where I was. I would signal him and catch his eye once he emerged again.

A minute passed, and then two. After five minutes of waiting for Porter to reappear, I began to worry. Was he in there alone with Niklas? Did Niklas suspect someone had been in his house? I started toward the house, not sure what I was going to do. But I had to do something. I was about to emerge from the trees when movement from an upstairs window caught my eye. A white curtain twitched aside, revealing a face peering through the glass. Something disproportionate about the head. It was too large at the top. The nose too long. The skin too pale. A black square with a red light shining from one corner held in front of one eye. My breath stopped in my throat, and for a split second I felt a sense of...not unreality, but hyper-reality, a jarring pivot toward understanding, like the moment you remember something—a word, a name—you've been struggling to recall. But the curtain closed before I could get a decent look at the face in the window, and the moment ended with the abruptness of a balloon popping, before I could determine whether what I thought I saw was what I had actually seen.

Before I could be certain the face peering out at me had not been human, but the face of a wolf. A white wolf holding a video camera.

Niklas. Had he been upstairs the entire time I was in the house? He must have heard me prowling around.

A door slammed, nearly startling a yelp from my throat. Then I saw Porter on the porch steps, a hand raised to wave goodbye to someone. My chest eased. He was out. He was safe. He started down the gravel road toward the sanctuary office, glancing around furtively, trying to spot me. I didn't dare come out of the woods until I was out of sight of whoever was in the house besides the masked figure in the upstairs window. I cut through the trees, figuring I could catch up with him on the dirt path that led past the animal enclosures.

But when I emerged from the trees, it was not Porter I found. It was Niklas.

When he saw me, he stopped as abruptly as if he'd hit an invisible wall, momentarily too surprised to hide his face behind his shaggy hair. I got my first good look at him, and realized that his disfigurement was not as severe as I had first thought. The skin on the right side of his face was taut and shiny, as though it were stretched beyond its limit, and the shape of his nose, eye, and lip didn't match up with the unmarred left hemisphere, but he was not the mutilated comic-book villain I'd first taken him for. Nor was he the man in the wolf mask filming from the upstairs window of his house. He could not be here and there at the same time.

So who was in the house?

"Hi, Niklas." I took a step closer to him, but stopped when he tensed. I held up my hands to show I wasn't dangerous. The gesture was symbolic. Just having someone look at him and talk to him was clearly painful for Niklas, and I was already doing that.

"Not supposed to talk to you," Niklas mumbled, his

voice more heavily accented than either of his parents', as though his avoidance of speaking had preserved it.

"Do *you* want to talk to me?" I asked.

He turned his head slightly to the side, so I could only see the unmarked half of his face, but he didn't respond.

"Do you know why I'm here?" I tried again.

"You want to find the missing women," he said.

I nodded. "My sister is one of them now. Can you help me, Niklas? Can you help me find her?" He didn't say anything, but his shoulders hunched, his posture defensive. "Maybe if we find her, we'll find Annika, too. She was your friend, wasn't she?"

He hesitated a few seconds, and then nodded. "She was nice. Not to everyone, but to me."

"Niklas, was she in the woods with you the night of the fire? Is that how she burned her hands?"

He was quiet so long I thought he had decided to ignore me until I went away.

"She needed to see the wolf," he said finally.

"One of the wolves here at the sanctuary?"

He shook his head. "Not one of ours. The one in the woods."

I blinked at him, struggling to maintain a neutral expression. "Are you talking about the *Ulv Konge*?"

He tilted his head in a minute nod.

"Why did she want to see it?"

He met my eyes, but still his gaze somehow remained disconnected. He was looking at me, but not seeing me. "She wanted to make it stop. She wanted it to leave her alone."

"How do you make it stop?" I asked, but the answer was obvious. "The fire," I said. "That's why you started the fire."

"Not me," he said. "Annika…she started it. I tried to stop her, but she wouldn't listen."

My eyebrows rose. He might very well be lying, but I needed him to think I was on his side, that I believed him completely. It was the only way to keep him talking. "Why did you take the blame?" I asked.

He shifted uncomfortably from foot to foot, lowering his eyes to the ground. "People wouldn't understand. She'd get in trouble."

"But not you."

"I'm different," Niklas said, his voice barely above a whisper. "Everyone knows there's something wrong with me."

"Are you the *Ulv Konge*, Niklas?" I asked gently.

He shook his head vehemently, eyes still glued to the ground. "No," he said sharply. "The *Ulv Konge* wanted to hurt her. I would never hurt her. *Jeg elsket henne.*"

"I don't understand," I said. "Please, Nik. I need to know what happened that night. It has something to do with why Annika went missing. I know it, but I can't prove it without your help. I can't find her unless you tell me—"

A sudden hiss interrupted my words. I looked to my left and saw Tocsin slinking out of her den, her head low and hackles raised. She hissed again and her lips pulled back to reveal the yellow knives of her teeth.

"What are you doing here?"

The woman's voice startled me more than the sudden appearance of the two-hundred-pound cat, and I turned to see Helene jogging down the trail toward her son and me, her eyes blazing with anger.

"Nik," she said, "I told you not to talk to her. *Ga hjem!*"

Niklas said nothing, merely turned and started walking quickly up the trail, almost running. He glanced back at me once, and I thought I saw regret on his face. He wanted to tell me the rest, unburden himself of the truth he'd hidden for so many years. If Helene hadn't shown up, he would have.

Helene folded her arms over her chest, her jaw clenched. "Why are you talking to my son?"

I considered telling her the truth, that Nik was my main suspect, that all evidence pointed to him as the one who'd made my sister and four other women disappear. But that was a terrible idea. This woman was fiercely protective of her son. If she knew I suspected him, she would try even harder to shield him from me.

"I got separated from the search party and ended up here again. I was just asking Nik if he'd seen—"

"There you are!"

Porter came around the bend in the trail, and I exhaled in relief.

"I've been looking all over for you," he said when he reached us. "I thought you were going to wait for me at the office."

"You're with *her*?" Helene asked, sounding skeptical. "You didn't mention that."

I assumed she was referring to whatever Porter had told her at the house. So it must have been Helene who showed up and forced Porter to ring the doorbell.

Porter nodded and looked at his watch. "We'd better get back to the checkpoint. It was nice to see you, Helene. Thank you again for letting me use your landline. Things are getting hectic at the inn."

Porter started away, but I didn't move. "Helene, did Anders come back here with you?"

She nodded, eyes dipping guiltily toward the ground. "Yes, I'm sorry. I wish we could have stayed and searched longer, but we had to get back to work. We have several tours scheduled for today."

"I understand," I told her, but I didn't. Neither Niklas nor Helene could have been upstairs. Niklas hadn't been in the house at all, and Helene had been downstairs talking to Porter.

That left Anders.

40.

Walking back to the checkpoint, I filled Porter in on what I'd found in the Larsens' house, the ledger with the large deposits, and the projector in the basement, cued up to play Annika's disturbing, deviant sex scene from *The Girl and the Wolf*. I omitted mention of the face in the window, though I wasn't entirely sure why. Maybe because I wasn't certain anymore what I'd seen. Had my perception simply been distorted by distance? Had the person peering out at me really been wearing a wolf mask or holding a video camera? I'd glimpsed the face so briefly, it would have been easy to transpose a mask onto it in my mind.

And there was that instant of hyper-reality, of near-revelation, over so quickly it might simply have been the product of a rush of adrenaline.

Porter was quiet after I finished talking. He seemed to be having a hard time looking at me. I could tell he wasn't happy about the position I'd put him in.

"Well," he said, rubbing the bridge of his nose under

his glasses, as though he felt a headache coming on, "as far as the ledger goes I don't know if there's anything uncommon about small business owners occasionally paying themselves larger sums of money. I do that with the inn from time to time, usually just before the end of the year. It makes sense that the Larsens would pay themselves more before a pricey surgery."

"And the projector? Do you find it strange that Niklas had a DVD cued up to the moment when Annika gets fucked in *The Girl and the Wolf*?"

Porter cringed at my use of the word *fucked*, which I found somewhat amusing, considering he'd seemed pretty interested in reenacting the scene in front of the wolf enclosures. Then I remembered that Porter had known Annika, had admitted he had a crush on her, and I felt like an insensitive asshole.

"It could mean something," Porter admitted. "But it's a provocative sex scene, and he's a grown man, so maybe it's nothing."

"You mean maybe he was just down there beating off to the memory of a teenage girl who is probably dead?"

"That's a very crass way to put it," Porter said archly.

"Sorry," I muttered.

"I don't want to talk about this anymore."

"Fine," I said, irritated by his prudishness, and at the same time finding it endearing. Unfortunately, he didn't seem to feel the same cognitive dissonance about my filthy mouth. He stared straight ahead, frowning.

We didn't speak again until we reached the Dark Road, and found chaos.

*   *   *

There had to be fifty cars jammed bumper-to-bumper on the shoulders of the Dark Road. People from town and people who could only be from LA milled around the sheriff's checkpoint. A constant stream of traffic snaked toward the town, a mix of hybrids and power cars that cost as much as a three-bedroom house in the Midwest. Film people. The festival attendees arriving en masse, slowing to rubberneck as they cruised past the checkpoint. A few stopped in the middle of the road to call out questions to Sheriff Lot and his deputies, or to take pictures with their phones. If they weren't aware of Gemma's disappearance before, they would be now. They were probably thrilled, the producers anxious to find cell service so they could start making calls, vying for exclusive rights to Gemma's story, actors envisioning themselves in her tragic role. Who would they get to play me? Amanda Seyfried? No. Amy Schumer was more likely. Gemma would get Seyfried or Witherspoon or maybe even Lawrence if the script was good.

I wondered if Desiree was already fielding calls about the rights. And just as I wondered it, I saw her.

Her back was to me, clad in a camel coat that extended to the backs of her knees, but I knew her immediately in the way you can always recognize someone you dread seeing. She was talking to the sheriff, and as Porter and I approached she turned to point at the single search and rescue dog, a golden retriever, sitting patiently at its trainer's feet. I stopped walking abruptly. Porter, behind me, ran into my back.

"What is it?" he asked.

I tried to find my voice, form words, but nothing came out. Desiree caught sight of me, lowered her arm. She gazed at me with no feeling. No warmth. I hadn't seen her in person in years. I didn't know until that moment that I hoped, after this extended absence from each other, she might have built up some sort of affection for me. But there was nothing, and it struck me how unnatural that was. How monstrous to feel no love for the life she'd created. I had lived inside this woman, and she acted like we'd never met.

The last thing Gemma had said to me before she went missing still echoed in my mind. Desiree had not been the same mother to her that she had been to me. She had seen me as the true talent, Gemma as the understudy. While I despised being shaped and molded and styled and whittled down to the bones, it was all Gemma had wanted. To be seen by our mother. To be valued.

Desiree folded her arms and waited for me to come to her. She would never come to me. I knew that. I didn't want to go to her, either. I wanted to run in any direction but toward her. I couldn't run from her, though. Not in front of Porter and Sheriff Lot and the paparazzi camped out along the road.

I waited for a break in traffic and then crossed the road. Desiree sized me up with unmistakable condemnation. I knew what she saw. The years on my face. The thirty pounds I'd put on since my heyday. The carelessly chosen clothes that made me look like a regular person. No one special. And if I wasn't special, I was of no use to her. She was, above all things, pragmatic.

I wanted to look at her with the same appraisal, adding up her flaws. The tightness of her skin from too much Botox. The excess makeup for this hour of the morning. The loose skin at her neck, which was probably already scheduled for removal and tucking by a Beverly Hills plastic surgeon. The sun damage on her hands, where discolorations were starting to form, something else she would have lasered into oblivion. But when I looked at Desiree, what I saw most of all was her disapproval of the entirety of me. There was not a single thing about me she loved.

"I was just talking to the sheriff about his efforts to find Gemma," Desiree said, without greeting, as though we spoke regularly and this encounter was nothing abnormal. "Apparently this search party has been going on for hours, and no one has found a trace of your sister. It's unacceptable."

"What about the dog?" I asked Lot, nodding at the golden retriever.

The sheriff shook his head. "She found Gemma's scent, but the trail was from yesterday, and the rain confused it."

"Then get more dogs," Desiree said in the same sharp, clipped tone she used with an agent who tried to lowball her on the rental of one of her daughters. "I could make a single call and have a dozen superior animals here within the hour."

"Ms. Hill, I assure you—"

"I've heard enough from you," Desiree snapped. "As I understand it, four other women went missing on this road, and none were ever found. Don't give me your false assurances."

To his credit, Lot held his own against Desiree. But the second she turned her back to him, focusing all her attention on her phone, he let his confident posture sag. I felt sorry for him. I guessed, now that he'd met my mother, he felt sorry for me, too.

"There's no service out here," Desiree snarled at no one in particular. "How can there be no service? This is America, isn't it?" Without another word, she marched to her pearl-white Lexus, got in, and screeched away.

I went limp when she was gone, my energy vacuumed

into Desiree. For all her bravado, she didn't actually seem worried about Gemma. More...inconvenienced.

"That was your mom?" Porter said, looking at me with pity in his eyes.

"Yep."

A peal of thunder rumbled overhead. Out among the burnt trees, the searchers were making their way back toward the checkpoint, Wheeler and the other Bullshit Hunters among them.

"I called them back," Lot said, reading the question on my face. "It's about to pour, and I didn't want people caught out there in the rain."

"There's really no trace of her?" I asked.

Lot shook his head, his expression grim, his mouth pulled down at the corners. The morning had aged him. "Just like the others."

But this wasn't like the others. Gemma was blond and beautiful like the rest of them (like Annika had been before she altered her look), but she was older than everyone but Annika—by over ten years—and her disappearance had come too soon after Annika's.

Annika's disappearance had broken the pattern.

Maybe that was because Annika had started it in the first place.

41.

I had officially reached the point in the investigation where I had no clue what to do next. Should I play "you show me yours and I'll show you mine" with Lot again? Admit my B&E, tell him what I'd seen in the Larsens' house? And what about Soren? The guy exhibited questionable behavior, but it didn't necessarily connect him to the missing women, with the exception of Annika Kron. I couldn't help thinking that if Soren was really such a monster, Porter would have nothing to do with him.

With the search party on hold until the threat of rain passed, I said goodbye to Porter, who was anxious to get back to the Eden Tree, got in my car, and headed back to Stone's Throw Village. I hadn't eaten anything (0 calories), and I could only run on adrenaline for so long.

Overnight, Stone's Throw Village had woken from its coma, coming alive with the influx of out-of-towners. The circular main street was jammed tight with cars, sidewalks congested with a combination of twenty-somethings wearing stylish, overpriced rags, thirty-somethings wearing slightly more overpriced and slightly less stylish rags, and normcore forty-somethings in mom jeans, blazer/T-shirt combos, and sneakers, who were likely too wealthy to be bothered caring about their appearance.

I chose the least busy café and ordered my food to go. Everywhere I looked, people sat at bistro tables, eating pie and drinking coffee or wine or bottles of hard cider. I took my food and coffee and found a free bench in the courtyard in front of the October Palace. The marquee now listed a few of the headlining films that would be screened, along with the special-event screening that was by invitation only, the one to which Soren had promised me Gemma's ticket.

While I ate, I contemplated whether or not to attend Kron's opening-night gala. It was both inappropriate and insensitive for me to show up at a party when my sister was missing, but this might be my only opportunity to explore the Red House. To see where Annika Kron had lived briefly and where Soren had grown up.

By the time I finished my sandwich (450 calories), I'd made a decision. I would attend the party, but not with Porter. I needed to be free to explore without giving him an explanation or dealing with his naysaying every time I made a decision. I'd be wearing a mask, so hopefully no one would know who I was. But first I needed to buy a mask, along with a dress and shoes.

I wandered through Stone's Throw Village until I found an upscale boutique. I bought the first dress and pair of shoes I tried on, even though the shopkeeper urged me to try half a dozen more cocktail dresses, all of them twice as expensive as the simple black sheath dress I'd chosen. But I did peruse the display of glittery masquerade masks that had been laid out on the glass countertop. I chose a raven mask with a prominent beak. It was the one that would give me the most coverage, and was most likely to keep my identity hidden.

·   ·   ·

Back at the Eden Tree, a few paparazzi were camped out in the parking lot, which was now nearly full to capacity. Luckily, with so many guests arriving at the Eden Tree, it was easy for me to slip inside the building unnoticed.

Once in my room, I flopped onto the bed and closed my eyes, wishing I could take a nap. But there was no time for sleep, and even if there were, every time I closed my eyes I saw images that charged me with nervous adrenaline. Desiree's apathetic expression as she sized me up. Annika Kron, her chin dripping blood. The obscured visage of a wolf in the Larsens' upstairs window.

Follow the white wolf. That's what @AnnikaKron told me to do, and that's what I had done, but all I'd found were more questions.

I dragged my body off the bed and removed the body camera from its hidden location on my jacket. I plugged it into my laptop to download the footage and charge the battery, and then set up my camera on its tripod and starting rolling, not bothering to check how I looked. If Internet trolls wanted to chastise me for being too hideous to rape, bring it on.

"My sister Gemma Hill has been missing for close to twenty-four hours now," I said to the camera. "A search party spent the morning combing the woods for her, but found nothing to hint at her whereabouts or what happened to her. I haven't given up hope, but considering the fate of the other women who disappeared on the Dark Road, it isn't looking good. *Please*, if anyone out there has information that could help, contact me immediately. Your identity will remain private. All I want is to find my sister."

I uploaded this brief update to social media, not bothering to edit in any of my footage from today. There was little I could share legally, or without broadcasting my illegal activities.

When my body camera footage had finished uploading, I scrubbed through it from start to finish, pausing at the moment when I'd seen the face in the Larsens' upstairs window. But the camera hadn't been pointed in the right direction, and the lens wasn't wide-angle, so I couldn't see anything above the first floor.

I minimized the footage and opened Twitter to check for significant tweets or messages in response to my plea for help, and saw the following tweet:

The Dark Road claims another victim. Bullshit Hunters join the hunt for truth ONLINE! http://www.bullshithunters .com/darkroad #unsolved #mystery #bullsh?thunters #investigation #gemmahill #darkroad

The Bullshit Hunters had uploaded their first guerrilla-style webisode.

I watched it with a sinking stomach.

The production quality blew mine out of the water. Their episode was shot better. Edited better. Had better sound. Worst of all, Sasha had positioned herself as leader of the Hunters, and she brought an energy and focus to the show that had been absent for a long time. An energy and focus that I'd never provided. Three was the perfect number for their gang. The show was better off without me.

I made one brief appearance in the episode, though. The

editor had cut around my exchange with Sasha, only including the part where Sasha implied that Gemma going missing was a convenient coincidence, suggesting that it was all a publicity stunt, the way people had insinuated when Miranda disappeared. All part of the show.

The *Bullsh?t Hunters* online episode energized the trolls, who launched new 140-character tirades against me, accusing me of being a phony, telling me I'd played them, and, of course, letting me know that I needed to be raped, tortured, and murdered as punishment.

I was ready to throw my laptop against the wall when Twitter pinged with an alert. A direct message from @AnnikaKron.

AK: Did you follow the white wolf?

LH: Yes.

AK: Did you see me in the basement?

LH: I saw your scene. And I talked to Niklas. He says you started the fire. He says you were trying to stop the Ulv Konge.

LH: Is it true?

I waited. No response.

LH: Are the white wolf and the Ulv Konge the same?

AK: There are many wolves.

LH: What are their names?

No response.

LH: If you want to help me, then help me!

AK: Have fun at the gala. Say hi to the wolves for me.;)

42.

I called the front desk and asked if Porter was available. The attendant sounded confused by my question, but eventually agreed to tell Porter the occupant of room nine needed to see him as soon as possible. Fifteen minutes later, there was a knock on my door.

Porter looked and smelled like he'd showered after our trek through the woods, and he'd changed from hiking clothes into his innkeeper uniform: khakis, a blue blazer, a white shirt, and a blue-and-green-striped tie. With his boyish face and glasses, he looked more like a glee club member than a responsible business owner.

"Is everything okay?" Porter asked once he was inside and the door was closed. He glanced suspiciously at the bed, like he thought I might have lured him there to seduce him again.

I cleared my throat. "I can't be your date for the gala tonight. It's not right for me to go to a party with Gemma missing. I'm sorry."

Porter frowned and shoved his hands in his pants pockets. "I understand, but I can't say I'm not disappointed. What are you going to do, then? Stay here all night?"

I nodded. "I'm exhausted. I'll probably do some research online and be passed out by eight."

"All right," he said coolly, glancing at the bed again. "I guess I'll leave you to it."

He turned to go, but I grasped his arm, keeping him with me. "You're angry."

He shook his head. "It's been a long day."

"Okay," I said, knowing there was more to it than that. He was hurt, and not just by me bowing out as his date. I'd racked up quite a few offenses against him today, especially considering his aversion to nonfictional adventure. I wanted to make it up to him. I moved my hand up his arm to the back of his neck and pulled his face toward mine. He resisted for half a second, and then gave in and kissed me. The taste and texture of his tongue were already becoming familiar, like we'd been doing this for years. Like we'd never not known each other.

"I have to get back to work," he murmured against my mouth.

"Not yet," I said. I wanted more. I wanted to devour him. "I need you to fuck me," I told him, and this time Porter didn't wince or recoil. This time he made a sound like a growl in the back of his throat, an involuntary rumble. One of his hands found my breast and squeezed so hard I whimpered and nipped at his lip like a wounded dog. He spun me around, releasing me to unbutton his pants, while I unzipped my jeans and shoved them down. Porter bent me over the desk. His hand on the center of my back pushed me down so my ass was in the air. He positioned himself and thrust into me, gripping my hips hard enough to leave bruises. He grabbed my hair and yanked my head back, and I gasped, loving it. Hating it. Hating him for hurting me, and hating him felt good. Right. It was what I wanted. To feel something other than that vague satisfaction I usually experienced during sex. This, to me, was true connection. This felt like a memory even while it was happening.

Tie me up and hurt me.

When he pulled out and came on my bare ass, I felt relief. Not that it was over. Relief that I felt anything at all.

I pulled up my jeans and turned around. His cock was still out, still hard. I thought how vulnerable he looked, blinking behind his glasses. How easy it would be to hurt him in that moment. Penises were so fragile. Even the word sounded soft, undercooked. Why was I thinking these thoughts? Where did they come from? My head was a mess. *I* was a mess, just like Annika Kron.

Tie me up and hurt me. Make me feel so bad that I—

What? What did I want?

Make me feel so bad that I remember why I feel so bad.

Breathing hard, eyes shining, Porter put his dick away and straightened his clothes. I walked him to the door, where he stopped, looked at me. "I'm falling for you," he said, but I couldn't return the sentiment out loud.

"I'm glad," I said. Maybe it was the truth. *I'm scared* felt truer.

"I wish you would come with me tonight."

I kissed him goodbye, and he left. With the door closed and locked, I leaned my back against it, closed my eyes, and jammed my hand into my underwear. I came quickly, and the manic feeling that had gripped me began to fade.

Only then did I notice the dress bag and shoe box I had left on the bed, in plain sight of Porter.

*   *   *

I took a long, hot shower, telling myself it would help me think through everything I had learned that day. But all it did was make me so drowsy I couldn't keep my eyes open. I gave in and crawled into bed, just to rest, but the second my head hit the pillow I was out. I dreamed that something was chasing me through the burnt forest. I didn't know what it was. I couldn't pause long enough to look back and see. All I knew was what it wanted to do to me, that if it caught me it would make me suffer before it ended me. But I could feel it getting closer, gaining on me, grabbing for me. I couldn't run fast enough. Time was tar, impeding each step. There was no escaping the thing behind me, and I knew it. I gave in. I glanced back and saw a man with the head of a white wolf reaching for me. And behind him ran an entire pack of men with the heads of slavering wolves, their jaws snapping, cameras held up to film me, flashes exploding as they captured my image and then—

And then the forest was gone, and I was in a bedroom, lying naked on a mattress covered in plastic sheeting. My wrists and ankles were bound. There was a mirror on the wall across from me. I saw myself in it, and I was no longer Liv Hendricks. I was Olivia Hill, the teenager, the girl, not the woman. A boy with the head of a white wolf loomed above me, naked to the waist. He had a camera pointed at me, red light bright. He filmed me, licking persistently at his muzzle.

I tried to scream, but no sound emerged.

I tried again, and this time I managed a whisper. "Miranda," I said.

And she appeared at the wolf's side, her mouth moving soundlessly, like she was on the other side of a glass wall.

The wolf turned his attention to her. She tried harder to speak to me, shouting, pleading, crying. She reached for me. I could almost hear her, but the wolf began to snarl so loudly that it drowned out her voice. Then he opened his mouth and bit into her throat.

I finally heard her voice.

Heard her scream.

* * *

I woke up soaking wet, gasping for air to feed my empty lungs. I sat up, eyes searching, but there was no one in the room that I could see. No wolves. No cameras. No one. I checked every corner anyway. Had to be sure. Had to be safe.

It was seven o'clock. The gala started at eight.

I took another shower, cold this time, to wash away the feverish sweat I'd worked up while I slept. Under the spray, I started to cry, desperate, hiccupy sobs. I didn't even know why I was crying, whether it was for Gemma, or Miranda, or me. I had lost myself long before I ever lost my sisters. I had never not been lost. But this was something else. Something to do with the dream. That room with the plastic sheeting over the mattress. The wolf with the video camera. It didn't feel like a dream. It felt like it was happening, or like it had happened before, and now it was happening again. But that couldn't be right, because there were no boys with the heads of wolves. That wasn't real. That was *Anathema*, Kron's first film, not my life. Not my memory.

I stayed in the shower until my sobs subsided to an exhausted shudder. Then I washed away the tears, pulled myself together, got ready for the party.

I zipped myself into the black dress I'd bought and

pulled my hair back into a twist. Then came the most important part: my body camera. I clipped it inside my raven masquerade mask, where it was handily concealed by a fan of feathers jutting backward from the top.

Standing in front of the mirror, I examined my reflection, troubled by what I saw. I looked like I was playing a part in one of Jonas Kron's surreal, horrific films. After my nightmare, the idea seemed all too plausible.

43.

Guests in cocktail dresses and dark suits congregated in the lobby, most of them already masked in anything from glittering, gilded, feathered masquerade masks like my own, to more elaborate porcelain or wood or papier-mâché masks. There were animal faces: birds and cats and bears, and a few wolves that looked like Niklas's work. Some of the masks looked like they'd been purchased in other countries: Africa and Japan and the Middle East. One group of partygoers all wore World War II gas masks, which I thought they'd regret as the night wore on and they began to swelter.

I kept my head down, spoke to no one, determined not to draw attention to myself. I overheard someone saying that a shuttle service would deliver us to the Red House. I went outside and found three passenger vans idling in the lot.

I sat silently in the back of my van as we ascended into the foothills, trees obscuring our view until we crested a rise and the forest thinned to reveal the Red House, a sprawling, fairy-tale castle painted the color of dried blood. Surrounding the house were topiaries in the shapes of wolves. Two of them guarded the front door. The dream of Miranda surfaced in my mind like a murdered body dumped in a lake. A tremor started in my limbs, a shaking I could not control.

Say hello to the wolves for me.

The party had already started. Packs of masked guests roamed the gardens, carrying glasses of champagne, conversing with faces hidden. They could be anyone, and so could I, or I could pretend to be. It was what I had always done, my lifelong coping mechanism, pretending to be someone else. Even when I was playing "me" on *Bullsh?t Hunters* I was only a version of myself, a mask over a mask over a mask. Who or what was underneath all the disguises I'd worn, I had no idea. Maybe there was nothing at my core. Maybe I was no one, a vacuum devoid of personality beneath all the layers I donned.

I queued up to enter the Red House, standing between the topiary wolves. The doorman found my name on the guest list and waved me inside. Stepping into Kron's house was disorienting, like falling asleep at noon and waking at midnight. The interior was lit only by candles and oil lamps, uncontaminated by the harsh blaze of artificial light. Only the warm, natural glow of open flames, such a blatant fire hazard it seemed deliberate. A bonfire in the waiting, as if this town hadn't had enough fire. Masked strangers surrounded me, the roar of their voices filling the interior.

"Champagne?" a waiter asked, appearing at my elbow. Even he wore a mask, a featureless white egg with two round holes for the eyes and a dark dash for the mouth. Looking around, I saw that all of the waiters wore the same mask.

I plucked a glass from the tray, thanked the waiter, and finished the champagne in one continuous gulp. It was so good it would probably ruin all other champagne for the rest of my life. It was wasted on chugging, but when it hit my stomach I instantly felt looser, more comfortable in my skin. I snaked my arm over the waiter's shoulder and deposited my empty on his tray, then helped myself to another glass, and drained that, too.

I moved farther into the house. Much of the furniture was antique, the wood dark and oily with history, not the bright, warm tones Scandinavians favored. Kron was all about the Old World. Chairs and curio cabinets and sideboards and sofas that had absorbed generations of life. The walls were crammed with art, collages of paintings in mismatched frames, ranging from the size of a deck of cards to the length and width of a child's first mattress.

"Your first time in the Red House?" a woman's voice purred into my ear, her face concealed behind an elaborate unicorn mask. She wore a body-skimming silver dress with a neckline that plunged to her sternum.

I turned to her, nodded. "It is. Yours, too?"

"Second," she said. "I had a supporting role in Jonas's last film. He invited me and some of the others to spend a weekend here with him."

"He's quite the entertainer," I said, but she laughed at that.

"Not really. We barely saw him during our stay. He told us to make ourselves at home, and then he disappeared. I think he observed us, though."

"What do you mean?"

"You know those old movies where someone watches you through the eyeholes in a painting? The actors walk past, and the eyes follow?"

I glanced at the paintings on the wall nearest us, and she shook her head. "He didn't watch us through the paintings.

At least, I don't think he did. But that was the feeling we had, that eyes were following us. My guess is, he has hidden cameras installed all over the house."

"Why would he do that?" I asked, my paranoia growing.

She shrugged. "I can only guess. To study our interaction? To get inspired? Or maybe he's just an old pervert who gets a thrill from spying on people."

"You don't sound bothered by it."

"It's part of his artistic process," she said. "Besides, I'm an actor. I'm used to being watched. It comes with the job." She touched my arm, her fingers cool and slender, long nails painted the same metal as her dress. "And what or who are you?" she asked, her voice lowering, a husky tease.

"Nothing and no one," I said.

"You're not going to tell me your name?"

"Tonight I don't have one," I said, and she laughed again. I startled when her fingers stroked down my spine, unable to repress an involuntary shiver. I felt disconnected from myself. From my body. From reality. A girl with no past and no future. Something about the mask, the way it sheltered me, made me feel free. I was tired of Liv Hendricks, the way I'd been tired of Olivia Hill. I was tired of being seen. Tired of being judged and found wanting by everyone around me. Too pretty. Not pretty enough. Too skinny. Not skinny enough. Too young. Not young enough. Too real. Not real enough. Too slutty. Not slutty enough. Too drunk. Not drunk enough.

It was exhausting. I was exhausted.

"Jonas, hello," the unicorn said, breaking me from my daze. "It's nice to see you again."

I turned and there was Jonas Kron, a knife-thin figure in a dark suit and maroon tie, a tiepin in the shape of a wolf's head in the center. He was the only one at the party not wearing a mask. What, I wondered, was the significance of that? Was he trying to tell us that he was the only real person among us, that the rest of us were all characters in his living theater? He was the director, and we were the players?

He took my hand and gave a little bow. "May I steal you for a moment," he asked in his quiet, musical accent.

"Yes," I said absently. Did he recognize me? How could he?

Ignored by Kron, the unicorn drifted off into the crowd, looking for a new plaything.

Kron offered his elbow and I took it. "Would you like a tour of the house?"

I nodded, linked my arm through Kron's, and he escorted me through the crowd, which parted for us as if he were a ship cutting through a school of fish.

"Do you know who I am?" I asked when we were clear of the crowd.

"Of course," he said. "Ms. Hendricks. I asked the attendant at the door to notify me when you arrived."

I nodded, relieved that I hadn't been recognized so easily. "I was hoping to fly under the radar. My being here might seem inappropriate, considering the circumstances."

"Yes. I was sorry to hear about your sister. I wish to take back the things I said about her last night. That was unfair."

"You didn't know she had disappeared."

"Nevertheless, I was thoughtless. I apologize. And I understand that you're here on business, but I hope you're enjoying the party as much as one can."

"It's like nothing I've ever experienced," I assured him.

"Good," he said, nodding. "They say at the end of your life, you will only regret the things you did not do."

"I might be the exception to that rule. I've done plenty of things I regret."

"That's good. You cast off your innocence. Innocence is for children," Kron said matter-of-factly, as though his opinion were the only one that mattered. "You can only truly live through experience. Your life is your story, your most important work of art, and art must be fed like a hungry animal. Otherwise it will either die, or try to kill you. If something scares you and you look at it, you are either a pervert or an artist. If you are a pervert, you will take it in and seek more. If you are an artist, you will create."

"What if you do both?"

He chuckled rustily. "Then you're a genius."

We broke free from the crowd and entered a less packed section of the house, a room set up as a kind of shrine to Kron's films, display cases positioned throughout the floor, each of them containing a piece of Kron feature film memorabilia. It was a Kronophile's holy temple of worship. I paused in front of one display case containing a lifelike wolf's head mask, and I felt that queasy, roiling, sinking sensation again. The little rectangle of paper inside labeled this as having come from his first film, *Anathema*, the one that had inspired a homicide and postmortem mutilation. I averted my eyes and moved on quickly. Another, smaller case on the wall displayed the bone-handled hunting knife the killer in *The Reddest Red* used to slay his first victim. The white dress with the Peter Pan collar that Annika wore in *The Girl and the Wolf* and the nameless girl's red-and-white swing dress from *A Stranger Comes to Town* were both displayed in glass cases on the wall. I paused to study them.

"You could have been the one to wear that dress," Jonas said, standing close beside me. Too close. The wool sleeve of his jacket brushed my bare arm. "You were the one I wanted."

I looked at him, inched slightly to the side so we were no longer touching. It was the first time he'd brought up the fact that I'd turned down the lead in *The Girl and the Wolf*. I felt a vague sense of guilt, like everything for Annika could have been different if only I'd accepted the part, saved her from what working with her uncle did to her. He could have broken me instead of her. Either way, I had ended up broken. If I'd undertaken the role of Joelle, perhaps I wouldn't have been driving on Mulholland Drive the night Miranda disappeared. One yes instead of a no and everything in my life could have taken a different path.

"But then you wouldn't have made the film you made," I pointed out. "Some people say it's your definitive work."

"Most people, not some," he said drily. "My best work is behind me. I accept that. I don't like it, but I accept it."

"I know how you feel. It's kind of funny when you think about it. We both peaked at about the same time."

He smiled, amusement in his eyes. "You're still young. You may surprise yourself someday."

"I hope you're right."

"Come with me," Jonas said, leading me from the room. "There's something I want to show you." He steered me toward a staircase and took hold of the polished banister.

I hesitated. "We're going upstairs?"

He nodded and began to climb the stairs, not waiting to see if I followed.

But I did follow.

At the top, we turned down a long, wide corridor that seemed to stretch for eternity like a hallway in a dream, the kind in which you can run forever. The corridor was lined with closed doors, maybe a dozen of them. Kron walked to the last door on the left, opened it, and flipped a switch. A tapestry of twinkle lights blinked on overhead, just like the canopy of imitation stars I'd seen over Niklas's bed.

"This is—was—Annika's room," Jonas said. "I haven't changed a thing since she left. All these years, I hoped she might come back. I picture her as she was when I last saw her. Eighteen. Hair as long as her spine. Freckles in the summer. Chipped fingernail polish. Laughing one minute, brooding the next. She was like her mother that way. Unpredictable. Erratic. She was quite un-Norwegian, not at all stoic or reserved. She burned brighter than most. That was what made her shine on screen."

And according to Porter, Jonas had stoked the fire in Annika until it consumed her. Until she nearly burned down the Wolf Wood, if Niklas was to be believed.

I turned in a circle, taking it in. There were few indications that this room had belonged to a young starlet in the making. Her accommodations were not glamorous. The bedroom could have belonged to any teenage girl in America. The twinkle lights overhead. The collection of photographs and postcards and drawings pinned to a corkboard near her desk. The books filling a small bookshelf were a mixture of pulp, literature, and classic children's novels. I moved to the corkboard and looked at the photos, at a print of Annika and her friends back in Norway. A pretty girl with her life ahead of her. A girl just starting to take shape. Gemma and I had never been such girls. By the time we were sixteen, we had seen too much, lived too much. We had never been sixteen. We had been whatever we were told to be. I envied this Annika, but not the Annika in the photo next to it, a black-and-white production still from the set of *The Girl and the Wolf*. In it, Annika stood alone in front of the wolf enclosure, her right hand grasping her left elbow, her posture radiating fear. She wore her white dress and red knee socks. I guessed this photo had been taken before the famous sex scene was shot, or maybe just after. The scene that had been cued up to play in Niklas's basement bedroom. Had Niklas been present when that scene was shot? Had he watched as Annika's costar lifted her dress to fuck her from behind; as she crouched naked inside the wolf's enclosure, pretending to rip it open, feed on it until blood painted her chin and chest?

How could Jonas, her uncle, a man who was supposed to love her and protect her, ask her to do what she did in that scene? Would he have asked the same of me, or worse?

"What did you think of Annika's aspiration to be an actor?" I said, turning back to face him.

"I supported it, obviously," Jonas said without hesitation. "It was her dream. I wanted to help her achieve it. She had the talent and the ambition. All she needed was an opportunity, and I gave her that."

"I've heard you write the scripts for your movies as you film them," I said.

He nodded. "Sometimes I write the day's pages the night before. Sometimes the morning of."

"So it wasn't like the script for *The Girl and the Wolf* existed before you cast Annika. You wrote it for her."

"No. I wrote it because it was the story that wanted to be told."

I raised an eyebrow. "So you don't think you have any control over what you end up filming? That the story simply exists, and you take it down like dictation."

One corner of his mouth curled in a dry smile. "Something like that. I sense you don't approve."

"I don't approve of the things you made her do."

"I didn't make her do anything. She could have said no."

"She was barely an adult, and you were her uncle. She trusted you to look out for her best interests."

"Like you and your sister trusted Desiree Hill to look out for yours? Annika didn't want me to look out for her best interests. She wanted me to make her a star. I pushed her to take risks so she could grow."

"And now she's gone."

Jonas held my gaze for a long moment before lowering his eyes. "Yes," he said softly.

"Jonas, do you know what Annika was doing in the Wolf Woods the night of the fire?"

"What?" He blinked at me and shook his head minutely. "I don't...who told you that?"

"Did Annika ever say anything to you to indicate someone was harassing her?"

"No. She never—"

"Did she ever tell you she believed in the *Ulv Konge*?"

"What? No, that's ridiculous! Where did you hear this?"

"Is it any more ridiculous than turning an entire town into your set? Is it more ridiculous than improvising a film that turns your eighteen-year-old niece into a sex object and then claiming you had no choice in doing so? Is it more ridiculous than this house and this party, or than people who worship you coming to Stone's Throw to pay homage, running around the woods in wolf masks and—"

"Jonas." The director and I both startled, turning toward the open doorway, now filled by a figure nearly as tall and lean as the director, his face obscured by the mask of a white wolf. Soren Kron.

Say hello to the wolves for me.

I realized I wasn't breathing, forced myself to inhale. Not to give in to the panic that wanted to take hold of me.

Soren cleared his throat. "You're needed downstairs."

"In a minute," Jonas said.

"Sheriff Lot is here," Soren insisted. "He says he needs to talk to you."

"About what?" Jonas sounded annoyed.

Soren glanced at me, eyes so pale inside the holes in the wolf's face that they seemed to emit their own icy light. "That is something you'll want to speak to him about in private. We wouldn't want this to end up on the Internet."

I felt a jolt go through me, like a shock of electricity. Did he know about the body camera?

"Please excuse me," Jonas said curtly. "I hope you enjoy the rest of the party."

44.

While I'd been away the tone of the party had shifted from civilized to hedonistic, the voices turned up and the laughter too loud. Everyone drunk on champagne and atmosphere. The waiters in their featureless masks wove through the party, silver platters perched on their hands, offering dangerous-looking hors d'oeuvres, meat laced on skewers that could put out an eye.

I tried to follow Jonas and Soren to eavesdrop on their conversation with Sheriff Lot, but I lost them in the crowd. I searched the rooms on the first floor but couldn't find them anywhere. Flushed with the heat of all those bodies, I plucked another glass of champagne from a silver tray and downed it in a single gulp. I was a flood of nerves and adrenaline, my heart pounding too hard, too fast. I couldn't seem to draw a deep breath. My brain gave birth to a throbbing headache that tried to escape through my eye sockets. My vision dimmed with every heartbeat.

What had happened to Annika? Why had she come back after all these years? And what did any of it have to do with the rest of the missing girls? With Miranda? No—*Gemma*. Miranda was long gone. Gemma was less gone. I could still find her. I was so close. I felt the answers dangling just out of reach, but every time I grabbed for them they moved backward an inch. Questions piled on top of questions. My headache multiplied and spawned a new ache at the back of my skull. I filled my stomach with champagne in lieu of painkillers. The party took on a surreal quality. The room had begun to smell like a zoo, a musty, fecal odor, like the tunnel that housed the wolf sanctuary care stations.

Why wolves? That was a question I wanted to ask Jonas. Why the obsession with that particular apex predator? But now that I'd accused him of exploiting his niece for the sake of art I wasn't sure I'd have another chance. I could guess at the answer based on what Jonas had told me about his view on the creative process. Jonas's art was a "hungry animal" he had to feed or it would turn on him. His art was his wolf, dangerous and intelligent and enigmatic, like his films.

Maybe Jonas was right. Maybe we all had a wolf to feed. I had certainly been feeding something ravenous for the last fifteen years.

I cut through the crowd until I found a door, escaped into the topiary garden, sucked in a clean breath of night. The crowd here was not as dense. There was room to move. I felt the eyes of masked strangers watching me, and I headed away from them, following a dirt path through a maze of topiary, around the side of the house into darkness, where I would no longer be seen. No longer be observed.

I continued on the trail until the voices were behind me, but in the distance I saw a subtle red glow. There was some kind of structure tucked into the trees out behind the house. I made my way toward it and a hundred yards later found another house, much smaller than the Red House. A fairy-tale cottage with a sharply peaked roof, round windows, a domed door. The cottage was painted the same blood-clot red as the big house, but in the night it looked black, except for the light coming through the windows.

The light was red.

It was yet another place I had already visited through light and pixels. This miniature Red House was one of the *Stranger Comes to Town* locations. It was where the heroine had stayed after the townspeople found her on the road, beaten and bloody and missing a toe.

Wobbling in my heels, I moved toward the house, hearing muted strains of music coming from inside. I stood on tiptoe to peer through one of the round windows, but there was a curtain obscuring my view. I could make out movement inside, a collection of shadows shifting through the interior.

A hand touched my back. My heart rammed against my rib cage. I whirled around.

"Shall we?" It was the woman in the unicorn mask. She reached for the doorknob.

I stepped into the tiny house and was bathed in red light, finding myself in a quaint living room that connected to a kitchen. The furniture was whimsical, like it had been chosen by a child, bright, primary colors and curlicue embellishments, but the red lightbulbs in the sockets painted everything in a whorish light. A few people lounged on a purple velvet sofa, or lingered against walls, chatting, bodies close as they sipped champagne. But on the kitchen table, a woman in a butterfly mask, wings hiding her eyes, lay with her dress hiked up to her thighs, a man in a black leather mask buried between her legs. I tried to ignore the hot, immediate pulse of excitement between my own.

"Come with me," the unicorn said, taking my hand and leading me farther into the house, down a narrow hallway toward an open door. Toward the bedroom where the name-less girl had stayed until the townspeople fed her to a monster.

I heard the sounds they were making before I entered the room. Moans, gasps, grunts, cries of pleasure laced with pain. There were a dozen people packed into the tiny bed-room, most of them clothed only in their masks, naked bodies twined and writhing.

I took a step backward toward the door, stumbling a lit-tle on my heels, but the unicorn blocked my way.

"Where do you think you're going?" she asked, her voice both playful and subtly threatening. She didn't know that my mind had gone vacant. No thought. No feeling. I was adrift, outside my body.

There was a restraint system attached to the wrought-iron bed frame. A naked woman in a black lace mask had her wrists and ankles bound, wrenched so it looked like her shoulders might dislocate. A naked man in a white wolf mask hammered into her like the point was to hurt her, make her bleed.

Something clawed from the depths of my mind, a creep-ing, black widow spider of memory. I reared back from its bite, turned my face from the man and woman on the bed, the dream of the wolf-headed boy flashing behind my eyes, his camera pointed at me, his teeth sinking into Miranda's neck.

Another man sat in a chair on the other side of the room, wearing a white wolf mask and a black tie. So many wolves. The room was filled with them. Wolves every-where I looked. A girl crouched between the sitting wolf's legs, her head bobbing up and down. The wolf saw me watching and met my eyes. He waved cheerfully.

The unicorn wound her arms around me from behind, one hand cupping my right breast. "He wants you," the unicorn said, starting to unzip my dress in the back.

I jerked away from her, alarms going off in my head. I pushed past the unicorn and fled the room. The fairy-tale cottage. Ran back down the path toward the Red House, my mind and memory on fire. I tore my mask from my face. I couldn't stand to wear it anymore.

The wolf masks. The red light. It was all too familiar, but not like something I had watched in one of Kron's films.

It felt like something I'd lived. Not a dream. An event.

What had happened to me?

What did they do to me, these forgotten wolves from my past?

I was so close to knowing. So close to the truth. I might have found it tucked down inside of me, but when I reached the big house, what I found instead were more red lights. Blue ones, too. And they were flashing.

I arrived just in time to see Sheriff Lot open the door of his sedan for Jonas Kron in handcuffs, ducking into the backseat, the place where the suspected criminals sat.

"Liv, is that you?" I stared in confusion, spotting Wheeler cutting through the crowd toward me. I grabbed his arm, feeling the need to hold on to something steady and stable. Something real.

"What's going on?" I asked him.

"The sheriff received some kind of anonymous tip about Gemma," he said.

"Did they find her?"

The look on Wheeler's face turned my stomach into an anchor.

"They found shoes in the trunk of one of Jonas's cars.

Not pairs. Just shoes for the right foot." He paused, looking dismayed, casting his eyes about as though there might be someone else nearby to say the rest.

"Wheeler." I dug my fingertips into his arm.

"There was a severed toe inside each shoe," he said. "That's all I know."

OLIVIA HILL

2003

17 YEARS OLD; 109 LBS.

45.

Russel, Jimmy, and I stood on the front step of a one-story midcentury modern house that could have been an actual Frank Lloyd Wright design, or just a solid knockoff. The front yard and walkway were enclosed by a high wooden fence. The front gate was unlocked, but the windows of the house were dark. The only vehicle we could see was the black SUV parked in the driveway.

"This doesn't look like much of a party," Russel said, the three of us clustered together on the front porch. "Maybe we got the address wrong."

I put my ear to the door and listened, heard faint music coming from inside, something cinematic and eerie, a movie score that was vaguely familiar to me, though I couldn't quite place it. Either way, it was definitely not party music.

I tried the knob, not bothering to knock first. The door opened on an unlit foyer. I looked back at Russel *and Jimmy to make sure they were still with me. They shrugged, shared a glance, nodded.*

Jimmy maneuvered himself ahead of me and stepped inside. "Hello?" he called. "Anyone here?"

No answer. But if there was someone in the house, they'd have a hard time hearing us over the dramatic, sweeping music, which I now recognized. It was the score from Jonas Kron's first movie, Anathema. I'd watched that film and several of Kron's others within the last few months when his casting director tapped me to play the lead in his next film. Then Desiree turned the part down without even asking me if I was interested, and it went to another actress, an unknown from some other country, making her debut.

We entered the house, and found ourselves in a vast living room with a wood ceiling and wood-paneled walls. Wood everything, except for the very back wall of the house, which was entirely glass and looked out on a spacious patio with a pool. There were no other lights on inside the house, no lamps that I could see. The moon offered just enough illumination to reveal that the living room was empty. No furniture whatsoever, only a cold fireplace.

"Doesn't look like anyone lives here," Jimmy said, his kryptonite-green eyes the brightest thing in the room.

Nervous sweat gathered in my palms. This wasn't a party. The thought played over and over in my mind. This wasn't a party, and my sister was somewhere in this house with a man who told her it would be. A man who should not be alone in a darkened, deserted house with my inebriated, foolish, underage sister. I had to find her. I had to get her out now. I just hoped I wasn't too late to save whatever piece of her would be missing after the man was through with her.

I followed the music to a long, dark throat of a hallway off the living room that ended with a closed door. A line of red light shone along the bottom, giving it the diabolical look of a gateway to hell in a cheap horror movie. I took a step toward the hallway, but Russel put an arm out to hold me back and went ahead of me. Jimmy reached forward and took hold of my sweaty hand, squeezed it to reassure me. I glanced back at him appreciatively. I still couldn't figure out where I'd met him. When this was over and Gemma was safe, I would have to ask, even if it embarrassed him and made me seem like an oblivious bitch.

Russel turned the knob. Just before the door swung open I had the urge to turn and run in the other direction. Some internal alarm in me went off, blaring *You are not safe.*

But I didn't run. I couldn't. Maybe playing a teen detective had made me think I was something I wasn't, a person capable of facing real danger. A person who didn't listen to her instincts telling her everything was wrong, wrong, wrong, because if she did that, then there wouldn't be a show. If she did that, she wouldn't be the hero.

Or maybe I was just stupid.

Russel pushed the door open on a room drenched in red light. A boom box sat on the floor, blaring the Anathema score, a lamp next to it, the regular bulb replaced by a red party bulb. There was only one piece of furniture inside: a bare mattress on the floor.

And on that mattress lay Gemma, stripped to her

bra and underwear, a gag stuffed into her mouth and her wrists and ankles tied with rope. Her wide-open eyes rolled toward me. Russel tried to step inside, but I dropped Jimmy's hand and elbowed my way in front of him, darting to Gemma's side.

I knelt beside her. "It's okay, Gemma. I'm getting you out of here."

Gemma moaned something and jerked her head toward the corner of the room. I looked and saw a video camera on a tripod, facing the mattress.

My gut clenched.

Then something thudded against the back of my skull.

The red room turned to black.

LIV HENDRICKS

2018

32 YEARS OLD; 138 LBS.

Facebook Fans: 14,455

Twitter Followers: 49,126

Instagram Followers: 8,210

46.

Sheriff Lot and his deputies found no bodies at the Red House, only four little toes, all of them severed from the right foot of a different woman. Only one of them was fresh, most likely severed within the last twenty-four hours. It had to be Gemma's. But there should have been five toes. Five missing women, one toe from each. So whose toe was missing, and why? Yet another question with no discernible answer.

Jonas Kron had been arrested for the abduction and suspected murder of the Dark Road girls, but he had lawyered up and was admitting to nothing, maintaining that he had no idea how the toes and shoes of the missing women had ended up in his car. Yes, one of his most famous films had featured an outsider coming to town, scant her right shoe and the little toe on her right foot, but this was not an admission of guilt. It was his art, and art inspired copycats.

"I don't think he did it," I told Wheeler, who sat on the sofa in my room at the Eden Tree. Danny was too busy planning for how they'd cover the Dark Road story now that a suspect was in custody to keep tabs on Wheeler. We had changed out of our gala clothes and into jeans and sweaters. Wheeler brought the mini bottles from his room (even though Danny had warned him and the rest of the Bullshit Hunters not to dare touch them). He gave me the Maker's Mark and kept the Jack Daniel's for himself. I washed down four Advil with a swig of bourbon.

It was after midnight, but I was more awake than I'd ever been. We had hung around the sheriff's station for two hours waiting for news, but the tiny office was swarming with reporters and paparazzi. And Desiree Hill led the charge. My mother ignored me at the station, refused to even glance in my direction. The entirety of her attention was focused on grilling Lot and demanding answers.

Sheriff Lot finally lost it and blew up at the whole crowd, roaring at everyone to leave and come back in the morning. He'd have more information then.

But the town and the press and the Internet had already made up their minds. Jonas was guilty. Jonas had taken the girls. It was the only thing that made sense. Everyone seemed to have forgotten about the fact that Jonas was on location shooting films in other countries during most of the disappearances. He had ironclad alibis. And they didn't know what I knew, that Jonas had paid me to figure out what happened to his niece and the others. I would come clean about that if he contacted me and asked me to do it. Until then, I'd continue to keep our connection a secret, as promised.

"How can you say he didn't do it?" Wheeler asked. "The man is a lunatic. He makes movies so disturbing they hand out barf bags at his premieres. People have sued him for giving them recurring nightmares. How could he *not* be the guy?"

Because he wouldn't hire me to catch him and then not let me catch him.

"Wheeler, I've met him. I've spoken with him. He's an arrogant son of a bitch, but he's not the least bit insane. Or if he is, he channels it into his films, not into his real life."

He feeds it to his wolves.

"Okay," Wheeler said, cracking the top on a can of Diet Coke and pouring it into a glass half full of whiskey. "Let's say he didn't do it. Who did?"

"Probably whoever called in the anonymous tip that led the sheriff to his car."

"Which would mean it was the same person who actually put the shoes and toes in his trunk."

"Exactly."

"And who would do that?"

"If I knew, I would be handing that person over to the sheriff now instead of sitting here drinking my feelings."

The bottle of Maker's was already gone. I twisted the cap off the Absolut bottle next, but Wheeler stood and came to sit beside me on the bed. He put his hand over mine to keep me from raising the bottle to my lips.

"Gemma might still be alive," he said softly. "All of them might be."

I shook his hand off. "People who abduct women don't take trophies," I said. "People who kill them take trophies."

Toephies. That's what people online were calling them, like it was all a big joke. Like my sister most likely being dead was grounds for a fucking hashtag.

I downed the vodka, but I was too anxious for the alcohol to take effect. What was I missing? I was on the verge of understanding what was really going on in Stone's Throw. I was sure of it. But until I found the missing pieces, I couldn't see the picture as a whole. It was like an old grindhouse film with missing reels. The plot wouldn't make sense until I found them.

In lieu of a plan, I connected my body camera to my laptop to upload the footage and recharge the battery. Wheeler switched the TV on and turned it to the local news, which was dominated by ongoing coverage of the developments in the Dark Road story. Most of it was filler, the same information repeated over and over again. I logged on to Twitter and checked to see if anyone had contacted me with new information. I scrolled through the tweets quickly. They were mostly condolences from people who assumed Gemma was dead and wanted to let me know how sorry they were. Others wanted to tell me they always thought Jonas Kron was the abductor, and I was stupid for not catching him when I had the chance. #toephies

I switched to my direct message feed. Nothing new from @AnnikaKron.

Had Jonas created the Twitter profile for Annika? Had he been the one messaging me all along?

My body camera footage finished uploading. I dragged the file to my editing program and scrolled through the footage, pausing on the section filmed in the red cottage out behind Kron's mansion. I turned the volume all the way down and shifted my laptop so Wheeler couldn't see what I was watching. The light was low, but I had captured plenty of explicitly pornographic images from inside the cottage. When I came to the section from the bedroom, the white wolf orgy, I forced myself to scroll backward, play it again. As expected, my guts squirmed at the sight of the men in their wolf masks, but I forced myself to keep watching, straining toward that feeling of long-submerged remembrance.

And then something in the footage caught my eye. A

flicker of light reflecting off metal. I scrolled back a few seconds and was about to hit PLAY when Wheeler barked at the TV news, "Hey, they're using *Bullshit Hunters* footage. Can they do that without permission? Danny better make them pay for it. I'm tired of doing my own makeup."

I glanced up, watching as the screen filled with a shot of Sasha, Wheeler, Tate, and Blitz standing in front of the half-blackened remains of the Wolf King's cottage in the woods, Sasha delivering exposition about the films Kron had shot there. The footage was from that afternoon. I knew because Sasha wore the short tight dress I'd criticized. The Bullshit Hunters entered the cabin, and Sasha led the cameraman to a crudely drawn chalk mural of the *Ulv Konge* on the back wall, its head grossly overlarge, its back bowed, and its arms long enough to drag its claws on the ground, though it walked upright.

A single sentence scrawled in chalk accompanied the drawing: FOLLOW THE WHITE WOLF.

My laptop dinged with an incoming DM.

> **AK:** Your sister misses her toe. She's still alive, but…maybe not for long.

> **LH:** Where is she?

No answer.

> **LH:** Annika?

No answer.

> **LH:** Annika, please!!

No answer.

I stood, trembling all over. "Wheeler," I said. "We need to go."

He looked over at me. "Where?"

I pointed at the TV. "There."

"Now? It's the middle of the night, and you want to go for a hike?"

"I'll explain in the car. Get your coat," I said, yanking mine on and looping a scarf around my neck. Forgetting that flash of silver I'd seen on the wolf orgy footage, I unplugged my body camera and attached it to my jacket collar.

Wheeler headed for the door.

"One more thing," I called to him. He turned back around, looking hopeful, like maybe I'd changed my mind. Hated to disappoint him.

"Where's Blitz?" I asked.

"In his crate in the van."

"Do you have keys?"

"Oh, Liv . . ." he groaned. "You're going to get me fired."

"We'll have him back before anyone notices he's gone." I hoped.

Once Wheeler left, I removed my gun from under the mattress, checked to make sure the safety was on, and slipped it into my coat pocket. This time, if any wolves showed up, I'd be ready to say hello.

47.

By the time I parked at the head of the White Wolf Trail, I had told Wheeler everything I'd been holding back with the exception of Jonas Kron being my backer. I turned off the ignition and looked at him. He stared straight ahead, saying nothing. I handed him the flashlight—I only had one—and clipped a leash to Blitz's collar.

"Ready?" I said, reaching for the door handle. Blitz scrambled around in the back of my car, eager for an adventure. He exploded from the backseat as soon as I opened his door, but Wheeler remained where he was, his arms stubbornly crossed.

"This is crazy," Wheeler said. "It's crazy and it's dangerous."

"I won't argue with that. Are you coming, or do you want to wait here alone in the dark?"

Wheeler cursed loudly as he got out of the car, clicking the flashlight on with a huffy sigh. "I still don't understand why we had to bring the dog," he muttered. "It's not like he's trained to track a scent or protect us or anything actually useful."

"You don't give him enough credit," I told Wheeler. "If he hears or smells something strange out there, he'll let us know. That's good enough for me."

"What do you think is out there?" Wheeler scanned the trees, as though he suddenly felt eyes watching him from the darkness.

"That's what we're here to find out," I said, heading down the White Wolf Trail. The straight black torsos of the trees closed us in. Blitz attempted to bound ahead, but I kept a tight hold on his leash. At the sanctuary, the wolves were howling, and I could tell the sound put Blitz on edge. Wheeler trained the flashlight beam on the forest floor two feet in front of us. Luckily, the moon was out and round, and provided wan yellow light to break up the inky darkness.

After about half a mile, Wheeler halted abruptly. "Did you hear that?"

We stood in silence, listening. Blitz strained against his leash, and I reeled him backward.

And then we both heard it, somewhere up ahead: the distinctive, broken-bone snap of a branch.

Blitz roared a bark and lunged toward the sound, nearly wrenching my arm from the socket. I lost my grip on the leash, and an instant later Blitz was gone, tearing through the underbrush.

"Blitz!" I called over and over, but the sound of his paws galloping across the ground quickly grew faint. I ran after him, and heard Wheeler's footsteps pounding the ground behind me, his flashlight beam jouncing wildly. I leapt over a jutting root that tried to catch my foot. Wheeler stumbled and went down on his hands and knees.

I stopped to drag him to his feet. I didn't want a repeat of my separation with Gemma the day before. We stood together, listening for the sound of Blitz's paws or barking or anything to tell us where he was now. But there was only silence.

"What do we do?" Wheeler asked, looking helpless and angry. "Danny is going to fire me. I'm so screwed."

"He'll come back when he's finished chasing whatever he's chasing," I said with more confidence than I felt. "Don't worry. He'll find us. But we have to keep going."

Wheeler sighed. "All right."

We backtracked until we reached the trail, and set off again in the direction of the cottage.

"Thank you for coming out here with me," I said after we'd walked for a few minutes in a tense silence. "I thought I could do this alone, but I can't. This sounds lame, but I miss being a part of a team, even a pretend one."

"You're doing fine," Wheeler said, still sounding irritated. "If the things that happened to you over the last couple of days had happened to me, I would be long gone by now. Turns out I don't just play a coward on TV. I really am the 'Shaggy.'"

"I don't think that's true," I protested weakly. It was definitely true.

He looked at me. "If I had any guts, I would have stood up for you all those times Danny yelled at you. I would have told him I quit, too, when he fired you, or said I was out when he decided to come up here and fuck with your investigation. And I sure as hell would have told you no when you said we should bring Blitz out here. But I didn't do any of that. I just went along with it."

I squeezed his arm and smiled at him. "You're out here with me. That matters."

His return smile was tentative, but I could tell he appreciated the praise. He got precious little of it from Danny or the *Bullsh?t Hunters* fans, who enjoyed abusing him online almost as much as they had me.

Ahead I spotted the diagonal line of a roof. "There it is."

As we entered the cottage I felt my nerves crackling with foreboding at what I would find inside. The interior was cramped, the windows boarded up, but moonlight found its way in through the gaping hole in the roof where the tree had fallen on the house. I shone the flashlight around.

Gemma wasn't here. No one was here.

I put a hand to my head, shaking it. I had brought us out here in the middle of the night and had possibly lost Blitz, which could get me sued and Wheeler fired, and it was for nothing. Maybe I was wrong about Jonas. Maybe he was the perpetrator who had abducted all those women. Maybe Gemma was dead. Maybe @AnnikaKron was just some troll having fun with me.

Either that, or I was still missing something.

Unlike a typical set piece, which would be torn down at the end of shooting, the Wolf King's cottage was sturdily built, which was probably the reason it hadn't crumbled years ago. Kron intended his sets to last. The dirt floor was littered with dusty, broken bottles, crumpled chip bags, faded candy wrappers, and one lonely-looking used condom, shriveled like an abandoned snakeskin.

I stepped toward the chalk mural on the back wall to examine it more closely, and as I did I heard a groan from behind us. Wheeler and I turned at the same time to see the cottage door swing shut.

We looked at each other with wide eyes. My mind desperately grasped for a best-case scenario. *It was the wind. A sudden gust of wind blew the door closed, that's all.*

Then from outside the cottage came a sound that made my guts drop: a sharp pounding, a hammer striking a nail and driving it into wood.

I rushed toward the door and tried to push it open, but it wouldn't budge. Someone strong held it fast on the other side as they continued to drive nails into the wood. This, like so much else in Stone's Throw, was a familiar scene. Jack and Joelle had done the same thing to two of their classmates in *The Girl and the Wolf*, trapping them in the cottage and threatening to burn it to the ground.

Wheeler and I hit the door at the same time. Together we shoved against it with all our weight. The wood shifted slightly but did not open.

The hammering stopped suddenly, and I smelled the oily, distinctive odor of gasoline just before glass shattered against the outside of the door, and I heard the whoosh of fire bursting into existence.

Wheeler and I stumbled backward, sharing a look of alarm. Wheeler's eyes were wide and bulging.

"The windows!" I shouted, and we broke in two different directions, heading for windows on opposite sides of the cabin. I banged my palms against the wooden boards covering one of the windows and bit back a yelp at the pain that shot up my arms. The boards were thick, nailed down solidly. They didn't even rattle when I hit them.

I pulled out my gun and unloaded five rounds into the wood, then tried shoving against it again, hoping the boards would bend and break. But the bullets did nothing but make a few tiny peepholes.

Wheeler was still pounding and pushing against the boards on his window, but I could see they weren't going to break loose. Whoever had nailed them there, they hadn't done a shoddy job. I checked my cell phone and saw a single bar. I dialed 911, but the call ended less than a second after I hit SEND. Wheeler was now trying his phone as well, and apparently getting the same results, because he began to shout "Come on, come on, come on, come on" at the screen.

"The roof," I said, grabbing his arm. His eyes rose to the hole above our heads. Smoke began to obscure what we could see of the sky around the trunk of the fallen tree, turning it the color of dirty cotton.

"I'll boost you up," Wheeler said grimly.

"Who's going to boost *you* up?" I had to shout to be heard over the roar and crackle of the fire eating through wood.

"I'll figure something out." He knelt, linked his hands together, and signaled for me to climb on. "Once you're out, run and get help, or run until you find service."

"I'm not leaving you here!"

"You have to! I can't squeeze through. I won't fit."

I shook my head. Wheeler wouldn't be here if it weren't for me. He should be the one to get out and run for help. But I saw his point. The space was barely big enough for me to wriggle through.

"Liv," he said, turning his head to cough out a lungful of smoke. "Let me do this."

Without waiting for permission, he grabbed me around the waist and hoisted me up toward the hole in the roof. Even though I knew it should be me who remained behind, I grabbed on to the edge of the ragged hole. I had logged enough torturous hours at CrossFit to ensure I could do at least one real pull-up. I did that one, and lifted myself high enough that I could wrench my body through the hole, the trunk of the fallen tree scraping down my back. I felt the roof bow under my weight, and for one terrible second I thought it would collapse on top of Wheeler. I spread myself out flat so my weight was equally distributed, and swiveled to peer down into the hole at Wheeler. I held out my hand to him. The roof bowed another inch.

"Go!" Wheeler shouted.

I would not let Wheeler die in this cabin. I slid on my butt to the edge of the roof, lowered my body over the side, and dropped the remaining five feet. My boots hit the ground, and I ran around to the front of the cabin to see if there was any way I could put out the fire. But flames had consumed the front of the structure. Luckily, the wood, already charred in so many places, was not burning as quickly as it might have. It bought us time.

"I'll be back soon!" I shouted, but I didn't wait for his response.

I ran through the woods in the direction of the wolf sanctuary, where I knew they had a landline. Without a flashlight, the forest was a gauntlet of branches trying to tear my face off, clothesline me, knock me on my back. The ground was just as bad, roots and ill-placed stones catching at my feet. I fell once, hit my knee hard on a jagged rock and tore open my jeans, but I was up again in an instant, hurling myself forward with blood soaking my leg. A sharp branch caught my cheek and razored across it, so close to my eye that the shock made me freeze in my tracks. With my heart exploding and my lungs shredded, I clapped a hand over my right eye, feeling blood pool in the palm. When I dared to take my hand away, I blinked and assured myself that I had not just gouged out my own eye. I tentatively fingered the tear in my skin, and my stomach rolled at the depth of the cut, a trench stretching two inches, soaking the right half of my face with warm blood. But it was fine. It didn't matter. I'd deal with the cut later.

I already had one massive scar on my face. What was one more?

It was as good a place as any to check my cell reception, just in case. I took out my phone and almost started to cry when I saw there was still only one bar, but when I dialed 911 this time an operator picked up.

"Nine-one-one, what's your emergency?"

My knees almost buckled in relief. I opened my mouth to answer her, and then I heard a familiar, shrill shriek that turned every nerve in my body into a live wire. It was Tocsin, the mountain lion. I must be near the sanctuary again. A chorus of lowing wolves joined the female shriek of the mountain lion. The combined sounds made me feel like I was losing my mind. Howling and screaming. Screaming and howling.

"My name is Liv Hendricks," I said. "There's a fire in the Wolf King's cottage. I don't have an address. I don't think there is one. It's in the woods off the Dark Road—I mean Dag Road. The house is on the White Wolf Trail. There's someone trapped inside—"

That was as far as I got before a figure moved into view ahead of me, a statuesque woman with hair so blond it was almost white. She wore dark jeans and a black jacket. There was a long black gun propped in her hands.

"Helene," I said, and took an automatic step backward, away from her. There was a series of beeps in my ear as I lost the call. I lowered the phone, keeping my eyes on Helene as I pressed the button to redial. But this time the call ended immediately.

The Norwegian woman's narrowed eyes moved from my bloody face to my bloody knee and back to my face again. "What happened to you?"

"Why do you have a gun?" I countered. My right hand inched toward the Glock in my coat pocket.

"It's a tranquilizer gun," she said. "For Tocsin. The wolves are howling and upsetting her. Sometimes it is the only way to make her stop her cries."

Her method of quieting the mountain lion seemed excessive, but I didn't have time to worry about animal cruelty at that moment. Wheeler could already be unconscious—or worse—from smoke inhalation.

I took a step toward Helene again and raised my phone to redial. "Helene, there's a fire at the cottage in the woods. My friend is trapped inside. We need to get the fire department out here as quickly as possible. Will you please run back to your office and call them on your landline? Tell them what I told you?"

Helene nodded but didn't move. She took a deep breath and sighed. Then she pointed her tranquilizer gun at me and pulled the trigger.

There was a sound like someone spitting out a seed. Then a hard, sharp sting in my thigh. I looked down and saw a dart sticking out of the front of my jeans.

"I'm sorry," Helene said. "I didn't want to do this."

I blinked once. Dropped my phone. Dropped to my knees.

And then I was gone.

48.

Wake up, Liv. Please, wake up!" A frantic female voice brought me back.

I pried my eyes open, wincing though the light was a feeble yellow emanating from a bare, low-wattage bulb overhead. A headache lanced through the center of my soupy brain, and I shivered violently. Someone had stripped me to my bra and underwear. Sharp bits of straw poked into my back.

A woman knelt beside me, touching my arm. A woman with stringy blond hair, her body and face streaked with grime.

"Gemma?" I rasped her name in wonder.

"Oh, thank God!" Gemma smoothed the matted hair off my forehead, tears pooling and shivering in her eyes. Her face was pallid, bloodless, strangely shiny. She was only slightly more clothed than I was, in a grimy white tank top and white underwear.

I dragged myself upright so I could look around. We were in a room with rock walls, a man-made cavern. I had been here before, in one of the care stations in the tunnel behind the sanctuary enclosures. Only last time I had been on the opposite side of the bars.

We were in a cage. Helene Larsen stood on the other side of the metal bars. She no longer carried the tranquilizer gun. She didn't need it. The bars were enough.

But there was a new addition to the care station, a digital camera affixed to a tripod, its round, black eye apathetic and impartial. The red light wasn't on, so this was not being filmed. Not yet.

My neatly folded clothes sat in a pile on the floor next to the tripod. On top of the pile lay my gun. I wondered if my body camera was still recording.

There were two other piles of folded clothes on the floor. Helene picked them up and dropped them through the bars.

"Put these on," she said.

I swallowed to moisten my parched tongue, which felt like a piece of sun-bleached driftwood that had washed up in my mouth. "Help me up," I said, and Gemma scrambled to her feet and hauled me to mine. I trembled, my knees determined to buckle. The spot where Helene's tranquilizer dart entered the front of my thigh was as tender as if it had been injected with poison. Blood oozed from my knee, where I'd torn it open when I fell, and the blood on my face had hardened to a muddy crust.

Gemma kept a firm grip on my arm. I wanted to ask her how she'd come to be here, what had happened to her, but that would have to wait.

I tried again to clear my raw throat, which felt coated with soot. Wheeler...had the 911 operator heard anything I said? Had someone gotten him out?

I moved to the bars. Helene was three feet away. Just out of reach. She didn't seem the least bit afraid that I might get out, which was disheartening. It probably meant there *was* no way out.

"What's the camera for?" I asked Helene.

"I think you can guess the answer to that," Helene said, an almost undetectable tremor to her voice. "I need you to put those on," she said again, nodding at the outfits she'd passed through the bars.

I looked down at my body, and for the first time in years, maybe for the first time ever, I loved it. The pooch under my belly button. The ripple of cellulite on the fronts of my thighs. The bumpy red rash of razor burn at my bikini line. The slight sag of my breasts, giving in to gravity. I should have treated this vessel better, should have appreciated it, abused it less. I had to find some way out of this, save my imperfect body so I could do right by it.

I picked up one pile of clothes, Gemma the other. I found that I had only one item of clothing, a retro swing dress, white smeared with red. The dress the nameless woman wore in *A Stranger Comes to Town*. Gemma also had a dress, but hers was a white baby-doll dress with a Peter Pan collar and red knee-high socks. The costume Annika Kron had worn in *The Girl and the Wolf*. I thought, crazily, of asking Gemma to switch with me. It seemed more appropriate for me to wear Annika's wardrobe. But it probably didn't matter which dress I wore. Things ended badly for both characters.

The only thing I could think to do was cooperate and stall in the hope that the fire department had arrived to save Wheeler, and that he would figure out where I was. I pulled the dress on over my head, and Gemma did the same. She whimpered as she attempted to shove her right foot into the red knee-high sock, and I saw the place where her toe had been severed. There was no bandage, only a raw, red plane where it used to be. But the flesh at the base of the wound was angry with infection. That explained the colorless sheen of Gemma's face. She probably had blood poisoning. She needed antibiotics.

"Why are you doing this?" I asked Helene once I was dressed as the nameless girl, gripping the bars to keep myself upright. "Are you helping Niklas? Or is it Anders?"

"You think I would get my family involved in what I'm doing here?" Helene shook her head. "They know nothing."

Gemma moved up beside me. I could feel fever heat coming off her even though we weren't touching.

"I never hurt anyone," Helene said. "I want you to know that."

"Then what did you do?" I asked.

Helene's eyes shifted left and right, as though looking for an escape. Not from the room, but from the situation she was in. "I provided a location. That's all. I never touched a single one of those girls. I never even saw them."

I thought of the ledger I'd found in her house, the occasional large sums of money deposited into the Larsens' personal account. If I checked the dates on those deposits, would they correspond with the dates the girls had gone missing? I should have thought to look. "Someone was paying you," I said. "Who?"

Helene shook her head, looking miserable. "I don't know. I've never known. He makes donations to the sanctuary, and in exchange I..." She rubbed nervously at her lips. "I leave the keys to the enclosures where he tells me to leave them. Then I pick them up the next morning. I don't ask questions."

"You just cash checks," I finished for her.

"For my son," she said, squaring her shoulders and raising her chin. "I did what I had to for Niklas. I never hurt anyone," she reminded us again, and tears began to run down her cheeks. "I never intended to."

She picked up my gun, removed the safety, aimed at me, and pulled the trigger.

The right side of my chest exploded in pain. I didn't realize I was falling until my back slammed the floor. Air exploded from my lungs. I searched my chest for the brightest source of agony and found the hole where the bullet had entered, near my right shoulder. My chest was on fire. Blood cascaded down my arm and soaked my shirt. I pressed the heel of my palm against the bullet hole to stanch the bleeding, biting back a cry of agony.

Helene turned the gun on Gemma, who hissed in a breath, as though she'd already been shot. Her face contorted in rage, and I saw the Gemma I knew from so long ago, not the poised, self-possessed starlet who'd replaced her.

"This isn't supposed to happen," she said, or I *thought* she said it. I could barely hear her over the sound of my own heartbeat chugging in my ears.

"He doesn't want any loose ends," Helene said, and pulled the trigger again, but there was only a hollow click.

Gemma laughed. She sounded insane. "Nice try, bitch."

Helene pocketed the gun. "Her blood will be enough to bring them," she said quietly. Then she moved to the wall of the care station, where there was a hand crank attached to another set of bars, these covering a surface-level hole, a rough, distended oval. From beyond the bars came the low thunder of growling. Two pairs of yellow eyes floated in the darkness.

Gemma wasn't laughing anymore. She pressed her back against the bars.

"You can scream," Helene said. "I think he wants you to. But you'd be surprised how little sound escapes this cavern." She pushed RECORD on the digital camera, and the red light blinked on. She staggered toward the door, holding her stomach, looking like she might be sick. "I have to go now. I can't watch."

Then she left us alone with the wolves.

49.

When Helene was gone, I peeled myself off the floor and climbed to my feet. Gemma didn't offer help. She kept her distance from me, the source of the tantalizing blood. When the wolves came through, they'd go for me first.

I wanted to ask what Gemma had meant when she told Helene this wasn't supposed to happen, but I couldn't worry about that right now. I still wasn't sure I'd heard what I thought I heard.

"What do we do?" Gemma asked, her eyes like two cigarette burns in her face, round and red and feverish.

"I don't know." I clutched my wound, pulsing out blood, my mind flipping rapidly through conversations I'd had with Blitz's handler about establishing oneself as dominant against an aggressive animal. Stand up tall and hold your ground. Look the dog in the eyes and know that you are the one in charge. Most important, feel no fear. That was a big ask. I was bleeding all over the wolves' den, and as they crept closer I saw their lips pulled up to show tongues whipping from between their teeth, tasting my blood on the air.

"We're going to die," Gemma said, her voice trembling. I didn't look at her, didn't want to take my eyes off the wolves. "I want to tell you something."

"What is it?" I was barely listening to her. It took all my energy and focus just to stay on my feet.

"I did call you that night," she said, her eyes blazing, wide and manic. "The night Miranda disappeared."

I forgot about the wolves, turned to Gemma, blinking away the black spots starting to burst in my vision, which probably meant I was losing too much blood to stay conscious much longer.

"Why did you lie?"

Gemma's chin trembled, and tears began to fall. Was she acting? Was this real? Was any of this real? It felt like a nightmare. No, not a nightmare. A Kron film, and I had unwittingly been cast as the lead.

I grabbed Gemma's shoulders, crying out in pain as I tried to use my right arm. The wolves snarled at my sudden movement. "Do you know what happened that night?"

Gemma nodded, and I felt like I took my first deep breath in fifteen years. There was an answer. An explanation. I would not die without knowing. She would finally tell me the truth.

She opened her mouth to speak, but before she could utter a single syllable she was interrupted by a loud click, followed by a creaking sound. We turned at once to see the door to the care station opening, and Niklas stepping inside. Gemma and I both gaped at him in disbelief as he crossed the room quickly and inserted a key into the lock to our cage. He turned it and flung the door open, waving frantically with one arm.

The wolves lunged at the same time we did, but Gemma and I were safe on the other side of the bars by the time they reached us. Niklas slammed the cage door just as the wolves hit the bars, snarling in ravenous fury.

"Thank you," I panted.

Niklas's eyes widened as he realized much of the red on my swing dress was my own blood. "Follow me," he said, and walked past us to the door.

I hesitated, glancing at Gemma, who wouldn't meet my eyes now. She hurried after Niklas, giving me no time to question her further about her revelation moments before. I grabbed my coat off the floor and pulled it on over the bloodied dress. I was shivering so hard I felt like I was having a seizure. My feet were cartoon anvils, my whole body seeming to densify to dark matter like a dying star, growing heavier with each step.

"Where is she?" I asked Niklas. "Where is Helene?"

"I don't know."

"Do you know what she did?"

He glanced back at me with the unscarred side of his face, his good eye filled with some sadness, but mostly bewilderment.

"Not until tonight," he said softly. "Annika emailed me the videos of—" He took a shuddering breath. "Of them. Of all of them. The missing girls and the wolves. Everyone but herself. And you," he said, nodding at Gemma, and then lowering his eyes again. "She must have killed them. My mother."

I didn't argue with him about whether this was true, or whether it had actually been Annika who'd sent him an email. I'd had plenty of my own correspondence with Annika, or whoever was pretending to be her. I wanted to ask what the videos showed, but just then I heard the door opening at the other end of the tunnel. Helene had returned. She must have realized Niklas was here with us now, and she'd come to stop him. Because the tunnel was curved, she wouldn't see us immediately when she came inside, but as soon as she realized our cage was empty she'd come for us. Niklas froze for one instant and then grabbed the nearest doorknob and ushered Gemma and me into a care station, easing the door shut.

There was an inhuman shriek that made every hair on my body prickle. We were in Tocsin's care station.

"She's going to hear," Gemma hissed, and snatched up the tranquilizer gun racked on the wall, the same kind Helene had used to shoot me in the woods. But instead of pointing it at Tocsin, she aimed it at Niklas.

"Please, give it to me," Niklas said softly. "I know how to use it." He took a step toward Gemma, reaching for the gun.

"Seems simple enough to me," Gemma said, and pulled the trigger. A dart hit Niklas in the center of his chest. His eyes went wide, and then immediately began to droop. He sagged to his knees, and then slumped to his side, long hair falling to hide his face.

I stared at my sister, uncomprehending. She had come unhinged. Maybe it was the fever cooking her brain. Or maybe this was the real Gemma, the one who'd been kept like a secret prisoner for so many years and had finally been set free.

"I'm going to feed that cunt to her own wolves. That fucking bitch. Those fucking assholes!" Gemma babbled. "I was supposed to escape. I was supposed to be the hero. That was the plan. That was the fucking plan!"

"Wh-what are you...talking about?" I could barely hear my own voice, and Gemma ignored me anyway.

She bent and fished in Niklas's pocket until she found the keys he'd used to unlock our cage. Then she checked to make sure the tranquilizer gun had more darts ready to go. On the other side of the bars, Tocsin continued to yowl shrilly. Gemma smiled at the lioness. "Good kitty. Let her know exactly where we are."

I sagged against the wall. "Gemma, what did you do...?" The black spots popping in my vision were now more like dark, swimming squid, inking out my consciousness.

Gemma backed up until she could not be seen through the little window that looked into the room, but Niklas would be clearly visible lying on the ground. Rapid footsteps approached, paused outside the door.

A second later, the door flew open and Helene dove to her son's side. She didn't even look in Gemma's direction until the tranquilizer dart struck her in the arm. Then she let out a strangled cry, clawing at the dart a moment before collapsing next to her son.

Gemma gave a gleeful, witchy cackle and set the gun aside. She grabbed the sedated woman's ankles and started dragging her toward the door, which had swung closed on its spring.

"Hold the door open," she commanded me. When I didn't answer, she finally looked in my direction and found me pointing the tranquilizer gun at her, my arms quivering as I fought to keep it trained on my sister.

"Put it down," Gemma ordered, eyes cold and stern. "This isn't the time."

"It's the only time. What did you do, Gemma?"

My sister released Helene's ankles and faced me, looking like someone recently bitten by a zombie, halfway to becoming a monster. All the urges waking, but still contained inside a vaguely pretty package.

"I'll tell you since you're about to bleed out anyway.

This time I'll make sure you're actually dead. Not that you were supposed to die at all. You were supposed to live, *Olivia*. It was all about *you*. Miranda shouldn't have even been there that night. I never gave a fuck about Miranda. She was nothing. She was nobody. *You* were the one who was always in my way, always showing me up, getting the lead. I was the poor man's Olivia Hill, even though I was prettier and thinner and every bit as talented as you. Everyone wanted to watch *you*. They were going to cut me from *The Hills Have PIs*. Did you know that? Just cut me, make you the solo face of the show! I would have ended up a plotline, another disappearance for you to solve. It was always supposed to be the two of us! But the studio heard I was drinking too much, partying. I had become an insurance risk, but I only did those things because *you* were making me crazy. I needed to take you down a few pegs, so I asked a couple of friends to help me out. They were just as excited to fuck your shit up as I was, Liv. You really rubbed a lot of people the wrong way. You didn't even remember meeting them. You're such a self-involved snob."

Her tirade left me reeling. I struggled uselessly to recall these "friends" of hers, people I'd apparently met before, but the only thing that came to mind was a pair of bright-green eyes.

"Who...who were they?"

"For you, just two more guys fawning over you at one of those stupid fan mixers Desiree made us go to. For me, they were far more useful. I saw the way you brushed them off. Their attention meant nothing to you. But one of them was obsessed with you, and you crushed him with your disinterest. But not me. *I* talked to them. *I* listened. *I* understood that they were more than fans. They were special.

"We made a plan to get you alone, somewhere nice and private. I called you from a burner phone. I pretended to be drunk, but I hadn't had a single drop to drink that night. I asked you to come and get me, come and save me like the hero of the story, and you fell for the whole thing. My friends were waiting for you at the party. A party I never even went to. The whole thing was a trap, and you fell right in. The only problem was that you took Miranda with you. She was never supposed to be there, so... I guess it's your fault she's gone."

"She... she's dead?"

Gemma shrugged. "You still believe she's out there somewhere? God, you're an idiot. You always thought you were the smart one, but you're so fucking naive. My friends killed her, bashed her head in with a rock and got rid of her body. They had to. She'd seen too much. There was no other choice. But I wasn't involved in any of that. They took care of everything."

I couldn't stay on my feet any longer. Gemma's admission had sapped the rest of my strength. I lowered myself to my knees, sat on the backs of my heels, still leaning against the wall. Still pointing the tranquilizer gun at Gemma. But gravity was pulling the muzzle toward the floor.

"What about Helene? What was supposed to happen with her?"

"What was supposed to happen was that I would let her keep me in captivity for a few days, make it look like I was one of the Dark Road girls, but that someone else had sedated me and stashed me here. Then I would escape, and you would be a wolf snack. I had to cut my little toe off to make it seem real. I didn't mean for the fucking thing to get infected, but I've been hiding in one of the empty animal dens since yesterday, and it was disgusting in there.

But blood poisoning will make my story even more sympathetic."

"You coming here, pretending to help me...that was all part of it?"

"It was a last-minute agreement, but I could hardly say no." Her smiled turned bitter. "Not without consequences."

"Who...arranged all of this?"

"He likes to be called the Wolf King." She took a step closer to me. "I'm not a monster, Liv. Believe me when I say your career was the only thing that was supposed to die."

She grabbed for the gun.

I wrenched the muzzle up and used the last of my strength to pull the trigger. The dart went straight into her eye, and Gemma let out a scream that matched Tocsin's banshee shrieks. Then her scream faded and she joined Helene and Niklas on the floor.

I knew I should make an effort to drag myself from the room, lock Gemma and Helene inside so I'd be safe from them, but I had neither the blood nor the energy to make that happen.

I lay down on the cold floor, touching my coat pocket where the body camera was still securely fixed. Still recording. No matter what happened, I had gotten Gemma's confession on camera, and Helene's, too.

I closed my eyes. The last thing I was aware of before darkness swallowed me was the distant sound of a hysterically barking dog.

50.

The next time I opened my eyes, I was in a moving ambulance. Wheeler sat across from me, his face blackened from smoke and his eyes red as two raw bullet holes. He looked like a coal miner who'd been trapped underground for a few days. But he was alive, and appeared to be unhurt.

I tried to sit up, but I was strapped to a gurney with an IV needle stuck in my wrist, connected to a bag of blood on a stand.

"Lie still," Wheeler said, touching my forehead. "You've lost a lot of blood."

"H-how?" I said, my voice a dry croak. "How did you...find me?"

"Blitz," Wheeler said. "It was a good call bringing him. He found me at the cottage and barked his head off until the fire department and the cops arrived. Then he led everyone to the sanctuary and you."

I nodded. "Told you not to...sell him short. Or you." I touched his hand. "Wheeler, I need you—" I coughed.

Paused to swallow, wet my sand trap of a throat. "I need you to...find my coat."

"Your coat?"

I nodded. "Body camera. Gemma...she confessed."

His eyes widened. He began to search around the back of the ambulance until one of the paramedics turned around and asked testily, "What do you need, sir?"

"Just looking for her coat."

"It's in a box under the bench."

Wheeler fished around under the bench until he found it. He held it up. It was soaked in blood.

"The left pocket." I lowered my voice so the paramedics wouldn't overhear. "Give it to the sheriff, but not until you've downloaded the footage onto my laptop."

. . . .

Stone's Throw was too small to have its own hospital, so I was taken to the nearest medical center thirty miles away. An emergency room surgeon dug the bullet out of my shoulder, and an intern with a semi-steady hand stitched up the lacerations on my face and leg. I would have scars.

Hydrocodone was my best friend the following day, when I woke in a dim room with curtains pulled over the window.

A foggy blur of a man sat in a chair in the corner of the room. I blinked at him a few times before my eyes cleared, and the blur became Sheriff Lot. Seeing my eyes open, he stood and came to the side of the bed. He offered me a sip of water from an insulated mug with a plastic straw protruding from the top. I attempted to sit up, but fell back at a roar of pain from my shoulder. I hissed through my teeth, but batted the sheriff's hands away when he tried to help me.

"I can do it." My lips were parched. I tried to moisten them, but my tongue was about as useful as a strip of Styrofoam. I used my good arm to take the mug from Lot and continued to sip at the water until I could speak without sounding like a throat cancer survivor.

"So," I said, eyeing the sheriff, who waited with his arms crossed over his chest, never taking his eyes off me. "Did I earn my paycheck?"

"Yours and mine both," the sheriff said drily.

"I accept PayPal."

"Hilarious. Do you mind if I open the curtains?"

He didn't wait for my answer before parting them. I squinted in the light, but I didn't mind the sudden onslaught of brightness. I'd been in the dark long enough.

I remembered every word of what Gemma told me before I shot her with the tranquilizer dart. I thought her admission might jog my actual memories, but I still couldn't remember anything. Not her phone call. Not her friends who'd set a trap for me. Not the crash. Nothing.

Nothing but green eyes without a face to go with them.

Miranda was dead. At least now I knew. I still had unanswered questions in regard to her death (Where was her body? What were the names of Gemma's friends, the ones who'd done the actual killing? Where were they now, and how would I make them pay for what they'd done?), but the most important question had been resolved. And I'd been right about Gemma all along. That truth was less satisfying than I had expected it to be. Knowing my sister had conspired to destroy my career and had, in the process, gotten Miranda killed would take some processing.

Lot leaned against the wall by the window. His skin

looked looser today, like it no longer fit him. The sag of his cheeks made his acne scars appear deeper, but he was still handsome in that Marlboro Man way that had never appealed to me. Maybe it was time to try something new, though. Be a new me. Not Olivia Hill and not Liv Hendricks. Someone else entirely. I could feel her taking shape inside me already.

"Did Wheeler give you the footage from my body camera?" I asked.

"He did indeed."

I took in a huge breath that expanded my chest and hurt my wounded shoulder. But I could handle physical pain. It was the emotional variety I'd never been good with.

"Where's Gemma?" I asked.

"Here in the hospital," Lot said. "Recovering. The stump of her toe was badly infected. She had sepsis, and she lost the eye you shot her in. I don't know if that's what you were aiming for, but you hit the bull's-eye. Literally. The tip went dead center into her pupil."

This news should have brought vindication, but I only felt remorse. Not for Gemma's eye. She deserved worse than the loss of her peripheral vision. What I regretted was that I had relinquished who I was and become her, the irresponsible, self-indulgent train wreck, and that gave her the freedom to become me. Maybe the universe demanded that kind of balance. Or maybe we were just a couple of fucked-up ladies raised inside a fucked-up system. When it came down to it, Gemma was a hollow girl just like me. A series of masks and facades and archetypes and clichés we had embodied more often than we had been ourselves, for so many years that there was no self anymore. Our identities had never belonged to us. I had never been who I thought I was, and neither had she.

We'd never truly been sisters. We'd only played them
on TV.

"You okay?" Lot asked.

"Pretty far from it, if you want the truth."

"That's understandable."

"Is my mom here?"

"She and her lawyer are keeping your sister company
now."

"What about Helene?"

The sheriff's mouth compressed to a tight, straight dash.
No doubt he was feeling a measure of embarrassment that
I had done what he couldn't, found someone who was
at least tangentially involved in the Dark Road disappearances. But I'd also been left a trail of bread crumbs to lead
me in the right direction. I'd had help from @AnnikaKron.

"Helene we arrested. We released Jonas Kron. He told
me to tell you thank you, by the way. He'll probably offer
you a part in his next film to show you his gratitude."

I said nothing. I'd lived a Jonas Kron film over the last
three days. I felt like I was still living it. Unresolved plot
threads remained...

"Did you arrest Gemma?" I asked.

"We will," he said. "I'm not sure when or for what.
We still don't know exactly what she did, and she's not
talking. Right now her lawyer has her on lockdown. No
one but her doctors and I have access to her. But I can
tell you she's not answering questions about anything,
not just the stuff she said to you last night. She won't
talk about her abduction either."

"Because it was fake. She was never abducted."

"I know that, but she claims everything she confessed
just before you shot her was caused by her fever, that she
was delusional and doesn't remember saying any of it."

"She's lying."

"The Internet agrees with you."

"What do you..." I trailed off, remembering vaguely what I'd asked Wheeler to do before he handed my body camera footage over to the police.

"Your friend Chris Wheeler had a busy night," Lot said. "Your sister's lawyer has demanded the video he posted be taken down, but it's already viral. Even some national news channels have picked it up."

"What about Niklas and Anders?" I asked. "How are they doing?"

"Considering they just found out Helene was renting out the wolf sanctuary for illegal activities, I would say they're doing exactly as you'd expect."

"Do you know yet what went on there? How much did she tell you? Did you find out who was paying her?"

He shook his head. "We don't know much yet because, if she's to be believed, she doesn't actually know much. The donations were made through a shadow corporation. She says her only contact with the person who paid her was through Kronophile chat rooms, where he went by the screen name WolfKing18. But we don't have the—"

"Did you say WolfKing18?"

He nodded. "Does that mean something to you?"

"I don't know. Maybe." I shook my head. "I'll let you know when I figure it out. What else have you got?"

He hesitated. "I shouldn't tell you. It hasn't been made public yet."

"You owe me, Clarice. I handed you a really big quid."

He sighed. "I'm swearing you to secrecy here. If you tell anyone or use this on your series—"

"I won't. Trust me. The series is done."

Something in my tone must have convinced him, because he took a breath, wiping his fingers over his eyes. "It's starting to look like the previous sheriff had dealings with the Wolf King, too. One of the things Helene did tell us was that this Wolf King assured her she would have no problems with local law enforcement."

"Jesus. You're starting to look like a real saint. Did anyone ever try to buy you off?"

"Only you."

"I did not."

"You kind of did."

"Whatever." I waved a hand at him, a gesture that was not worth the pain it caused in my shoulder.

Lot glanced at the clock and began to edge toward the door. "Look, there's still plenty we don't know, but eventually we'll sort this mess out. I'll update you again when I can."

"You don't need to take my statement?" I asked.

"Your statement is all over the Internet," he said. "Get some rest, Liv. I'll go pick up whatever scraps you left for me."

⁕   ⁕   ⁕

I turned on the TV mounted across the wall from my hospital bed and flipped through the news stations, watched as my footage was broadcast for the entire country to see. I muted the volume and used my room phone to call the Eden Tree. I asked for Chris Wheeler's room, but the phone rang without answer. I hung up, figuring Wheeler was sleeping. He'd had a long night, too.

I turned off the TV and closed my eyes, fatigue settling on me like a fog. I didn't mean to fall asleep, but it didn't seem I had a choice. My body insisted.

I woke up when a nurse came to check my bandages and give me another dose of pain medication.

"You had a visitor while you were out," she said. "Porter Morrison. I told him you needed to rest. He left this for you." The nurse patted a white envelope lying on the night-stand. My name was written on the front.

I opened the envelope. Inside was a single ticket to a special-event film screening at the Stone's Throw Film Festival. The title of the film was *Girl on a Dark Road*.

51.

Wheeler showed up right as I was walking out of the hospital. The whites of his eyes were still red and irritated, but he had showered and no longer smelled like a piece of smoked meat.

"Shouldn't you be in bed?" he asked.

"The doctor said I was free to go." This was a lie. I hadn't asked for permission to leave. I'd simply gotten out of bed, pulled the IV from my arm, and walked out in my hospital robe. There was no way they'd discharge me already, but I wasn't their prisoner.

"Does that mean we're going home?" Wheeler asked.

Home. It was my beacon, my stakes, my whole reason for coming here. Los Angeles. My loft. My excuse for a life. I had fought to keep it, and it appeared I had won. But I didn't feel that way yet. And I wasn't even sure I wanted my life—or anything resembling it—back.

"Not yet," I told Wheeler. "There's one last thing I have to do."

Wheeler drove us back to the Eden Tree in my car with

air from the broken window keeping us chilled, waking me up and sharpening my thoughts, which had been dulled by pain medication. He listened in silence as I told him what I'd learned from the sheriff, and frowned deeply when I showed him the ticket Porter had dropped off for me.

"Liv, you almost died last night. You can't go to a film screening."

"I'm going."

"Give me one good reason why. You did what you came to do. Do you know what people online are saying?"

"No. I haven't seen my phone since Helene shot me with a tranquilizer."

"They're calling you a hero. They want more of you, more investigations. You did it, Liv. You're done. Let the police deal with the rest of this mess."

I shook my head, staring at the invitation in my hands. "It's not over here."

"How do you know?"

In my head, I saw those electric green eyes again.

"I just know."

*   *   *

When I looked in the mirror back in my room at the Eden Tree I hardly recognized myself. My hair was streaked with dried blood, and a bandage covered the laceration under my eye. I peeled it back and winced at the black stitches underneath. I was probably going to need some kind of cosmetic surgery. Maybe I could convince Kron to foot the bill for that, too.

I asked Wheeler to go the front desk and retrieve a couple of trash bags so I could cover my bandages in the shower. While he was gone, I opened my laptop. I needed another look at the footage from the fairy-tale cottage out behind Kron's Red House, which Wheeler had thankfully not included in the edit he uploaded. I scrubbed through the video until I found what I was looking for, the detail I had noticed the previous night. I peered closely at the man in the wolf mask who had been sitting in the chair, the one who'd met my eyes and waved at me like we knew each other, like he was a friend saying hello. It was barely visible, but there…a glint of metal in the center of his tie. A round tiepin, black in the center, ringed in silver.

My stomach knotted, and my eyes slid to the film screening invitation sitting next to my laptop.

I went to my Shot in the Dark profile next. There were hundreds of messages in my inbox, most of them with subject headings that suggested my next investigation. I ignored them all and clicked on the most recent message from Jonas Kron.

Dear Ms. Hendricks,

I have wired another $20k into your bank account, as promised. Thank you for clearing my name. There are still many unanswered questions as to the fate of my niece, Annika, but you almost died trying to find out the truth. You earned the second half of your payment.

I know you are recovering from your injuries. However, I want to make you one last offer. You received the invitation to tonight's special screening, did you not? I would very much like for you to attend. If you are able to make it and stay for the entire film, I will pay you another $10k. Plus, you will receive a special bonus surprise after the credits. I promise it's one you won't want to miss.

I hope to see you soon.

Best,

Jonas Kron

I closed the Shot in the Dark website, opened *LA Femme Online*, and found the post Freya McBride had written about me, the one that had exploded my life. "A Star Burns Out: Whatever Happened to Olivia Hill?" I scrolled to the comments section, where there were now over a thousand posts, and scanned the screen names until I found the thread I was looking for.

WolfKing18 Liv Hendricks is the best thing about Bullshit Hunters. She deserves her own show. I'd watch that.

1NeverApologize Like anyone would give this train wreck her own show

WolfKing18 She doesn't need anyone to give it to her. These days all anyone needs is a camera. She should pitch something on Kickstarter or Shot in the Dark. I'd back her.

I opened a new browser window and went to Twitter, clicked on my direct message feed. I typed a message to @AnnikaKron.

> **LH:** I know who you are.

Maybe a part of me had known even before I saw that silver tiepin on the man in the wolf mask. The signs were there. I hadn't wanted to see them.

@AnnikaKron responded within seconds.

AK: Finally ?

The message included a video attachment. I clicked PLAY. A woman dressed in a familiar black sheath dress, wearing a raven's mask, entered a small bedroom filled with people in various states of undress and various states of copulation.

The woman in the raven mask looked straight at the camera, and then turned around and walked out.

The woman, of course, was me.

* * *

Wheeler helped me get undressed and fashion a waterproof casing out of the trash bags for my bandaged chest and leg. I stepped into the shower and let water run over my hair and body. The bottom of the tub turned the color of Jonas Kron's house. I took my time showering but didn't have the energy to bother with my hair and makeup, or to put on anything dressier than jeans and a hoodie. I'd been shot less than twenty-four hours ago. That gave me license to keep it casual.

Wheeler sat on my bed, his back against the headboard, his laptop open on his thighs as he monitored the ongoing news about the Dark Road and tracked my upward mobility on social media, calling out occasional tweets of support and devotion. There were even a few apologies from haters.

@Director_ElliotHoyt tweeted:

> I was wrong about @LivHendricks. Forgive me, Liv?

I was not currently responding to anything on social media, but I asked Wheeler if he'd mind tweeting back to @Director_ElliotHoyt.

> @Director_ElliotHoyt Go to hell.

Wheeler closed the laptop and sighed when he saw me dressed and ready to go. "Can I at least come with you?" he asked.

"I only have one ticket."

Someone knocked on the door then. I answered, and was not surprised to find Porter on the other side, looking polished and more sophisticated than usual in a dark-gray suit, white shirt, and black tie. No tiepin this time. I supposed he didn't need it anymore. It had served its purpose.

"I called the hospital," he said. "They told me you'd left." I said nothing, and he shifted uncomfortably when I didn't let him in. "I guess you're probably not going to the premiere after . . . everything."

"I wouldn't miss it," I said.

He smiled. "Can I give you a ride?"

I thought about saying no. That was the smart thing to do. But there were questions I needed answered, and Porter was the only one who could do it.

I just wished I still had my gun.

* * *

"You're not wearing your hidden camera," I said, keeping my eyes on Porter as he drove us through the dark orchard toward town.

He stared straight ahead, and for a moment I thought he might pretend not to know what I was talking about. Then a guilty, slightly gleeful smile broke across his mouth. He looked at me with his plain, unremarkable brown eyes. For some reason brown seemed the wrong color. In my mind, I saw those green eyes again, the color of kryptonite. *My* kryptonite.

He reached over to put his hand on my knee. I moved my legs out of his reach. The idea of him touching me— that he had ever touched me—made my skin writhe. He was not the kind, nerdy, small-town fanboy I'd begun to fall for the moment I met him. I still wasn't sure *what* he was. That's what I needed to find out. Not for money. Not for Jonas Kron. Just for me. I had to know what was behind his mask.

"You were at Kron's party last night, in the cottage out back," I said. "You were one of the wolves. I didn't realize it was you at the time, but I was wearing a body camera inside my mask. I looked at the footage when I got back from the hospital. I saw that tiepin you're always wearing."

"I never claimed to be a saint," he said, still smiling. "And you can hardly blame me for blowing off a little steam at the party after you canceled on me at the last minute. And lied to me about it, it turns out, because you *were* there."

"You knew I would be. You saw the dress bag on my bed when you were in my room yesterday."

"Did I? I don't remember. I was too busy screwing your brains out, as you requested."

My cheeks flushed, and I was disgusted by the thrill of

hot nerves that swarmed in my stomach at the memory. "That was before I knew who you were," I said.

"Who am I?"

"You're WolfKing18. You've been manipulating me from the start. From before the start. You planted the whole crowdsourcing idea in my head with your comments. You filmed me while I slept my first night here and sent me that video. You left the trail of bread crumbs for me to follow. And you're the one who paid Helene for use of the Wolf Sanctuary. She told Sheriff Lot the screen name of her mysterious benefactor from the Kronophile chatrooms. WolfKing18. That's you. Not that you don't use other handles when it suits your needs, @AnnikaKron."

He turned his eyes back to the road, staring straight ahead.

"You didn't think I would figure it out," I said. "You've been one step ahead of me the entire time I've been here."

He snorted a laugh.

"What's funny?"

"Me being one step ahead of you," he said. "More like fifty. You've barely scratched the surface."

"Okay, then tell me what I'm missing," I said. "I'm not wearing any recording devices. It'll be my word against yours. I just want to know what happened to the Dark Road girls."

I didn't expect him to admit to anything, but when he glanced at me I saw arrogant delight dancing in his eyes, and I realized he *wanted* to tell me his big secret. He wanted to take off his mask. I knew the feeling.

"Why should I trust you?" he asked.

"You probably shouldn't. But I think you want to."

He hesitated, but only for a moment before nodding. "I'll give you a little behind-the-scenes sneak peek, but that's it," he said, a smile tugging at the corners of his mouth. "I don't want to spoil the main event. What do you want to know? Ask me anything, and maybe I'll answer. Or maybe I won't."

"Are they dead, the girls you abducted?"

"First of all, I didn't 'abduct' anyone," he said, growing serious. "Second, to assume they're dead is a failure of imagination. Those girls chose their fates. They came to me, not the other way around."

"You expect me to believe that?"

He shrugged. "It's the truth."

"Explain."

He took a deep breath. "Well, we don't have much time before the show begins, so I'm going to give you the short story, which is this: Many years ago, I met a nice young lady in a Kronophile chat room. She said it was her dream to be in one of Jonas's films. I told her I could offer the next best thing. I invited her to come to Stone's Throw so we could film an homage to Kron in the locations where he had shot his most famous scenes. Only our homage would not be limited by the strictures Jonas had to abide by. We agreed not to fake anything. The blood would be real. The pain would be real. The penetration would be *very* real."

I stared at him, my stomach clenching in horrified realization. "You made Kron porn? That's what this was all about?"

He looked offended. "You make it sound so pedestrian! It was more than that. More than porn. More than a fan film. It was a continuation of the stories Jonas told. It was real women embodying his characters and story lines, but also making them their own. *Our* own. I turned life into art. Reality into plot."

"You told me you weren't a writer," I pointed out. "You said you'd never finished anything."

"I hadn't when I told you that." He smiled. "Now I have. But it would be disrespectful to make scripted art inspired by Jonas Kron. You don't *write* a Kron story. You create a catalyst for drama, and then you capture it as it unfolds. That's what I did, with the help of a select few like-minded Kronophiles over the years. It wasn't easy to find the true acolytes, the ones who would give it all. The ones who would offer themselves as willing sacrifices to the Wolf King, and let him decide their fate."

"Did you kill them?" I asked again, and once again Porter looked insulted.

"Liv, please…if I tell you that it will ruin the twist. Ask me something else."

"Fine," I said. "What does Soren have to do with all this?"

"Poor Soren." Porter sighed. "He was doomed to disappoint his father. But I'm hopeful that might change tonight. I couldn't have done any of this without his help."

"Or his money," I said. "Is that what you meant when you said he was executive producing?"

"Someone has to write the checks," Porter said. "Besides, I could only be in so many places at once. I have a business to operate. I can't be running around town in masks, waiting for you to show up. The independently wealthy have a lot of time on their hands."

"Soren was the wolf at the cottage," I guessed. "And in the window of the Larsens' house. While he was there, I'm guessing he set that projector up to play Annika's scene from *The Girl and the Wolf*."

"We had to give you a suspect to chase," Porter said. "If we didn't keep you busy, you might have started to look too closely at Soren and me. I gathered from our conversations you were already suspicious of Soren. Maybe you should start doing this full-time. You have good instincts. But you should understand, Soren and I did what we did for different reasons. I wanted to create something great, something bigger than me, and my inn, and this town. Soren wanted to stick it to dear old Dad. He thinks all of this will be a slap in the face to Jonas. I'm hoping it will be the opposite. I want Jonas to see what we've made as the ultimate tribute."

"I'm guessing he's not a big fan of cover bands."

Porter turned a cold gaze on me, and I felt a twinge of fear. I readied myself to grab the door handle and bail from the moving vehicle if it came to that.

"When you see what we've made, you'll understand," he said, and faced forward again. "You may not like it, but you'll have to appreciate it."

I relaxed slightly and moved my hand back to my lap. Porter wasn't going to try to kill me in this car. He was too anxious for me to witness his masterpiece.

"You say you didn't abduct any of the Dark Road girls. So what *did* you do to make them disappear?"

He clucked his tongue. "See, that would be a spoiler."

"I don't mind spoilers."

"But I do. I've worked hard on this, Liv! You have no idea how many years, how much time and effort and thought went into all of this. Don't get me wrong. When Soren and I started our first project, we had no idea what the scope would be. All we knew was that we wanted to make something. We had access to everything we needed. Cameras, lights, edit bays, even actors. Though our principal characters didn't actually know they were participants in our project."

"Was Annika your lead?" I asked, thinking of what Niklas had told me about Annika and the *Ulv Konge*, how it wouldn't leave her alone. How she had set the Wolf Woods on fire to make it stop tormenting her.

"In the beginning, yes," Porter said. "I really thought the story was about her. When I saw Annika on the set of *The Girl and the Wolf*, I knew she had true talent. She made acting, even in Kron's improvisational style, look effortless. I have to admit, I was a bit obsessed with her, but the feeling was certainly not mutual. She had no interest in friendship with Soren and me, even though she was living in Soren's house. She preferred Niklas Larsen, which Soren and I both found insulting. So we decided to teach her a lesson, humble her a little. It started out innocently enough, a few mysterious phone calls and notes, a little LSD dissolved in her vodka. We didn't intend for it to go as far as it did." He glanced at me. "Sorry, here I go with the spoilers again. The point is, sometimes inspiration strikes and you simply go where it leads." He smiled over at me. "That's what happened with you, Liv. I doubt you'll believe me when I say this, but you're my muse. When I first met Annika, I thought she was going to be my greatest inspiration. But she wasn't even Jonas's first choice for the lead in *The Girl and the Wolf*. It was you. It *should* have been you. And this story, *Girl on a Dark Road*, isn't Annika's story. It's yours. It's always been yours."

We entered Stone's Throw Village, and Porter pulled to the curb in front of the October Palace, where there was a line out the door, people waiting to enter the theater and see the mysterious masterpiece.

"This is where we say goodbye," Porter said.

"Aren't you coming in?" I asked.

"I'll be watching. Just not from here. I'm sorry to say this, Liv, but this might be the last time we speak in person for a while. I would kiss you goodbye, but the way you're looking at me now I think I'd like to remember a different kiss as our last."

"What makes you think I won't call Sheriff Lot the second I'm out of this car?" I asked.

He smiled. "Because then you won't see how the story ends. I promise, you've been waiting for this a very, *very* long time."

52.

I filed into the lobby with the rest of the guests, gazing around in appreciation at the revitalized interior of the old Hollywood-style theater, art deco detailing and merlot-red velvet draped on the walls. There was a bar set up in the lobby, and bartenders in white shirts and black vests poured champagne and handed out slices of pie. For once I was not tempted to hit the bar.

I scanned the faces in the lobby, found the one I was looking for.

Jonas Kron stood amid industry players, mostly balding men in expensive suits, though there was one woman with a severe haircut, elbowing her way into the group, leaning in with all her might. Jonas gazed over their heads at nothing in particular, clearly paying no attention to what was being said to him.

I made my way through the crowd and waved my hand to catch his eye. He stared at me a moment before shooing the Hollywood vultures. They dispersed, eyeing me hungrily. I saw one of their mouths make the word *biopic*.

When they were gone, I asked Jonas the question I should have asked the first time we met. "Did you hire me?"

Jonas blinked at me, confused. "Hire you to do what?"

"That's what I thought." Even when we were alone, he'd never spoken of our arrangement. Kron hadn't backed my project. I had been a pawn from the very beginning. At least I wasn't the only one.

"Jonas, have you seen *Girl on a Dark Road* yet?"

Jonas shook his head. "No one has. Soren curated it. I don't even know what the film is about."

Just then the lights dimmed, and a bell chimed, urging the guests to take their seats. The crowd flowed eagerly toward the theater entrances.

The show was about to begin.

*   *   *

There were only a few seats left by the time I entered the theater, so I was forced to sit on the front row, the last place I wanted to sit. This was the kind of antiquated movie theater with a stage and a plush red curtain hanging in front of the screen. The seats were newly upholstered in matching red velvet. The sconces that lined the walls and the ornate, filigreed design on the ceiling looked to be the original art deco details.

It was a gorgeous theater, but I had a feeling we were about to see something on the screen that was anything but beautiful.

The lights lowered. The curtain went up. Cinematic music blared, and an image appeared on screen.

It was us. The audience. We were being filmed at that very moment, and the footage was being projected onto the screen. For a full minute, we stared at ourselves, shifting in our seats, growing more and more uncomfortable. We were here to watch, not be watched. Then the lights dimmed completely, and the image on screen faded to underexposed footage filmed through the windshield of a car driving on a narrow road at night. The car accelerated suddenly and caught up to a red BMW.

I recognized both the car and the road.

The road was Mulholland Drive in Los Angeles.

The car was mine.

No. Not mine. It was Olivia Hill's. I knew it even before I read the license plate.

Cut to a black screen, and the title of the film:

> # Girl on a Dark Road

The title disappeared, and a caption took its place:

> ## Prologue: Annika Kron
> ## 2003
> ## 18 years old

The caption dematerialized as an image faded in, a stunning young woman with white-blond hair that hung needle-straight down her back. I couldn't see her face. Whoever was filming her was following her from a distance. I guessed she didn't know she was being followed. Didn't know she was being filmed. But I would have recognized her even without the caption to identify her. Even if she hadn't been wearing her wardrobe from *The Girl and the*

Wolf, the white baby-doll dress and red, knee-high socks.

Of course it was her. Annika. She was the beginning. She was, as the caption stated, the prologue to this whole story. But not its ingénue.

Annika carried a single item in her right hand: a two-gallon can of gasoline.

The camera angle changed. The cameraman must have found a way to get ahead of her, because now we saw her from the front, walking toward the camera. A black line obscured part of the view. I thought, but couldn't be entirely certain, that the cameraman was filming from inside the Wolf King's cottage, through one of the windows.

Annika stopped when she reached the cottage. Even from a distance, I could see her eyes were livid, wide open as though her lids had been pinned back. I'd seen that look on the faces of certain homeless people in LA, the ones who lived in a different reality from the rest of us. The ones who were surrounded by whispering demons who wanted to drag them down to hell.

Annika dropped her gas can. "*Jeg er her!*" she shouted at the cottage in Norwegian. "*Kom ut, Ulv Konge!*"

Subtitles appeared as she spoke: I'M HERE. COME OUT, WOLF KING.

When nothing happened, she crouched and picked up two rocks and hurled them at the cottage door. The camera jostled as the rocks crashed into the wood.

"*Kom og ta meg!*" Annika shrieked.

COME GET ME.

For a long moment, there was only silence, and then a low, grating rumble answered Annika's call.

"Take off your dress," said the voice of the Wolf King in English, processed through some kind of voice modulator. "Get on your knees and bow to me, girl."

"*Nei!*" Annika shouted back. "Fuck you! You can't have me!"

She twisted the cap off the gas can and began splashing gasoline wildly in a circle around the cottage. She spoke in rapid, hysterical Norwegian as she did it. When she was finished she tossed the gas can aside and reached into her pocket, withdrawing a silver Zippo lighter. She flipped it open, put her hand on the igniter. I could see that her hands and arms were shiny with sprinkles of gasoline. Her chest rose and fell as she panted, excitement making her eyes shine.

She was smiling, proud of herself. Completely manic.

The image cut to black, and a young man's voice said softly, "*Annika, stoppe.*"

A new caption appeared.

> **Part I: Olivia Hill**
> **2003**
> **17 Years Old**

The caption disappeared, and a new image faded in, a shot of a much younger Gemma Hill. Barely sixteen. She lay on a couch wearing a short denim skirt and a white tank top with no bra, nipples hard enough to pierce the fabric. She was startlingly thin, clutching a half-empty bottle of vodka between thighs whittled to the femur. I could tell she was already beyond drunk. Her eyelids drooped, more closed than open.

"Why are you filming me?" she asked, mugging into the eye of the camera, swaying like she might topple at any moment.

Jennifer Wolfe

A male voice from off screen. He sounded young. Familiar. "Tell us what you want us to do to your sister."

Gemma swigged from the vodka bottle, then leaned forward so the lens framed her lips. "I want you to ruin Olivia Hill. I don't care how you do it. Just get her out of my fucking way." She flopped back on the couch, giggling hysterically.

"What do we get out of it?" A different guy asked this question. There were two of them.

Gemma let her legs fall open, revealing the crotch of her panties. "You get this."

"I've already had that," the second guy said, and Gemma slammed her legs shut, lower lip jutting into a pout.

"What do you want, then? Money? I have money."

"How about this?" the first guy said. "We'll teach your sister a lesson that shrinks her ego to a manageable size, and we'll make sure we have video evidence of it. You can use it against her in whatever way you want. But you'll owe us a favor. We can collect on it anytime we choose. This video is our collateral to make sure you don't renege. Deal?"

Gemma leaned forward again, but this time she used a rolled dollar bill to snort a line of cocaine off the surface of a coffee table. Her eyes widened and she smiled and thrust her hand toward her offscreen "friends" to shake on it.

"Deal," she said.

The scene cut abruptly to a bedroom filled with red light. A teenage girl with long blond hair lay on a mattress, her back to the camera. Someone in a wolf mask entered the frame, close to the camera, looking straight into the lens as he adjusted it. He had eyes so unnaturally, radioactively green that even the red light in the room couldn't turn them any other color. Then he stepped out of frame, and the girl on the mattress was revealed once again. She stirred, sat up, and looked at the camera, eyes dazed and blinking.

"You're awake," the wolf said off camera.

She was.

I was.

OLIVIA HILL

2003

17 YEARS OLD; 109 LBS.

53.

Pain was the first thing I became aware of, an aching knot in my head, pulsing in rhythm with the sound of kettledrums. An orchestral score, almost a war march, blared in my ears. I dragged my lids open and saw a haze of red, like my eyes were filled with blood. I started to remember. The empty house. The boom box and the lamp with the red lightbulb. Gemma bound and gagged and nearly naked on that mattress. The video camera pointed at her.

Something hard crashing against my skull.

I sat up and blinked until the blurry images in my line of sight sharpened into focus and tried to make sense of what I saw: a man with the face of a wolf, dressed all in black. He stood a few feet away from me, next to the video camera, its red light shining.

"You're awake," he said, his voice pitched unnaturally low, like he was trying to convince me he was older than he was. I thought of Russel and Jimmy, the

guys who'd brought me there. What had happened to them? What about Gemma? Where was she?

I shook my head, trying to clear it, but all that did was make the world tilt and spin. I held my breath, waiting for the dizziness to pass. I'd never had a concussion, but I was pretty sure this was what it felt like. I turned my head slowly, taking in my situation. I was on the mattress now, but Gemma was gone.

I looked at the wolf-faced man again, and now that my eyes had focused I saw that he did not actually possess the head of a wolf. He wore a mask in the shape of a white wolf's head, one large enough to cover his entire face.

"What did you do with my sister?" I asked. My voice came out slurred, delirious.

"She's here," the wolf said. "My associate is keeping an eye on her. What we do with her depends on you."

"What do you want?" I asked. "Money?"

He laughed. "Not money. I just want you all to myself for a little while. No distractions. No paparazzi. No managers. No fans….except me, of course."

I gulped a breath, my mind and heart racing, trying to come to grips with the situation.

"Okay," I said, fighting to keep my voice calm when what I wanted to do was scream. But if I did, Miranda might hear me and come to the door instead of going for help. "Let Gemma go, and then I'll do whatever you want." They were brave words, but I wasn't sure they were true. They sounded like lines I'd been scripted, words I was supposed to say to protect my reckless sister, even though she'd gotten us into this mess.

He shook his head slowly. "That's not going to

work for me. See, if I let her go, then I don't have any way to make sure you behave yourself. But if I keep her handy, guess what? She's the one who suffers if you don't do what you're told. I know you, Olivia. I've been watching you for a long time, and I really, really like you. I feel things for you. I might even be in love with you. But I think you can be a bit of a stuck-up, arrogant bitch sometimes, and that's what this is all about. I'm going to make sure that by the time you leave this house you're nice and humble. I want you to treat people like me with the decency we deserve from now on. Because you are nothing without people like me. I'm the whole point of your existence. If I didn't watch you, you wouldn't exist."

I glared at the wolf, but I was trembling all over. "So what do we do now?"

"We get started," he said. "First things first...take off your shirt."

I hesitated, only for an instant, and the wolf tsked.

"I can tell you're not taking this seriously yet," he said, and then called out. "Cut off Gemma's little toe!"

"No!" I shouted, and grabbed the hem of my shirt, ripped it over my head. "There! I did it!"

But Gemma, in another room, was already screaming. The scream tapered into gasping sobs. "Liv, please!" she cried. "Don't let them hurt me!"

"I'll do whatever you say. Stop it!" I pleaded with the wolf. "Just tell me what you want me to do."

"That's more like it," the wolf said. I could hear the smile in his voice. "Believe me, Olivia, I didn't want it to be this way. When we first met, I hoped you would feel the same way about me that I do about you. But you didn't even give me a chance. You blew me off like

I was some pathetic nobody. Just another fan. But I am so much more than that."

I remembered what Jimmy had said back at the party where I'd gone to find Gemma, how we had met before, and I had pretended to remember him to keep him on my side, wanting to help me. But apparently the damage had already been done.

"Jimmy..." I said tentatively. "Is that you? I'm sorry...I didn't realize—"

"My name is not Jimmy," he snapped, cutting me off. "I told you my name when we met, but I bet you weren't even listening."

"I'm sorry," I said meekly. "I didn't mean to hurt your feelings."

"Aren't you sweet to apologize. It doesn't change anything, but I appreciate the effort. Now take off your jeans. And if you're going to address me as anything, call me Wolf King."

This time I didn't hesitate, though I did start to cry a little as I unbuttoned my jeans and pushed them down.

The Wolf King clucked his tongue at the sight of my plain, utilitarian underwear. "I would have thought you better than a sports bra and granny panties, Olivia. Get rid of them."

I did as I was told, crying harder now.

"Stop it," the wolf said, and I froze in the middle of pulling my bra off over my head. "Stop crying. Right. Now."

I swallowed my tears and pulled my underwear down over my hips. I tried to cover myself with my arms, but the Wolf King shook his head. "You know better," he warned.

It took all my will to let my arms fall to my sides. A sob bubbled in my throat, but I choked it down.

"Wow," he said, looking at me through the viewfinder and adjusting the angle. "Look at you. Underneath all the designer clothes and hair and makeup you're so much smaller. So vulnerable. I like seeing you this way, Olivia. I feel like I'm looking at the real you now. No costumes or characters or sets. You're just a body, like me. Now we're the same. Imperfect. Flawed."

My teeth clenched involuntarily behind my lips.

"Now you're going to perform for me, Olivia, and I want you to wipe that disgusted look off your face. Enjoy yourself, or at least pretend to. You're an actor. A good one. I'm sure you can manage it."

He told me what he wanted me to do to myself. Again, I made the mistake of hesitating, and the Wolf King laughed. "It's okay," he said. "Gemma has two little toes, but neither of them is essential. She'll live a fine life without them."

"No!" I shouted, and rushed to do as I was instructed.

"Slow down," he said, his voice lowering to a gruff croon. "Show me that you're having a good time."

I bit my lip, hoping I looked sexy, not like I was about to vomit, which I was. I tasted acid at the back of my throat, but I kept going, kept doing what I was told, and my mind began to retreat backward into the holding space where it lived when I let a character take me over. I became someone else, someone who wanted to be here, a sensual, sex-crazed submissive who craved someone telling her what to do. Someone who didn't care that all of this was being captured on video, who *actually found it that much more exciting. The Wolf King watched me in silence, and I knew he was happy with what he was seeing.*

"Stop," the Wolf King commanded suddenly, and I ceased my act. He reached into a brown paper grocery bag at his feet and removed a coil of rope.

"Get on your knees and turn around," the Wolf King said, walking toward me.

I shook my head, tears pooling in my eyes, but I was already sinking out of sight, letting that other girl have control of me. I wondered what her name was. I'd think of her as Liv. Liv could deal with what was happening to her. Liv was tougher than Olivia. She didn't mind being degraded. A sick part of her wanted it. But Olivia...she'd never even had sex. She was too busy for sex. Too haughty for some casual hookup. Too special for her first time not to be as exceptional as she was.

Moving as though in a dream, I knelt, as instructed, and felt the mattress dip as the wolf climbed onto it. He grabbed my hands and yanked them behind me, and I felt the rough scratch of the rope on my skin as he bound my wrists together. He pressed a hand into the center of my back and pushed me down until my face was against the mattress. I heard his zipper come down, and he positioned himself to enter me, but it felt like something that was happening to someone else. To Liv, not Olivia.

The pain was Liv's.

Olivia was safe. Liv was going to keep her that way.

Then the Wolf King was inside her (me). Olivia drifted in her safe place, only distantly aware of the things being done to her. She was beyond it all.

She had no idea how much time passed before the wolf stopped moving on top of her.

"What is it?" the wolf said, and she (I) looked at the door to see another guy dressed all in black, also wearing a wolf mask. Russel, or whatever his real name was.

"I heard something," Russel said.

The Wolf King pulled out of her (me) and shoved her (me) down flat on the mattress. "Where?"

"Outside. Someone's creeping around the house. What should we do?"

The wolf stood, staring down at her (me). "Stay here and don't move or we'll cut off one of your sister's nipples," he commanded, and then the two wolves left the room, closing the door behind them.

She (I) floated while they were away, our mind in some purgatory between dreaming and consciousness. We didn't hear the door open again. Didn't hear the soft footsteps rush across the floor toward us. Someone tugged frantically at the ropes binding my wrists.

Then we heard her voice. "Olivia, get up. Put your clothes on. We have to get out of here."

It was our sister. It was Miranda.

I came back to myself, or as much as I could. I still felt Liv in there, ready to take over if it all became too much for Olivia.

LIV HENDRICKS

2018

32 YEARS OLD; 135 LBS.

Facebook Fans: 56,128

Twitter Followers: 105,399

Instagram Followers: 17,013

54.

I didn't take my eyes from the screen, even though I had never wanted so badly to shut them. To hide my face. To look away from the sick, sadistic brutality. All of it real. All of it a reality I had experienced. That I had lived.

I'd been dissociated from myself for fifteen years, but now, watching my exploitation and rape on screen, surrounded by a rapt audience, I felt my two selves merging. Olivia Hill and Liv Hendricks began to fuse in furious agony. My heart, my brain, my lungs, my limbs...everything was on fire.

I clasped my sweaty hands in my lap and kept my eyes on the screen, and let myself burn.

Porter was right. This is what I'd been waiting for. This was what I had needed all these years. To know what had happened that night. To know why it had turned me into the person I was now.

Knowing would come with its own cost, but nevertheless... I watched.

OLIVIA HILL

2003

17 YEARS OLD; 109 LBS.

55.

Miranda's hands worked fast to free me from the rope that bound me. The urge to scream continued to clog my throat, making it hard to breathe, but there was no time for hysterics. We had to get Gemma and get out before the wolves returned.

"Where are they?" I whispered when I was free, grabbing my clothes off the floor and wrenching them on. I didn't bother with my bra, underwear, socks. I yanked on my jeans and T-shirt, shoved my feet into my shoes.

Miranda put a finger to her lips, tilting her head. I heard them then, distantly, the wolf boys outside, exploring the perimeter of the house, moving from front to back. Miranda tiptoed to the bedroom door, waving urgently. I grabbed her arm, and she winced as one of my fingers pressed into the gouge she'd opened up earlier, when we were driving. I felt slick blood. She must have been picking at herself while she was in the car, waiting for me to return, which I never did.

"*Did you see Gemma?*"

"*She's with them.*"

"*I know. They're holding her hostage to make me—*"

"*No, Liv. I mean she's with them. She's not tied up. She's fine. I saw her through the window when I was trying to figure out how to create a distraction. The one with the red hair . . . he was in our house that night I told you about. I didn't recognize him before because his hair was blond then, but he's the one Gemma was screwing.*"

The truth hit me, and I doubled over, biting back a sob. The pain of her betrayal was as visceral as a kick to the stomach. Jimmy and Russel. I should have realized why their names were familiar. They were the names of the male students in To Die For, Gemma's favorite movie. The names of the characters who helped Nicole Kidman off her husband, who was getting in the way of her career.

"*Come on.*" Miranda took my hand. "*They'll be back soon.*"

We bolted from the bedroom toward the front of the house. Out the front door. Down the front walk. Through the high fence that surrounded the house. I froze when we reached the street, remembering the camera. The video footage of me naked. Exposed. Doing things that would ruin me, even if people knew I'd had no choice. If that video got out, it would be over for me. The humiliation would be too much. Gemma would win, even if she lost. She would have destroyed my career, because having that video in the world would destroy me.

But there was no time to go back for the video. I had to let it go. Let me go.

Miranda pushed the car keys into my hands, and we ran. I'd parked down the street, and as we sprinted to my BMW I kept expecting to be grabbed from behind, but we made it. Tumbled into the seats. I shouldn't be driving. I still felt lost inside myself. In shock, probably. I almost asked Miranda to trade places with me, but then I saw them.

They rushed through the gate, all three of them, Gemma included. She spotted us in the car and jabbed a finger at us. I cranked the keys in the ignition, shaking so hard the motion could hardly be described as shaking. It was more of a full-body convulsion. I put the car in drive, hit the gas, peeled out as we sped away from the house, for once thankful that my mom had forced this high-octane vehicle on me.

It wasn't until we reached Mulholland that I began to gain control of my breathing. We'd made it. We'd gotten away, but I continued to clench my fists on the wheel like someone might try to tear it from my grasp. I could barely keep my eyes on the road, I was too busy checking the rearview mirror.

I had begun to think we were safe, that they weren't going to follow, or that I'd managed to lose them. Then headlights burst to life behind us. A black SUV. The black SUV that had been following us earlier. They'd been driving it without lights and now they were right on my bumper. The SUV accelerated and rammed into my car. My head whipped forward. I jammed my foot down on the gas pedal and tried to lose them, but they pulled up alongside me. For a moment I saw them, still wearing their wolf masks, the one in the passenger seat filming. And then they swerved sharply and rammed into my

BMW from the side. I lost control. And then there was no road beneath us and we were flying.

Flying off the side of the road.

Neither of us screamed as we began to plummet down the hillside. I had time to look at my sister, tell her with my eyes that I was sorry. So sorry I'd dragged her along with me tonight. Sorry I'd dragged her along through the insanity of my life, which would end here.

A tree expanded in the frame of the windshield, branches filling my vision.

And then... impact.

And then nothing.

LIV HENDRICKS

2018

32 YEARS OLD; 135 LBS.

Facebook Fans: 56,137

Twitter Followers: 105,651

Instagram Followers: 17,084

56.

The blazing fusion I'd felt after watching my onscreen rape had cooled to violent chills. Now that the gap of emptiness that had plagued me for fifteen years had been filled, I trembled like I'd been hosed down with ice water.

Whoever was filming—either Soren or Porter, I realized now, although no one in the audience would have any idea it was them—had managed to capture the crash on video. It was funny how much less dramatic the crash appeared on screen than I had expected. Somehow I'd managed to forget that this was not a movie. This was real life. No matter how much Porter maneuvered me and positioned me for drama, in the end all of this had been my life, and reality didn't look like a movie. It was stranger than fiction, but it was also uglier, and crueler, and it made less sense.

As I watched my former car veer off the road, I thought I remembered my last moment with Miranda before it slammed into the tree that caught us. I saw myself reaching out and grabbing her hand, telling her how sorry I was that being my sister had made her life unlivable. But maybe that was wishful thinking, me wanting to believe I'd had time to apologize before she was gone for good.

I couldn't take my eyes from the screen as the boys in their wolf masks made their way down the embankment toward the smashed ruin of my BMW.

"Shit, man!" Soren said. I recognized his voice now, though it had deepened with age. "Do you think they're okay?"

"I don't know," Porter said, strangely calm. He was the one holding the camera. He moved closer, filming through the window of the BMW to get a shot of me bleeding out from the branch that split my head open. So much blood already. How could there have been any left in my body?

"We should have let them go," Soren whined, sounding on the verge of tears. "They couldn't have identified us."

He was probably right. Soren had dyed his blond hair that rusty maroon for their con, and Porter had traded his glasses (I assumed he'd always worn them) for those electric green contacts. And even if I had wanted to identify them, I would have known what they had on me. That disgusting video. The things they made me do. They could have used it to blackmail me into silence, and it would have worked, because I could not have allowed the world to see me that way.

"I think they're dead," Porter said, his voice trembling slightly now. This was not part of his plan. He hadn't wanted to kill me. I didn't think he even cared about blackmailing me for Gemma, or ruining my career. More than anything, Porter had wanted to be in control of my story. He had wanted to be *in* my story. He'd tried to do it the old-fashioned way, but that hadn't worked. I'd seen him as another fanboy, nothing more. So he had to try a different tack.

"She's moving!" Soren said, pointing at Miranda, who was beginning to stir in the passenger seat. "She's alive. What do we do?"

Porter hurried around to the passenger-side door, still filming. He covered his hand with his jacket sleeve as he pried the door open. Miranda raised her head to look at him, her eyes dazed, blood oozing from a cut on her forehead. Porter unbuckled her seat belt, and my sister spilled out of the car and onto the ground at Porter's feet.

Porter picked up a rock and handed it to Soren. "Knock her out. We're taking her."

"Why?" Soren asked. He sounded nervous, and he kept looking up the hill toward the road. It was only a matter of time until a car drove by and saw the accident.

"She's seen our car. She might have seen our faces. We need to get rid of her."

"Maybe not."

"Olivia!" Miranda cried, fully awake now. "Olivia, run!" Like either of us was capable of such a feat. My younger sister began to crawl across the ground away from the wolf boys.

Beside her, Soren hesitated, looking at Porter, who held the camera pointed at him. "Why are you still filming?" Soren asked. "It'll be evidence."

"It's not evidence," Porter said, sounding distant, like his mind had moved on to a more interesting matter than the possible manslaughter and assault at hand. "Don't you get it? This is the story. We have to follow it through to the end. That's what Jonas would do."

Soren, wearing his wolf mask, started to nod. "Yeah. Yeah, okay."

Miranda found her voice then and screamed for help,

but the sound cut off with a meaty thud as Soren brought the rock down on her skull. Her body went limp.

My ribs felt like they'd constricted around my lungs, a shrinking cage squeezing tighter and tighter until I could barely draw breath. My fingers ached from gripping the armrests. I wanted to pry myself from the theater seat, run from the flickering images flashing in front of me. Get in my car and drive to anywhere but the places I'd been. Leave Los Angeles. Leave everything.

But an overriding thought repeated in my mind.

They didn't kill Miranda. They didn't kill Miranda. They didn't kill Miranda.

The screen went black for a beat. Then:

> Part III
> Liv Hendricks
> 2018
> Facebook Fans: 56,128
> Twitter Followers: 105,399
> Instagram Followers: 17,013

At least this story held no surprises, even though some of the scenes had been filmed without my knowledge. I wasn't the only person in town with access to hidden cameras. Porter had been wearing a camera hidden in his tiepin during every encounter, including the times we'd had sex. Plus, footage I had filmed had been edited into this cut. The edit was rough and choppy, which made sense. Soren and Porter must have been working on it up until the last minute.

My story didn't end with Gemma's confession at the wolf sanctuary, as I'd hoped it would. It ended with a shot of me asleep in the hospital, a hand placing an invitation on the table beside me.

Then the screen cut to black. Another caption.

> Epilogue: Annika Kron
> 2003

Annika's scene picked up where the prologue left off, revealing the owner of the voice who had interrupted Annika as she was about to set fire to the forest. Niklas Larsen, his face porcelain-smooth, unmarred, but not for long.

"Let me take you home," Niklas said in Norwegian, with subtitles.

Annika shook her head, backing away from him and shaking her head. "I have to stop the Wolf King."

"Annika, the Wolf King isn't real. Your uncle made him up."

"He *is* real. He comes to me in my dreams. He says I have to give myself to him, or he'll never leave me alone!"

"No, Annika. You're not well. Let me help you…" He reached for the Zippo lighter, but Annika darted backward away from him. And while all this was happening, the cameraman hiding in the cottage slipped out the back window and began to creep away, continuing to film as he made his escape.

"He says if I don't sacrifice myself to him, he'll take another girl like me. And another. And another. And another. He'll keep taking them until he has what he wants. I can't let that happen!"

She flicked her thumb on the igniter, and the flame burst to life. At the same moment, Niklas lunged for the lighter, trying to knock it from her hand. He succeeded in sending the lighter flying, right into a puddle of gasoline, and in an instant fire was everywhere. It raced across the ground and climbed trees.

It was difficult to see what happened next, it was filmed from so far away. It looked like Annika sat down in the clearing. Maybe she wanted to observe the destruction, watch the cottage burn and hear the Wolf King's screams. Or maybe she intended to be the Wolf King's last sacrifice. If that was the case, Niklas had no intention of allowing her offering. He grabbed her under the shoulders and dragged her kicking and screaming to her feet.

"Leave me!" she shouted at him, and shoved him away from her. He stumbled backward, tripped over a fallen branch, twisting as he fell to catch himself. But his upper body splashed down into a puddle of gasoline that had yet to light up, and that puddle joined another puddle that was already aflame. In the next instant Niklas was on fire, screaming. Annika rushed to him, babbling incoherently in panicked Norwegian, slapping at the flames to try to put them out. But all she managed to do was set her gasoline-splattered hands on fire. She fell to the ground to beat them out, and Niklas began rolling to squash the flames eating him.

Cut to black.

For a moment I sat there, stunned. That couldn't be the end. What about the missing girls? What about the end to Annika's story? To Miranda's?

I almost sighed in relief when the next scene faded in again, but I realized quickly that this was only a montage. There was no dialogue, only a crackly country-western song sung by a man who sounded like he'd bitten half his tongue off. Credits began to roll over the montage, the shots filmed at a variety of famous Kron locations throughout Stone's Throw, but mostly at the wolf sanctuary. And each shot featured one of the missing women as they reenacted grotesque, pornographic versions of scenes from *The Girl and the Wolf*, a shocking collection of sexual acts performed by girls in Kronsplay on a man in a white wolf mask. The montages were cut together in a choppy pace so frantic it was almost like watching time lapse. There were more than three of them. Far more. At least a dozen women had participated in the films, but apparently not all of them had been required to vanish.

The red velvet curtain rustled, and then three women filed out onto stage, all of them blond, all of them in Kronsplay. They were older than they'd been when last seen, but I recognized them as the missing women. Allison Sargent, Camille Banks, and Mary Elizabeth Woodson. They had returned to Stone's Throw for their premiere, less a little toe, which they had offered to the Wolf King to further the narrative.

It really had all been a hoax. One unfathomably long hoax, and the joke was on all of us. The audience. The people of Stone's Throw. Even on Jonas Kron, because the one story line he'd wanted resolved had been denied him. We still didn't know what had happened to Annika Kron. She was not among the three no-longer-missing women assembled on stage, smiling and radiant, clearly proud of what they'd been a part of. They joined hands and bowed.

That was when the applause began. Tentative at first, and then louder, more enthusiastic. The audience stood for an ovation. I rose, too, and the people around me patted me on the back and told me congratulations on my most convincing performance, exclaiming about how they'd been fooled by the whole thing, how it must have taken so much careful planning to pull off such an elaborate and shocking hoax fifteen years in the making! Bravo! Scanning the audience, I spotted only a few people whose expressions told me they understood that all of what they'd just seen had been real.

A choked sob came through the speakers, and I looked back at the screen to see an Easter egg scene at the end of the credits.

I stopped breathing. The audience quieted.

It was the bonus that had been promised to me. It was Miranda.

She was the age she'd been when I last saw her, wearing the same clothes she'd worn the night she went missing. There was an open wound on her forehead. Her face was covered in so much blood she was hardly recognizable.

A voice off screen said, "What's your name?"

"Miranda Hill."

"Do you like being on camera like your sisters, Miranda?"

She shook her head. "N-no. I hate it."

"Really?" the voice said. I thought it was Porter. "That's a shame. Well, Miranda Hill, I don't know what we're going to do with you."

"You could let me go home," she said, her eyes dissolving in tears. "I won't tell anyone what happened tonight."

"That's pretty hard to believe," Porter said. "Besides, why would you want to go home now? Your sister Olivia is dead. Your other sister is, well...I don't know if I believe in evil, but Gemma definitely lives somewhere in that neighborhood. And then there's your mom. *Wow.* It must have been rough growing up with a mother like her."

Miranda nodded, and unconsciously began digging at the hole in her arm. The camera zoomed in on the wound.

"What happened there?" Porter asked. "Did you do that to yourself?"

"Y-yeah."

"Do you hurt yourself often?"

She hesitated only a second before nodding.

"You must be really unhappy."

"Yeah," she whispered, tears spilling over her lids. She lowered her eyes to her lap.

"And things are only going to get worse. So the way I see it, we have two choices. We can kill you—"

Miranda's head jerked up, eyes going wide with fear. She didn't want to die. At least there was that.

"Or...we can make you disappear. You'd get to start over somewhere else. You could have a whole new life away from your mom and Gemma. Away from all the things that make you unhappy. We'll even foot the bill to help you start over, won't we?"

"Yep!" Soren's off-camera voice said eagerly. "We'll take care of everything."

"You'll have to change your look, of course," Porter said. "And you can't ever, ever come back no matter what. If you do, we'll have to release the video we made of Olivia, and you know she wouldn't want that, right? If people saw the video, that's all they would remember her for. That's the only thing people would think of when they hear the name Olivia Hill. So what do you say, Miranda? Do we have a deal? Will you disappear?"

57.

LA FEMME ONLINE
Liv Hendricks: Girl on a Dark Road

Freya McBride
1 day ago—Filed to CELEBRITY
4,398 Likes—287 Comments

You might remember my post a month ago about Liv Hendricks, aka Olivia Hill. It garnered a lot of attention for the former child star, much of it negative, and resulted in Liv losing her previous job as a co-host on *Bullsh?t Hunters*. For that I apologize. It was never my intention to cause problems for Liv. The silver lining is that my article may have started Liv on a journey that helped her gain closure to the mystery that plagued her for nearly half her life: the disappearance of her sister Miranda Hill, who was fourteen when she vanished. Hollywood conspiracy theorists have long claimed that Miranda Hill's disappearance was all an elaborate publicity stunt devised to up the ratings on *The Hills Have PIs*. Turns out that wasn't so far from the truth.

Oh boy. There is so much to this story, I don't know where to begin. How about this? If you are one of the uninformed who has not been following the saga of what happened in Stone's Throw, California, instead of forcing me to do a recap, just go to shotinthedark.com/livhendricks and watch her investigation into the Dark Road girls. Do that instead of watching *Girl on a Dark Road*, the movie Porter Morrison and Soren Kron uploaded to the Internet, which features a lot of terrible things happening to Liv and former actress Annika Kron, among others. Just . . . have some respect and don't watch it.

Yes, if you must know, I did watch it, but only as preparation for my interview with Liv. And yes, you might be surprised to learn that Liv was willing to speak to me after what I wrote/posted about her last time around. But after a few apologetic phone calls from me, she did agree to an interview as long as she didn't have to be on camera. We met at Ledlow Swan, one of her frequent haunts in downtown LA. Her former costars Chris Wheeler and Blitz (the Doberman pinscher who now belongs to Liv) were present for the interview as moral support.

So, without further ado, here's what she had to say:

Me: So, Liv, I think the first thing everyone wants to know is how you're doing.

Liv: Better. I don't know why I've avoided mental hospitals for so long. It was exactly what I needed, and Jonas Kron was kind enough to pick up the tab.

Me: So you're...okay now?

Liv: They let me out, didn't they?

Me: I didn't mean—

Liv: Listen. What I went through was enough to drive a sane person insane, but my entire life has been pretty insane. What Porter Morrison and Soren Kron and my own sister did to me...it worked. It destroyed me for a long time, but that's over now. I'm not going to be the person they created. I'm going to decide my own fate now. I'm going to make a choice every day to stop suffering. I'm not going to feed the wolf anymore.

Me: I think that's amazing.

Liv: Can we talk about something besides my mental health?

Me: Okay. Have you heard anything from Porter Morrison or Soren Kron? They are currently awaiting trial for criminal mischief, and are out on bail, is that right?

Liv: Yes. They have good lawyers. They'll cut a deal. I doubt they'll serve any time. The statute of limitations is up on the worst of their crimes. And they claim they had nothing to do with Annika Kron's second disappearing act.

Me: Do you believe them?

Liv: The fact that they've taken credit for everything says something. If they did do something to Annika, they would have tried to film it. Neither of them is interested in tormenting people for the sheer fun of it. If they're going to hurt people, they'll keep a record of it.

Me: Do you have any theories about what happened to Annika Kron?

Liv: Maybe she reinvented herself again, started over. Maybe, before she could do that, she had to return to where it all started to get closure. Or maybe she's dead. I don't know. I hope she's out there somewhere with a new name, new hair, living a quiet, private life. We'll probably never know, and that's for the best. Her life belongs to her, not us.

Me: How about you, Liv? Was this your last case? Do you want to go back to acting? What's your plan? Where can we look forward to seeing you in the future?

Liv: I think the world has seen enough of me for the time being.

Me: Okay, last question... Have you heard from your sister Miranda?

(Liv pauses, then signals the waiter for the check.)

Me: Liv?

Liv: No comment.

ACKNOWLEDGMENTS

The Parable of Wolves claims there are two wolves inside of us that are always at war with each other. The bad wolf represents things like greed, hatred, and fear. The good wolf embodies kindness, bravery, love, that sort of thing. The wolf that wins the internal war depends entirely on which one we choose to feed.

I have a very bad wolf inside me, a voracious beast. I might feed it three square meals a day if not for the people in my life who encourage me to let it starve as much as possible and focus on the good wolf instead.

Thank you to my masterful editor, Lindsey Rose. Your notes hit the mark every time. You have every ounce of my trust.

Thank you to my agent, Doug Stewart, for loving every draft and never giving up on this book, and for being hilarious and witty and so damn cool.

Thank you, Libby Burton. You saw this book's potential and you made it happen. One of these days we'll get that drink.

Thank you and thank you and thank you to Gabrielle Zevin, for your insight and friendship. You inspire me and make me a better writer. You chase away the "Jennui."

Thank you to Mary Elizabeth Summer for reading this book in its craziest form and planting new ideas in my head. Just so you know, I need you, too.

And, finally, thank you to the Wolfpack, my strange, brilliant, insane, and, let's face it, pretty pervy critique group. Your wise criticism helped me rein in the things that needed to be reined and unleash the things that needed to be unleashed. Gretchen McNeil (BAMF), Brad Gottfred (Cyclops), James Raney (Hef), Nadine Nettman (Nayyyy-deeeen), and Julia Shahin Collard (Froolia)…Red Snow loves you.

There will always be a bad wolf inside me, and I will always give it regular snacks, but you lot help me keep my good wolf fat and happy.

ABOUT THE AUTHOR

Jennifer Wolfe worked as a phlebotomist, a fiction writing teacher, a copywriter, and ran a concert venue before quitting to move to Los Angeles and teach herself how to write screenplays. She performed odd jobs in the film industry for a decade, everything from Craft service and wardrobe to producing short films and music videos, before deciding to write about the movie business.

Jennifer grew up in a small town in Utah, where her father owned a video store, giving her access to all the movies she could get her hands on. She had a particular taste for horror movies, and still does. Every October, Jennifer watches a horror movie each day of the month. She now divides her time between Los Angeles and Portland, Oregon.

WATCH THE GIRLS is Jennifer's debut thriller. She also publishes young adult fiction under the name Jennifer Bosworth.